Choose your Lane to love!

Readers loved *Candy Man*

"Dearly beloved, we are gathered here to celebrate the wonder of Amy Lane and the fabulousness of this freaking story—*Candy Man*."
—Joyfully Jay

"There are two Amy Lanes – the very angst-filled, need a bunch of tissues Amy and the very sweet and happy Amy. This story is firmly in the second Amy camp and my favorite kind of Amy to read."
—Hearts on Fire Reviews

"*Candy Man* is sweet, without being syrupy, and the gentleness of Adam and Finn's love story was heartwarming."
—Rainbow Book Reviews

"I highly recommend picking up this sweet novella and savoring the tasty bits of love and life inside."
—Prism Book Alliance

"I love when Ms. Angst-and-Pain-Amy-Lane writes a sappy sweet holiday tale! I mean it! … *Candy Man* was just…adorbs!"
—Boys in Our Books

"I've said it before and I'll say it again, when Amy Lane is on, she writes killer books. This is one of those killer books."
—Gay.Guy.Reading

More from Amy Lane

Immortal

"Leave it to Amy Lane to write a fairy tale that kicks my ass... Thank you Amy, for the gift of your words, for the gift of *Immortal*.
—MM Good Book Reviews

"Amy "angst" Lane has written a superb story in Immortal..."
—Prism Book Alliance

"A book that made me feel...made me live every emotional onslaught these men suffered! Bravo Amy Lane and thank you for giving me an unputdownable, gold star read I won't forget."
—Sinfully... Addicted to All Male Romance

Food for Thought

"This is a SWEET Amy Lane story, and those are my favorite... I loved everything about *Food for Thought*..."
—My Fiction Nook

Beneath the Stain

"...this was a very enchanting book and I hope to see these characters again in the future."
—Hearts on Fire

"It is truly storytelling at its best and I highly recommend this novel to you."
—Joyfully Jay

By AMY LANE

Behind the Curtain
Beneath the Stain
Bewitched by Bella's Brother
Bitter Taffy
Bolt-hole
Candy Man
Christmas with Danny Fit
Clear Water
Do-over
Food for Thought
Gambling Men: The Novel
Going Up!
Grand Adventures (Dreamspinner Anthology)
Hammer & Air
If I Must
Immortal
It's Not Shakespeare
Left on St. Truth-be-Well
The Locker Room
Mourning Heaven
Phonebook
Puppy, Car, and Snow
Racing for the Sun
Raising the Stakes
Shiny!
Sidecar
A Solid Core of Alpha
Super Sock Man
Tales of the Curious Cookbook
Three Fates (Multiple Author Anthology)
Truth in the Dark
Turkey in the Snow
Under the Rushes
Wishing on a Blue Star (Dreamspinner Anthology)

GREEN'S HILL
Guarding the Vampire's Ghost • I love you, asshole! • Litha's Constant Whim

Published by DREAMSPINNER PRESS
http://www.dreamspinnerpress.com

By AMY LANE (Continued)

Published by DREAMSPINNER PRESS
http://www.dreamspinnerpress.com

Bitter TAFFY
AND
Candy MAN

Amy Lane

Published by
DREAMSPINNER PRESS

5032 Capital Circle SW, Suite 2, PMB# 279, Tallahassee, FL 32305-7886 USA
http://www.dreamspinnerpress.com/

ISBN: 978-1-63476-287-8
Digital ISBN: 978-1-63476-288-5
Library of Congress Control Number: 2015905840
First Edition July 2015

Printed in the United States of America
∞
This paper meets the requirements of
ANSI/NISO Z39.48-1992 (Permanence of Paper).

Amy Lane

Candy
MAN

I will never write a book not dedicated to Mate in some way. And Mary. And, in this case, Chicken, Zoomboy, Squish, and Big T, who were the whole reason I stopped into Candy Heaven in the first place.

Author's Note

Mate was running a half marathon, and I was running back-up support. So he ran his fit, lithe body thirteen miles, and I hauled my lumbering, fat butt for what amounted to a 5K, back and forth from Raley Field to Old Sacramento. After Mate came in, we walked the (final!) trip back through Old Sacramento, and in the nest of shops on the old boarded walkway, we saw Candy Heaven—and went in. Hey, it was the day before St. Patrick's Day, and we didn't have anything for the little kids to wake up to. Convenience and desperation drive discovery. Anyway, Darrin, the proprietor, was funny, kind, and 6'6" tall. He was also fabulous in a very rainbow/tie-dye sort of way. Maybe it was that I was breathless, sweaty, and felt stupid, because, hello, Mate was the one running the marathon, but I *so* needed a Darrin right then. I determined that this year's Christmas novella would be about Candy Heaven and have Darrin in it. So if you're ever in Old Sacramento, look Candy Heaven and Darrin up. His shop is the one right across the river by the parking structure on the corner—you can see the bridge and Raley Field from the front. Meet the real-life Darrin and his crew of mismatched, wonderful, happy workers inside. Don't forget to take a free candy—the blue labels are for tasting. ;-)

Pixy Stix

DARRIN CHECKED his manicure and tossed his shoulder-length shag-cut hair back, shaking his head so it came clear of the dangly earrings. Yeah, it was a little grayer when he forgot to do highlights, but he still managed to look glamorous. Feeling cocky, and damned good about the coming Christmas season, he leaned forward against the high wooden counter and watched as Joni unlocked the doors.

"Think it's going to be busy, boss?" Joni had a buzz cut, dyed black, and a body as stocky as one of the barrels that held hard-candy sweets throughout the store.

"I hope so!" Small businesses in this climate weren't always a sure thing, but Candy Heaven had been around for a few years, and Darrin was clinging to his little store with every bit of strength in his long, manicured fingers. The store resided in Old Town Sacramento—a four-by-two block cobblestoned, boardwalked tourist trap formed in the pocket created by Highway 275, the Golden State Highway, the I Street Bridge, and the Sacramento River. The stores ranged from burger joints to fine-dining restaurants to antiques to importers to art galleries. They made their money from tourists looking for a quick bit of history at the railroad museum, and locals looking for a reliable place to get something specialized and unique. The candy stores—his wasn't the only one—were a sweet little perk and part of the area's appeal. They should do a brisk Christmas business, and Darrin thought about his crew of twelve or so employees and reflected that they might be down one for the holidays.

"In fact," he said thoughtfully, "I think we may need to hire some help."

Joni grunted. "I'll put out the sign, then. God, I hope we don't get high school students and shit. I *hate* premetacognitive beings."

Joni was twenty-four and working on her master's in sociology. Darrin was waiting for her to get old enough to think "premetacognitive beings" were adorable and pat them on the head and send them on their way with a cookie. Right now she was sort of abrasive—although that could have had something to do with her recent breakup. Joni's ex-girlfriend had been barely nineteen.

Darrin ripped the top off a Pixy Stix and dumped the contents on the counter, then drew a random picture in the sour sugar and imagined who would work for him. Six four, chest like a wall, heavy tattoos on his back and neck. Bold nose, rectangular jaw, brown eyes, flat and untrusting. A heart like… quicksilver—used to defending itself by pretending it wasn't there.

"Hm…," Darrin murmured. "Yes. Yes, his name is Adam. He's not going to be… friendly."

Joni groaned. "Aw, boss! Seriously—do you see anyone else in there? Five six, blonde, blue-eyed, big boobs, tiny waist—"

"No, dear," Darrin said, too intent on the man he saw in the Pixy Stix to be tactful. He saw a child huddled under a bed in the dark, the whip and slap of unkind voices echoing above his sanctuary. He saw a shining lifeline. Oh dear. And the lifeline led here.

Darrin licked his finger and then drew a little more. Staring at the picture, he tasted the sweet-tart powder on the end of his finger and grimaced.

More bitter than it should be.

"This one needs us. Needs sweetening."

Joni groaned. "Boss, can't we have, you know, a wide-eyed kinda hamster girl, smart enough to not be premetacognitive, dumb enough to want me?"

Darrin pulled himself away from his visions of sugar-humans and scowled. "*You* need to find someone who doesn't take your shit. You drove that sweet young thang away sure as I'm standing here. Forget cute with perky boobies. You need someone who will throw you against the counter, kiss you, and then tell you to stop being a bitch!"

Joni grunted and set the Help Wanted sign up in the window. "Can she have perky boobies too?"

"I am *not* doing a reading for you! Now start stocking—we need more of the magnets with my picture on them. There's going to be a run."

Joni rolled her eyes and went to do her job, and Darrin sighed and started to pick up his end. Sometimes it sucked being the boss.

For one thing, he wasn't going to *be* the one helping sweeten this man's sugar. But maybe that was okay. Maybe just seeing who *would* sweeten this man's life would be enough.

Lifeline

ADAM MACIAS looked at the smoking hulk of his engine and slammed the hood down. *Oh, for fuck's sake.* The Chevy Matiz—whose idea was it? Four doors, shaped like a shoe, and all the reliability of his grandmother's digestive tract. Whether she'd been constipated or had the runs, it was always ugly, and her mood had been to match.

And now, unlike his grandmother (dammit!), this damned car had apparently shuffled off its mortal coil.

He fought the temptation to bury his head in his hands and scream.

He kicked the car's tire instead. "Fuck-burger, shit-eating, rancid piece of dog cock!"

It wasn't going to make it.

The fucking car was the whole reason he was trying to drive from San Diego to Sacramento in the first place. The fucking car had broken down one too many times. Adam had missed his class, Adam had missed his job, and now Adam had neither class *nor* job, and no VA money coming in to help him pay for his tiny little apartment.

And now he had no fucking car.

What he did have—the *one* thing he did have—was an offer from his cousin, Rico, to let Adam house-sit his apartment off of F Street, in downtown Sacramento. Rico said straight up it wasn't a great apartment, but it was rent controlled, and Rico didn't want to lose it when he went to serve an internship at a firm in New York.

Rico also needed someone to walk his dog, feed his cat, and keep his fish alive—all of which he was willing to front Adam rent to do, but Adam had to *get there* first.

Which he could not do with his car in its current condition.

"*Argh!*"

He kicked the tire again and then grabbed his shit. He'd served in the military for eight years. He knew when to fish, when to cut bait, and when to ditch his car off at a U-Pick-It and buy a bus ticket out of Southeast of Hell.

U-PICK-IT PAID him $200 for the car, and Adam thought that the girl behind the counter was being generous because she was trying to land him for a date. When he told her that he had to get to Sac by the next morning, she shrugged philosophically and directed him to the nearest bus station, and he was grateful enough to smile.

God, he was pretty sure her panties flooded just from a smile, and he really wished he could take her up on it, but he was done thinking he could do that anymore. He took the $200, grabbed his duffel bag and his suitcase, and bought himself that bus ticket out of town.

There would be no more flirting with girls for him.

How many buddies did a guy have to blow before he realized that it wasn't just because he was bored, and it wasn't just because he was horny, it was because he actually *liked* guys, their cocks, their asses, and their stubble burn on his stomach when they were going down on *him*?

Well, the last guy really *had* been his friend, and Adam had been willing to come out of the closet so they could have a relationship, but Robbie hadn't. The resultant mess had been, well, less than stellar for Adam's career, and he'd taken the opportunity to not re-up when the time came.

He was going to use those benefits and go to *school*, right?

Except the one car he could afford had been that *thing* that had just died on him for the last time, and now he was on a bus with no heater the week before Thanksgiving, freezing his ass off on the way to free room and a little board.

God. And the guy next to him was looking… interested, to say the least.

"Hey, kid," the old man muttered, trying to talk under his breath. "You, uhm, feelin' lonely?" He accompanied that thought with a hand gliding roughly down Adam's thigh.

Adam lifted it firmly off. "Not that lonely," he growled. His phone buzzed in his pocket.

He picked it up, saw the text, and groaned.

My plane takes off tomorrow. Where are you?

Car died permanently. On the bus for Sac.

Fine. Key under the mat, am writing out instructions. Cat needs medicine twice daily. The dog may fucking eat you.

Adam fought a burning behind his eyes. God, he'd expected Rico to totally cancel on him. The two of them had spent long hours at Grandma's while their mothers both worked, and the bond had lasted through Adam's stint in the military and Rico's college years. When Adam had come out and Grandma and his mother had (thank God!) stopped talking to him, Rico had been the first person to text him— almost before the old bitch had slammed the door in his face.

High five! You know between the gay thing and the soldier thing, you may possibly have become cool.

Because Rico, easygoing Rico, had been beloved through high school—the jock, the swim team captain, the student body president. *Everybody* loved Rico. Adam had been the silent, brooding loner, trying really hard to hide his sexuality while at the same time trying really hard to solicit blowjobs from the unwary. God, he'd wanted someone to love him. Blowjobs had just felt like a way to do that.

And now Rico was Adam's last possible hope for reclaiming some sort of order from the crapfest his life had become.

He felt something crawling on his thigh again and, in a fit of irritation, swung around in his seat and pinned the old man against the headrest by the throat.

"Now listen, old man," Adam growled, "I may be fucking queer, but I am *not* up for grabs, do you hear me? You keep your hands to yourself and—" He held on to his gag reflex as the man expelled a gasp of fetid breath over greenish teeth. "—and breathe through your fucking nose, and you may live to see Sacramento, okay?"

The old man barely nodded, two silver tracks creeping their way down the wrinkled, alcohol-reddened skin.

"Didn't mean nothin'," he wheezed. "Just missing some company, tha's all."

Adam let go of him and threw himself back in his seat. Oh fuck. It was like looking through a time machine, because sweartagod, if he stopped trying and started drinking Ripple, that old man was going to be him.

"Well I'm shitty company tonight," he muttered. "Just keep your distance."

When the old man crumpled into a tearful, *non*predatory heap next to him, Adam picked up his phone and texted with the last of his battery.

Thanks cousin. I owe you. I SO need to get my shit together.

You got your shit together, A—just need a little help. Keep my babies alive and don't wreck my car. We're square.

No. Not square. But Adam wasn't going to waste this opportunity. He wanted a job, he wanted to get back in school, and he wanted to find his own place before June. Friends? Lovers? Pets? Need not apply.

The bus pulled into Sacramento just as the sun was rising, and for a minute, as the bus approached from the south, the city was backlit by the brilliant, thin gold of winter. The unimpressive skyline suddenly held character and charm, and the surrounding acres of flatlands and suburbs exuded a possibility that Adam wouldn't have given the place credit for eight hours earlier.

Nobody knew him here. He could make a new start. He wasn't even thirty yet—he still had things he could do.

An hour later, after he'd hauled his shit the mile from the bus station to his cousin's apartment off of F Street in the joint-freezing cold, he was hoping one of the things he could do was shower, and the other thing was sleep.

HIS COUSIN lived in half of the second floor of an old Victorian house. The house itself wasn't in bad shape—could have used some new boards on the stairs and a new coat of paint, but Adam saw Thanksgiving decorations in all the windows, including Rico's, and the winter lawn was neatly trimmed. Adam understood that was his job too, but he didn't mind.

Maybe if he worked hard enough, the super would recommend him to another apartment. Who knew, right?

The thought cheered him, and he pulled the key out from under Rico's doormat and let himself in with a little bit of optimism.

Which was quickly knocked out of him when something that looked like a cross between a boxer and a pony tried to knock him on his ass.

"*Clopper?*" he hollered, suddenly getting the name. Too compact to be a clodhopper, too massive and clumsy to be anything else, the dog wasn't even really trying to escape so much as it was trying to crawl into the crotch of Adam's pants nose first, entrance unnecessary. "Clopper, you asshole, knock it off!" He shoved the dog's head aside and hoped he didn't just condemn himself to a dog-bite neutering procedure.

Clopper didn't wag his tail, but he didn't growl either. The look he cast Adam was more like disappointment. *Oh. We can't get to know each other better? That's a shame. I wanted to be your friend. Are you sure you won't let me crawl into your pants and maul your family jewels?*

"No," Adam said out loud, feeling grumpy. It was the third unwanted advance he'd fended off in six hours. "You can't lick my balls. I have to know you longer than a nanosecond, you fucking perv!"

Clopper grunted and retreated to the far corner of the apartment, where a giant dog bed existed to serve his monster-dormancy needs.

Adam recovered his dignity and dragged his suitcase and duffel in the door, then slammed it shut behind him so he didn't let the dog and the as-of-yet-unseen cat out. Carefully he prowled around his new surroundings, deciding they suited him fine.

The apartment had been adapted from what looked to be the bed and bath portion of the house. To his right as he entered was a small kitchenette with a counter that divided the cooking area from the living room. A small breakfast nook attached to the kitchen, with a little white Formica table complete with yellow vinyl eggshell chairs. *Classy, Rico—here's hoping the internship pays better than the last job!* The hallway took off from the living room. From the front door, Adam could see three doors—he assumed two bedrooms and a bath.

Oh Lordy, compared to the shotgun single bedroom he hadn't been able to afford, this was like a luxury suite at the Hilton. Adam leaned against the door and closed his eyes. Six months here. Six months running distance from downtown and Old Town, biking and bussing distance from at least two colleges and several vocational schools. He could do it here. He could get a job and get a car and get his feet back under him again.

He pulled his charger and phone out of his pocket and plugged them both in, then waited a moment for his phone to light up.

I'm here. Has your plane taken off yet?

No—we must have just missed each other. Sorry cousin!

I'm sorry too. But I'll take care of your guys for you.

Has Clopper sniffed your balls yet?

Yup.

Good. It means you're home. Gotta run!

Adam wasn't sure what that feeling in his face was until he got out of the shower and went to brush his teeth.

That was when he saw it in the mirror. He was smiling. *Oh God, let this be, however temporarily, home.*

Sign in the Window

"YOU FOUND anyone yet?" Finn Stewart asked brightly, and Darrin smiled at him, liking his flirty, almond-shaped blue eyes and wide-mouthed smile. Finn could probably be underwear-model material, but he could never manage the whole broody thing. He had curly red-brown hair that peeped out of a fleece cartoon character hat, the kind with the chin strap and the button underneath. His body was all elbows and knees held together by long, rangy arms and legs, with wide shoulders and a torso shaped in a perfect capital V.

But och! That grin, with the dimples and the brackets in the corners of his mouth! Could light up the sky, it could—and he flashed it *everywhere*!

Right now the boy was flashing it as he delivered Darrin's daily lettuce-chicken wrap, and Darrin was grateful for both. True to his promise to Joni, the past two days had been almost miserably busy as people gathered big bowls of specialty candy for their Thanksgiving Day centerpieces and candy bowls. If it wasn't for Finn's father's sandwich shop, Darrin wasn't sure he and the rest of the staff would have had time to eat at all. He'd been running the store on full cylinders, working his employees as long and as often as he could, up to and including overtime, and they *all* needed a little help.

So Finn's arrival was worth taking a little break, if for nothing else than to see that smile.

"Still looking," Darrin said, thinking his new employee would show up damned soon. The Pixy Stix never lied. "In fact… ah! There he is!"

And sure enough, here was Tall, Dark, and Broody, with brown eyes under sunglasses, bold cheekbones, an equally bold nose, and full lips. The confidence of his no-bullshit military strut and haircut didn't quite compensate for the lines of anxiety around his eyes and mouth.

Darrin's next project was in dire need of some fixing up.

Finn looked over to where Darrin was looking, and in spite of the fact that the store was full of people, his little gasp of "Oooh" was unmistakable.

The door closed behind the newcomer, and Darrin raised his eyebrows. "Oooh" indeed.

Finn turned to Darrin with big, infinitely blue eyes. "Can I come back?" he asked, his knockout grin lighting up the store. "I want to meet this guy!"

"I don't know, sugar," Darrin drawled, playing for time. "Do you work tomorrow?"

"Tomorrow's Saturday, so that's a yes! See you then if you don't need me before!"

Finn saluted over his little puppy-dog hat (something to do with a cartoon show—Darrin was not ashamed to say he was too old to follow it) and hustled out of the front entrance, past Darrin's soon-to-be new employee. The store was crowded, and although Finn made an attempt to sidestep, the two of them were jostled together—and that was when Darrin saw it.

New Guy's eyes popped open just as he was raising his sunglasses over his head, and when he met Finn's merry blue eyes, a look that Darrin could only describe as wistful crossed his face. The whole world seemed to hold its breath, whether the people in the crowded store knew it or not. It didn't breathe again until Finn flashed his grin at Tall, Dark, and Broody and then skedaddled, dynamite in jeans and a hooded Sac State sweatshirt, delivering sandwiches from River Burger to the cobbled streets of Old Town.

Tall, Dark, and Broody had a moment of visibly pulling his shit back together, and then he seemed to remember the Help Wanted sign in his hand and the thing he'd set out to do.

ADAM LOOKED around the bustling little candy store, and he had to agree: Candy Heaven was *definitely* in need of help. He remembered visiting Rico on leave. Adam had liked the charm of Old Town Sac, the little tourist trap across the bridge from Raley Field. After a day of rest (and a chance to coax Rico's skittish tiger-striped cat, Gonzo, from under the bed), he figured he'd take a bus and start there.

This was the fifth place he'd gone into with a Help Wanted sign, but so far all the positions had been filled. He'd been a little disheartened—and very hungry—when he'd seen the sign in the candy store. And the kid he'd run into—the one with the bright eyes and knee-melting grin?

Yeah. That kid had smelled like sandwiches.

At least that was what Adam told himself, because the sizzle-spark-*zing* that had traveled his spine when he and the kid had danced, trying to get around each other, had no business taking up residence anywhere in his body.

Home. Job. School. C'mon, Adam—remember the basics!

So basically, Adam had to find the boss and ask for a job, and to that end, he had to find….

Well, the boss, right? Apparently, the boss was the guy on all of the little canvas candy bags, with the long hair and the Willy Wonka hat. And *that* guy was standing behind the counter and waving at him.

In that moment Adam had a supreme instance of dislocation.

He pointed dizzily to himself and looked behind him to see if Willy Wonka—or the guy with the long layer cut standing behind the counter—wasn't talking to somebody else.

But the guy kept smiling and gesturing, and then he reached behind the counter and pulled out an apron.

Adam drew nearer and the guy said, "You're here for a job, right?"

"Uh, yeah—"

Six people suddenly cut in front of him to wrap the already present queue around the stack of candy-filled barrels near Adam. He had to cut *back* through the line to get to the counter.

"Well great!" the Candy Man said. "Here, put this on so people know you work here. I'll clock you in later for twelve thirty, and what I need you to do is stand by the scale and weigh the candy while I check people out. Can you do that?"

"Uhm, yeah—"

Oh geez. Adam didn't even know how much this job *paid.* But at this moment, it *was* paying, and when Adam had walked through the store, he'd been making precisely dick.

"Okay, folks," he said, using his military training to sound like he meant it. "Everybody stand aside, coming through, we're gonna move this line a little faster, how's that sound!"

The huzzah of the crowd sounded good-natured and excited, and Adam figured what the hell. Even if he walked out of here with one day's pay to find a better job, one day's pay would at least buy his dinner and his bus fare, right?

SEVEN HOURS later, Adam wasn't sure he was going to make it until dinner.

"Uhm," he said, a little desperately, recognizing hunger spots in front of his eyes. "When do we close again?"

Darrin (his boss—he'd figured that out in the first hour) looked at him with worry in his eyes. He was actually taller than Adam, which was a feat in itself, but that didn't stop him from seeming really... kind. "Sweetheart, when did you last eat?"

"Last night," Adam confessed. Rico didn't have much in the cupboards, and Adam didn't have much in his pocket. He'd been going to buy a sandwich or something after he'd found a job.

"Oh Glory! Here, you go help Joni stock that barrel, and I'll call Finn for another delivery."

"Finn?" Adam asked, feeling hazy. "Like the cartoon character?" The kid he'd bumped into, the one who'd smelled like sandwiches, had been wearing a hat like that.

"Yup—our resident sandwich boy. Get some of the others to help you, and scoot. We need to stock or people are going to start eating the wood!"

He wasn't far off. Candy Heaven was one of those candy by weight places: on the bare floorboards sat big wooden barrels, each one filled with a different wrapped confection, and tied-dyed flags decorated the loft, where Darrin kept stock. For those (like Adam, actually) whose taste went more toward chocolate, there was a glass-covered refrigerated display cabinet in the back where a customer could pick truffles, fudge, or chocolate, along with a small refrigerator case with sodas and water. Darrin had purchased a bunch of canvas bags and had them stamped with his likeness—a thin-featured man with a winsome smile and long-layered red-brown hair—and gussied the image up with a purple top hat and tails. Those were a real plus. People would fill one of those and call that a quickie Christmas or Thanksgiving gift. It wasn't until Adam looked up in the middle of weighing what seemed to be his one-thousandth canvas bag that he realized, omigod, they were almost *out*, and many of the barrels were down to the last inch of candy.

Adam looked around as he walked the short distance from the register to the loft stairs. He saw a surprising number of employees in this little operation—he was pretty sure he'd counted at least five other people wearing brown Candy Heaven aprons, and they were all doing different things. The squat dark-haired girl with the crew cut and glasses was handing out free taste coupons, the sour-looking boy with the nose ring and goatee was behind the counter with the chocolates, and the foxy-faced girl with the skunk-stripe in her dyed red hair was currently stocking from the last batch that had been pulled down from the stairs. A good-looking kid with brown hair and big brown eyes was cleaning out the old boxes from the loft and throwing them out back, presumably to make it easier for Adam to get up there to stock.

Two new boys had walked in while Adam was working, both of them with sienna skin and curly, shiny black hair. The taller one had a mustache and the shorter one had a jowly face—every now and then when they weren't taking care of customers, they spattered Hindi at each other in an effort to give directions. In fact, they were the only two people *besides* Darrin whose names Adam knew. The tall one was Ravi and the short one was Anish. Adam had no idea how they were related, but he knew they probably couldn't exist for longer than an hour outside the other's pocket.

And given that he was going to need help and theirs were the only names he knew, they were about to become his new best friends.

"Uh, Ravi? Anish? Darrin says he needs stock—can one of you tell me what to look for, and the other stand here at the bottom of the stairs and take stock?"

They both looked at him, teeth flashing whitely as they smiled. "Yeah, sure," Ravi said with decision. "Anish, you shout the orders, I'll take the stock."

Oh, thank God. Help. Adam tried not to sway as he pulled himself up the stairs into the loft.

"Lemon sours!"

Adam searched until he found the last box, and ran that down the stairs to Ravi. As he was doing that, Anish called out, "Sanded cinnamon drops and sanded cherry drops!"

And then he repeated the process.

He was into it, breaking a sweat, in that place where hunger and tiredness didn't matter, when Anish called out for mixed sour balls. They were on the bottom shelf. He squatted down for them....

And fell on his ass.

As he was down there, wondering how he'd gone nearly a whole day without eating, he heard a perky alto calling out, "Darrin! Darrin, you said you needed food?"

"Finn! Yeah, here. Put the usual on the counter here, but do me a favor, would you? Could you run the burger with blue cheese and mushrooms up to the loft? My new employee just passed out."

There was a chorus of "What? Who? Is he okay? Who was that guy, anyway?" And Adam felt like he should contribute his two cents.

"Didn't pass out!" he said, but he could hear his own voice wandering. "Fell on my ass. Please tell me I'm getting paid. What time is it, anyway?"

"It's almost eight o'clock at night," said that perky voice. Adam looked to the top of the stairs, and there he was. The kid with the Finn hat, and he was carrying a box of takeout in a plastic bag.

"Finn," Adam said, literally so drifty he couldn't lock down his own brain. "Where's your goofy little dog?"

"You watch *Adventure Time*?" Finn said, sounding delighted. "That's awesome!"

"Someone at the base had boxed sets," Adam said, his brain flashing to the comfortable camaraderie of H-1, outside of Baghdad. Yeah, there was war, but there was a lot of boredom, and he and the troops had passed entertainment around with an almost religious intensity. Paperbacks were golden, and Lieutenant Crandall's boxed DVD cartoon sets from his kids had resulted in fistfights before Crandall had started showing them for an hour a day in his bunk. "*Futurama, Adventure Time, Archer. Adventure Time* was my favorite."

"Finn" came closer to him, eyeballing him with a certain wariness in the dim light of the loft, like he expected Adam to start foaming at the mouth or something.

"Your sweatshirt's wrong," Adam said soberly. "It should be dark blue. It's purple. That's off. What's your real name?"

The kid sat next to him and started pulling out the food. "Would it blow your mind if I said it was Finn?"

Adam started to laugh, suddenly in real danger of just losing it and giggling until he cried, detonating his entire emotional nut in the loft of a candy store he might or might not work at. "Would it blow your mind if I told you I was having the *weirdest* week?"

"No," Finn said gently. "Here. My dad's best burger. Darrin asked for it special."

He put the box in Adam's shaking hands, and Adam realized he needed to start eating what was in it or he really would pass out. For a few moments there was nothing but the sound of him getting a one-handed grip on the burger and cramming it into his mouth. At about halfway done, he set it down and closed his eyes, trying to catch his breath and let the food catch up to his stomach.

"Thanks, kid," he said, trying to get a better look at him. "Nice of Darrin to feed me."

"Well, it was nice of you to just start working on faith. I'm not a kid."

Adam raised his eyebrows in disbelief, and Finn rolled his eyes.

"Okay, I'm twenty-four. I keep an apartment over my father's store, so I officially live on my own, pay rent, and I'm probably about two years away from my degree. So, you know. Grown-up."

Adam nodded, his blood sugar still too up and down for real words, and took another bite of his hamburger. He swallowed. Thought, *This kid has never had his heart broken. Never sacrificed something for someone who didn't give a shit. Never tried his hardest and had his ass handed to him on a platter.* For a moment bitterness threatened to rear up and bite off the head of this sweet kid with the Finn hat and the goofy smile, but then Finn rooted in the plastic bag and came up with garlic fries.

"Here!" he said cheerfully. "They're still hot. Do you want some ketchup?"

The aroma of garlic fries almost made Adam whimper.

"Yeah, sure," he rasped, aware that he didn't get to bite the head off of anybody when anybody was feeding him and being human. He took one of the fries and fell into the temporary vortex of carbgasm, then resurfaced and tried to resume his questioning. "So, what are you going to school for?"

"Structural engineering," Finn said, like everybody said that every day.

Adam blinked. Figured. The kid was smarter than he was. Of *course* his life was better. "That's a good major," he said seriously. "Beats mine."

"What's yours?"

"Animation. Went to a school in San Diego, but I lost my grant." God, he did *not* want to talk about his stupid car and the fucking death spiral his life had entered in the past month. "What do you want to build?"

"Bridges, highways, and grain silos."

Adam laughed—he had no choice. "Grain silos?"

"Very phallic. After my last boyfriend, I needed a penis substitute."

Adam almost inhaled a fry, he was laughing so hard. Oh God, this kid! "So I guess you're lucky you're not making weapons, right?"

Finn shrugged. "Yeah, well, my idea of a sword fight is very, very different, right?"

"Oh absolutely."

They sat in silence for a moment, and Adam finished off his fries and sighed softly, leaning his head against his knees. "Well, Finn, it's been great talking to you, but I think I have to pay you and get back to work."

Finn shook his head. "No, no, like I said, Darrin took care of it. Don't worry about paying me. They were going under when you walked in. I think he's just grateful you took the job on faith."

Adam nodded. He wanted to ask *What is it with that guy?* because he figured *no one* could be that sweet and that *trusting* in this day and age, but Finn was getting up, and it was time for Adam to as well. "Well, I'm grateful for the feeding—and it's time I told him—"

"What's your name, anyway? Darrin didn't say."

"Adam, but—"

"Why were you that hungry, Adam?" Finn asked, barging right into his privacy without so much as a by-your-leave.

Adam shook his head. "Just got into town. Nothing in my cousin's fridge. Thought I'd get a job first."

"Wow. That's dedication." Finn stood and offered his hand down, and Adam took it after only a second's hesitation.

A little force, a little lever, and suddenly Adam was standing way too close to the cute sandwich delivery kid. What made it worse was that Finn backed up against a stack of crates and looked at him with big eyes in the suddenly intimate loft.

"Gee, mister," Finn said, licking his lips, "you are awfully tall."

Adam froze for a moment, thinking that Finn, for all his flirt, was probably not ready for what he and a few guys from his squad used to do in the darkened bunkers, between Humvees, or in the miniscule, sweating supply closet of his base outside of Baghdad.

"I'm, uhm, six four," he mumbled, taking two steps back. Finn was maybe five eleven, so not really short, but Adam felt sort of outsized, freakish, and awkward. "Uhm, I'll walk you down."

He was feeling the day now, in the soles of his shoes and the heaviness of his limbs. Maybe he could sign some paperwork or something, sit down, stop thinking about Finn's wide, pink mouth and the way his straight teeth glinted when he smiled.

"So, how long have you been in town?" Finn asked as they made their way down the stairs.

"Thirty-six hours," Adam replied shortly, thinking that it was probably closer to thirty-eight.

"What are you here for?"

"To watch my cousin's animals and get my shit together. Jesus, kid—"

"Where'd you come from? Did you leave anybody there?"

"San Diego, a school that is indifferent to me, and a grandmother that lights black candles to curse my every breath. Do you always—"

"What kind of animals do you have? I mean does your cousin have? I'm just asking, because if you're not used to dogs or cats, I can help. I mean, I'm not an expert, but my family has had tons of the critters. I've grown up with them. What about you?"

"I had a boxer in high school. My mom put him in the pound the day I shipped out. Rico didn't get there in time to save him. He was euthanized."

Finn's barrage of questions stopped cold. "Holy God, Adam, do you have any *happy* answers?"

Adam got to the bottom of the stairs and looked around the store, which was almost miraculously cleaning itself up with the help of the hipster elves that seemed to be working there this evening. "Yeah," he said, bemused. "Ask me if I got a job."

Finn's grin lit up the entire wooden room. "You got a job?"

"I'm pretty sure I do, but let me go talk to the boss man. You got a problem with that?"

"Nope. I'll be waiting when you come out of the office."

"Don't you got a job to do?" Adam asked, confounded. Jesus, who *was* this kid, and would he ever stop talking long enough for Adam to gently but firmly disengage?

"Nope. This delivery was my last task of the night. Dad's cleaning up, I'm off the clock, and, you know, you just got done here—"

"He still has paperwork to sign," Darrin intervened smoothly. "But you're welcome to stay and give him a ride if he needs one."

They both looked at Adam expectantly, and Adam tried to think. "Uhm, I took the bus here, but it wasn't that far. I can probably walk—" It was four miles, but seriously, four miles to a guy from the military? Nothing.

"I can take you," Finn said confidently. He hopped up on the wooden stool behind the register, tucked his hands into his purple hooded sweatshirt, and swung his feet. The whimsical smile on his face had more than a hint of steel, and Adam looked at Darrin a little desperately.

"Okay, uhm, paperwork?"

"C'mon," Darrin said kindly, giving him a little shove. "It won't take long."

Darrin took him behind the stairwell to the left, where a tiny office attached. In the back of the office was a little restroom, and to the left of that stood a door to what was probably an alleyway or a courtyard. Two office chairs sat in there side by side, and Darrin pointed to the one with the little pile of papers on it.

"My office manager, Carolyn, set these out before she left today," he said. Adam had a vague memory of a motherly woman with short red hair and eyes that twinkled behind her jeweled glasses. She'd been in and out all day, getting Darrin's signature on something and then disappearing.

"Okay." Adam swallowed and sat down, filling in the forms by rote. When he got to "address," he wrote in Rico's address and wondered if he'd still have this job when he had to move in six months. "It was really great of you to give me a job. All I did was walk in the store."

Darrin laughed softly and shook out his hair. He was wearing a bright red turtleneck sweater—something classic and soft and not quite feminine but not butch either. It went well with the flared jeans and eelskin cowboy boots. "All you did was walk into a madhouse and start weighing candy," Darrin said. "You were great, sweetie. Now here—make sure you sign the *whole* packet, even that last one there, you got that?"

Adam did as told and then risked a glance out into the front of the store, where Finn still waited. "He's really going to just give me a ride home?"

Darrin nodded. "This surprises you?"

"He barely knows me."

"True, but he knows me. I haven't hired a serial killer yet."

"But… but why *me*?"

Darrin smirked. "Oh baby—they do have *mirrors* where you come from, don't they?"

Adam rolled his eyes. "It's muscles, not sex appeal." He yawned. "But I'll explain the difference when he drops me off."

Darrin laughed throatily, a sweet velvet kind of sound, and Adam found himself smiling in response. "Yes, Adam, I'm sure that conversation will go over well."

Adam squinted at him, tired, a little confused, and worried about the animals. Rico said the cat needed medication twice a day, and she hadn't gotten it yet, and the dumb dog had been taken on his walk to crap once already, but Clopper was pretty big. He'd probably left a giant steaming helping of trouble just waiting for Adam when he opened the door. (Rico had left specific instructions and a buttload of cleaning products should that happen. What frightened Adam was that the cleaning products were all half-empty, and the scrub brush well used.)

"Why did you give me a job?" he asked, because the thought of caring for Rico's animals still terrified him. "I mean, I just walked in the door and—"

"Didn't you *need* a job?" Darrin asked, blue eyes regarding him kindly.

Adam tried to guess how old his new employer was, and failed. Anywhere from twenty-five to fifty? Probably closer to fifty, Adam would hazard—not because he *looked* middle-aged but because his voice was kind and patient, and those were things Adam had always hoped for in his elders but seldom found.

"Yes," he said hoarsely, suddenly wanting to open his heart to this kind man and spill everything. "Thank you. Uhm, when do you need me next?"

"Well, we're going to be pretty busy until Thanksgiving, and then Friday morning is like D-Day around here. How about ten 'til six for the next week and a half. I'll have a schedule for you tomorrow. And get here at six in the morning on D-Day and expect to work a twelve-hour shift, paid overtime, then? Carolyn will get you a regular schedule after that. I'm afraid it's not much more than minimum wage—"

"It's awesome," Adam said firmly, his voice growing a little more solid at the thought of a job that paid regularly and had decent hours.

"Of course once you start school, you'll have to let us know what your hours will be—we can work around them." Darrin stood up then and grabbed a leather trench coat off the post in the corner. In a move of sheer elegance, he swirled the coat around his shoulders and started locking the back door and turning off the lights.

"I don't… I'm not a student anymore," Adam said, feeling foolish.

Darrin arched expressive eyebrows at him. "Then I suggest you start making inquiries, young man. I hired you because you had a future."

"Yeah, sure, boss," Adam mumbled, because explaining was just too hard. "Anything you say."

He turned and followed Darrin out of the darkened room, and then remembered why he couldn't accept Finn's ride home. "I appreciate you waiting," he said to Finn, who was resting his chin on his two fists and peering moodily over the counter. "But really, I can walk from here. I've got to stop and get food and—"

"No worries. I know where the nearest market is." Finn straightened in his seat and smiled, looking about as tired as Adam felt.

Adam looked around and realized that everybody else had cleaned and finished stocking while he'd been in the office with Darrin.

Suddenly Darrin, the boss himself, straightened up. "Oh hell, I forgot to do the counts—what was I thinking? Damn. Ravi? Are you still here?"

"Yeah, yeah." Ravi popped up from behind the stairs, where he'd been stocking little bags. "You need me to help with the counts?"

"Yes, you know math isn't my thing."

Ravi shuddered. "We *all* know math isn't your thing. Come on, Anish—I'll do the counts, you do the paperwork. Boss'll lock it in the safe."

Anish was standing behind the chocolate counter, straightening the money drawer there. "Yeah, in a minute."

Adam looked around and saw the stout girl with the spiked black hair and the pretty thirtyish girl with the long ponytail and the skunk stripe finishing up in the back of the store.

"Does anybody need to be walked out?" he asked, figuring he was the most like hired muscle.

But Ravi looked over his shoulder on the way to the office and shook his head. "We'll take care of them. You go home. Tomorrow we might even get to train you!"

And with that, Finn grabbed Adam's hand and dragged him semireluctantly from the store.

"What?" Finn asked when they had finally started a normal gait down the raised boardwalk of Old Sacramento, heading toward the south entrance. "You act like I'm going to ravish you or something!"

Adam shook his head. "No. Not ravish. Just… you know. Just got here. Don't know you—"

"So I'm a stranger? Hey, we ate in a romantic little hideaway, I can't possibly be a stranger!"

Adam let out a partial laugh. "If that was romantic, no wonder you're building your own grain silos."

"Hmm," Finn said suspiciously. "I have several responses to that, but first things first. Don't forget to take your apron off when you get out to go shopping—that's first."

Adam looked down at himself and felt his face heat. Sure enough, the brown apron with the little logo road to Candy Heaven was still gracing his front. He groaned and pulled the damn thing off, folding it neatly as they walked. "And second?" he asked, thinking that if this kid could keep him from looking like an idiot, it might be worth living with the nonstop verbiage.

"Second? Oh yeah, the second thing. Wear a coat!"

"You first!" Adam retorted, surprised. They were both, in fact, wearing hooded sweatshirts, except Adam's was a basic blue zipper hoodie, and Finn's was the rather enchanting purple one that said CSUS in rainbow letters across the front.

"Yeah, but we're heading for my car!" Finn blew on his hands, his breath smoking around his face in the damp cold rising from the nearby river. "I mean, if you were going to walk home like this, you'd need a hat, a scarf, some gloves. Didn't your mother ever nag you about that stuff?"

When you gonna pay your part of the rent, kid! You're not a baby anymore, and you're eating like a fucking horse!

Make yourself scarce! I got a date tonight and it's no kids allowed, okay? Don't give me no crap about where you gonna go. Call your cousin, he'll sneak you inside.

Yeah, you go ahead and leave. I ain't gonna take care of your fuckin' dog when you go, and my boyfriend thinks it's a pit bull. He'll put it to sleep, you little fucker, so don't be shitty to me.

"No," Adam said shortly. "Nobody nagged me. Sweet of you to do so now, though. It's a real welcome to the neighborhood."

"Right?" Finn asked rhetorically. "You came to the right place!"

"Sacramento?" Adam asked dubiously. "Kid, this place is pretty much the end of the road for me. It's like my version of Last Chance Motel."

Finn shrugged and then crossed the nearly empty street as it dead-ended to the off-ramp. "Well, yeah, but here's your chance, right? If this is Last Chance Hotel, you still have one!"

Couldn't argue with that, and Adam was actually too tired to argue at all.

He followed Finn through the quiet of Old Town, past the statue of the Wells Fargo pony, and into the pricey parking garage.

The kid pulled a monthly pass out of his wallet as they neared a battered green minivan with peeling paint and side panels that looked like somebody took a rake to them after a day on the golf course.

"Wow," Adam said, glancing from bright and shining Finn to the suburban mom-mobile.

Finn smirked and pulled out the key remote to unlock the door. "Don't laugh. This here is the best thing to happen to an American boy since the condom."

Adam couldn't resist. "Do tell," he asked as they both swung in.

"Well, when my friends and I want to go to lunch, it seats six. If somebody needs to move, I take the seats out and it's almost a truck. Took it camping once without the seats, and it rained, and we slept on the floor just fine. It doesn't go beyond ninety, so I'm not tempted to street race, and most importantly…."

Finn grinned, anything but coy, and Adam was forced to smile back. "I'm dying here. More importantly…."

Finn stuck the keys in the ignition and swiveled, smiling brightly when the engine turned over, purring like a kitten. "When I turn the car on, it runs."

Adam remembered his last car dying on the side of Highway 5 at eleven o'clock at night. "You got me there. The apartment is on Eighth and F—any store you can stop at between here and there is good."

They ended up at a tiny Safeway off J Street, and Finn followed Adam inside while he ran around the store and bought bread, peanut butter and jelly, a gallon of milk, and two packages of noodles.

"That's it?" Finn asked, appalled. "No veggies? No fruit juice? Jesus, buy some cereal!"

"That right there is going to have to last me until I get paid," Adam said shortly. "It'll do."

"Fine," Finn muttered. "Stay there in line. I have to get something."

He was back in a moment with a paper bag full of apples, and Adam refrained from questioning until they'd both been rung up.

"They're for you," Finn said as they gathered their groceries and walked toward the car.

Adam swallowed. "I knew that. You shouldn't have."

"Consider it a welcome to Sacramento gift."

"Apples are nice."

"I couldn't get you a family or a car."

"You brought me a hamburger. Apples are real good. Thank you."

"You're not used to asking for help, are you?" Finn asked as they got back in the car.

"Nobody's ever given it to me," Adam said, feeling stupid and pitiable and like he shouldn't be having this conversation.

"Well, ask us. Darrin's a good guy. He likes it when his people are happy."

Yeah, Adam had gotten that impression. "That's nice and all, but I've sorta got to get my shit together. Happy isn't part of the equation."

Finn grunted like Adam had hit him. "You can't mean that!" he said after a few blocks of darkened streets.

"Right there," Adam said, not wanting to answer the disappointment in his voice.

"Adam?"

"You're a sweet kid," Adam said as Finn pulled to a stop in front of his apartment building. "But not everybody gets Mom's minivan and a happy life. Thanks for the ride. Appreciate it."

And with that he opened the door and gathered his stuff and went inside, to where the gods had been extra merciful, because the dog hadn't crapped and the cat was still alive.

The Lay of Alien Territory

GONZO THE cat did *not* like Adam. He hid in corners, under the bed, in the back of the closet, behind the toilet. The morning after Finn dropped Adam off—the morning he woke up to an alarm, thinking, "I need to walk the dog before I go to my holy-God-I-have-a-job!"—Gonzo displayed the depths of his enmity. That was the morning the cat distinguished himself from all the other creatures in the world who hated Adam's guts, by leaping on Adam's head from the top of the refrigerator when Adam ventured into the kitchen for a glass of milk and a peanut butter sandwich.

It took a minute for Adam to fight him off—he was trying not to hurt the damned animal—and by the time Gonzo was thrown *gently* across the room, Adam was bleeding from several scratches along his jaw, his neck, and his shoulders.

"God*dammit!*"

And *that* was when the dog ran in, jumping and barking, and tripping Adam on the way to the bathroom, where he hit his head on the corner of the counter and slid to the floor, seeing stars.

He made it out to walk the dog, which helped him get hold of his temper so he could pin the damned cat to the couch and shove medicine down its maw, but by the time he got a good look at himself in the mirror, the scratches and bruises were in their full glory.

Way to make a second impression.

Darrin's eyes widened as Adam trotted into the store, a small backpack with an extra sandwich and a refillable bottle of water on his back, so he could eat lunch and not embarrass himself *more* this time around. He'd also thrown his sketchbook in, because through eight years in the military, he'd *never* gone without one. He wasn't going to start now.

Unfortunately, his face drew more than enough attention.

"Is there an abusive spouse we should know about?" Darrin asked in all sincerity.

Adam shook his head. "My cousin's cat... fuckin' dog...."

Darrin nodded. "Carry on, then. We didn't finish the stock last night, and as soon as we're open, I need you to go walking with the free-taste coupons, okay?"

Adam stared. "*This!*" He flailed his hands around his mauled face. "*This* is what you want to be the face of the company?"

Darrin shrugged. "Everybody can have a bad morning," he said philosophically. "Let's see if we can have a sweeter day."

"Oh God."

"Don't be so pessimistic, Adam. I mean, yesterday you walked into a store and found a job. Maybe you'll walk the streets and find some optimism, what do you think?"

"I think I'm more of a grunt than a front man," Adam replied honestly. "But *as* a grunt, I'm really frickin' good at taking orders."

Darrin grimaced and shook his head. "By Christmas you will be a compliant house elf. Of this I swear."

"Yeah, you do that. I'll work Christmas Day if you want, just let me keep the damned job."

"Go," Darrin ordered, glaring. "You're funking up my nice little store. But don't go too far, and be sure to smile at people so they don't call an ambulance."

"Will do, boss. I'm outta here."

The thin sunshine barely penetrated the riverfront cold, and Adam was grateful for the cheap pair of thin knit gloves he'd gotten from the dollar store and the peacoat he'd had sent to Rico his first Christmas overseas. God, he missed his cousin. They'd both been inmates of Grandma Macias, but Rico used to show up with Legos and board games in his backpack. The two of them would disappear for hours, the better to stay out of Grandma's line of fire when her soap operas didn't go her way. Rico was the idea guy—which was what he was doing now, working for an ad firm, pitching ideas—and Adam had been the person who'd drawn his ideas out. And the more they'd worked like that, Rico giving ideas, Adam drawing like he saw on the TV, the more he'd wanted to do that.

When he'd gotten out of the military, the idea of sitting behind a draft table, creating something bright and happy and beautiful, had been the only thing on his mind.

Keeping his car running so he made it to his classes and didn't lose his VA loan didn't seem to have any bearing on his direct future, but he'd been wrong about that, hadn't he?

So he wasn't planning to blow this chance, even if it meant smiling at people when he knew he looked like a disaster victim while passing out tickets for a free taste of candy over at Candy Heaven. Most people took the coupon from his fingers and didn't look at his beat-up face at all, and for a little while, he forgot about his appearance and concentrated on giving people a little bit of sweetness for their day.

Until a now familiar burst of enthusiasm practically knocked him on his ass.

"*Adam*? Holy *cow*, Adam, what happened to you? Did you get beat up? Pushed out of a car? Held hostage by the mo—?"

"Jumped on by a psychotic cat and tripped by the dog?" Adam supplied before Finn could get to "abducted by aliens." His newfound friend still had the fleece *Adventure Time* hat on, but in deference to the chilly morning, he was also wearing a bright blue wool coat, a thick handmade wool scarf wrapped several times around his neck, and fleece gloves. His apple cheeks were red with the cold, and his breath came out in steamy puffs, which made Adam think he was probably pretty warm in all that gear.

A little part of him was glad. All of that happiness—it needed to be protected.

"Is that all?" Finn asked, but he was smiling and not particularly disappointed. "My friend, you need to work on your story. The least you could say is that your second job is feeding the monkeys, and they demanded more bananas."

Adam couldn't help it. He smiled. "I was gonna work on my 'abducted by aliens' schtick, but you caught me before I had it ready."

Finn's wide, mobile mouth could sure stretch a smile into the stratosphere. God, he was a good-looking kid. "Well, I'll leave you to it. But hey—" Casually, Finn grabbed his bicep, and Adam let himself be turned. "If you go down that way and then turn left, you'll see my dad's deli, River Burger." Finn reached into his pocket and pulled out a coupon, which he showed to Adam like a grade school teacher would show a student. "This here is a coupon for free garlic fries and a drink, no purchase necessary. I'll be behind the grill this morning, so when you get lunch, come by for some garlic fries, okay?" He nodded earnestly, but God, Adam hated charity.

"Finn, naw, I can't let you do that. Those are for customers and—"

"And friends," Finn said. His hand was practically burning through Adam's coat, and without so much as an apology, he reached under the hem of the thick blue wool and shoved the coupon in the pocket of Adam's jeans. Adam gasped because that hand was more than a little personal, and because, oh God, he hadn't been touched since Robbie, and his body was so *not* going to ignore this beautiful kid with the apple cheeks being this close.

Finn dropped his hand and grinned, still holding on to Adam's arm. "Okay? So I'm going to see you on your lunch hour?"

Oh hell. "Well, you know." Adam swallowed and smiled shyly. "Those fries were pretty good."

Finn whooped out of nowhere, throwing one fist in the air and bouncing on his toes. "Score one for my team! Yes! See you at your lunch hour!" He came back down to the boardwalk from the stratosphere. "Now, you know, I'm not going to take *my* lunch break until I see you, so if you try to get out of this, you're sort of screwing me over."

Adam groaned. "Oh, now, Finn, you don't want to go counting on—"

But it didn't matter. Finn had finally let go of him and was turning in the direction of the deli, talking to Adam over his shoulder.

"Now see, you can't ditch. You don't like charity, so this is worse, right? That's a promise!"

And he was disappearing, so Adam had no choice. "Yeah, fine," he muttered. "But remember, I didn't get a break last night until I fell on my ass!"

"Well remind Darrin today! Don't let me down!" And then he was gone, trotting down the boardwalk as the stores around him opened.

"Why's it matter so much?" Adam asked, but he didn't shout it, and he wasn't planning to go back on his word. With a sigh, he kept up his walk around the perimeter of the little three-block area, greeting as many people as possible with their free coupon.

He walked to the end of the boardwalk, took a right, then walked past more shops until he came to the Railroad Museum on his left and the same parking garage Finn had used in front of him. The garage was in the shadow of the overpass, but instead of feeling the presence of the freeway, Adam felt like all of that concrete sheltered them from the big bad world. It wasn't until he saw the parking garage that it occurred to him to ask what Finn had been doing on the riverfront walk.

"Naw," he muttered to himself. "Why? Seriously. Kid, why you gotta...." But he didn't finish that sentence, and continued back to Candy Heaven, because Darrin said he had half an hour on coupon duty, and it was someone else's turn to freeze their ass off.

But when he walked into the store, Joni, the shorter, stouter girl with the buzz-cut dark hair, said, "Hey, did Finn find you? He was over here looking before he opened up the grill."

"Yeah," Adam muttered, setting the basket of coupons down on a stool near the riverfront entrance. The other entrance was back behind the two cash counters, which made for a nice flow of customers from one end, through the barrels, around the chocolate counter, to the register. Adam was starting to get a feel for how the business moved. "He found me. Thanks."

"What'd he want?" Darby asked, her red-streaked ponytail swinging behind her as she poured barrel-shaped root beer candies into an actual barrel. "He's not usually so insistent."

"He wanted me to come by on my lunch hour," Adam said, a little rattled by all of the attention.

"For what?" Anish asked. He was in the chocolate corner again, but instead of working with chocolate, he was using tongs to put sour gummi tape into a cellophane bag. When it had been weighed, the little bags would be wrapped tightly and put into barrels for purchase.

The customers were trickling in, and Adam guessed they had another half an hour before the place was wall-to-wall people like it had been when he'd arrived the day before. "I don't know! He gave me a coupon. Honestly, I was gonna take my sandwich there and eat my fries, that's all I know!"

"Children," Darrin said dryly from the counter, "can we give our new student a chance to settle before we ask for his report?"

"Yeah, but Darrin, you know that Finn's just getting over Perry! We don't need him breaking his heart over Tall, Dark, and Military, you know?"

Darrin looked at Joni thoughtfully. "Who says he'll break Finn's heart?"

"Well Jesus, it's not like he's gay!"

The whole store shut down, customers included, to look at Adam, who swallowed and looked away. Absurdly, he remembered that moment in the barracks, when Heller and his fucking trash talk had finally gotten to be too much. Robbie couldn't even meet his eyes after that—the memory just ripped him raw.

"Man, could you knock off the bullshit about faggots already! Jesus, Heller, it's legal in the service and everything!"

"What's your problem, Macias? It's not like you're one of them."

"That's not what your cock said when I sucked it last year!"

Deafening, condemning silence, because Adam had said what nobody said. He searched out Robbie's eyes, thinking that yes, Robbie wanted to come out, wanted to be a couple, and this way they could be, and nobody could gainsay them.

Robbie looked away, curled his lip, and Adam heard the word before he uttered it.

"Faggot."

Adam looked around at the little store with the rainbow banners and the rainbow candy, and thought that this *had* to be easier than that last time. "No one said I wasn't," he said quietly. "Gay, that is. Nobody said I wasn't gay. 'Cause I am. So, you know. There's that."

He looked up and met Darrin's eyes steadily, not wanting to talk about it. Any of it. "Where do you need me, boss?"

Darrin's smile was nothing but kind. "Help Anish with the weighing. We're pretty low on the premeasured packets, and we need as many of those as you can churn out."

"Awesome."

Adam ignored everything—the silence, the emerging chatter—and went to help Anish with the task. He got so intent on weighing the sour tape and wrapping it in the cellophane that he almost didn't hear Anish address him.

"What?" he asked, pulling himself out of those terrible last months of eating alone, of Robbie's recriminatory looks, of knowing Robbie and Heller were sneaking behind the Humvees, and it was all okay because neither of *them* said the word "gay" and made it stick.

"It's always hard," Anish said softly. "It always takes bravery. Making a statement about yourself is never easy. Even if it's 'Dad, I don't want to study business.' Joni knows that—I'm sure Darby is chewing her out as we speak."

Adam nodded and shrugged. "Thanks," he said quietly and went back to weighing candy. But he felt better, and he made extra sure to smile at Anish when he could manage it. Because Anish was right. Making a statement—or an overture of friendship—was never easy.

Business didn't exactly taper off, but it *did* become more manageable around two in the afternoon, when Darrin started giving out breaks. Adam took his last, because he still felt like a little bit of a weenie for almost passing out the night before, and it was three thirty by the time he and Ravi went jogging out to the sandwich shop. Ravi was picking up for Darrin, who was going back to count drawers and do paperwork, as well as for himself and Anish.

There were a lot of food places in Old Sac. This one had sort of the standard elements. A glass display case with sample meals, sandwiches, and desserts separated the employees from the customer seating area, and a register sat on the counter near the back. This particular deli had five or six tables, the small metal kind that made Adam think of ice cream parlors, and chairs to match.

Finn was preslicing meat on the back counter as Adam and Ravi walked in, but he looked up almost immediately, turned the slicer off, and smiled. "There you are!" he crowed. "Here, let me put fresh fries in."

The enclosed space was pretty warm after the late afternoon chill of outside. Adam slid his coat and backpack onto a chair and pulled his sandwich, water, and sketchbook out of the pack.

Ravi nodded at him and went up to order while Adam sat down and made his PB&J disappear. He was down to the dregs of his water and starting a sketch when Ravi sat down across from him to wait for his food.

"What is that?"

Adam shrugged. "Just something I do." *Something I thought I was going to make a living doing.*

"Can I see?" Ravi watched in fascination as a quick sketch of Candy Heaven took shape, and then laughed, his white teeth flashing in his sienna face. "That is very good—there's Anish and Miguel and Darby and Darrin—" He stopped and grinned. "That is *amazing*, Adam. Did you go to school to learn that?"

Adam shrugged. "I was. Car broke down, lost my job, lost my grant...."

Yeah. It didn't sound any better when he said it out loud than in his own head.

"Well, you need to find a way back to school," Ravi said with conviction. "That is much too good a gift not to share."

Adam shrugged again. "We'll see," he said, because it hurt to commit to things when you were afraid you couldn't get them done. He kept working, since Ravi didn't seem to mind watching him, and when Finn called him up to pick up his order, Adam signed the sketch and ripped it out of the book.

"Here—you can keep it, or give it to Darrin or whatever, 'kay?"

"This one I'll give to Darrin," Ravi said decisively, and then he smiled wickedly. "But you need to draw one of Anish and I so we may give it to our grandmother—we'll frame it and everything. We can even pay you for it, if you like."

Adam's palms actually started to sweat. Oh God—money. He could buy his own damned fries. He could come here and watch Finn work, and not eat free like a charity case.

"That would be great," he said, feeling a tiny metal string between his shoulder blades uncinch. "Tell you what, I'll bring you something nice and inked tomorrow—you pay me what you think it's worth, okay?"

Ravi grinned. "Excellent. Anish and I will be sure to get in our good sides." He grabbed his bag and left.

At the same time, Finn washed his hands and called back to a middle-aged ginger-haired man working in a small room behind the counter, "Dad, I'm on break!"

"Hear ya!" came the reply, and Finn trotted around the counter, a suspiciously full tray in his hand.

Adam glared at it. "You'd better be eating most of that," he said seriously.

Finn's eyes were as wide and as guileless as an infant's. "Oh, I'm sure I'll eat some," he said, nodding like someone with his physique could eat two hamburgers and two orders of garlic fries.

"But Finn," Adam began, not even sure how he was going to finish that sentence. He took a deep breath and the PB&J in his stomach laughed mockingly at him. Oh man, those hamburgers did *not* smell any worse than they had the night before. In fact, now that Adam knew how good they tasted, they might even smell *better.*

"Tell you what," Finn said, picking the food baskets off the tray and putting a hamburger most *definitely* in front of Adam. "How about you draw a picture for *me*, and I'll consider it payment."

Adam looked around the little deli, thinking that he'd like to put Finn—the real Finn—behind the counter, and the cartoon Jake from *Adventure Time* sitting at one of the tables.

"Yeah," he murmured, wanting that burger really badly. His stomach gurgled, reminding him that he hadn't been eating a whole lot *before* he'd left San Diego either. "Yeah, okay. I can do that."

"Good," Finn said, and took a bite of his own burger. He chewed and swallowed while Adam was putting his sketchbook away, and then added, "That way I know I'll see you tomorrow."

Adam pulled the drawstring on his little day pack and turned back to the burger. "How do you know my company is even that good?"

Oh my God—that grin. Should be put in a bottle and used to disarm enemies, or solve world hunger or something.

"'Cause it's been pretty worth it so far. Now tell me, how was your day?"

Adam looked at that young, earnest face and swallowed. "Well, you know. I delivered coupons, weighed candy, came out to my new boss—all in a day's work."

Finn didn't startle at the "came out," but his grin increased in width, amperage, and all-around lethal capability. "*That* sounds like a good day's work, amigo. Now give me details."

Adam took a bite of his burger, chewed, swallowed, and said, "Yeah, sure. But maybe when we're done eating, 'cause this? My friend, this is a masterpiece."

Adam had spent so much time alone, both his last few months in the Army and the time after that in San Diego, and while he worked on his burger with what should have been single-minded dedication, he also found himself captivated by Finn's bold monologues.

"So like a bridge, right? But something amazing, like, say, the one in Australia or the Golden Gate, but I want it to go across a *city*, right? Why can't we do that? I mean New York does it, but they do it across the rivers, but I still think we should just do it across a city—"

"But aren't those, you know, overpasses?" Adam hated to rain on his parade.

"But no! This would be a whole different concept in urban development. It's like the tunnel, right? That leads from here to K Street? Except the *opposite* of that! And way the hell bigger."

Adam looked at him, nodding excitedly, and thought of another picture—this one of Finn, the real boy, without his fleece hat, building a giant bridge over the meager Sacramento skyline. "Yeah, sure," he said helplessly. He had no idea if it was a good idea. He'd just agree to anything this kid said so he could see that manic spark of enthusiasm in his eyes.

"So it's either that or, you know, an aquarium like the one in Baltimore, with the solid stratified core of marine life, and a tunnel through the center, and a bridge overhead, and maybe a second tower, and a... tunnel bridge, a, you know, a chunnel, connecting them, like England to France, except in water, or we could go to the bottom of the Monterey Bay and build one, except"—Finn's face fell—"that's probably not environmentally sound." He sighed. "It would be cool, though!"

"Oh absolutely," Adam agreed. The picture of Finn had changed, and now he was proudly displaying a chunnel surrounded by fish on the bottom of the bay, like a water city except better.

Because Finn was there.

And fish.

Oh God.

"So, good burger?" Finn asked, and Adam became aware that he'd been done for a few minutes, and he'd just been sitting there, staring at this irrepressible kid, daydreaming about how he should be drawn.

"Excellent." Oh man. How long had Adam been there? He didn't even look at his phone. Judging by how much he wanted to stay, it had been too long. He started gathering the paper and the napkins from his lunch. "I gotta go. I mean, lunch break don't last forever. I mean, you know, time to go back to work. Don't want to lose the job on the second day. But thank you for the food—it was real good. I'll bring that picture by tomorrow."

"I'll pay you in food!" Finn said brightly, and Adam shook his head.

"No, no, you already paid me in food *and* company. I'll just bring you the picture, okay? If I got money, I'll get something. But I gotta go. Thanks for the company. Gotta go."

And with that he threw on his coat and backpack and practically raced out the door, dumping his trash in the can on his way out.

He couldn't bear to look at Finn and daydream about him anymore. Of all people, he knew that cartoons weren't real.

DARRIN LET him go at six thirty that night, which meant he had two eight-hour shifts on his time card, and he felt pretty good about that. He trotted back to the apartment in the stone-cold dark, grateful for the physical exercise and for a breather away from all the people in the store, and from Finn.

Especially away from Finn.

The kid's company was addictive, pleasant, exciting, and Adam's body, which had been hanging out in sort of an injured dormancy after Robbie, was starting to wake up and notice.

He got back to the apartment and took Clopper on his second walk for the day, getting used to the big animal's energy and getting *really* used to telling the big doofus, "Down, boy!"

And whenever his imagination strayed to that wide mobile mouth and the bright blue eyes, he tried to tell himself the same thing.

When he got back to the apartment, he had another PB&J, some milk, and an apple, and sat down at the kitchen table while the television played in the background.

He had two commissions: he needed to make good.

The first one was easy. Ravi and Anish were bright, smiling, ink-and-paper worthy, with only a hint of caricature in their presentation of bags of candy. He thought maybe that would be the sort of picture a good grandmother would want. Not that he had any experience with that.

He's a bad boy, just like his mother. Rico comes out and says please and thank you. This one hides because he's afraid.

And thus, eight years in the Army to prove that he was not. God. Grandmothers. So Adam hoped that the picture was good for them. He even added a hint of color in the faces and the brightly colored background of the store, and then cut it carefully off of the art book with an X-Acto knife. Rico had left a box of cereal in the cabinet, so Adam pulled the bag out of the box and folded the cardboard over the picture to keep it safe.

And then he went to work on Finn's.

The first one, or, well, four, he couldn't use. He couldn't bring himself to tear them up either, but he couldn't use them.

They were too....

Personal.

One featured Finn in the hat, as he appeared sitting next to Adam in the darkened loft, knees drawn to his chest. The other was the Finn he remembered backed up against the pallet in the stock room, eyes wide, lips slightly parted, like he was anticipating a kiss. The third was Finn fist-pumping the air when Adam agreed to come eat, and the last one was Finn, eyes bright over his hamburger, spinning bridges out of air and a future out of a solid faith there was a future to be had.

All of them lingered on things—the crinkles at the corners of his eyes; the fullness of his lips, even when his mouth was wide and smiling; the little bump in the bridge of his nose; or the slight dent that interrupted the even bevel on the bottom of his chin. Things. Inappropriate things.

Finally, as the eleven o'clock news came on and Adam fought not to tear his military-cut hair out by the roots, he ground his teeth and knuckled down and drew what he'd intended to in the first place: Finn looking up from the cutting machine to grin at the Jake cartoon character across the store. It took a while—the store was a place of multi-perspectives and a lot of little details that Adam lavished his time on, since Finn was small enough that he couldn't spend his time on *Finn*, and when he looked up, it was twelve o'clock, and he was done, and tired....

And he'd forgotten to medicate the fucking cat.

Oh, shit, shit, shit, shit, shit....

"Gonzo.... Gonzo... here, kitty, kitty. Where you hiding from me now, you homicidal little fucker? Gonzo...." Oh God. Under the bed, on top of the closet, behind the toilet—oh, hey, hello, *in the bathtub*, lying still, panting, and not looking good *at all*.

Adam barely had to hold Gonzo down to give him the medicine, and he started to panic. Oh hell. He imagined the text. *Rico, your cat isn't looking too good. In fact, I think he died in the bathtub. Please don't hate me, I promise to do better with the dog.*

He left the cat in the tub with its water bowl and a bowl of soft food, mushed carefully, and went to bed, hoping for the best.

Rico, I'm sorry, man, I'd take the cat to the vet, but I got no money, and you didn't leave me your vet's name, and....

Okay, erase *that* text.

Rico, who's your vet? The cat isn't looking fantastic, and I'd like to take him in if he gets any worse.

Okay. Better. Not alarming, but concerned. And not a word about the money, so Adam could write a hot check for the rat bastard cat if he had to, and Rico wouldn't know that his stupid fucking cat was going to break him. Good. That would work. He could live with that.

Or at least go to sleep with that. It could work.

It was all he had.

Sunset by the River

ADAM WOKE up in the morning with the cat sleeping by his head. When he stumbled into the bathroom to take a leak, there was a big pile of cat crap in the bottom of the tub. Not the most pleasant way to spend five minutes before his shower, but it wasn't on the rug, and it wasn't a cat corpse, so Adam was calling it a win.

He made that a conscious choice for the rest of the day too. Joni ran coupon duty until the deli was open, so he had no accidental-on-purpose run-ins with Finn, and if Adam avoided the deli while he was doing his own duty during lunch rush, well, that was probably an accident.

Probably.

His lunch half hour rolled around and he gave Anish the carefully cardboarded picture to run to Finn when he got Ravi's lunch. For himself, Adam asked Darrin if he could go out in the back courtyard to eat.

Darrin found him there, shivering, five minutes later, as he swallowed the last of the PB&J and washed it down with more tap water.

"He's here, Adam, and he brought you fries, so you may want to quit being a chickenshit about it and go say hi."

Adam tried to smile at him, which should have been easy since he was dressed in a brightly colored shawl-collared Christmas cardigan, with evergreen reindeer running across the horizontal stripe in the middle, but he was pretty sure what came out wasn't happy. "Oh. Uhm. I, uhm, didn't think…."

"Didn't think he'd want your company again after stalking you two days running?"

"He's not stalking!" Adam defended. "He's just being nice to the new guy."

Darrin narrowed his eyes. "Okay, so, new guy, go out and be nice to your new friend."

If this is what having a real parent was like, Adam could see why Rico moved out of the house as soon as possible. "Darrin, he's getting a crush on me!" he said after a moment, sounding petulant, even to himself.

"Yes, Adam, and I think the feeling's mutual. Now go out there and face that little boy like a man." Darrin plucked his brows with an unmistakable arch, and his very skepticism cowed Adam even more.

"I'm gonna break his heart," Adam muttered. "He's barely old enough to be allowed out of the house."

"That's bullshit and you know it, Army. Now go spend your lunch break with somebody who wants to know you better."

"Oh Jesus," Adam muttered. "I'm an *employee*! You've known me three days."

Darrin nodded thoughtfully. "That's true. And look at me, falling into the hole in your life where you needed a Darrin. I'm *awesome*!" He spun his hands at the wrists, ending up with a vogue in which he framed his face with elegant fingers. "Now go let Finn fall into the Finn-sized hole in your life. You'll almost be hole-less."

Adam glared at him impotently, because there was no comeback to that. Hell, there wasn't even a *language* for that. "Are you sure you weren't waiting for someone *else* to come be your winter help?"

Darrin laughed throatily, closing his eyes and tilting his head back so his hair fell behind him. "Oh, Adam. You think you're only staying for the winter? That's adorable. Now scoot!"

Adam cast a hunted look over his shoulder, unable to say why Darrin's sweet smile should be so terrifying. Then he went to face the music.

Finn was waiting out in front of the store, arms crossed, a takeout bag dangling from his hand.

"Uhm, hey, Finn. I, uhm, didn't you like the picture?"

"The picture was fine, you coward. A little impersonal, but fine. Do you not do close-ups?"

At that moment Anish walked in from coupon duty. "Oh no! He does wonderful close-ups! You should see the one he did for our grandmother. I cannot wait to put it in a frame. She'll think we actually *thought* about her present for once!"

Finn glared at him, and Adam wished he'd stopped to put his coat on.

"None of your close-ups came out," he mumbled. "I can try again tonight."

"Have you eaten?" Finn demanded.

Adam thrust his hands in his pockets so he wouldn't take the fries. "Uhm, you know. The usual."

"I was there when you bought the groceries. Now here, take the fries and walk with me, okay?"

Adam didn't know how to fight that. Not without being rude, and Finn didn't deserve that. He squared his shoulders and enjoyed the warmth of the fries through the takeout container, and hoped his hooded sweatshirt would do him in the chill off the river.

Which was exactly where Finn was taking him. Across the cobblestone street, past the restrooms, and over the landmark bridge. The wind coming off the river cut through the bone in the winter afternoon, and Adam shivered, but he kept following Finn over the bridge. Riverfront Park was essentially a nice little walking path in a corner of green overlooking the river. Finn headed toward the wrought iron fence that bordered the drop-off, and Adam kept up, trying to keep his teeth from chattering.

Finn heard him, though, and made a sound of exasperation. "I would have waited while you went and got your coat!" As he spoke, he busied himself with the button at the chin strap of his fleece hat, and before Adam could protest, the hat was over his ears, warm and cozy and smelling of Finn.

"Thanks."

"Oh my God, was that so hard to say?" Finn demanded, unwrapping his Doctor Who scarf from around his neck and winding it laboriously around Adam's when he was done.

"You didn't have to," Adam said, his voice dropping miserably.

Finn's angry motions stopped, and the air around them stilled. Behind Finn, the sun was setting over the river, and Adam could either squint into it or peer into the quiet shadows of Finn's face. He chose Finn, and they stared at each other for a heartbeat while Adam tried not to notice the quivering of Finn's lower lip.

"I just want to get to know you. Is that so bad?" Finn asked, his voice a raspy whisper, not quite too quiet to be heard amid the traffic over the bridge and the day-to-day sounds on the boardwalk.

"I'm not really used to...." Anything.

"I know, Adam. I get it. I mean, two minutes with you and I got it. You... whatever is going on in here"—Finn waved his hand in the direction of Adam's chest—"it's dark and sort of sad and hard for you to get over."

"I'm not some charity case," Adam muttered, hating the gentleness, hating the compassion.

"I'm not giving charity," Finn snapped, shaking his head.

"Well I don't see what you get out of it!" And that, that right there, was Adam's entire problem with the past three days. A job out of nowhere, a friend—a sweet, sexy one at that—literally landing in his lap and delivering him hamburgers. What did these people get out of it? What was there to be gained by giving Adam Macias a break? It certainly hadn't benefitted anybody before, had it? He and Rico had history—a long one—of Rico helping Adam behind everybody's back and Adam being exhaustingly grateful.

The only history Adam had with Candy Heaven and Finn was walking through the front door.

"Maybe you just seem like a decent guy," Finn said with dignity. "Can't you just deal with that?"

Adam grunted and turned toward the river. Without talking, the two of them resumed their walk, and Adam delved into the fries before they could get cold.

"So," Finn said as they approached the fence near the bottom of the walk, "what was your morning like?"

Adam shrugged. "My cousin's cat is still alive—that's something." And with that he related the misadventures of Gonzo, the ancient tiger-striped cat, and how apparently the medicine regulated Gonzo's blood sugar and *absolutely needed* to be given every night and every morning.

"Oh no!" Finn gasped, clearly taken with poor man-eating Gonzo's fate. "What did your cousin say when you texted him?"

Oh Lord. Adam didn't even have to consult his phone to remember the text verbatim. *Please don't freak out. The cat was a rescue and old when I got him five years ago. If it's his time, it's his time. Not your fault.*

"He said the cat was old and to just keep doing my best. But you know? Rico's my only family. It's not like I want him to come back in June and have no cat, right? It would be a shitty way to pay him back when he's done me a solid by letting me stay at his place."

"Well, yeah. But he doesn't expect the impossible from you, Adam. Maybe just give yourself a break about it, okay?"

Adam shook his head. "I mean, unless I can get back in school, I don't know what else I got, right? It's like this stupid cat and the big-assed dog are my last chance to prove I'm useful as a human being!"

Finn stared at him in horror. "Jesus, Adam, how old are you? Thirty?"

"Twenty-seven."

"That's even worse! You're barely older than me—you can't possibly hinge your whole existence on the life or death of an aging cat. C'mon, find something else! I mean, so Rico's your only decent family. You can draw, and it's great. You're pretty smart, because you walked into a job knowing nothing and made yourself useful pretty fast, and you have a sense of humor, because you were going to say you were abducted by aliens instead of beat up by a cat—"

"Only to make you happy," Adam admitted, feeling bad.

"But that's *awesome!*" Finn said, practically dancing. "That means you want to impress *me!*"

Adam stopped, folding up the empty fry container and shoving it into the bag almost automatically. "You know, we should probably get back to the shop. I think my break is almost over."

"You do, don't you?" Finn asked after they'd turned around and started walking back.

"Do what?" Adam responded, but he knew.

"Want to impress me?"

Adam swallowed, thought about how the kid had just showed up and insisted Adam pony up. He owed Finn. "An embarrassing amount," he admitted.

Finn pumped his fist. "Woot!" And Adam's mind took a picture of that moment right there. He was so happy. Adam wanted to freeze time. He started planning the drawing as he dropped the trash in the bin and let Finn lead the way back to work.

He didn't realize until he got inside that Finn hadn't taken his silly fleece hat back, or his hand-knitted Doctor Who scarf. Adam wore them on the jog home and on his walk out with Clopper. The whole time he had that kid's smell, that happy, sandwich smell, keeping him warm.

THE NEXT day he brought Finn the picture—and his hat and scarf back—but even he could see that the deli was busy when he stopped by. Ravi and Anish had given him twenty-five dollars for his drawing, and he made it up to the counter to order a turkey sandwich (because the garlic fries were giving him gas), but as soon as Finn saw him, traffic stopped.

"You came? You came, and we're busy? Oh my God! That sucks! But you *came*!"

Adam glanced around him, wondering if he was going to get grief because he was apparently blocking the entire line.

"Well, uhm, yeah. I owed you a picture. And you need your hat. And your scarf."

"And you need…," Finn led and Adam blushed.

"A turkey sandwich. Just chips this time."

Finn nodded soberly. "The garlic makes you fart, doesn't it? Yeah, me too, but they're nice to have some of the time. Okay, with coffee and the discount that'll be $5.45."

Adam opened his mouth to protest the discount, because Finn knew damned well that was about half what his order should cost, but arguing about it would just make Finn look bad in front of the crowd.

And judging by the way Finn was grinning at him while he called the order to the woman behind him, he knew it too.

Adam gave him the money, scowling, and the woman—who had hair very much the color of Finn's, and big blue eyes framed with strawberry blonde lashes as well—gave Finn a droll look as she took the tag from him.

"Now go sit down and wait. I'll have time to bring it out in a minute," Finn said, handing back the change.

Adam growled and shook his head, and then took the last seat and sat down. While he was waiting, he pulled out his sketchbook and started working. Some of those more personal pictures of Finn needed fleshing out, but he figured that wasn't safe to work on here—not when Finn could see him. Instead he pulled up a newer page, one he'd sketched the night before and inked in, featuring Darrin's store in bold lines and bright primary and secondary colors. Working at every juncture in the store was a chibi version of one of the employees—a short, squat Anish, a less short and squat Ravi, a Carolyn with bejeweled glasses, a Joni with spiky hair and lots of piercings, and so on. All of the employees he'd met so far—the boy with the nose ring, the girl who liked pigtails and striped socks—all of them were there in their squat little cartoon versions, and Adam thought it was a good piece. Maybe he'd give it to Darrin for Christmas, and to say thank you for the job. He was looking forward to that. Ravi had taken the first one he'd drawn and pinned it up behind the register. This one was better, and Adam hated indebtedness.

"Ooh," Finn said behind him. "Nice. That'll look good in the store."

Carefully he set down Adam's order, plus a hot chocolate, and Adam looked up at him, knowing his smile was a little shy and unable to help it. "Sort of a thank-you to Darrin, you know?"

"That's a good idea. Here, let me see!"

And before Adam could protest, Finn had taken the sketchbook from his hand.

"Uhm, yanno, that's sort of like a diary, really, and—"

Oh no. Finn hadn't looked directly behind his own pictures. No, even worse, he'd gone to the beginning of the sketchbook, where Adam was still working out things from Baghdad, and the things he'd drawn....

Finn's bright, shining face sobered, went dark, as he looked at a picture of bodies in the desert, bones protruding, a child's hand flopped backward in a parody of elegance, rags of clothing fluttering about the corpses like moths.

"Oh, Adam. I'm so sorry."

"That's, uhm, you know. Sort of private," Adam said, more clearly this time. "I don't want you to see—I mean some of that stuff is pretty ugly." He went to take it from Finn, but to his surprise, Finn didn't let go.

"That's fine," Finn said, trying to make eye contact while Adam was bent on looking at the plant in the corner by the trash can. Finn's hand on his shoulder, warm and a little moist from just being washed, finally made him look up. "No, Adam—it's fine that this is a diary. I'm sorry I intruded. But don't think you have to protect me from this, okay? I'm not really Finn from the cartoon, you know? I'm a grown-up. If you served active duty, I know you had to see some awful stuff. Don't hide it from me because you think I can't take it."

Adam nodded and reached for the book. "Uhm, thanks." God, could this moment end?

"No. Adam, I mean it." Finn put the book in Adam's hands and squeezed his shoulder again. Then he broke Adam's world by bending down and placing a warm, chaste kiss on Adam's temple. "I'm a big boy. I can deal with this too."

Adam couldn't answer. He was busy gaping and trying to contain the shivers that racked his body in the aftermath of that careless kiss. He managed a nod and gratefully put the sketchbook in his pack.

"The sandwich looks, uh… really good."

Finn shook his head and sighed. "I really just fucked with your head, didn't I?"

Adam nodded and talked through a full mouth. "'S a great sandwich."

"Yeah, Adam. You enjoy that."

Adam looked fixedly at the plant. "I did," he confessed. They both knew he wasn't talking about the sandwich, but he didn't have the words for anything else.

Finn started talking—rambling, really—about something, anything, and Adam could only be grateful. It was uncanny the way the kid knew how to settle Adam down. When Adam was done with lunch, he wiped his mouth and managed a twitch of his lips for Finn, who had worked really hard not to let silence take over the table.

"It was real human, you know? To sit and talk to me. Oh!" He'd almost forgotten. He reached for his backpack again and pulled out a little cardboard packet, which he shoved at Finn, embarrassed. "Here. It's, well, more personal than the last one—"

"Do you have any in your diary?" Finn asked, so dead-on Adam knew his Latino-mocha skin washed ruddy just from the heat in his face.

"Of, uhm, *you?*"

Finn shook his head. "Asked and answered. That's okay, then. Even if this one isn't personal, I know you're thinking about me." He smiled then, luminously, and Adam was possessed with the desire to spill his sketchbook out for Finn to see, to share his secrets, to invite this kid into his heart.

"But I hope you like this one," he said weakly.

Finn looked at the picture with avid eyes. "That's the other night at sunset, isn't it?"

"Yeah."

"We were standing closer than that," Finn told him surprisingly. "I know because I realized how brown your eyes are."

Adam's face heated all over again. "Yeah, well. Macias. Mexican. You know."

"Hot," Finn said playfully, raising his eyebrows.

"Yeah, it is getting that way in here. You know, I gotta—"

Finn's face fell. "Yeah. You gotta go. Hey, when do you get off tonight?"

"Seven, wh—"

"Good. I get off at six thirty. I'll pick you up."

"Where're we—"

"Movie. My treat. Popcorn too."

"I gotta walk the dog!" If Adam had paws, all four of them would be splayed out, just like Clopper's when Adam tried to pull him away from some especially tasty-smelling dead thing. *Abort, abort, abort! Friendly human is taking me somewhere I don't want to go!*

"Good! I'll go with you. We can dose the cat, walk the dog, and *then* go to the movies. Now hurry, you're going to be late. Don't forget to wait for me!"

And Finn got up and left, returning to work and the line of customers who hadn't diminished one bit, even though other people who looked much like Finn were busy serving them.

Adam was left gaping after him, aware that he'd just been hauled into a date by the collar.

The people at Candy Heaven were *not* sympathetic.

"So," Darrin said delicately as Adam returned from lunch a few minutes early, "how is Finn?"

"He's fine. He's terrific. I think he's taking me on a date. Does that bother anybody else? That should bother you. It bothers me. Is *anybody else freaked out about that?*"

Darrin listened to him ramble as Adam put on his apron and stationed himself behind the counter at the weighing bowl. Then Darrin pulled a gummi lemon sour from a pile of them, extracted it from the wrapper, and while Adam was in full cry, asked, "Are you allergic to lemon or sugar?"

"No, but did you hear what I—omph!"

Adam's entire face tried to squeeze shut, and he fought not to swallow the little round ball of goo down the wrong pipe. It took him several minutes of rolling the thing around in his mouth before he sucked in a mouthful of spit, tucked it between his teeth and his cheek, and managed, "What in the hell is the matter with you!" before he had to swallow again.

"Well, my boy, I figured if you didn't stop talking and go out on your date, you'd become a sour old man in no time at all. This was just a taste of it."

Adam squinched his eyes shut and wondered how in the hell those kids who ate this shit by the pound could manage it. As he did that, he had a vision of his grandmother, nose wrinkled, eyes narrowed, looking *just like* she'd been sucking lemons all day, while she told Adam's mother what a loser he was and how he was going to turn out *just like her*.

"It's awful," he said after another moment, although the candy itself was starting to grow on him.

"Yes, well, you will be too if your whole life is about being alone."

Adam regarded him suspiciously, rolling the squishy thing around in his mouth as it disappeared. God, some people *chewed* those things. The thought boggled him. "You say that, but I don't see *you* parading anything hot through the hallowed halls of Candy Heaven."

Darrin's smile was perfectly self-contained. "*I* could be entertaining an entire brothel of sweet young things for all you know. I find that the more people know about my personal life, the less people are apt to listen when I am giving them *perfectly wonderful* advice. Now keep sucking your lemon, Adam, and I'm going to go into the back room and do paperwork."

"You don't do paperwork. You watch Carolyn do paperwork."

"Yes, well, that will be fun too."

And with that Darrin disappeared, leaving Adam in charge of the counter, feeling strangely bereft now that the candy had gone.

"He's right, you know," Joni said from the chocolate counter. "Finn's a great guy. I mean, at worst you get to spend an evening out. What's the harm?"

"I got nothing to offer him," Adam muttered. "What kind of candy was that? Can I get a few?"

Joni sighed, moved to the appropriate barrel, and took out a handful, which she thrust at him. "He seems to think otherwise. God knows why, because right now you are irritating the *fuck* out of *me*. But then, I'm not all that crazy about things with peen."

Adam couldn't decide whether to glare at her or thank her. He popped a candy in his mouth, closed his eyes and squinched up his face, and decided on option B.

When he could see again, he said, "Well, thank you—and I promise to keep my peen to myself."

She nodded in her particular "no bullshit" way, and together they turned toward the customers who had made their way up to the counters.

Bad Habits of Sweets

FINN TOOK him out to an animated Christmas movie, which delighted Adam to no end. He'd forgotten why he'd gone to animation school, the particular blend of art and storytelling that he could lose himself in forever.

But that didn't stop him from breaking down the component parts of the animation and explaining them to Finn as they left the building.

"See, the water? That's stop-motion animation, so the action looks really sped up, but it's not, you know, computer G or pen and ink. So they had to do something mechanical for that, and I think it was like, two layers of painted glass and flickering lights, and between that and the skipping every tenth frame, it *looked* like real water, right?"

Finn nodded, smiling at him, a little bemused. Adam realized he'd been talking from the time they left their seats to the time they got back to the minivan. Finn probably didn't know Adam knew that many words. "That's amazing that you know that. How far did you get through your program?"

"Only a year. I had two more to go and—" He was tired of whining about his fucking grant. "I'd sort of been counting on that money."

"Yeah. That's really unfair. Have you thought of other ways to get through school?"

"Through that one? No. It's pretty expensive, even though they have one here. I could probably get a BA at the state college, but I might need to retake some of my general education. It doesn't always count when you transfer, and they usually don't have degrees in animation, so it would have to be art or art history or something."

"What would a special school get you that a state college wouldn't?"

Adam shrugged, trying not to let this hurt. "You know, internships, connections. I mean, I could get the degree in art and even be really good, but generating that whole network thing you need to get your dream job...?" He shook his head and summoned up the same optimism that had sent him to Sacramento on a bus. "But, you know, maybe you just adjust the dream and keep going, right?"

Finn's smile at him was not up to its usual wattage. "Wow," he said quietly.

"Wow what?"

"I mean, here I was, thinking you were pessimistic as hell—"

"I am."

"No! You're not! Look at you. You're ready to start again, start from scratch. That's amazing."

Adam swallowed, feeling somehow like he'd let Finn down. "You don't sound amazed," he observed tentatively.

"Yeah, no." Finn unlocked the doors and slid into the driver's seat. "I'm amazed that you're optimistic about the future, I'm just depressed that you don't seem to be optimistic about *people*."

Adam blinked slowly. "Well, I didn't doubt you'd show up tonight. That's something."

Finn's troubled expression lightened up a notch. "That's true. In fact, that's *awesome*. Okay. I take it back. I can have a little faith."

Adam's heart did a backflip, stopped beating, and started up again with a ragged little limp. "You were gonna give up?" he asked, a pain he'd been trying to avoid for the last two years blooming in his chest.

"No!" Finn protested, sounding shocked. "No—Adam, you're a tough nut to crack, but you've drawn me two pictures and taken a walk with me. I think we're okay."

Adam thought about it for a minute, the pain receding but not quite going away. "You deserve more," he said, feeling wretched. "How bad was the last guy that I'm something to hold on to?"

"Wasn't bad, really," Finn said, starting the car and pumping up the heater. "Just, well, I've got about two more years on my degree, right? And Perry zipped through his degree, because hey, Humanities, no waiting, and then just didn't ask me or anything. Went to Virginia for his MA and doctorate. I mean my *family* is here, and yeah, maybe I'll have to leave them eventually, but he didn't even ask me. Just said, 'I'm going, and you can come with me or we can break up.'" Finn let out a grunt. "I mean, it hurt. We'd been together for three years. He was my first boyfriend after high school. I guess—I guess I thought my life would matter too."

"It should have," Adam said gruffly, thinking about Robbie and their plans to come out, their plans to leave the Army together. Adam had already put in his papers. Robbie never did. "Those sort of promises, they should matter."

Silence fell, and then Finn took a deep, fortifying breath. "Are you going to tell me?"

Aw hell. But he'd been losing faith. *Finn* had been losing faith. Suddenly Adam felt the need to give him faith, something real.

"See, I was a real slut in the Army," Adam started out, because hey, let's be honest. "I pretty much blew anyone who didn't look at me straight."

"Yeah? So you're pretty good at it?" Finn asked, sounding like he was *willing* Adam to be the god of all blowjobs.

"I got no idea," Adam muttered. "It was...." He blew out a breath. "See, I joined the Army 'cause my grandmother is a real bitch, right? And she spent my entire childhood telling me I was a coward, and I sucked, and I would never amount to anything. So I joined the Army because she would respect that. But I never admitted I was gay, and I never told anybody that I didn't like girls, and I just—you know—some guy in high school looked at me funny, pulled me behind the bleachers, and next thing I know, I got a dick in my mouth, and if I'm gonna suck, well, that's the way to do it, right?"

"Holy God," Finn said, and Adam was doing this wrong, but at this point, he couldn't stop.

"So military was the same thing. But then Robbie and I, suddenly we're not just blowing each other. Suddenly we're—we're *important* to each other, and I say the word, yanno? The big scary word?"

"Love?" Finn hazarded.

Adam shuddered, reluctant to burst his bubble. "Gay. *That's* as far as I got. Said we were gay. And we were going to come out. So that was the plan, right? And we were going to put in our papers, and not re-up, and there you go. A boyfriend. A couple. Ta-da!"

"And...."

"And we were in the barracks and some guy I'd blown half a dozen times was using the word 'faggot' like it's the word 'like,' and I came out. Said maybe not use that word anymore, since I'd blown half the guys in the unit. And I looked at Robbie and...."

"Oh, Adam."

"He called me a fag." Adam blew out the breath. "Which, I guess he wasn't wrong, you know?"

"I'm so...."

"It was a lonely fucking way to spend the last months of my assignment," Adam confessed. "I…. You're real nice. But I don't know how much trust I got in me."

"Yeah," Finn said softly. "I can see that."

"I'm sorry," Adam said, looking out the window of the minivan. It had been a really nice time—maybe what dates were all about.

"Don't be. You up for some ice cream?"

Adam looked at him and shook his head. "Naw. You can just take me home." It was over. It had to be.

"Okay, if that's what you want."

Adam didn't answer, and he watched the bright lights of downtown J Street flitter in front of his eyes before Finn took a right on Ninth. In another moment, he pulled up in front of Rico's apartment, put the car in park, and left it on idle. Adam prepared himself for the brush-off, for Finn saying they could still be friends, and he was surprised by the bare hand on the back of his neck. Finn must have taken off his gloves, for one thing, and for another, the pressure was intimate and insistent.

Adam turned to look at him and realized he'd taken the armrests up and was sitting sideways on the bucket seat.

"Adam?" Finn said softly.

"Yeah?"

"I don't want a blowjob right now."

"Then wha—"

A kiss. A simple kiss. Mouth on mouth, Finn's tongue slipping softly inside, Adam opening wide for his invasion.

Finn groaning, pushing Adam back against the seat, and Adam tunneling his fingers through Finn's curly strawberry blond hair, shuddering with the want that had just punched him in the nads.

Oh God. Oh God, oh God, oh God, oh… oh my *God*!

Finn pulled back, panted for a moment, and studied Adam in the light from the streetlamp four houses down. "You want this, don't you?"

"So bad," Adam admitted for the first time, even to himself.

"We'll kiss some more, but not further. Not tonight."

"It's your rodeo," Adam conceded, because nice boys like Finn got to call the shots. Adam was easy. He'd bend over for Finn in a heartbeat, or take him if he asked. Either way, didn't matter. Adam had no moral code about sex. But he found he had a moral code about *Finn*, and his moral code went that whatever Finn said, *that* was the code.

So when Finn pushed his hand under Adam's coat and rucked up his sweatshirt, letting Adam feel the coolness of Finn's fingers against his stomach, all he could do to that was suck in a breath and close his eyes. Finn's hand went higher, along his ribs, and then he pulled back again.

"You are all muscle and bone, aren't you?"

"I work out," Adam confessed breathily, and Finn chuckled against his lips.

"So do I. Wanna feel?"

Oh *hell* yes. Adam fumbled with Finn's waistband, finding the smooth skin of his back and digging in slightly. Finn flexed, and Adam felt them, muscle groups, biceps, triceps, the latissimus dorsi. Yes indeed, Finn did work out, and his flesh under Adam's palms was intoxicating. Adam pulled Finn closer while Finn continued the kiss— and continued to grope his chest—and in the meantime, the swelling in his groin, the heavy ache of arousal, grew bigger, more painful, and harder to ignore.

Finn maneuvered, and for a moment the awkwardness of necking in a minivan helped Adam control himself. Then Finn hit the seat latch, sending Adam flat on his back with Finn on top of him. They lay there, surprised, smiling at each other, groin to groin. Adam groaned and rocked his hips up, the better to push against Finn, to ease that pain. Finn's delighted smile sobered, grew serious, and he took Adam's mouth again with as much passion as intent.

Adam slid his hands from Finn's back down under his waistband. He dug his fingers into the muscles of Finn's ass and pulled down, thrusting his groin up against Finn's while Finn continued to explore his chest and, oh God, his sensitive, sensitized nipples.

He brushed them a couple of times with his thumb, and Adam groaned some more, pulling harder. Through the plackets of their jeans, he felt Finn's no-bullshit erection, and just the *thought* of Finn desiring him made him even harder.

The kiss went on, and Finn stopped brushing Adam's nipples and started pinching.

A sound that wasn't entirely human ripped from Adam's lungs.

He arched his back and ground up against Finn so hard it actually hurt, right in his throbbing balls, but the pain was enough.

Adam's orgasm washed white-blind behind his eyes, and he sobbed for breath inside Finn's mouth as his hips thrashed, caught between the seat and Finn's unyielding body.

He must have hit Finn just right, though, because he moaned softly, buried his face in the hollow between Adam's head and his shoulder, and bit Adam hard on the side of the neck. The edge of pain, Finn's mouth on his skin, that was enough to send Adam off again, shaking, his come flooding his underwear, making it sticky and cold within moments.

Finn collapsed weakly on top of him, panting in Adam's ear. "That's probably a good place to stop," he muttered.

Adam nodded, dazed, disoriented from the force of desire and raw need. "Yeah, sure," he mumbled. He moved his trembling hands from Finn's ass to the back of his head so he could smooth his hands through that curly hair again, feel the silk of it between his fingers. "Probably best," he said, lost in the comedown. He opened his eyes enough to take in the surroundings—the dark interior of the minivan, the glare of the streetlight from far away, the stoop of Rico's apartment building, where no lights were on.

The hopeful glint in Finn's eyes as he stared at Adam and *willed* him to come back to ground and acknowledge what they'd just done.

Adam closed his eyes and kissed Finn's forehead. "You're amazing, you know that, Finn?"

"Yeah?"

"You're like magic. Like… like a magic potion, like green goop."

Finn choked, his breath tormenting Adam's ear, and Adam wished they were in a bed or something so he could see Finn's eyes, that amazing blue.

"No," Adam explained. "See, when I was a kid, if we skinned our knee, got a sunburn, whatever, Rico's mom had what she called green goop. It was, like, aloe and lidocaine. It was great shit, you know? Cured all ills. Nasty burn, get the green goop. Fall off your bike, get the green goop. Well, you're like that, but better. You're like green goop for my heart, you know?"

Finn made a suspicious sound. If Adam didn't know him, didn't *trust* him, he'd say it was laughter. But because he *did* know him, he knew that it was more like tears. "Those are really good words, Mr. Cartoon Man. I wish you could draw those words for me."

Adam smiled because he knew he'd done good. "I'll try. I'll bring the picture by tomorrow."

Finn kissed his cheek, and then kissed his temple, and then kissed his forehead. And *then* he pushed himself up on his elbows and kissed

Adam briefly on the mouth before rolling over and maneuvering himself into the driver's seat. Adam pulled the lever and shot the back of the seat straight up, so he had to manipulate it a bit so it wasn't absurdly upright. Finally he was ready to go, with his hand on the door handle and everything.

He and Finn met eyes, and he wondered if Finn's underwear was as icky-clammy as his own.

"Tomorrow?" Finn asked. "You promise?"

Well, even Finn would need reassurance. Adam reached out and feathered a touch down his cheekbone. "Yeah. I promise." He pulled Finn into another kiss, this one lingering for just a breath, before he separated and opened the door to the frigid winter air. "Night, Finn. I had a real good time."

"Night, Adam. Me too. Dream of me, okay?"

"Yeah. No worries there. I don't got a choice."

And he didn't.

Not Thankful

TWO DAYS later Adam let Finn down for the first time, and he wasn't planning to and wasn't even sure how it had happened.

It seemed like such a simple thing, right?

"So, you doing anything for Thanksgiving in two days?" Finn asked.

Adam had done another commission, this one for Darby, who had brought her five-year-old in. She wanted a picture of him to give her mother for Christmas. To celebrate, Finn took Adam to the grocery store on the way home. They were wandering Safeway, arguing over whether Adam could afford the decent spaghetti sauce because it was on sale.

"Sleeping in," Adam said promptly, putting the cheap sauce in his cart and scowling. "Dosing the cat. Taking the dog for his twice-daily dump." Adam actually enjoyed exploring the neighborhood. It wasn't fantastic—some of the sidewalks were cracked, and not all the lawns were kept. The cars on the street were older, and there were a few oil stains. But it wasn't a shithole either. There were no working girls on the corner, no drug addicts in the alleys, and the homeless were polite and didn't knock over the trash cans. Adam had started to leave a half a sandwich on top of the can every morning, like he had down in San Diego, because he knew that if Rico hadn't given him this break, he'd be the guy looking for food.

"So, since you've got all *that* planned, do you have any time to go to my parents' place for Thanksgiving? They live, like, ten blocks away from you, up on Twenty-First and H."

Up where the neighborhood started getting considerably better. "Wow—that's actually pretty close. Me and Clopper probably passed the place." Adam started wondering which one it was. He had a vague idea of a bunch of houses with bright stained glass and pastel paint jobs, wind chimes from the eaves and doohickeys on the lawns. He could only imagine that people who spawned a Finn would live in one of those places—it was inevitable.

"So, do you want to go?"

Him? In one of the Willy Wonka houses? Oh no. No no no no no. "Finn, you and me, we've only been, uhm, what are we doing?"

"Dating, Adam. The kids call it dating these days."

"That's not funny," he said wretchedly. It should have been, but it wasn't, because he *didn't* know, because he didn't know from dating, and that was his point. "But it's only been a little bit of time. Maybe, you know, wait some before you bring me home to Mom and Dad, okay?"

Finn's grunt sounded unmistakably hurt. "Lots of people are coming. I mean, nobody will worry about how long we've been dating. It's just... food, family—don't you want that?"

"Just because I want it doesn't mean I know how to have it," Adam grumbled. Coming out to his grandma and mom the Easter after he'd been discharged had so *not* been a great idea. He'd carried the cut on his head from the door slamming in his face for a month. "I'm not—not a good person to have around your family, Finn. Not right now. I—you know, I barely remember the names of the people at Candy Heaven."

"That's not true," Finn snapped.

Adam put his pasta in the cart and soldiered on. He needed more milk, and maybe some salad mix. He was missing greens, and he'd finished off the bag of apples. "It's... I'm... you just don't know, I mean, family shit.... I... it doesn't end well, Finn. It's not...." He closed his eyes and stopped moving. "I just got into town a week and a half ago. I hope it's okay if I stay home and think of you happy, instead of go to your family's house and maybe make you uncomfortable."

When he opened his eyes again, Finn stood right next to him and was regarding him steadily from their five-inch height difference. How did he manage to make Adam feel small? "I can live with some discomfort, Adam. I'm not sure how much longer you can live being lonely."

Adam twitched his lips and hoped it passed for a smile. "Well, one more holiday is going to have to do it, okay? Right now you and me are—we're a sketch. And we could be a real great picture someday, with ink and oils or watercolor, and hell, we may even be a movie. But not right now."

Finn narrowed his eyes. "I swear to God, Adam, every time I think this is hopeless and I was deluded to even try to get close to you, you say or do something that is so fucking beautiful it's like I've got no choice."

Adam risked a look down into those beautiful blue eyes. "You got a choice. You always got a choice. I'm just glad you picked the other thing so far."

Finn nodded. "Me too." He stretched up on his toes then, and Adam was the one with no choice but to close his eyes and bend down into a brief kiss that grew longer, involved more hands, and eventually Adam wrapping his longer arms around Finn's tight, fit body for real.

The sound of an infant crying broke them apart. Adam whipped his head around to see an ungainly woman wearing flannel cat pajamas and a weary expression, pushing a cart with a screaming baby in the car seat carrier in the front.

For a moment they stared at each other, and then Finn spoke up. "Uhm, colic medication is, like, three aisles down."

The woman nodded, lines and sags on what was probably a young face giving a new meaning to the word "exhaustion," and said, "Thanks. Oreos?"

"One aisle over, by the freezer," Finn supplied helpfully. "Milk's down at the end, with dairy."

"You're a lifesaver." The woman nodded at Adam, just to be cordial, probably, and resumed her push of the crying baby. When Adam looked down again, Finn's expression was pure compassion.

"My oldest sister—man, both her boys. Colic until six, seven months. Constant screaming. I mean, we'd all go over to her house and clean and rock the baby and give her a chance to sleep, but it's hard. She used to tell me that she'd put them in the car and just drive around until they fell asleep, but by then she'd be so tired she wasn't sure if she could get back. She'd stop at the market and buy cookies and milk to keep herself awake."

"God," Adam muttered. "That's rough."

"Yeah. Her husband would take his shift too. They were good at sharing the misery, you know?"

"That sounds more like cutting it in half, but that's real nice. You got a good family there."

"Yeah, I'm lucky." Finn smiled tentatively, his open face just inviting confidence, but Adam didn't want to give him too much of his own family bullshit.

"You are. Not everyone gets that."

"You didn't."

"No."

"How did your family take your coming out?" Finn asked, proving once again he was fearless.

"By slamming a door in my face," Adam muttered. "How about yours?"

Finn regarded him carefully, and together they started walking through the store again. "Well, honestly, they came out to me first."

Adam had to laugh at that. "As what?"

"As flaming liberals. They called the whole family into a circle when I was about twelve, and sort of addressed all of us—there's five—and my mom started talking." Finn did a good job of impersonating a mother, speaking in that low, singsong, controlled voice Adam had heard from television moms but not from his own. "Okay, we know that you are all at the age when your peers start to ask certain questions, and in this town, everybody is going to make certain assumptions about us politically, but we need you to know something."

"What?" Adam asked, hooked in spite of himself.

"We want you all to know that we're liberals. So in spite of anything your peers might be afraid of from *their* parents, perhaps there are things you may want to confess to *us* that we won't be quite so upset about. Would anybody like to start?"

"And you said you were gay? At twelve?"

Finn laughed. "No, no. My oldest brother, Peter, who was in college, said he'd tried marijuana but he hadn't liked it. My other brother, Christopher, said he didn't want to study law, he wanted to study environmentalism, and since he was still in high school, who really cared. My oldest sister, JoBeth, said she was planning to run away and get married the next week because she was pregnant."

Adam couldn't help it. "Oh my God! Really?"

"Yep. She was twenty at the time, and she'd been dating Greg for a year, so it wasn't that big a deal. And my youngest sister, Mari, who's about two years older than me, said, 'You guys, you all know this was supposed to be a way to let Finn come out of the closet, so you idiots and your bullshit just screwed all of that up!' and my mom turned to JoBeth and said, 'You were going to *elope*?' and Dad turned to Pete and said, 'We knew about the pot, son—we flushed it and substituted oregano.'"

By this time Adam was laughing so hard, he forgot what he was shopping for. He had to stop on the endcap aisle and hold on to the shopping cart while he tried to pull himself together. "Oh my God! Oh my God! That's… that's—"

"Fucking hilarious, I know. But it's not perfect, right?"

Adam gulped in a breath. "Christ, no."

"Yeah." Finn snaked a hand around his hip and stood up on tiptoes to kiss his temple. "We're not perfect. Nobody's perfect. It's a shame you don't want to come to my family's house. You'd like them."

Adam closed his eyes. "Christmas," he said gruffly. "If I don't screw this up by Christmas, I'll meet them then."

Finn kissed his cheek and they resumed their trek around the grocery store.

That night, they necked some more in the car. Right when Adam thought his head was going to pop off, he felt Finn's hands worming under the waistband of his jeans.

He almost hurt himself unlocking the door and rolling out of the minivan.

In the car, Finn shoved himself up from the floor, where he'd fallen and almost gotten wedged, and glared at him. "You could have just said no!" he snapped.

"Yeah, I could have, if I didn't want it so bad!"

"Well if you want it that bad, why don't you pretend we're grown-ups and ask me in!"

Adam grunted. "Uhm…."

Finn shook his head and waved his hand. "No. Never mind. That's my bad. You're trying to be smart and take it slow, I get it."

Adam scrubbed his face with his hand and leaned into the car so he could be face to face with Finn. "I want it," he said gruffly. "But slow. Please? I'm getting there. I'm getting used to this being my life now. And that I can keep making changes. We get paid next week—I'll submit my application to Sac State and one of the junior colleges then, okay? And then I'll be on my way. I'll be, like, committed here. I won't be a drifter who lucked into a place and a job, okay?"

Finn reached out and touched his cheek. "Yeah. Okay. It's a good plan. It's got hope. I like that in a plan."

Adam smiled a little. "Yeah?"

"Yeah." He kissed Adam one more time, chastely on the lips, and Adam got into the backseat for his groceries and went. He knew the routine by now: medicate the cat, take the dog for a walk, and plan, just plan how he was going to take Finn out on a real date, and maybe make him spaghetti and salad, and maybe kiss him on a couch until they had their hands down *each other's pants*. Then, maybe, if he did all that right, he'd get to see Finn naked, eager in the moonlight, stretched out on the bed and wanting, and Adam could have him, the beautiful boy who wasn't really a boy, had always been a man, and he could be Adam's for real.

It was a nice dream. As grand, in its way, as a college education, but even better, because it was Finn.

Adam thought he could have that dream—it was as hopeful as he ever got.

The next day they got off early, and Finn had time to take him home but no time to hang out. Finn had to help his parents with the predinner preparations, and he said he would have asked Adam, but he figured if Adam was reluctant to go to the actual dinner, the predinner would probably be a nightmare.

"I don't mind a little work," Adam said, knowing it was stupid to feel hurt.

"Darrin's going to be there tomorrow," Finn told him. "Just commit to tomorrow and then you can come help us tonight. It'll be fine!"

"Darrin?"

"Yeah—half of Candy Heaven is coming. My parents are getting propane heaters and everything so people can go out into the backyard. Are you *sure*?"

Adam thought of all those people, and a part of him wanted to be with them, and a part of him shuddered. He leaned in and kissed Finn's cheek. "You'll have to tell me all about it," he said gruffly, and he made sure Finn was out of the way before he shut the car door and went inside.

THE NEXT day he did everything he said he was going to do. He slept in, he took care of the animals, and he cleaned the house a little. He took the old bread and made some peanut butter and jelly sandwiches, wrapped them in bags, and put them on top of the dumpsters on the corner for the people who might not be so lucky to have a home or a family or someplace to go. When he was done, he made himself some sandwiches and sat down to watch the football game, and listened, the whole time, to the silence inside the apartment.

In a way it really was nice—no clatter of the boardwalk, no voices bouncing off the lacquered floorboards of the store. No clamor of customers, no city sounds. The dog sat on the floor and rested his chin on the couch so Adam could reach out and scratch him behind the ears, and the cat? Well, Gonzo had been sitting on the back of the couch and kneading his hair. It was peaceful, he decided, dozing there with his sketchpad on his knee and his phone on the table.

He missed Finn, but it was real peaceful.

He was not prepared for his phone to buzz at three o'clock. He picked it up and read Finn's text, then read it again.

You'd better not be naked, because we're almost to your place with dinner. Don't worry, I mingled with the fam, but Candy Heaven and I are on our way.

He bolted upright, and the cat latched on to his neck and slid down, claws extended. While he was still crying bloody murder—and dripping blood—the doorbell rang.

He opened his door and a Bing Crosby movie flooded into his cousin's apartment, armed with grocery bags, a boom box playing Christmas music, and a case of beer.

Finn was the leader of the gang, which didn't surprise him, but Darrin was second banana, and Darby with her son, Joni, Ravi, and Anish followed in short order, as well as a man who looked like Finn's older brother, and the woman Adam had first seen in the store that one day, holding a toddler tightly by the hand.

"What in the holy fuh-lllaming cow," Adam corrected, staring at the toddler and the five-year-old at the last minute, and clutching the dog. The boy he knew already, a thin boy with dark eyes in a mocha face and a surprising, sudden smile. The toddler—a pudgy kid who probably looked a lot like Finn when he was that age, with strawberry blond hair and big blue eyes—was new, but when Adam stared, he stared soberly back.

Finn came up behind him and put a hand on the small of his back. "Don't panic," he said firmly. "Everybody else is here just long enough to—"

"*No!*" hollered the older guy who looked like Finn's brother. "*No, no, you dumb motherfuckers, no!*" He had avoided the whole group presentation thing and sat himself down in front of the game. Lucky bastard.

"Pete, stop swearing around Josh, or his father is gonna kill you." This from the older sister. For a minute Adam thought she must be JoBeth, but she didn't look that much older than Finn, and he'd probably seen JoBeth working at the restaurant, so she must be Mari.

Pete looked over his shoulder and grinned at the toddler. "Wanna come sit on my lap, Joshie? We gotta watch USC win, okay?"

Joshie broke away from his mom and hauled ass to sit on his uncle Pete's lap. Adam looked for Darby's kid, Cameron, and saw him seated right in front of the dog—like *right next* to Adam. The dog was licking him politely on the head.

Working hard at not joining Cameron, Adam tried looking *at* the other faces around him. "Uhm, good to see you all. You're here why?"

Darrin grinned and patted his cheek. "Don't ask why, sweetheart. Just dig in to the chow!" With that he turned toward the game, grabbed a beer, and proceeded to root for the other team.

"Here, come help me," Finn said, grabbing his hand and hauling him into the kitchen. "That way you can just pretend there's people in the house and you don't have to worry how they got here."

Clopper took that moment to escape Adam's grasp around his collar, escape Cameron, and go rushing into the living room, apparently to lick *all the things*.

Like the other kid, who laughed, and the uncle, who invited the big doofus to sit on the couch when there were people sitting on the floor, and the cat, who was hiding in the corner and who hissed and fled for the back bedroom.

"Clopper—hey, man…."

But Clopper didn't give a shit, and Finn hauled Adam around the counter into the kitchenette.

"Surprised?" he asked, pulling out a wrapped plate of turkey and a big container of potatoes.

"Very much," Adam said, looking into his living room again. Darrin caught his gaze and winked, then waggled his eyebrows. Anish and Ravi were arguing over whether or not USC could pull it out, and Darby, Mari, and Joni were lavishing all of their attention on the kids and dog. Five minutes ago Adam couldn't have predicted Rico's little apartment would *hold* all these people.

"Well, you shouldn't have been," Finn said, standing on tiptoes and kissing his cheek. "My parents' house was a zoo. My mom had, like, three turkeys and a ham going, and there was no place to sit.

Darrin asked where you were, and when he found out you were here, *alone*, with all this space, he said you were a selfish bastard who should share, so we decided to go with that."

Adam half laughed. "That's considerate of you," he said gravely. "Thanks for letting me off the hook."

Finn started to unload the next bag. "Not a problem. Will it make sure you're not alone for Thanksgiving?"

"I do not seem to be alone now," he said.

Finn smiled softly at him. "Well, mission accomplished," he said, looking very smug and pleased with himself.

"You're a force of nature."

"I am. Hey, do you have any bread? Mom was out of rolls."

Adam shrugged. "Naw. I used the last of the old loaf today."

Finn stopped pulling a banquet out of the bags and stared at him. "How many sandwiches can you eat?"

"I made little packages and put them on the dumpsters," Adam said, embarrassed. "You know. For the homeless? I mean, I at least got a place to slee—"

Finn tackled him, pushing him back against the refrigerator and kissing him until all of the scary people faded into the background. He backed off when both of them were breathing hard, and shook his head. "Surprised? Good. Every day you say something that surprises me."

Adam knew he was blushing. "I'm... uhm... you know...."

Finn kissed his cheek. "It's good, Adam. It really is. It's a sign." He turned back to unloading the bags, and Adam couldn't help it.

He hoped. He looped his arm around Finn's shoulders and gave thanks.

He could have done it—he'd been doing it practically his whole life. He could have spent this holiday alone, watching television, thinking that human contact was for other people, but he had a meal and a roof over his head, and that was plenty.

But now he had people in his living room, and a dog, and a psycho cat, and it was an embarrassment of riches, and he was going to have to deal.

He put his hand on the small of Finn's back and closed his eyes as the warmth seeped into his palm. Then he kissed Finn's temple, in that same way that Finn used that usually blew his mind.

"Thanks. It was a nice thought," he said, just loud enough for Finn to hear. "I'm not sure how fair it was to all the people you dragged with you, but it was really sweet."

He walked away then to gather plates (mostly paper) and glasses (a lot of Rico's glassware consisted of plastic souvenir cups from some of the finest gas stations in the greater Sacramento area) and reusable plasticware.

Well, it was something.

IN THE next two hours, he and his new house of people ate, told jokes, cheered USC on to humiliating failure (and groaned when Darrin preened because his team won), and played spoons with the deck of semi-X-rated playing cards Darrin pulled out of his pocket.

Finn looked at the cards, which had Sharpie marks in all the convenient places on the pictures, and said, "The jack of spades will never be the same."

Darrin smiled smugly. "Think of it as a loincloth and play."

Joshie sat on Pete's lap and gave away all his cards by the end of round three, but Cameron got his own hand, although his mother gave him pointers during the play. Adam resigned himself to drinking his cereal out of the bowl because his plasticware was now all in the trash.

And Clopper lay on his back in the corner, drunk off of more turkey and stuffing than any dog should eat ever. Every ten minutes he'd pass a giant gas bubble that would send him barking around the room, angry at the big farting monster who had dared impose on his dreams.

In his entire life, Adam could not remember laughing so much. It was like Thanksgivings were supposed to be in movies, on television.

For perhaps the first time in his life, he felt truly blessed.

FINN HAD driven one of the two cars, so he was part of loading everybody up and taking them back to his parents' house. He let the rest of the horde tromp into the car and start the ignition, and turned to Adam as he stood on the stoop, looking down the steps into the cold, foggy night.

"It was okay?" he asked again, sounding so uncertain Adam's heart broke a little.

"It was great," Adam said. Without thinking about it, he lifted his hand and palmed the back of Finn's head, loving the texture of his hair and the way his eyes got big and shiny in the moonlight. He lowered his head, tasting Finn, and he didn't taste pumpkin pie, which was the last thing they'd eaten. He tasted joy.

He pulled back and smiled a little. "Tomorrow's gonna suck." Black Friday always did, no matter what retail business you served. In the case of Candy Heaven, Darrin said most of the business would be from people coming in for a break after shopping at the rest of the stores, and he said the day would be fierce.

"Yeah. And I've got papers and shit due on Monday. I won't see you for a couple of days."

Adam grimaced. "Okay. Well, we should make that kiss better, then, okay?"

Finn grinned and pushed up against Adam, and this kiss turned urgent and demanding. Adam closed his eyes and wished. Hope and joy and faith—all of those things, right? He could have all of them.

Someone beeped the horn of the minivan, and Finn pulled away to groan theatrically. "Gotta go—my family's waiting."

And then he was gone, trotting down the stairs and across the yard like he had all of the hope, joy, and faith in the world. He must have—he'd given some to Adam, right?

And it lasted all the way until bedtime, when Adam looked around for Gonzo and didn't find him. After searching the apartment three times, he realized that the worst must have happened: in all the flood of people leaving, the fucking cat must have run out the goddamned door.

The Things We Live Without

"YOU LOOK like shit," Darrin said bluntly as Adam walked into work at six o'clock the next morning. Morning crew was already there—had probably been there for hours, getting everything as absolutely stocked and ready as possible. The truck had arrived about ten minutes before he walked in. Ravi and Anish had complained bitterly about being on truck duty, and Adam had looked forward to showing up to help.

But that was before the big cat disaster.

"I am aware," Adam muttered, and guzzled the extra-large coffee he'd bought, hoping it was laced with something stronger than caffeine.

"Seriously, did Finn go back or something and take you out clubbing?"

Finn. Oh God. Adam could not even take the thought of Finn right now. He'd be all full of help and sympathy, and Adam? Adam wanted to rip someone's face off. He *really* didn't want that person to be Finn.

"No. Fucking cat got out. Was out until one looking for the little fucker. Didn't show."

Darrin closed his eyes. "Oh—oh hell. I'm sorry, Adam. I saw him go. I didn't know he was supposed to be inside only."

Adam swallowed hard on that whole face-ripping impulse. "Yeah, well, I think the people freaked him out. Not your fault. Mine. I've never had a cat before. I don't know cats for shit. It was a bad idea to leave him with me."

"Oh no...." Darrin narrowed his eyes and his voice turned speculative. "Oh no no no no no... you are *not* going to use this to... to...."

Adam didn't want to hear it. Of course he was. It was like *God* was talking to him. When God talked to you, you listened, right? His grandmother had always said God hated bastards, and God hated fags, and he was both, so he was proof. He was the faggot bastard who let Rico's cat out, and damn if he could find a reason to think well of himself after that. "Boss, don't I have to work or something? Where do I need to go?"

"Help the guys load the stock up in the loft. And if you're thinking about using this as an excuse to break up with Finn, stop thinking period and wait a few days."

"Can't really break up," Adam said pertly. "Haven't made any promises. Nothing to break."

"Just his heart, you jackass!" Darrin snarled, and Adam turned away.

"Naw. Now it'll just bruise a little. Better bruised now than broken later."

"Adam, goddammit—"

But Adam was already running up the stairs, not sure if someone had coked his coffee or if fear was just a really big motivator.

Probably A. He couldn't possibly be afraid, could he? Nothing could hurt you if you didn't let it in.

THE DAY sucked, but he got through it, pulling on his military discipline to sell candy and not be a complete dick to the people who came into the store. Like Darrin promised two weeks before, it was one of those days where everybody stayed long, and he was just clocking out when Darrin called out to the store. "I'm ordering from River Burger, if anyone wants to put in a request!"

From across the store, Adam met Darrin's slightly derisive look, but he didn't let it stop him from swinging his coat over his shoulders and running the hell away.

He looked under every car and in the shadow of every shrub on his way home, and when he walked up the familiar rickety stairs to the stoop with the worn welcome mat, that goddamned cat was curled up in front of the door.

He wasn't breathing so good.

Fuck. Time to text Rico.

Rico, your cat escaped last night and I just found him. He's not breathing well and he's hardly moving and he looks like hell. Where do I take him?

Adam, if he's going to die, just let it happen. There's a little garden behind the apartment—it's sort of the small animal graveyard. Avoid the bald spots—there's a lot of dead gerbils in there.

But RICO, it's YOUR CAT!!!

Do you think it doesn't hurt? Jesus, Adam! But every time you love something, you run the risk that it's going to leave you.

Adam hadn't eaten, and he couldn't feel much beyond the exhaustion. He carried the cat in, and Clopper avoided his customary body tackle, moving instead to sniff at Gonzo's still little form.

Gonzo reached out with a paw and patted the big dog's nose. Adam had a sudden "Finn" thought, about how they probably had a friendship going on since they were alone in the house a lot when the humans were not.

The thought was gone quickly, and Adam set the cat on the corner of the couch, wrapped in a towel and tried to dribble a little bit of medicine in his mouth. Poor thing just let the medicine drip to the other side, falling on the towel, before he licked at his palate to maybe get the taste away.

Oh. Fuck. Fuck fuck fuck fuck.

Adam managed to make himself a lettuce wrap of leftovers, which he ate while doing a perfunctory walk around the block, making sure Clopper did what he had to do. For his part, Clopper didn't need any encouragement or extra blocks like he usually did; Adam could only be grateful.

He and Clopper eased quietly back inside, and Gonzo hadn't changed. He lay sprawled on his towel inelegantly, his chest rising and falling, seemingly slower with every breath.

Oh God. Adam had a horrible thought. He could take the cat outside, lay him down under a bush, and he could die right there. Adam reached down and picked up the little nightmare, and that limp weight rested trustingly in his arms.

With a sigh, he sat down, the cat on his lap. Clopper did what he usually did—sat on the ground and rested his head on the couch while Adam petted the cat gently and reached for the remote control. He found a program in reruns and thought, *Oh yeah, I like this one!* and then he put down the remote control and continued petting the cat.

When he woke up an hour later, he had a crick in his neck, the program was over, the news was on, and Gonzo the cat had breathed his last.

Adam continued to stroke that still body for a good ten minutes, his eyes burning, the breath coming short in his chest.

Finn would make this feel better.

Finn needs to be nowhere near me.

When he finally rewrapped the cat in the towel and took him out to the back flowerbed with a flashlight, he still didn't have an idea which voice won.

But he knew he sobbed his heart out over that stupid furry terrorist. Goddammit, Adam still had scratches on his face and his back from the awful animal—how was he supposed to go in the ground?

There weren't any answers to that one either. But as Adam laid Gonzo the cat to rest in the apartment burial ground at eleven o'clock on a moonless November night, Adam did know one thing.

Nothing he'd learned in the past two years had done him any good. He was as alone as alone could be.

THE NEXT morning he woke up to his phone chirping merrily on the charger next to the lamp.

Hey—missed you last night. Did you survive the rush?

Oh God.

Yeah.

That's it? Yeah? Did you miss me?

Oh geez. He couldn't even lie to Finn by text.

Yeah. But I need to get used to that.

Why?

Okay. Deep breath.

And his phone rang.

"Why?" Finn's voice didn't sound "just woken up" at all. God, he must have been up for hours.

"Finn? Look, you and me, I mean, it's great for me but not so good for you, so maybe you should not count on me, okay?"

"No, not okay—where's this coming from? This is *not* where we were on Thursday night!"

"Well I hadn't killed the fucking cat on Thursday night!" Adam exploded. "But the fucking cat is dead now, and if I can't keep him alive, how am I supposed to keep you and me together? So maybe it's just me alone because that's the way it should be. I've never needed anybody before now. I gotta learn...." Oh God. That was a *sob*. He'd sobbed. His voice had cracked and he'd *sobbed*. Like, cried. Like a baby.

"The cat died?" Finn asked, his voice absurdly gentle.

"Finn, I gotta go. I… all the shit inside me is stupid and ugly, and I don't need you to see it, okay? Just… just pretend the last two weeks never happened."

And he hung up, buried his face in his pillow, and howled.

Personal Things

HE LOOKED like shit again at work, but he did his job and did it competently, and didn't give anybody any crap.

And when the friendly neighborhood sandwich guy showed up, Adam heard his tread on the boardwalk, sort of a happy tripping sound, and ran for the loft before anybody knew where he was to start with.

He heard Finn's distraught voice and Darrin's soothing tones, probably calming him down. It didn't seem to work, though, because Finn's shouted "*Coward!*" echoed through the store before he stomped away, the happy tripping all gone.

When Darrin came up the steps, Adam was sitting cross-legged between the same pallets he'd been sitting by two weeks before, when Finn had first sat on the floor and given him a hamburger.

"So the cat died," Darrin said softly.

"Yeah." Adam leaned his head against a big box of giant sour gumballs that were maybe one of his favorite things in the store.

"Wasn't your fault. Finn said he was old."

"It's what Rico said." Adam had texted Rico that morning, with maybe his thousandth "sorry" included.

Rico had texted back, *I'm sorry more. I didn't mean to leave you this job to hurt you.*

Adam didn't have anything to say to that, because how do you tell someone that maybe you were just too hurt long before you even lost your car and your job and your school grant? Maybe you were too hurt years ago, hiding under the bed in the guest bedroom and listening to your mom and your grandma argue over whose fault it was that you were such a colossal pain in the ass and waste of effort.

"Then why is this such a big deal—I mean, besides the fact that I think you liked the animal. Why do you have to lose Finn too?"

Darrin sat down cross-legged next to him and wrapped an arm around his shoulders.

Adam looked at him, trying to be grateful, but he found he didn't even have that in him. "Man, why's it matter so much? Finn is meant for people. He's great with 'em. Maybe I was just supposed to be like the damned cat, you know? Maybe I'm supposed to just go lose myself and die cold and alone."

"Oh, honey! Is that how the cat died?"

Adam couldn't resist him anymore. He sighed and laid his head on Darrin's shoulder. "No."

"How did the cat die?"

"On my lap."

"So you're saying the cat had you."

"Yeah, I don't know what difference that makes."

"He came home to see you, Adam. It means you're the human he most wanted to be with."

"I was a poor replacement for Rico, who had to leave."

"Maybe you were the better replacement—you ever think of that?"

Adam straightened and glared at him. "Why in the hell would I think of that?"

Darrin's eyes were kind, even in the dim light of the loft, and he shook his hair back out of his face before he answered. "Because that's who you are to Finn."

"Augh!" Adam growled, because he'd exhausted all his good words.

Darrin pulled him close and kissed his temple, and Adam wondered what it was about these people—how did they know it was his comfort thing?

"Adam?"

"Yeah?"

"Finn told me about you and making the meals for the homeless people."

Adam sighed, glad for the non sequitur. "So? It's like, you know, the bread was going stale anyway."

Darrin nodded. "Yeah. I do know. I know you're a better boyfriend for Finn than his ex ever was, and I know you need some sleep and a chance to think to see it. Go home—"

"But I need the—"

"You got in a seven-hour shift. Go home. See how empty it is. Let the silence drive you bugshit. Candy Heaven will be here tomorrow."

Adam scowled, but he had to admit, he was wrecked and done. "You sure?" he asked, and Darrin shook his head grimly.

"Have a sweet day," he said, but it sounded more like a punishment than a benediction.

RICO'S APARTMENT was really boring. Yes, television and stereo, and Adam had the computer he'd used for school, but mostly it was off-white carpet, off-white furniture, and sort of white walls.

He needed pictures.

Adam sat at the table that night, Clopper's head dejectedly on his knees, and drew. He drew the dumb cat—when it was alive—and the dumb dog taking off after a squirrel and dragging Adam behind him. He got out his pastels and added the tawny color to the cat's fur and the silver highlights to the dog's short, floppy ears.

He drew Candy Heaven—a picture for him and not for Darrin, where he captured the easy, human way that Darrin laughed and the way Joni smiled brightly at every child who walked through the door, no matter how bitchy she was to her coworkers. The way the dark wood floors and rainbow sugar seemed sort of like home.

He stared at the picture of Candy Heaven and sighed. There was one thing he hadn't drawn yet. He really needed to draw it, because he needed to be able to *see* it, even if it was something he couldn't have.

He turned the page in his sketchbook and there was no paper left.

Fuck.

Almost desperately, he flipped back to those preliminary sketches of Finn and thought about how badly they sucked. They weren't good enough. His chin was squarer and his jaw was a little asymmetrical. His eyes were more almond shaped and less round, and his mouth wasn't that wide unless he was smiling, and that big water spot wasn't there on his forehead.

Or that other one on his cheek.

Adam shut the book abruptly before any more of those could happen, and then he clutched Clopper's massive, patient head to his chest. It was too late to go get another sketchbook, but he got paid tomorrow. He could do it then.

For now it was a great idea to just sit on the couch and stare at the television. Clopper lay next to him where he wasn't supposed to be, whining for the furry person who had disappeared from his life.

ADAM GOT in from his run with the dog the next morning and found a steaming cup of Starbucks coffee and a muffin on his porch. The bag with the muffin had writing on it in ballpoint pen. *Miss me yet? Bet you do, right? Don't deny it.*

Adam had to *force* himself to not smile, and his stern expression didn't last through the giant mocha and the banana muffin.

Yeah, Finn. I'm missing you. Just knowing you were here makes it better.

Work was actually a little slow that afternoon, which was good because it made dodging Finn that much easier when he came in with Darrin's lunch. After Finn shouted, "You miss me! Admit it, you stupid-head!" and stomped out, Adam came down the stairs tentatively, like nobody in the store would know that was aimed at him if he pretended he'd never run into the loft in the first place.

Ravi, Anish, Joni, Darby, Miguel, and Darrin all glared at him as he slunk from the base of the stairs to the counter, where he had customers waiting.

He ignored them and rang up the customers, pretending he didn't notice their curiosity and bemused smiles, and then he carefully wiped down the candy dish on the scale. Finally he could stand it no longer.

"What?" he demanded.

Darrin walked up to the counter and dropped one of their cellophane prewraps of six medium-sized jawbreakers on the shiny brown surface. "In case you forgot you had any," he said, his eyes flinty as he glared at Adam.

"I got two," Adam mumbled, embarrassed.

"Fine." Darrin walked back to the jawbreaker barrels and came back with another cellophane wrapped bag—this one with two *giant* jawbreakers in it. "This is in case you need *bigger ones.*"

Adam glared at him and grabbed a Tootsie Roll from the go-back box, unwrapped it, and stuck two gumballs at the base. He held it upright, thinking it looked like an extended middle finger, and asked, "Does *this* remind you of anything?"

Darrin smirked. "Yes, darling, I had one of those last week, except a lot bigger!"

Adam gaped, and he felt a long-delayed blush traveling from his toes all the way up to the top of his head. "It was supposed to be... you know... the bird... flipping... I mean, not that I want to flip off the boss but... oh hell...."

Everybody broke into raucous laughter, including the two grandmotherly types buying the specialized *Star Wars* candy tins Adam had always thought were really cool.

Reluctantly, Adam felt another smile working on his face. His second of the day—it almost hurt.

But the smiling, the camaraderie, must have seeped in, softened the parts of his soul made brittle by pain, because as he was leaving into late-afternoon twilight, he didn't run when the familiar happy-trippy tread on the boardwalk zipped up behind him.

"Don't talk," Finn said, grabbing his bicep and hauling him across the cobblestones and up into the tree-shaded walk.

"But—"

"No talking!"

Adam shut up and let himself be hauled across the street, then across the bridge to the wrought iron fence that marked the edge of the park. The two of them stood there for a minute, looking out across the river. The last of the sun shot out over the horizon, and Adam turned in time to see Finn, eyes closed, face illuminated by the thin gold light.

Fading freckles stood out on his cheeks, and his nose was almost absurdly small for a grown man.

Not perfect. No.

But so beautiful.

The sunlight disappeared and a burst of wind kicked off the river, making them both shiver. Finn opened his eyes and looked into Adam's, the expression on his face simple and poignant. "This is real," he said, and Adam knew what he was talking about. "The sun, the river, and us."

Adam opened his mouth, not even sure what he was going to say, but Finn didn't let him. He stood on his tiptoes instead and took advantage of Adam's open mouth, pulling him into a sweet, lingering kiss. Adam let a moan slip out, warm for the first time in three days, and Finn deepened the kiss, not letting him back away. Adam had no choice. He wrapped his arms around Finn's shoulders and clung, kissing him back, *needing* him.

Finn pulled back and panted, which was when Adam came to his senses. He dropped his arms and avoided Finn's grim glare.

"This isn't over," Finn said seriously. "You and me. We're as real as the sun and the river. Think about me."

He turned and trotted away.

Adam stayed for a moment, taking deep breaths and trying to get his heartbeat under control. It wasn't working. It was like all that laughter in the store really *had* made him more susceptible to happiness.

And the pain that came when it walked into the frosty dark.

Sunrise

TWO DAYS later, Adam had filled half a brand-new sketchbook with pictures of Finn, and he was worried as hell about the damned dog.

Clopper, who nose-humped strangers and body-tackled friends, had apparently devoted his life to apathy and depression. He sat, listless, in a corner, head on his gray-and-white paws, eyes wandering the house looking for Gonzo, who had probably spent his days jumping on Clopper's head for fun.

He's lonely, Adam texted to Rico. *He hasn't eaten in three days. I'm worried.*

Get him a friend.

Adam gaped. A… a…. *A WHAT?*

Go adopt another cat. That way, when I move back, I'll get to know your cat like you got to know mine.

But Rico!

No—it'll be good. We always shared toys when we were kids. We can share pets now.

You trust me to get you a cat?

Why not?

Adam flailed as he sat at the table and petted the depressed dog. Jesus, Rico had *been* there—they'd shared the same childhood, right?

Because I'm the loser? he texted after his flail.

Shut up.

No, I mean—you heard the same shit I did!

I heard two bitter harpies blame all their fucking bullshit on an eight-year-old who would sooner hide under the bed than hurt a fly.

But I proved them right, didn't I?

SHUT UP. Jesus, Adam. You served your fucking ungrateful country, you came out in that fucking house of bile. You're the bravest person I know.

Adam thought of Finn and that moment by the river, when Adam hadn't given him any hope at all.

I'm a coward, he texted with feeling.

Then be brave. Come on, Adam—save Clopper's life.

What if I pick wrong?

Gonzo was a fucking asshole cat who ruined my best shoes right before my first job interview.

He tried to kill me at least twice.

See? How much worse could your choice be?

Adam thought about Rico—shaved head, high cheekbones, full lips, and big brown Mexican-chocolatey eyes. He was everything Adam had wanted to be as a kid. His job in advertising seemed to make him so much more than Adam could reach for as an adult.

Suddenly getting Rico a cat and saving his dumbass dog's life made him feel like, just in a little way, he could be as good as Rico.

It was Tuesday, which was apparently going to be his permanent day off, but he didn't sleep in. Thanks to Rico, he had plans to make.

He dragged Clopper on his walk in the morning, taking him up the block to H and Twentieth, walking around the block and searching out the pretty houses, the ones with the rainbow trim around the windows and the bright Christmas-themed flags on the porch. Was that one Finn's parents'? Was that one? Oh, hey, this was embarrassing, was it the violet/blue one *with Finn's minivan parked in front of it*?

Abort! Abort! Abort! Friendlies on board! Finn was here! *Oh my God, Finn might see him*!

Adam was going to backpedal—he was. Two things stopped him.

One of them was Clopper, who could be turned right or turned left but could not, under any circumstances, be turned around to go the opposite direction.

The other was the text from his cousin. Rico thought he was brave. *Rico* thought he was brave. Finn thought he was worth it.

The least he could do was walk in front of Finn's house!

And wave when Finn came galloping out, fleece hat falling off his head, one shoe in his hand, one bare foot and one stockinged foot mincing across the frosty sidewalk.

"Hello!" Finn gasped, chest heaving, eyes bright. He only had one arm in his bright blue coat—the rest of the coat flopped down behind his back. "What are—" Pant. "—you doing here?"

Adam had to laugh, and he slid the loop of Clopper's nylon leash down his arm and grabbed the back of Finn's coat.

"I actually just came wandering by," he said, helping Finn find the arm and slide the quilted blue felt up his shoulders. Clopper, true to his recent depression, just sat, regarding them both with somber eyes. "I didn't expect you to be here."

"Yeah, well, my cousin came in from out of town with his family. We gave him my apartment, and I'm back here until after Christmas."

"That happen on Thanksgiving?" Adam asked, conscious that it could be a sensitive thing to talk about.

But Finn chose to ignore that. He nodded. "Yeah—I didn't get a chance to tell you. Anyway, I've got to run my last paper in to my professor this morning, but after that, I have the day off."

"Really?" Adam asked, sincerely surprised. "It's mine too. I mean, did you do that on purpose?"

Finn grinned. "Yes." He was brilliant. Brilliant, bold, and unrepentant. Adam wanted to be like him when he grew up.

"I, uh, I sort of have to go get a friend for Clopper," Adam said. "Want to, you know, come with me?"

"Or, you know, you and Clopper could ride with me. And we could spend the day together and wrap it up with an evening spent at your apartment, during which we eat a wonderful dinner and then have some variation of sexual relations."

Adam blinked. "Some variation?"

"Yup. It can either be hot monkey lust or sweet sweet lurve. We'll have to see."

"I, uhm… aren't we moving a little fast?"

Finn paused. "Yeah. That is fast. But I've known you for three weeks and I'm already emotionally invested. So maybe we'll just make out. Maybe I'll fall asleep in your arms and wake up and know that you're not going anywhere."

Adam swallowed, unexpectedly moved. "Maybe that last one," he said softly. "I'd really like that last one."

That radiant smile undid him.

"Yeah. I think that's the best option." Finn stood on his tiptoes again and kissed Adam's cheek. "But not our only one. It depends on how much in love with me you are by the end of the day. Stay right here. In fact…." He grabbed Adam's hand, and although Adam did his best Clopper impression with splayed limbs, Finn still won. Adam ended up towed into the house, the dog perking up enough to prance at his heels.

The door was still open from Finn's precipitous exit, and Finn cleared the threshold hollering, "Mom, Dad, this is Adam! He changed his mind and we're a thing again!"

Adam glared at him. "Thanks, Finn. I promise, I'll get even for that."

Finn grinned and took him into what was probably a breakfast nook where two perfectly nice people in late middle age stopped drinking coffee and stared at him in surprise. Adam had a chance to take in blond hardwood floors, a white kitchen table, and a giant cornucopia in the center. Finn's parents were both reading something from tablets, but he'd heard voices as he'd walked in and assumed they'd been talking as well. Nice people. No yelling. Happy faces.

Terrifying.

"Wow," said Finn's mom, her ash-blonde hair perfect, her Finn-blue eyes wide and round. "That's, uhm—hello, Adam. Nice that you're back in our daily dialog."

"Nice to"—oh God—"meet you. Hiya, Mr. and Mrs. Stewart. Sorry for just barging in—"

"I'll be right back!" Finn called, running down the hallway for what, God only knew. He was still missing a sock, and his hair didn't look combed, and his breath hadn't been awesome.

"If he's going to the bathroom, he's going to take at least twenty minutes," Mr. Stewart said. Adam recognized him from River Burger, but they'd never spoken. He must have been the seminal redhead, because his graying hair was still ginger and his thin, ruddy face bespoke a lot of sunblock in the summer.

"Yes, and if you have to pee, Adam, be sure you use the one upstairs." Adam almost choked on his tongue, because such a nice-looking woman just said pee, but she didn't seem to notice. "And don't let him tell you it's whatever he ate the night before—it's a total lie."

"I'll, uh, keep that in mind."

At that point Mari walked into the kitchen, laughing. "Oh my God, Adam, I hope you knew what you were getting into. Joshie saw you walking down the street and yelled 'Clopper!' and the next thing I know, Finn was dragging his pants on in the living room. I've never seen someone move so fast."

Adam smiled at her, relieved. "I was going to text him today," he said, knowing it was the truth. He couldn't imagine spending one more day without knowing Finn was in his life. "I… I mean, I was thinking about how to make up to him. I, uh, didn't know I just had to walk by the house."

To his shock, Finn's sister walked right up to him from the living room and hugged him. His free arm, the one without Clopper attached, flailed for a minute, and then he put his hand between her shoulder blades and just endured.

"I'm sorry about the cat," she said softly. "I mean, I've got kids and pets. It's always the most frightening thing, thinking, 'I can take care of this creature.' What if you can't? Who's going to help you? What if you fail? But really, all you can do is your best. It's all anyone asks of you."

Adam grimaced. "So, uhm, you and Finn talked a lot about that, did you?"

Mari's grin was just as infectious as her little brother's. "Yep. The only way I could get Finn to buckle down and finish his finals was by telling him you needed a little time and a little encouragement."

Adam shook his head. "Your entire family is insane."

She nodded maniacally while crossing her eyes, and Adam cracked up. He couldn't help it.

"Yeah, well, you like me," Adam said, laughing. "Must be nuts."

He turned back to the Mr. and Mrs. Finn, who had been watching Mari charm him with indulgent smiles on their faces. "I'm real grateful for the Thanksgiving dinner," he said, hoping they'd know he was sincere. "It was a real nice thing."

"So were the sandwiches on the trash can," Mrs. Stewart said. "You know, we volunteer at Loaves & Fishes during the winter. Would you like to come with us someday?"

Adam's breath caught in his chest. "That... that would be really great," he said, unsure of how to put it into words. "If it wasn't for my cousin, I'd be living in my car this season. And that thing died on the way from San Diego. It's like... I owe the world, you know?"

Finn's mother looked at him thoughtfully. "I think that's extraordinary," she said, a small smile on her face. "And it speaks really well of you. Have you given any thought to school, since you have a place to stay right now?"

Adam shrugged. "I've been applying online. Still waiting for someone to get back to me. People have been paying me for my drawings. If I can do that for a second job, I might be able to afford tuition. It's a work in progress."

Finn's dad grinned at him. "As all lives should be. C'mere, Adam—pull up a chair. Mari, could you get Finn's friend some coffee?"

"Yeah, sure. Adam, you want a bagel? They're fresh, and Mom bought lox. It's good stuff."

"You don't have to—" But before he could even politely refuse, she had coffee in front of him and was pointing to sugar and cream on the table. The bagel showed up—with tomato, avo, lox, and cream cheese—and he was suddenly enjoying a pleasant conversation about his options as a cartoonist and how he'd loved to draw things for Rico, who had all the best ideas.

Finn emerged after a good twenty-five minutes, arriving just in time to watch Adam feed Clopper the last quarter of his bagel.

"You're going to make him fat," he chided, and Adam looked up and smiled widely. Seeing Finn fully dressed—jeans belted, warm knit sweater hugging tightly to the V of his torso, hair combed, loafers on with matching socks—was something. He looked freshly scrubbed and radiant, and Adam wondered if he always looked like this before he left the house, and if his curls didn't just escape and his clothes go askew as he happy-trippy walked all over the world like he belonged there.

"We'll do extra circles around the block," Adam said, still smiling. Suddenly he realized that he was in his old jeans and his hooded sweatshirt. "I... I uhm, didn't dress nice. I mean, we were just walking around the block. I... you look real good."

Finn grinned back, undismayed, and walked right up to where Adam was sitting. He bent and kissed the top of Adam's head, ruffling his hair. "You look fine. It's not an eating-out date, remember? It's just a day."

Adam shrugged. "Maybe let me swing by my place—"

"No," Finn said adamantly. "Nope. You're not getting away from me today. Let me go get my backpack."

Adam watched him go, sighing a little. He was always going to be one step behind, wasn't he? Just a moment away from catching up, watching Finn hop around and be quick and smart and full of life.

But then, Finn looked like he'd always come back for Adam, so maybe that was okay.

"He *really* likes you," Mari said softly, smiling.

Adam shrugged, blushing and standing up. "Good. 'Cause, mutual."

Finn returned, a full backpack over his shoulder and his bright blue coat over his arm. "Bye guys! See you tomorrow, 'kay?"

"If not, call us," Finn's mom said mildly, and Finn bounced around the table to kiss her on the cheek.

"Kk. Love you."

And then he turned and grabbed Adam's hand while Adam was still babbling thank you for the coffee. One step behind—there was no doubt about it—but loving the trip to catch up.

FINN PARKED at the big lot by College Town Drive, and they walked onto the campus through the back way, over the bridge across the river. Fog drifted over the campus, and the smell of the eucalyptus trees by the river was particularly strong. Adam liked this side of Sacramento—the muffled, quiet side. It was sort of a prickly town, he thought, but he liked that. There wasn't always a real spiritual presence here. All the conversation was done in grunts and laughter that didn't really touch the eyes.

Adam could identify with this city. He could see loveliness when it was dripping in fog and muted, the sound of people's laughter seeming far away.

He and Finn talked quietly as they walked about the campus, letting Clopper pee in every corner. Finn led the way to the engineering building—a square, blocky science building, although Finn said the other building in the department was much better-looking—and left Adam outside while he ran in to put the paper in his professor's box.

While Adam was standing there, a couple of kids passed him by, talking and giggling. They looked like the kids at the art school Adam had gone to, and when one of the girls turned to him in a burst of excitement and said, "Man, aren't you glad we're *done!*" he didn't have the heart to shit on that.

"Feels good, huh?" he asked, smiling.

She nodded and went back to talking to her buddies, but he thought then of the applications he'd turned in. *I can do this. If the state school doesn't take me, the junior college will. I can have a future, like Finn. It'll take a while, but I can do it.*

Finn came out and grabbed his hand, then went up on tiptoes to kiss his cheek. "You freeze to death?" he asked. Absently, like it was just a thing you did with dogs, he reached down and stroked the smooth fur of Clopper's forehead. Clopper gave a small doggy smile and leaned into him, and Adam thought maybe the day out had been good for him too.

"Nope," Adam said, squeezing his hand. "But that doesn't mean I'm not willing to move on to the next part of our day."

"Lunch?"

"Are you kidding? I just ate breakfast!"

"Oh, yeah—okay. Kitten first. I hear you."

Adam patted Clopper on the head again. "We'll get you a buddy," he said softly. "I promise."

AN HOUR later Finn came out of the special cat room of the PetSmart off of Watt holding a kitten in each hand.

"We've got two contenders," he said judiciously. "We've got this adolescent ginger tom, who is comatose and barely awake." He shook that cat, who bonelessly draped over his hand before closing its orange eyes and falling asleep. "And we've got this cat—hold still, you little bastard—who will probably slit your throat or tackle your junk as you sleep."

The tiger-striped kitten held firmly in Finn's hand was twisting and turning and bitching and moaning and biting and scratching.

Adam reached out and grabbed the tiger-stripe, which promptly ripped a chunk out of his hand and spat at him.

And *then* got a good look at the dog and wriggled free, skittering on the clean tile of PetSmart.

"Fuck, I'll get him," Finn muttered, shoving the comatose tom at Adam before taking off.

Adam watched them go with big eyes but figured he and Clopper were the *last* elements that situation needed. Carefully, he adjusted the ginger tom in his hand and squatted down to Clopper.

"What do you think?" he asked quietly. "I mean, I know Gonzo was a spaz just like that other guy. But this guy—he's gonna be nice to you. Probably just purr and knead your ass. What do you think?"

Clopper nosed the cat with interest, and Adam balanced the leash and the cat until Ginger Tom curled up in the crook of his arm. Clopper nosed him again and then extended a tongue and licked the animal.

Who purred. Adam held the cat up to his face and nosed his whiskers flat. The cat returned the gesture with interest, and Adam fell a little in love.

A few minutes later, Finn returned with the half-feral tiger-stripe in his hands, and Adam was filling out paperwork for the ginger tom.

"You're getting that one?" Finn asked in surprise.

Adam looked up from the cheap plastic table where he was signing his name to a zillion pages and getting ready to spend about half his check on one lousy cat.

"Yes," he said shortly. "Can you hold him and put him in the box while I do this? He keeps drooling on my sleeve."

Finn gave the tiger-striped kitten to the anxious volunteer so he could go back to his sulfur pit and mouse head collection, and took the unresisting ginger tom from Adam and cuddled it. The cat was apparently a slut and a half, because it didn't even change the tenor of its purr.

"He's awesome," Finn breathed. "But I thought you'd like a cat more like, you know, Gonzo."

While Adam paused and thought about it, Clopper moved from Adam's side to Finn's, where he nosed up Finn's thigh, looking for the kitten.

"No," Adam said thoughtfully. "See, the way me and Clopper see it, it's one thing to deal with a bad situation 'cause that's what you got stuck with from the very beginning. But if you're making a fresh start, maybe you don't have to carry all that bad bullshit with you. Maybe the stuff that hurts should be the first thing to go."

Finn grinned down at him and then bent and kissed him on the cheek. "I think that's really wise, Adam. And hopeful."

So beautiful. Adam could drown in those Finn-blue eyes. "Thanks," he said, knowing he was just gazing dreamily at Finn. "I... I have hope."

They just stared at each other until the volunteer behind the table cleared his throat, and Adam got back to sacrificing a lot of his hard-earned cash to keep Rico's dog from dying of apathy.

THEY SPENT the rest of the afternoon talking about everything from their favorite movies (Adam's was a cartoon, of course) to trying to determine a name for the cat. By the time they'd eaten lunch and then gone shopping for dinner, they had it narrowed down to Ralph or Jake—Ralph from *The Muppets*, to match Gonzo, or Jake from *Adventure Time*, to match Finn.

"Jake," Adam said as they entered the apartment in a flurry of animals and packages. "It's definitely going to be Jake."

He put the groceries on the table and straightened up, turning to watch as Finn let the new kitten out of the box. The kitten wandered around the apartment, smelling the couch, smelling the freshly cleaned and filled cat box, smelling down the hall.

"He'll be fine," Finn said with confidence. "So why Jake?"

"'Cause Jake goes with Finn. That way, you know, however we turn out, I'll always remember that you were in my life."

Finn gasped. "Wow."

Adam looked up from where he was setting the lunchmeat and the new bread on the counter.

"What?"

"It's like your superpower, Adam. You say things like that, and I will give you any chance you need."

Adam smiled. "Will you give me a kiss as I make our sandwiches?"

"Yeah. Absolutely."

His lips on Adam's tasted like the kind of wine they talk about in church. The kind that fills the soul.

THE BEST relationships are made of quiet times, Adam thought as the day wrapped to a close. Lunch, taking the dog out, cooking dinner, sitting to eat it in front of the television. Conversation that ebbed and flowed, the constant small touches that marked where the other person was and that they'd been absent for just a moment too long.

At the end of the night, Adam sat with his back up against the side of the couch, and Finn sat in his lap. The kitten claimed the back of the couch, curled into a little purring ball, and Clopper ate his second bowl of food since they'd arrived home. All was peaceful in the world. Adam felt himself nodding off and shifted one more time to keep that from happening, and Finn turned in his arms.

"Falling asleep?" he purred.

"Feeling happy," Adam apologized, then opened his mouth for what he thought would be a lazy kiss.

Finn devoured him.

Open mouth to open mouth, the subtle warming of Finn's body on his suddenly became an uncomfortable, steamy blaze.

Adam rucked Finn's shirt up from his waistband and fed his palms on the smooth skin of Finn's back, needing that feeling, the silk and the heat and the strength of the underlying muscles.

Finn groaned and kept kissing him, shoving his hands under Adam's T-shirt, groping his chest and petting the strands of silky hair. Adam tilted his head back and let out a whimper, and Finn showed him no mercy, kissing from the edge of his cleft chin down the stubble-roughened column of his throat.

"Augh, Finn!"

"Here, let's get this off, it'll make it easier," Finn panted, straddling Adam's hips and sitting up on his knees. He struggled with Adam's hooded sweatshirt for a moment, and then with the T-shirt underneath. In moments Adam was bare from the waist up and Finn was still fully clothed, nibbling determinedly from Adam's chin and down his throat. Oh yippee! Scruples or not, this was going someplace Adam really, really wanted.

Finn swept his tongue down to the waistband of Adam's jeans, and he undid the top button, looked up at Adam, and grinned.

Adam's breath caught in his throat. "Uhm… were you going to do anything about that?"

Finn flicked his tongue to the spot right above the button. "You ready to, uhm, variate this far?" He cupped Adam's cock and balls through his jeans, pushing just hard enough for Adam to grind up against him.

"Oh damn—Finn!" It was a plea nobody could argue.

Finn grasped his waistband in two hands while Adam arched his hips, and his jeans got shucked down to his knees.

For a moment Adam was afraid. Bare and vulnerable, under the eyes of someone who was supposed to care for him—Adam had been here before. It hadn't ended well.

Finn was oblivious. He lowered his head and licked the swollen head of Adam's cock, circling the bell, lapping softly at the top, dragging in a warm, wet line down the length. Adam let out a pained breath and shifted his hips up, needing.

Finn laved his testicles through the dark, springy hair and then dragged his tongue back up to where Adam's cockhead was cooling in the air. He lapped again at the slit, which was oozing precome, and Adam made a sound between a grunt and sigh.

Finn grinned at him. "Good? Because, wow!" And with that he opened his mouth and pulled Adam all the way in.

"Whoa," Adam breathed, not wanting to stop him *at all*—just stunned at how awesome it felt.

Finn didn't look up—he was too busy. Sucking, stroking, licking, tasting, laving—all of the good "ing" words, that was what Finn was doing to Adam's tender, vulnerable bits.

Including "loving," which Adam didn't understand until he fisted his hand in Finn's hair and stopped him, shuddering with need while his vision washed black because he was so close to coming.

"Finn!" he whined. "Finn, baby, I'm going to come...."

"Got any STDs?" Finn asked, looking up with his mouth covered in a glaze of spit and precome that did *not* help Adam get under control any faster.

"No! God no. Clean bill of health when I left the Army. No action since. But—*oh my God*!" Because Finn didn't wait for the rest, for any explanations about how Adam needed to take care of Finn first, or how he wanted time to explore Finn's body, or even how he was usually the one getting face-fucked and swallowing. Finn just dove right on in, shoving his head down until his lips tickled Adam's pubic hair and Adam's cockhead was lodged in the back of his throat. He was making "nummy" noises, humming sounds that vibrated against Adam's cock and heightened the pressure and the arousal even more.

"Oh God! Finn, I will come and it'll be over and—"

Finn lifted his head again and glared. But he didn't stop stroking Adam when he spoke. "It'll be over? Because you came? Not bloody likely. We have got some shit to do tonight, Adam. Don't even worry about it. Just close your eyes and trust, just once, that somebody will take care of you."

He didn't wait for an answer—greedy, like a starving man, he lowered his head again, and this time, he thrust his free hand deeper between Adam's thighs, bringing his fingers into play to tickle Adam's perineum and then, ever so suggestively, the little puckered entrance that Adam had not had touched, tenderly or no, since he and Robbie had leave together nearly two years before.

Adam arched off the couch, thrusting his hips, his vision washed by stars as Finn swallowed him down cleanly, and Adam's entire body blew into oblivion, made solid only by Finn's hard clasp on his thigh.

He came to himself, panting, disoriented, literally blown away, and Finn crawled up his body, come dripping down his chin, and smiled like an evil little pixie, small and cute but by no means a child.

Adam didn't fight the compulsion to stick out his tongue and taste the drop of come about to fall from Finn's chin to Adam's chest.

Finn glared at him defiantly and whispered, "Lick it all off, Adam. And then kiss me."

Yes! Adam sank into the moment, and the moment was good. He tasted himself running down Finn's chin, at the corners of his mouth, and then Finn kissed him, claimed him, set his mark on Adam's soul once and for all with a kiss that was both tender and ferocious, with a refusal to back down.

By the time the kiss was over, Adam had kicked off his jeans and peeled off Finn's shirt and sweatshirt, and the two of them were fumbling with Finn's belt and the buttons on his jeans.

Their fingers tangled more than once, and Finn laughed.

"Kk—let's go get into bed, okay? One of the perks of being grown-ups is we don't have to do this on living room furniture."

Adam nodded, thinking about the pleasure of having Finn naked to explore.

Uncharted countries, unnamed wonders.

Adam got to the bed first and pulled down the covers, then sat, beckoning Finn between his spread thighs. He wanted to kiss his tummy, which was perfect. Well-defined muscle, nicely cut oblique muscles—but that wasn't what drew Adam to it. The soft skin and the silky fur of the happy trail was Adam's favorite part, and while he was undoing Finn's belt and the top button on his jeans, he suckled mouthfuls of tender skin, delighting in Finn's every gasp.

He shoved Finn's jeans down perfunctorily—he was already lingering on the best parts. The jutting hipbones, the crease of his upper thigh, even the hairiness of his thighs and shins—Adam wanted to smooth his palms or his tongue over all of it.

But he hadn't even gotten to Finn's thighs before Finn tightened fingers in his hair and tilted his head back. "Adam, I swear to God, if you don't touch my dick, I'm gonna lose it!"

Adam's smile wasn't sweet—he knew that. "Lose it. Go ahead. Come all over my face. I'm hard again. This isn't done by a long shot."

"Nungh...."

But Adam took pity on him, engulfing the long, pale cock with his mouth, closing his eyes at the taste. Oh, man. He'd been good at this—*great*, if his demand as a covert companion was anything to judge by—but he'd never really *loved* it until now. Finn made another wordless begging sound, and Adam responded, licking the head, squeezing the shaft, using his other hand to knead Finn's backside and tease his cleft.

Unplanned, his dry fingertip made contact with Finn's pucker, and Finn whined.

"Lubricant—let me get my backpack."

It was good Finn had some—Adam didn't. He'd spent all his money on a cat and a new sketchbook.

Finn tore himself away and Adam shivered, scrambling under the covers in the brightly lit room. Finn's absence suddenly reminded him of all he was without shadows and warmth. Easy. Needy. Desperate. Despised.

By the time Finn got back, Adam was a heartbeat away from throwing on some clothes and pretending it had never happened.

But Finn had taken off his pants completely. He was naked, pale, his skin tinged pink and blotching, probably from arousal.

"Good idea," he said, hustling for the blankets and scrambling in. "God, is your thermostat on a timer or something? It's cold in here!"

And the feel of him, smooth skin, hairy shins, cold hands tickle-biting on Adam's ribs—sweet, natural, unforced, unjudging. Adam wrapped his arms around Finn's shoulders and covered that slender smaller body with his own.

"We'll keep each other warm," he murmured into the hollow of Finn's neck and shoulder.

Finn shuddered and shoved the lube into his hand. "I brought rubbers too," he said, gasping as Adam nibbled on his collarbone. "But I'm tested, you're tested…."

"I've never not used one," Adam mumbled, wondering if he shouldn't anyway. What if he shot come inside Finn's body and the bad parts of Adam, the parts that had hid under the bed in the guest room, the parts that had given it up for anyone who asked—what if those parts got Finn dirty?

"Good," Finn said, locking his lips around Adam's nipple and sucking hard before releasing it with a pop. "I'll be your first."

"Like starting again?" Adam asked, all of it, the apartment, the job, the dumb kitten, the boyfriend who seemed to think he was something—*all* of it—sliding into place around him in that moment.

"Yeah," Finn said, not conscious of the seven sorts of havoc he'd just wrought. He sat up then and straddled Adam, gesturing imperiously for the lube. "Gimme."

Adam handed it to him and Finn reached behind him. Adam watched in awe as he fingered himself, his face contorting, and Adam could feel it for him: *Stretch, stretch, ouch... oh... oh... yes!*

Finn moaned softly, his head back, and then he grasped Adam's cock behind his back and....

"Oh God!"

Slowly, smoothly, Finn lowered himself, and Adam threw his head back against the pillow and closed his eyes. Finn's body was tight and hot, and it clenched all of Adam's nerve endings in exactly the right places.

Finn sank down until he was sitting on Adam's hips, and Adam's vision went dark.

"Oh Jesus.... Finn...."

"Oh my God—*Adam*!"

Finn pushed up and sat down again, and Adam *oolf*ed because... oh man....

"Adam, look at me," Finn commanded, and Adam opened his eyes as Finn began to rock forward and back, forward and back. "It's good?" he asked anxiously.

Adam managed to clench his stomach. "It's amazing. Oh God. I need... harder... faster...." Not wanting to let Finn's warmth go, he clasped the lean meat of Finn's ass tightly and rolled them over. Finn grabbed his thighs accommodatingly, spreading himself open, and Adam looked down at their joining. "You're so hot," he muttered thickly, thinking it sounded shallow, but his whole body was hot, lit up inside by Finn's beauty and his sexiness and the way he needed the most primal part of Adam inside of him.

"Augh! Adam... need. *Need you. Need!*"

Adam couldn't deny him anything he needed.

He cocked his hips back and slammed forward, and Finn closed his eyes, tipped his head back, and screamed "*Yes!*"

Adam did it again.

God, again and again and again, and the sex blush blotching Finn's chest, shoulders, and throat got darker and sexier. Adam dripped with sweat, his heart clenching with desire and want. Finn was breath and heat and pain and fierce, biting joy, and Adam wanted it, wanted it, chased the core of Finn with his orgasm. Finn scrabbled for the sheets with one hand and scrambled for his cock with the other. He found his cock first and squeezed, begging *"Fuck me!"* loud enough to startle the dog, who started barking in the living room.

For once, Adam didn't give a damn.

He threw himself into it, fucking Finn in a frenzy, until Finn's cock burst white spend over them both, far and hard. Some of it caught Adam on the chin, and he licked it off. Hell, he was so ravenous for Finn he yearned to lick it from Finn's stomach, from his dick, from his chest and throat.

The thought of doing that, of sucking Finn's cock, of licking him all over, rimming him, used and dripping, all of it, along with Finn's breathless sex screams, sent Adam over.

Oh fuck. Oh *fuck*.

He lost himself. Blasted outside his body with his come, floated through into Finn, saw himself from the outside, from Finn's eyes, drenched with sweat, eyes squeezed shut, muscular body heaving, the cords on his neck popping out.

He was beautiful.

Inside Finn, he was beautiful.

The revelation leveled him, sent himself back inside his lightning-struck body, and he collapsed, shuddering, into Finn's arms.

Pretty Pictures, Pretty Words

HE'D NEVER lost time after sex before, but he must have. He woke up
and Finn was washing off his cock, the warm cloth both abrasive and
arousing. He sighed and arched his hips, massaging Finn's scalp
through his hair.

"Sorry," he mumbled, trying hard to focus. The cloth scraped the
tenderness of his cockhead, the mess of his pubic hair, and then gently
cradled his balls.

"For what?" Finn said softly. "For being a good lover?"

"Was I?" Adam asked, suddenly desperate to hear it.

"You were wonderful," Finn murmured, kissing his thigh gently.
He set the cloth on the end table and pulled up so they were eyeball to
eyeball. Adam must have been out longer than he'd thought, because
when they'd gone stumbling for the bedroom, every light in the
apartment was on, and now the place was dark.

"So were you," Adam said, brushing Finn's cheek with his
thumb. "You're fearless."

"I've never been hurt," Finn said baldly. "It's easy to be fearless
when you don't think anything can hurt you."

"I hurt you," Adam admitted.

Finn shook his head. "No. I mean, you would have if you'd kept
it up. But I still had lots of hope. But if you back away again now?"

Oh. "Hurt."

Finn nodded and swallowed. "Really, really bad."

Adam understood. "I will never hurt you," he promised. "Not if I
can possibly help it."

"It means you're going to have to be brave," Finn told him
soberly. "It means you're going to have to believe."

Adam closed his eyes on the words, let them ricochet around his
soul for a breath or two. "I'll do my best," he said after a moment. "Can
you risk it?

"I already am."

Adam kissed him then, deep, intense, satisfying. His body gave a throb, and Finn wrapped his leg around Adam's hip in another effort to crawl inside his skin. Well, they were taking a leap of faith to risk their hearts anyway—they might as well enjoy the high.

ADAM WAS a little bit tired but *very* energized when he went to work the next day. He smiled quietly and worked with great industry—and ignored the suspicious looks from his coworkers.

Around midday, he was dealing politely with a man in a suit who was buying Candy Heaven's logoed canvas bags for his entire office. The man surprised him by pointing to the picture hanging behind the register. It was the one Adam had given Darrin two weeks earlier, the thank-you for the job and for the hope.

"That's fun!" the guy said. "Do you know the artist?"

Adam smiled slightly. "Yeah. Me."

"Really? What are you doing working here with that kind of talent?"

Adam scowled. "It's a great place to work. It just might get me through school."

The guy held up his hands. "Sorry—didn't mean to offend." He smiled rakishly. He had the kind of sandy-haired, blue-eyed American-boy good looks that probably helped him get out of a lot of trouble.

"Just...." Adam looked around at the holiday crowds, most of whom were just plain happy to be there. "It's a good place," he said earnestly.

"Yeah. I can see that. And you're a good artist." He arched two sand-colored eyebrows almost seductively, and Adam sort of wished he was Clopper, who could unapologetically sniff someone's crotch and tell you if he was all good. "So, do you want a job?"

Adam narrowed his eyes. "Depends on what kind of job. I got a boyfriend who'd object to one kind of job but who wouldn't mind if I did some art for you."

The sheepish, human smile of rejection reassured him. "Well, I guess there goes asking you out for dinner. But would you still want to do some caricatures of my office staff? I've got sort of a good group. I was going to give them Christmas candy, but a hand-drawn portrait, even a quickie—that would be something."

Adam gaped at him and remembered how Finn had needed to bring the lube because Adam spent most of his pre-Christmas check on buying a new sketchbook and adopting a cat. "That would.... Uhm, tell me where you work. I get off at four."

"Don't you even want to know how much I'd be willing to pay?"

Adam never claimed to be a businessman. "Whatever you pay me, it will be more than I got now to get my boyfriend a gift," he said baldly. Sketch paper wasn't the only art supply he was running low on either. He grimaced at the thought. "But maybe tomorrow after work or during lunch—I've got to bring my supplies."

The guy squeezed his eyes shut and rubbed the bridge of his nose. "Okay. Here's my card—give me a call; we'll set up a time. I'll have you come in, introduce folks—I've got six employees. I'll tell them you're a client. Then you get back to me in a week?"

Adam nodded. "Yeah. Absolutely. That'll be good." Oh God. Absolutely not. He couldn't get to know people that quickly. "But, uhm, could I bring my boyfriend? He's better at the people stuff."

"Tell him to look up pricing for this sort of thing too," the guy said, still looking at Adam in disbelief. "Because one of you needs to be better at the business stuff."

The guy headed for the door, and Darrin caught his eye and arched his eyebrow. He got a second look, and then a third, and then *Darrin* got a business card too, and the guy got a suggestion to have a *very* sweet day.

Then Darrin parked his bossy ass in front of Adam's now empty counter and said, "Dish."

"He's got an art job for me to do."

"Excellent. Don't I pay you enough?"

Adam grimaced. "I want to get something for Finn."

Darrin wrinkled his fine, straight-arched nose. "Honey, Finn doesn't need something expensive."

"But he does need something."

"If you say so," Darrin grudged. "But you and people? You barely talk to *us*, and we're going on four weeks now."

Adam sighed. "Yeah, that's why I'm bringing him."

Darrin could make an insouciant shrug look damned sexy. "Okay, okay, he's your boyfriend—"

And Adam was compelled to speak the truth. Was that what you did in heaven, even Candy Heaven? "It's a chance to make money doing something I love," he said. "It's like, while I'm waiting to hear from schools, it gives me a chance to hope."

Darrin's expression softened, became sincere. "Well then, I'm pretty sure Finn will be more than happy. It was a good idea."

Adam preened, because Darrin seemed to love what *he* was doing, and maybe he'd know all about good ideas.

Finn was overjoyed. Seriously thrilled—he even did that jump-in-the-air fist-pump-to-the-sky thing that had captivated Adam so much.

"But why am I coming again?" he asked after Adam explained the setup.

It was hard to say—Adam thought he might swallow his tongue.

"I need help," he confessed after trying to make his mouth work. "I can't do this one by myself, and... you know. Money for Christmas is good."

Finn smiled sweetly. "You don't have to get me anything," he said. Adam didn't know if it was just the late-afternoon twilight coming off the river or the way Finn glowed from the inside out, but he always looked radiant, even when they'd both worked an eight-hour shift and were strolling slowly down the boardwalk.

"Yeah, but I want to get you...." Adam stopped, thinking about a Finn or Jake fleece kigurumi, or a new SUV that was a little cooler and used less gas than the minivan, or an apartment of their own when Rico came back, and a cat and a dog that were theirs to keep, and....

"What?" Finn asked, blinking those Finn-blue eyes at him.

"The world," Adam said simply, and Finn laughed.

"Well, all I want for Christmas is Adam," he said, nuzzling Adam's cheek as they walked.

"Okay. Well, that's all I got right now, so we'll have to make do with it."

Finn laughed and started to plan dinner after Clopper's walk, and for the first time, Adam thought that maybe he *was* good enough, and that if he was what they had to make do with, then he was up to the task.

But that didn't keep him from planning after he went into Derek Huston's office (that was the flirty guy with the business card) and talked to all the nice people who thought he was an investment client (hah!) and then drew their pictures. Huston cut him a nice check—Finn must have quoted a bigger price than Adam had in mind—but after Adam used it for a big bag of Clopper's food and his art supplies, he still didn't have much to shop with.

So he sat on it. He sat on the check and pondered, and worked his job, and lived his life—with Finn in it. Finn pretty much moved all his clothes into Rico's apartment over the next week, and Adam didn't object. He learned what it was like to wake up next to someone, and how sometimes they stole the blankets and sometimes they took *way* too long to have their morning BM and sometimes they woke you with a mouth on your cock, which made up for a lot of the other inconveniences. There was sex on tap—but more than that. There was a sweet touch on his hip when he was making dinner or a chattering voice telling him about Finn's day when they were walking Rico's oversize dog. There was a bouncy kid throwing a ping-pong ball for the comatose cat, sure that one day Jake would learn how to fetch, and a kind adult when….

When the Christmas card Adam sent his mom was returned with "No faggots allowed" scrawled on the back.

Finn didn't *act* like a grown-up then—he ripped up the card and flushed it down the toilet and swore over it. Then he hugged Adam and cried, and Adam spent an hour calming him down and telling him that the world wasn't like his parents, but Adam would never, ever let someone hurt Finn like the world had hurt Adam.

Finn looked up from that and hiccupped. "I'm crying for *you*, you dumbass. And I will *never* let anyone hurt you like that again."

"You already protected me," Adam said, wiping Finn's cheek with his roughened thumb. "Just now. When you got mad for me. Took all the hurt away, baby. Mission accomplished."

Finn smiled like the sun, and that took some more hurt away too.

And Adam thought harder for something to give him.

In the end, all he could think of was something that might hurt him more, but that, for Finn, would be beyond price.

HE AND Finn were going to volunteer at the shelter on Christmas Day and then going to Finn's family's place afterward, but Christmas Eve was theirs. Adam had the feeling that the family probably gathered on Christmas Eve too, but Finn was sparing him, and he was grateful. Finn told him to expect a present, and Adam had bought—with his employee discount—a small basket of wrapped sweets, with one of those very cool tins in the shape of R2-D2, which would be appropriate to bring to someone's house.

In his backpack, he had ready for Darrin and his coworkers the super-nice colored-in chibi version of Candy Heaven, with little chibi portraits of everyone he worked with, that he was planning to give to everyone when he went in for his half-day shift that morning. And he had taken his best portrait of Finn and drawn it again, adding pastels for color and spraying fixer on it so it would last longer. He bought a frame for it, and on one rare day when Finn worked and he didn't, he wrapped it all up, and that was what he would give Finn on Christmas Eve.

But it wasn't the real present. Not really. The real present was something he couldn't really be there for when Finn opened it.

Finn had Christmas Eve off, so Adam got up early and walked the dog. He came in chilled on the outside from the foggy cold and warm on the inside from anticipation, and even the dog seemed subdued, because what Adam was about to do, that was huge.

Adam put it off until after his shower because he and Finn had been up late the night before. Yeah, they'd had some *rockin'* sex, but after that they'd had one of those weird, dreamy conversations that happened when you were supposed to be going to sleep but there always seemed to be one more thing to say, one more precious piece of communication that *absolutely needed* to be shared.

It had been one of the most intimate moments of Adam's life, and he was going to put a capper on it now—right before he ran for the hills like the coward he knew himself to be.

When Adam got out of the shower, Finn was still sleeping, one bare pink shoulder peeping out from under the white comforter. Adam had started to wish heartily for enough money to buy some of his own stuff, because Rico's apartment was sort of boring—white and cream and ecru. Rico didn't have any Christmas decorations. Adam and Finn had spent a giddy, giggly evening gluing paper chains together to strew around the living room, but that was all they had. Adam loved color as an artist—and he hated to see Finn surrounded by anything less than brilliance.

Someday, he thought. Lights for Christmas and saturated colors in a home that was theirs. But not today.

Today he had one thing he could give Finn, and he was dressed and ready for the mile run to the bus stop and then the half-mile run to work. The time had come to give it.

He held the sketchbook tightly in his hands as he walked into the bedroom and stretched out next to Finn, savoring his smell and the mammal warmth that pervaded the room from his nest in the covers. The cat was curled up right behind Finn's neck, and Adam sort of loved that whenever Finn's usually active body went still, the cat was all over that action. Right now he reached out and moved the unresisting body so Finn could roll over without crushing him—not that Jake would notice.

"Finn? Baby, wake up a sec, okay? You can go back to sleep when I leave."

Finn smiled a little and peered up at Adam from bleary eyes. Freckles. Adam wanted to see baby pictures of Finn so he could see how many freckles he'd had as a kid, because not all of those had faded away. "What's up?" Finn mumbled.

"I got something for you, but I want you to look at it when I'm gone, okay?"

Finn squinted, refocused, and squinted again. "You want me to what?"

"Look, it's… it's like a Christmas present, but this one's sort of sad. The one that will make you happy is tomorrow, so I want you to look at this one today, okay?"

Finn pushed up on one elbow, his grumpy morning face settling into concerned lines. "Adam, is that your—"

"Yeah. It's my old sketchbook. Like… like me. Good, bad, ugly. Me. So, now it's yours. And I gotta go to work, so, if you hate everything in here, could you not tell me until after Christmas? Because I… I never had someone for Christmas, and I just… if you can't deal with me because of this, I would just prefer you pretend or something until December 26—"

Finn placed a bony, long-fingered hand over Adam's mouth. "Stop," he commanded quietly. Moving his fingers, he took the sketchbook from Adam's reluctant hands. "This is precious and important, and it's not going to scare me away."

Adam swallowed and nodded. "'Kay. Ain't nobody… I mean nobody has seen this before. Just… I know this is fast. A month. But you mean that much to me, Finn."

Finn nodded and pushed forward into a brief kiss. "Okay. It's okay. Go to work. It's in good hands."

Adam contorted his lips and hoped it passed for a smile, then made sure to grab his backpack before he bolted out of the apartment.

He wondered how he was going to make it through the day.

ADAM KNEW that the store closed early on the day before Christmas and opened early the day after, but he was not prepared for the two hours of cleanup after they closed to be one big office staff party.

Normally he wouldn't have cared—he would have taken his cookies and said thank you and walked away.

But now he had the silly little chibi drawings, and instead of Adam just handing them out discreetly and running away, they were part of the big gift-giving frenzy that the entire staff participated in at the end.

The frenzy had no rhyme or reason. If you worked with someone and liked them, you gave them a present. If you didn't know them, you didn't. No feelings were hurt, no fights broke out—people just got presents and were happy.

And everyone got the little scrolled chibis with a whole lot of happy. Adam was reduced to smiling shyly a lot and saying, "You're welcome. I'm glad you liked it," at least six hundred times.

And he was surprised to get some presents of his own.

Three people brought cookies, and he ended up with three plates—actual plates, not paper—of cookies, and one that held a hot-chocolate basket. When he realized that the plates matched and that the four gift-givers were Anish, Ravi, Darby, and Joni, he figured they'd gotten together and done it on purpose. Look! He had four plates and matching mugs—and cookies. And hot chocolate.

And a hooded Sac State sweatshirt from Darrin.

He looked at it, surprised, thinking that the bright green and gold made a change from the plain old dark blue hoodie he'd worn until the sleeves were ragged and the lining had all but disappeared.

"How do you even know I'll be able to get in?" he asked, feeling humble. It was a really great gift.

Darrin rolled his eyes. "Don't bother me with bullshit." He smirked. "I knew you'd walk through my door, I know you'll walk through that one."

Some of Adam's roiling worry about Finn disappeared, and he gave Darrin probably his best smile of the day. "Thanks," he said. "It's nice that someone's got some faith."

Darrin sucked on his Pixy Stix coquettishly and smiled. "Besides that guy, who has all the faith in the world, right?"

Adam heard a knocking on the locked door right then and turned to see Finn, his fleece hat buttoned firmly around his ears and a rather wistful smile on his face. Adam hustled to let him in, glad that they'd made plans for Finn to pick him up, because he didn't know how he'd get all the plates with food on them home if he didn't.

Finn took a step in and grabbed Adam by the shirtfront, then hauled him outside.

"Hey, all my stuff—"

Finn kissed him ravenously, like he'd been starving for Adam all his life. Adam reached under him, cupped his bottom, and hefted, happy when Finn hopped up and wrapped his legs around Adam's waist. They kissed until Adam's arms trembled and he had to set Finn down. They pulled away, resting foreheads against each other.

"That was awesome. What was it for?"

To his horror, Finn made a sound like a hiccupping child. When Adam peered into his face, he saw the telltale signs—red-rimmed eyes, slightly swollen nose—and hated himself.

"I'm sorry," Adam mumbled, using his thumb to smooth away yet another tear. "It's like this is all I'm doing to you. I didn't mean—"

"Sometimes tears are happy, Adam," Finn muttered, catching his hand. "Didn't anyone tell you that? It was the best gift ever. In a million years. It was all of you, and some of it hurt me and I wanted to burn it for you, and some of it was beautiful and…. Thank you. Just… you know. Thank you."

Adam exhaled shakily. "Yeah?"

"Yeah."

This kiss was less starvation and more harmony, which was okay. Adam needed that too.

The kiss ended, and Finn came inside and said hello to everybody. On their way out, Miguel stopped them, putting a hand on Finn's sleeve. Miguel was one of the guys Adam didn't know well, but he seemed pretty familiar to Finn.

"Finn—I didn't know you and Adam had hooked up. Go you! I've been trying to get his attention since he walked in!"

Adam blinked at him. He looked like a slightly browner, taller version of Finn—darker hair, same cheekbones, brown eyes, same build.

Different smile—this one a little more guarded, a little less open to the world.

"I had no idea," Adam said, slightly panicked, feeling sort of guilty.

Finn winked at Miguel and shrugged. "I'm not sure how it happened," he said. "But I'm really lucky."

Adam nodded at Miguel, a little embarrassed and a lot eager to be alone with Finn. He grabbed Finn's hand and let himself be pulled to the minivan, which was parked about half a block down by one of the meters.

"You totally lied," he said as he slid into the passenger seat, and Finn looked at him in surprise.

"How do you figure?"

"You totally stalked me. You said you weren't sure how it happened. You... you brought me food and made me come to your workplace and took me shopping and all but attacked me in the minivan, and I didn't have a *chance* against you! You were everywhere. I was going to totally fall in love with you whether I liked it or not, and it's just a good thing you were awesome, or I would have been fucking *doomed!*"

Finn was laughing hard—so hard that for a minute, Adam was afraid as he negotiated Christmas Eve traffic. But Finn had been born in this city—had grown up in his parents' house—and he was secure and comfortable when Adam might have been a little apprehensive. He took them directly home, although Adam thought they needed groceries. But when he suggested they stop for some, Finn waved his hand.

"No. I've got a plan."

"Well, I think we just covered that I like your plans."

"Good." Finn pulled in front of the apartment, lucky because there wasn't always space here. The week before, he'd had to park at his parents' house and walk. "Because I've made some plans for tonight."

He pulled Adam up to the apartment, and they braced themselves for the dog storming out. Adam had dreaded the dog's charge for the first couple of weeks, but now, after Gonzo, he sort of saw it as healthy.

That and Clopper listened to him when he said, "Down, dammit, down!" which meant it wasn't quite as bad as before.

Tonight the obedience was extra spiffy because, well....

"Wow," Adam murmured, trying not to choke up. He smiled over his shoulder. "Look what you did!"

"Had help," Finn confessed. "Mari and Peter came over, and Christopher brought the tree."

"It's…." Christmas. A tree—moderately sized, of course—stood strewn with popcorn and cranberries, paper ornaments, and, best of all, colored lights. In fact, the colored lights were twisted with the paper chains. The effect was busy and inharmonious and too bright and…

Beautiful.

"It's gorgeous," Adam said softly. "You and your family—something else. I'm…." Oh, it sounded like such a grand word, but it was all he had. "Humbled. I'm humbled. And really grateful."

"Me too," Finn said, pulling him into the brightly lit room. "Now sit down while I serve you Christmas dinner—"

Adam sniffed experimentally. "What's for Christmas dinner?"

"Stuffed chicken, gravy, salad, and garlic potatoes."

"Whoa!"

"Yes, Christopher *also* brought food from Mom, who says she's looking forward to seeing us volunteer tomorrow. Mom fundraises a lot for the homeless, Adam—you have yourself a fan right there."

Adam closed his eyes and remembered Thanksgiving. "Well, back at her. God, it smells good."

Finn shut the door behind him and came to nestle in Adam's chest. "So do you. Do you mind if we talk about the sketchbook after dinner?"

If Finn was here? And his? And unafraid? "Yeah, that'll be all right."

"Good. Go wash up and I'll start putting the stuff on the table."

Adam was getting used to eating regularly sized meals, and he wasn't going to pass up on seconds, not tonight. Finn told him about his day, about decorating, and how Mari and Joshie strung the popcorn, but Joshie and the dog kept eating it, and how Christopher and Peter had gotten into a big honking argument about how to get the tree up the stairs. "Did you know Rico has neighbors? I swear, I've been sleeping here for weeks, and I didn't know he had neighbors until this old woman across the porch from you poked her head out her door and started swearing at us in what sounded like German. Then the guy above *her* started swearing in what Peter says was Farsi, and he should know because he was in the Peace Corps. Anyway, you've got neighbors, and they all yelled at us today, but that's okay, because the living room looks great."

Adam smiled at him, savoring one of the last bites of stuffing. "It does. This is a real good present, Finn. Thank you."

"I got you something to open tomorrow, but, you know, like the sketchbook…."

"Yeah. Some of the best stuff doesn't come in a box."

"No."

Adam stood and took their empty plates to the sink and loaded the dishwasher. By the time he got back, Finn had wiped the table, poured them both a glass of eggnog from a carton, and pulled out the book.

And then the real work of the relationship began.

"So this is you, hiding from your mom and grandma?" Finn asked as Adam took his first swig.

The picture showed a small child-shaped stain in a dark space, with angry sounds beating against the fragile shelter.

"Yeah."

"This image shows up a lot."

"Yeah."

"Can… can we make a deal?"

"What?"

Finn covered his hand. "They say it takes twenty really good things to wipe out one bad thing, you know?"

"Yeah?"

"Yeah. Can we make a list on the back of this picture, this first one here? When we get to twenty good things, we can take this picture out of the book? Maybe burn it? We won't get rid of them all, you know, but maybe…."

Adam thought of those lonely days without Finn, thinking he didn't deserve anyone good in his life, thinking he would always be that helpless child, hearing how much nothing really meant.

"Maybe they won't be so much a part of me," he said softly.

Finn nodded and smiled. "Good. Yeah."

He flipped through some pictures from the Army—good ones. Soldiers marching in rank and file, looking earnest and brave. Young recruits in formation and seasoned soldiers wandering behind them, looking at the young ones with wariness and affection. A man at target practice with the M16, staring through his scope with sweat dripping in his eyes. Hard things. Warriors' pictures. Good moments of pride.

Robbie looking wicked, winning at Rummy, his short-jawed, pretty face alight with merriment because he'd just won Adam's best commodity, and Adam was happy to give it.

And then....

"Oh, I hate this picture," Finn murmured.

The lines were thick and dark, soldiers surrounding that child-shaped stain from the earlier pictures, raucous, angry word pictures coming out of their mouths.

Adam closed his eyes and looked away.

"I don't know what to do with this one," Finn murmured, taking his hand. "I want to rip it up, make it so it never happened. But it *did*, and that's going to hurt, and I can't stop it."

"You don't...."

"So maybe we let it sit, and maybe we'll forget about this book someday, and find it in the dusty bottom of years and years of your sketchbooks—pictures of the animals, pictures of me, my family, 'cause you have Thanksgiving in here already. Maybe someday we start writing the good things on the back of *this* picture, and it can go away too. What do you think?"

Adam gripped his hand and closed his eyes. "I think that picture is already getting further away."

"Good," Finn murmured, kissing the outer whorl of Adam's ear. "Then we'll just hope for the best here. Okay, moving on."

Past pictures of death in the desert because that was all Adam could see anymore, and past pictures of loneliness and desolation because that was all he had.

There was a gap then, because most of his drawings had been done for school, and those were in other sketchbooks.

Then there was Easter. His family—Grandma, his mother, Rico's mother and father, another auntie he barely talked to and her two kids, and they were all sitting at the long banquet table, looking in surprise at the closed door.

And Adam stood outside the door, with blood dripping down his forehead and nose, because Grandma had just slammed the door in his face.

Adam remembered that moment—*that* moment was yesterday.

"How did you get through that?" Finn asked quietly. "I might have stopped breathing."

Adam stroked the back of his hand with his thumb. "Rico texted me—probably right from the dinner table as the old bitch went off. Said I was finally cool."

Finn rubbed the drawn Adam's hurt forehead, and then the real Adam's scar.

"Then this one, we keep. But we rip it out. And every time you draw a picture of me or my family or someone you love at the holidays, we stack this picture under it. Until you have so many good pictures you have no choice but to let it go."

Adam smiled and closed his eyes, thinking. Letting the pictures parade through his head on the little movie theater in his brain. "Lots of different things to do with these pictures. What if we forget?"

"Then we still win."

Adam's smile widened. "What if all I want to do right now is take the dog for a walk and then take you to bed?"

Finn kissed each eyelid, a breath, a touch, and then Adam felt his lips, and the sweetest benediction Adam could ever imagine. "I think that sounds like an amazing plan," Finn murmured. "I think we should do that one."

Clopper was, of course, all for it. They walked the muffled streets of Adam's new home, and Adam felt more peace in his heart than he could ever remember.

Sleeping Pictures

THAT NIGHT Adam shucked his clothes and sat on the bed in his boxers, gesturing Finn to come stand, fully clothed, between his knees.

Then he proceeded to kiss Finn's stomach, his hips, his chest, delicate rubs of skin against skin, only the brush of tongue as Adam explored.

He discovered flat moles on Finn's back—five or six of them—and an odd sort of elongated freckle on the back of his neck.

"It's a stork mark," Finn murmured, sitting on the bed now in the V of Adam's thighs. He lowered his head to give Adam better access. "Mom says that's where the stork carried me."

Adam nibbled on it, thinking of a baby Finn being carried by an oversize bird. He could draw that, he thought. He would love to draw that.

Adam kept kissing, kept exposing little secrets in the lamplight, and Finn trembled with every touch of lips to skin.

By the time Finn was naked, stretched out in front of Adam with his hands over his head because Adam had put them there and asked him to stay, Finn couldn't talk anymore. He grunted and wiggled and spoke in half syllables and partial words.

"Ad… yeah… no… more… oh Go… ki… not the… *ah*…."

Adam drank him in, his trust, his need, his absolute confidence that Adam would give him whatever he needed.

Adam had that confidence too. Adam gave him *exactly* what he needed.

And when Adam was inside of him, possessing him, holding Finn's hands above his head and thrusting his sensitized, pulsing body into oblivion, Adam had the sense—the sublime, amazing revelation—that *this* was what sex was for.

So he could make love to Finn.

Finn came without touching himself, his moan of climax deep and resonant—a man's sound—and Adam had never been so happy to have a man in his bed. Adam came sheathed in Finn, his orgasm washing from his groin outward, like the electromagnetic pulse from a massive detonation, leaving him helpless, shorted out, quivering in Finn's arms without consciousness or care.

Finn took care of him when he was like this.

He would wake, barely, while Finn washed them both off and turned out the lights and then crawled into bed with him, curling into Adam's warmth so easily, so naturally, it was like Adam never had any doubts that he could give Finn what he needed.

He was starting to lose those doubts—but he'd never forget that he had them.

Maybe Finn had the right of it. Maybe you never really lost those pictures that hurt you. But maybe they could become less and less of all of the pictures in your heart.

THE DAWN was barely gray when Adam's phone went off, reminding him that it was time to get up and go help at the homeless shelter. He reached over Finn's shoulder to where the phone rested in the charger, and avoided crushing the cat, who had insinuated himself between them again, the better to snuggle with Finn at stork-mark level.

He'd no sooner recovered his phone than it buzzed with a text from Rico.

Merry Christmas from New York, Rico texted, complete with a picture of lower Broadway, the part that used to be all textile mills, taken through a window. It was decked out for Hanukkah mostly, but there was still the odd Christmas tree in the windows below, and Adam wondered how high up Rico was to take such an awesome scene. He wanted to draw it.

But first he pulled back just enough to capture the kitten tangled in Finn's strawberry blond hair.

Merry Christmas from Finn, my boyfriend, and Jake, your cat. He'd shown Rico lots of pictures of Jake—but this was his first of Finn.

They're both beautiful, Adam. You sound happy.

I am. Are you?

Very much. I don't have to go to San Diego and pretend anymore.

Pretend what?

That Grandma's an okay human being and I'm not mad at my mom for leaving you at her mercy.

Forget about it. You were my only good thing.

Pretend I let them slam you out of the house and I'm not just like you.

Rico sent that with a picture much like Adam's, except this was taken with his back to the window, and the sleeping features of a young, dark-haired man were illuminated by the snow-glowing morning behind them. Glittering on his chest was a tiny six-pointed star.

Adam thought, *Oh, Rico. You didn't tell anybody? Oh God. You must have been so afraid,* and his heart stuttered against his ribs.

He's beautiful too. Congratulations, cousin. I hope you're happy too.

I am. His name is Ezra.

You and me will always be family. Someday maybe I'll meet him.

I'd like that. I'd like that so much. Someday, I'd like to meet Finn.

Love you, Rico. Merry Christmas.

Love you too, Adam. Happy Hanukkah.

Adam sent a smiley face and then put the phone back and wrapped his arms around Finn.

"Mm... is it time already?"

"You know, we could sleep in if it didn't take you half an hour to poop."

Finn rolled over in his arms, and the cat hauled its lazy ass up the pillow to get out of the way. "I get some of my best thinking done that way."

"Yeah? What are you going to be thinking about today?"

"That I'm in love with someone who loves me back."

Adam nuzzled the hollow of his neck, which smelled like cat and eggnog, and a little like sex, and mostly like Finn. "You think about that as long as you want. I'll be thinking about it too."

"Merry Christmas, Adam."

"Merry Christmas, Finn. Let's get out of bed and see what kinds of memories we can make, okay?"

"Yeah. Let's make sure to take lots of pictures so you can draw them later."

Adam thought of the portrait he was giving Finn for Christmas. "Yeah. Let's do that."

So much hope. The first Christmas ever that he would have all the hope in the world—but, God willing, not the last by far.

Cherry Pixy Stix

THE DAY after Christmas, Darrin walked into his shop a little late and found that most of his staff had done all of the setup during the way way early. Well, yes, it was good to be boss, right?

People were pretty much at the "hanging around and waiting to open" stage, and Darrin looked over to the counter to see Adam perched on the sales stool, and Finn tucked up between his thighs. They were discussing apartments, and animals, and where Finn thought they could get the best deal in June, and Darrin warmed, just watching them.

Adam would be here for a while—three or four years, at least—but that was because Finn wasn't planning on moving away from him. Ever.

They would be happy, Darrin thought, remembering the Pixy Stix. They would have lives, careers, giant dogs, gentle cats, and maybe even children, sometime off in the hazy, hazy future of their own.

He wanted that for them, but he didn't doubt they would have it. He'd seen it. Pixy Stix never lied.

"Hey, boss," Joni said, coming up to greet him with a hug. "Did you hear about Miguel?"

"Yes—he finally took that internship instead of hanging around here, didn't he?"

Joni rolled her eyes. "I should have known you'd know. Are we going to need to hire anybody else?"

Darrin thought about it. "Probably not. At least not until June."

Unbidden, even without the Pixy Stix, he saw her. Feral, hair butchered and dyed too many colors, more piercings than was probably comfortable, flat eyes, and a real attitude.

She'd be perfect, he thought, looking at Joni. Joni's loneliness wasn't palpable yet, but by June she'd be in the perfect mood to maybe tame their new employee.

And in the meantime, Darrin's little store, his sweet little world, was happy, and so were the people in it.

He looked at Adam and Finn again, liking how Finn looked away at the last minute, because Adam's obvious worship made him blush.

It was a great way to make a living, overlooking the banks of the Sacramento River. You never knew what life's current would bring you, and never knew from whence it would come.

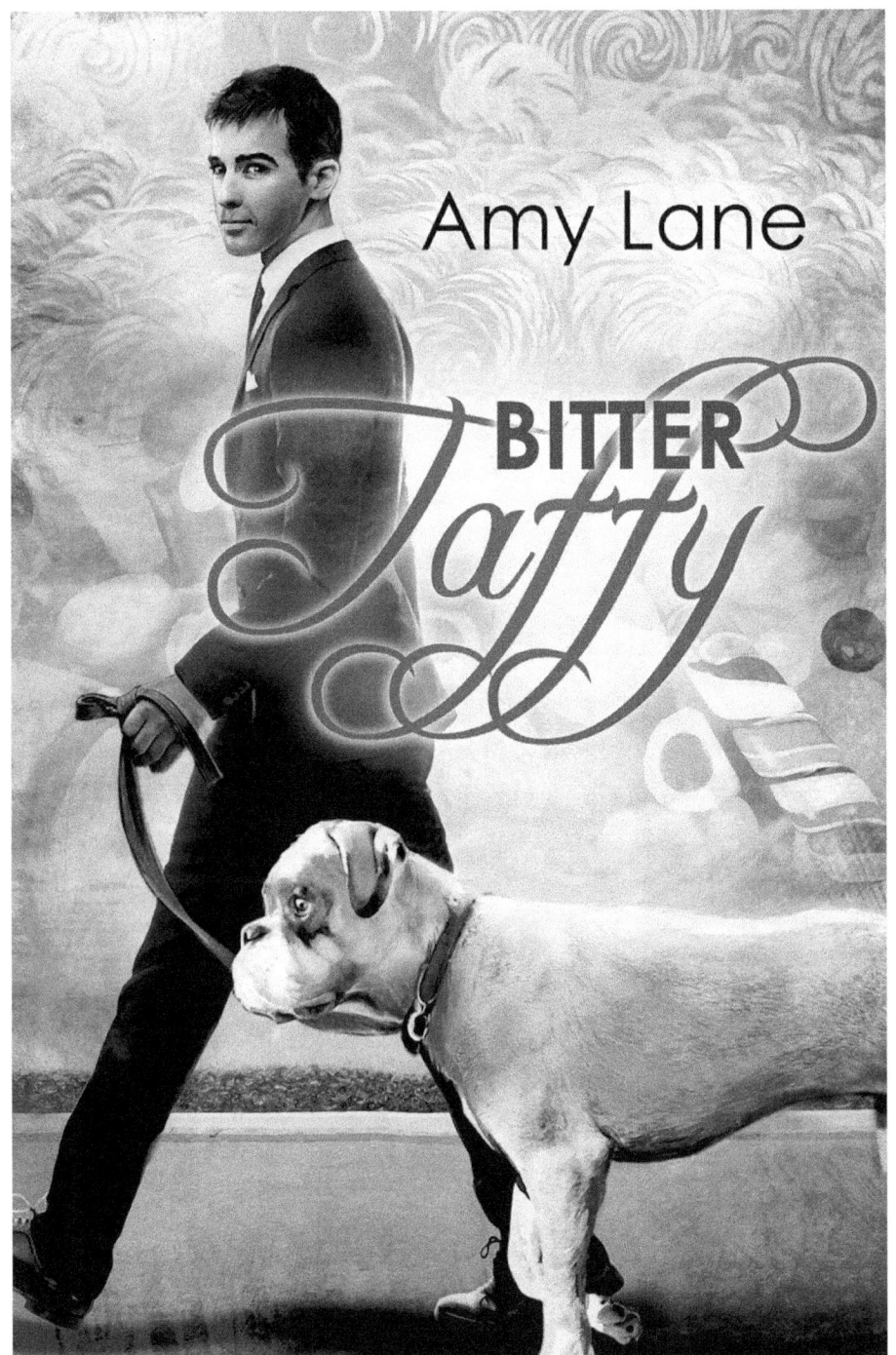

Amy Lane

BITTER Taffy

I put Mary through a lot last year in terms of fiction. I gave her drug addicts, Alzheimer's, murdered children, OCD/Asperger's/ADHD/bipolar disorder, and *two* cases of characters who didn't make it all the way to the end. This book was her reward. It was sweet. It was lush. There was nothing here that would rip her heart in twain. This book is MARY'S book. And Mate's too—because he'd take in a River Cats game in a hot second.

Acknowledgments

Thank you to the real Darrin from Candy Heaven and the real Roget from Rose-Eye Photography, who agreed to let themselves be in my book. Folks, if you want the real romance between these two, you're out of luck—they've never met in real life, but they have both made a tremendous impact on *me*. Thanks, guys, for good humor and a willingness to be fictionalized. You're sheer awesomeness—don't ever doubt it.

Amputee

OLD MAN Kellerman looked *pissed.*

José Ricardo Juan Gonzalves-Macias shuffled the ad copy he'd worked on all night and thought twice about the presentation he was about to make.

He'd interned at this company for four months—had done some really awesome work for them, if he said so himself—and he'd thought Artie Kellerman liked him. Of course the old guy was sort of an old-school backstabbing junkyard dog, with an iron lock around his family and a micromanaging streak, size macro, so "liked" was maybe a relative term.

But the way Kellerman stalked into the meeting room in the converted Manhattan warehouse made Rico think maybe he'd broken the cardinal commandment of bosses, be they hostile *or* friendly.

Kellerman's youngest son, Ezra, was at his father's heels, looking—for the first time in Rico's knowledge of him—mussed and out of sorts.

"Dad," Ezra said, a little desperately. "Dad, you can't do this—it's not his fault."

Ezra's dark blue eyes sought Rico's out over the heads of the rest of the marketing group, and Rico's stomach started pumping acid so fast he thought he was going to vomit right there.

Oh no.

Rico *had* broken the cardinal commandment of bosses. Thou shalt not *ever* sleep with the boss's son. *Especially* if thou wert a man.

"Not his fault that he *fucked* my son?" Kellerman shouted, and Rico knew his black-fringed brown eyes got huge because he could see them mirrored in Ezra's fashionable glasses.

"It was mutual!" Ezra shouted back, and even as he shouted, Rico caught his rolled eyes. It had, in fact, been *very* mutual. They'd been having sex for months before Rico even understood the concept of top and bottom as it applied to something besides bunk beds. As far as Rico was concerned, both positions felt good, and whoever felt the most like receiving did all the prep first. And if they both did the prep, well, that's what round two was about.

But that's not what Ezra was talking about now.

"It was mutual, Dad," Ezra said, darting a pained glance to Rico. "He... he didn't even know he was gay. *I* seduced *him*."

"SO YOU never even thought about it?" Ezra's smile glinted as white as the fat snowflakes falling around their faces in the December cold. "I mean, you're...." His smile went away. "You're beautiful. That was my first thought when you walked into Dad's office. That you were beautiful. That...."

Rico swallowed, and Ezra's vulnerability shivved open his gut, letting spill things he'd tried to tamp down for years.

"You, uhm...."

Oh God. Ezra's eyes were bright, his lower lip trembling. He'd been Rico's entrée to this amazing, frightening new city, and he'd given his time tirelessly to help Rico thrive in the challenging new job: marketing Kellerman's fabrics to the top fashion designers in the city.

"You...."

Rico closed his eyes and remembered his cousin Adam, who had told their family straight out that he was gay and that was why he'd left the service.

Their grandmother had grabbed him by the ear and thrown him out—she'd slammed the door in his face so hard Adam had needed a butterfly bandage to make the bleeding stop.

He'd shown up at Rico's hotel room that night, and Rico had applied the bandage, then given him a place to sleep, since Grandma Macias was out of the question. It was funny, but whenever Adam talked about that moment, he talked about Rico's text to him as he'd been thrown out the door. Weird how sometimes people needed reassurance more than food, more than shelter, even more than personal comfort.

"If I was gay," Rico said, trying to keep his voice kind and not wistful, "I would so want to kiss you."

Ezra must have heard something there—something Rico hadn't wanted to share but Ezra sensed nonetheless. "Would you kiss me right here on the street?" he asked winsomely.

And Rico... oh God. Those wicked blue eyes, that full mouth....
Years pretending that hunger for a man's touch, a man's body, didn't
exist, and here he was.

Right there.

Ezra's lips were so soft under Rico's, for a moment they felt like
another flake of snow.

RICO LOOKED at Ezra helplessly, and then at the guy who had been
his snarling mentor, telling him Rico could be the best marketing
director in New York if he stuck with products he believed in.

Well, the product, Rico believed in.

But he didn't believe in Artie Kellerman anymore, if he ever had.

"It *was* mutual," he said with a crooked smile. "We fell in love."

EZRA LAY on his stomach, looking over a pale shoulder sprinkled with
a constellation of small moles. "I know I'm a coward," he began, and
Rico put his fingers on Ezra's lips to stop that right there.

"Family's complicated," he said, meaning it. "I've pretended for
my whole life." He'd watched Adam struggle without even his mother to
protect him from the censure of their grandmother. Poor Adam—such a
good kid, grown into such a nice guy, and he'd been kicked in the teeth
again and again. "Nobody wants to stand alone," he finished roughly.
Because if he came out to his family, that's exactly where he'd be.

"I think I love you because you get that." A smile flirted with Ezra's
lips, and Rico thought that if he was a good guy—a truly good guy—he'd
comfort his lover and tell him he'd never let anyone hurt him.

But even then he'd known it wasn't that simple.

ARTIE KELLERMAN'S button eyes twinkled from puffy lids and what
generally looked like laugh lines framed his bulldog's face.

He only laughed for clients. When he wasn't laughing, he looked
pig-mean.

"Get out," he growled.

Rico nodded and started packing his briefcase. In his head, he was making the plans for disengaging his lease, packing his things, and buying the plane ticket home.

"Rico?" Ezra said helplessly, and for a moment—just a moment—Rico dared to hope.

"You could come with me," he said, smiling hesitantly. "I've got connections in Sac—we could make a life there."

He'd just been outed in front of his entire office, but he couldn't think about that—not now. He could only look hopefully at Ezra, and hope… hope…. *Oh, please, Ezra. Haven't the last four months in your bed been enough? Don't we have enough between us to make a go of it?*

Old Man Kellerman grabbed Ezra's arm—hard enough to bruise—and shook him. "Ezra, you'll go to my office. You're to have nothing to do with—"

"Shouldn't he answer?" Rico asked, wondering where the brave man in Rico's best knockoff Gucci loafers had come from. "I asked him. Shouldn't he—"

Ezra was looking bitterly at his father. "Just go, Rico. Just go. I'll take care of your lease. I know you're worried."

"I'm worried about *you*—"

"*Just go!*"

The shout came from both Ezra and his father, and Rico had no choice.

"You know where to find me," he said.

He got to his loft—another converted warehouse on lower Broadway—and put on a pair of cotton sweats to work in the apartment. When he realized he was wearing Ezra's clothes, he left them on…

Because.

He went on the Internet and started looking for plane tickets, but he put off purchasing…

Because.

Then he started to pack.

He pulled Ezra's shirts out of his dresser, stared straight ahead, and folded them in with his own things. He should separate them, he thought dully. Separate. They weren't living together. Ezra had his own apartment on the Upper East Side—separate.

But Rico *lived* here on lower Broadway. For the past four and a half months, he'd walked to Kellerman's Fine Fabrics every workday and some Saturdays, and Ezra had walked from his apartment to the same place. It was important, Ezra said, that they didn't look like they were together. That they looked like they were…

Separate.

Oh God.

He was actually grateful for the knock on the door, because the entire afternoon, from getting his box of things from his cubicle to the twenty-block walk back alone, had been like that pause between slicing off your finger and screaming bloody murder.

He was waiting… waiting… waiting… for the wound to hurt.

He opened the door to find Ezra, face stained with tears, flanked by Mario, Kellerman's driver.

Ezra shoved an envelope in his hand. "Plane tickets," he said gruffly. "For first class, at the end of the week. And a voucher for the moving company—they come in three days. And a hotel for the days in between."

Rico gaped, because in his analogy, he'd never guessed he'd be the severed finger, that he'd be thrown on a plane cross-country and shipped away from the body of his relationship while it screamed. "You could come with—"

"He'd come get me," Ezra said. "And besides…." He shook his head and looked away. "You pegged me when you got here, Rico. I'm spoiled. And I've lived with Daddy's money for too long. Go back home, brown boy." Oh, how the pet name seemed to wreck him. His voice grew thick, the words broken. "I'll… you… you were the best moment I've ever had."

And with that he thrust the paperwork at Rico and turned away, Mario's paw on his arm to make sure he made it where he was supposed to go.

"I love you, pretty boy!" Rico called, shocked that he had no shame.

"Me too—"

Mario shoved him in the elevator and that last part was cut off.

Like Rico's relationship. Like his career. Like his life.

THREE THOUSAND miles away, Darrin, proprietor of Candy Heaven and Rico's cousin's boss, broke off in the middle of his lover's best kiss and said, "Oh!"

"Oh? Oh what?" Ro looked around, microbraids swinging around his broad, open, handsome face. Ro kissed with enthusiasm and verve, and Darrin really *must* have been dreaming not to follow through on that kiss.

"Who is that man?" Darrin asked him, perplexed.

Ro's eyes grew huge, and he looked around Darrin's small apartment even more wildly. "*What man?*"

"No, no." Darrin stood up (what a shame—Ro was a good kisser) and walked the two steps to the overstuffed brocade chair and then the two steps back to the comfortable corduroy couch. "Not a man outside my apartment—a man inside my head!"

Ro raised his eyebrows and thrust out a cherry-chocolate-colored lip. "You've got another man in your head in the middle of my best kiss?"

Darrin patted his cheek. "Not *that* kind of man, sweetie."

"So the man in your head is straight?"

Darrin shook his head. "Not recently, no. But he did look awfully familiar. I think I'm going to meet him soon...." Darrin tapped a finger against his cheek. "I wonder who I know who looks like him...."

"Sweetheart," Ro said patiently.

Darrin shook his head. "Yes, yes, of course. Sorry, hon. You know, visions come and visions go—"

"But good sex waits for no man," Ro said seriously.

That seriousness about kissing was one of the things Darrin loved best about him.

"Then let's get busy," he replied, equally serious. Ah, the taste of someone who loved him.

Almost as sweet as candy.

Not Like Home

BY THE time Rico walked off the plane and caught the cab to downtown Sac, he was so tired he could barely focus.

In his entire life, nobody had ever told him how exhausting heartbreak could be.

He'd started crying when he'd gone back into the apartment after Ezra had left, and as far as he could fathom, he'd been crying every moment alone after that.

Not even when he was a kid and he'd broken his leg at the beginning of baseball season had he cried as much as he had in the past five days.

And he'd had a crush on his first baseman then, too.

This felt like more than a crush.

It felt like he was *being* crushed.

He'd been planning to come out for this guy. He *had* come out to Adam, his cousin, who hadn't held his silence against him, not once. But he hadn't come out to his mother and father, or to his grandmother, or anyone else in his rather awful family, and now he wondered if he would be locked in the closet forever.

The only one with the keys to that thing is you.

Not his words, actually. Adam's words. He'd texted them not a month ago, when Rico had confessed that if it hadn't been for Ezra and his beautiful, needy eyes, Rico might have stayed locked up in his own heart forever.

God, his cousin. For a guy who'd been told he was a loser again and again, Adam was probably the smartest guy Rico knew.

Oh God! His cousin!

It wasn't until the cab made that last corner onto F Street, a few Victorian houses down from where Dorothea Puente had become famous for being one crazy serial-killing old bat, that Rico remembered one really important thing he *hadn't* done in the past five days.

He hadn't told Adam he was coming home a month and a half early, and Adam was living in Rico's apartment with his boyfriend.

Oh crap.

Rico grabbed a suitcase in each hand after the cab driver pulled away, and managed to tiptoe up the stairs of the old apartment house fairly lightly. He got to his front door and stopped to listen. It was eleven thirty, but he didn't hear any telltale sounds of, uhm, personal business going on, so he pulled out his copy of the key and let himself in.

His giant, silver-furred scary freak-of-nature dog didn't even woof.

He *did*, however, trot across the kitchen floor in the dark and sniff Rico's crotch.

"Clopper," Rico crooned, comforted beyond words to have his big cow-dog there to pet. "How you doin', guy?"

Clopper sat down on his haunches, regarding Rico patiently, as though Rico were the one who had some explaining to do. Rico squatted and rubbed Clopper's ruff to see if the big doofus would forgive him for leaving four months ago. It was looking like the answer was "maybe" when a skinny white blur wielding Rico's favorite bat came screaming down the hallway at the top of its lungs.

Rico stood up in a hurry and backed into the kitchen so fast he tripped and landed on his ass. Clopper started jumping around excitedly and barking, and something grabbed the white blur abruptly around the waist, saving Rico's head from a *very* uncomfortable meeting with a Louisville Slugger.

"Hey, hey, hey, Finn, calm *down*, man! It's okay! It's Rico! Otherwise Clopper woulda eaten him!"

"You *knew* that?" Finn rounded on Adam, bat held easily in one hand. Now that he wasn't hauling ass down the hallway, Rico could see that Finn wasn't skinny, just slightly built and not as tall as Rico's freakishly tall cousin.

"Well, not until I saw him," Adam answered in his typically terse way. "And he let his hair grow out." Adam looked up at Rico. "If you were going to come home two months early, the least you could have fucking done was tell me you had hair."

Rico let out a short laugh and, for the first time in five days, realized he could do something besides cry.

And that made his eyes burn again. God*dammit*.

"Well," he said, his voice broken, "it's been sort of a weird week."

Adam grunted, and Rico saw the unmistakable tenderness of his hand on his boyfriend's waist. "Finn, baby, you maybe want to go into the other room, get some sleep? You got class tomorrow."

Finn made an indeterminate sound and looked suspiciously from Rico to Adam, then back to Rico. "I could make soup," he said, seemingly out of the air.

Adam smiled—something Rico hadn't ever seen him do as a kid—and kissed Finn's temple. "Tomorrow night you can make soup. I have the feeling Rico's gonna be sleeping on the couch until we can find our own place."

"Oh." Finn looked back at Rico and grimaced. "Sorry, Rico. This was...." He shook his head, and for the first time Rico saw that he was a young man, not much younger than him and Adam, and not a boy. "You're Adam's only family, and this was *not* the kind of impression I wanted to make."

Rico shrugged and smiled. "Yeah, me neither. But it's nice to meet you. I'll, uh, see you in the morning."

Finn stood on his tiptoes, pretty and lithe in his briefs, and kissed Adam's cheek. "Don't talk too long. You've got work in the morning."

Adam turned his head, caught his lips briefly, and then smiled. "I hear you. Night."

They both watched Finn pad down the hallway, Clopper at his heels, and Rico saw Adam grimace as bedsprings creaked *way* too loudly for just that one slightly built man.

"Are you letting my dog sleep on the *bed*?" Rico asked, scandalized. "I'm gone for four months and you ruin my dog? And wasn't there supposed to be a cat?"

Adam grunted. "Why do you think the dog's on the bed? The cat's there. Dog wants to sleep with cat. Adam isn't in the way. Finn's a pushover. You can have your dog back when I go back to bed."

Rico smiled in spite of himself. God, it was just so... warm. So friendly. That time in Manhattan, the only thing *really* warm had been Ezra. "I still say you ruined my dog."

"Yeah, well, you kept telling me I couldn't fuck him up too badly. You have only yourself to blame. Now sit. I'll make coffee. *And* heat up the soup. You look like shit. Let's talk."

God. Their grandmother and Adam's mother had pretty much acid-blasted all of the small talk and confidence out of Adam when he was a kid. But apparently *nothing* could take away the sweetness that had always appealed to Rico. Adam had always been the best playmate because he was never mean. He'd been willing to take direction, but he always had good ideas of his own.

And he'd always thought Rico walked on water, and Rico had to admit, that sort of guileless admiration had given him all sorts of fucking courage when they'd been growing up. He could run for student body president because Adam thought he was a god. He could apply to the big colleges because Adam looked at him like he could do anything. It wasn't until Rico went away to college—Adam's gift of a peacoat insulating him from the Bay Area chill—that Rico had the distance to see that Adam's adulation had come at a terrible price to Adam.

Rico had been the golden boy, the oldest legitimate son, the one with two parents—however distant—and the one everybody had the expectations for.

Adam had been the kid crying under the bed while his mother and grandmother screamed about how much *nobody* wanted him around.

Rico wanted him around. Rico had been *so* relieved when Adam had quit the service and come home. When he'd walked into Easter dinner and said, "You all might want to put away my table setting. I'm gay and I know how much you hate that," Rico had wanted to stand up and cheer, because in their entire childhood, he'd *never* seen Adam stand up for himself.

Adam's reward for standing up for himself had been getting thrown out on his ear.

When Adam's VA grant got pulled because he missed one class (and the draconian justice of *that* made Rico bristle all over again), Rico had been *so* happy to give Adam a break. Just one break—*God*, that was all Rico's cousin had ever asked for from life.

And Adam had run with it. He'd gotten a job, a boyfriend, and he'd be enrolled in school come fall. One little bit of kindness and Adam was here to put on a pot of coffee, feed Rico some *rockin'* chicken fajita soup with homemade bread and butter, and listen as Rico unloaded the worst moment of his life.

"Oh *man!*" Adam said, enthralled as a kid while Rico told about the staff presentation that turned out quite differently than he'd expected. "That's…." He shook his head. "Oh man, Rico. *That's* fucked up. I mean… I'm sorry. That's harsh."

Rico nodded and took another bite of the exquisitely flavored soup. "Who made this?" he asked. It had come out of a Tupperware container Rico had never seen.

"Someone in Finn's family," Adam said. "They cook for each other. Finn never makes just one loaf of bread—he makes six and then gives them to his parents, and *they* spread them around. His sister makes soup in like a fifty-gallon drum, and we get enough for a week. You shoulda been here at Easter. Apparently his mom makes these dessert cookies for *weeks*."

Rico smiled, thinking that Adam had been getting love, and he was glad. "Sounds dire."

Adam nodded and grinned so wide his cheeks appled. He had a dimple Rico had seldom seen, even when they were children. "Finn got *fat*," Adam whispered. "We had to run Clopper around the neighborhood double-time for a *month*."

"I heard that!" Finn mumbled sleepily from down the hall, and Rico had to laugh.

He pressed his palms up under his eyes to wipe them—again—and Adam handed him a napkin without a word. "You're so happy," Rico said, genuinely joyful in his heart for this. "Our whole lives, I've never seen you happy."

Adam ducked his head and then looked at him shyly. "And I've never seen you hurt." He reached awkwardly across the table and took Rico's hand. "I'm so sorry, Rico. I'm so sorry you got hurt. You're the best guy in the world—all I ever wanted was for you to be happy."

Rico tried to smile, because that was the sort of emotional honesty Adam wouldn't have been brave enough to share before this past Christmas. Before Finn. But that thought just hurt more, because Rico had honestly thought he was going to be able to be brave like Adam. He'd have Ezra and his new job, and he could tell his family that he was gay too, and they could love him or ostracize him, but they couldn't change him because that was just who he was.

To Rico's horror, his smile collapsed, and then so did he, shoving his empty soup bowl and his coffee cup out of the way as he laid his head on the table and came undone.

Adam draped his warm, solid body over Rico's back in the mother of all bear hugs and held him as he sobbed out the last of his helplessness—and the last of his hope—for the love and the future that he'd hoped would set him free.

He wasn't sure how long he cried, but he had a hazy memory of Adam shoving two ibuprofen and a big glass of water at him before telling him to get undressed while Adam got sheets and blankets for the couch.

"I'm afraid you're stuck with us for a while," Adam apologized.

Rico grunted. "I have no job—you may be stuck with me so we can all make rent together."

To his surprise, Adam grinned. "You say that like it would be a hardship. Dude, I'm sort of in love with your fuckin' dog, you know that? I was wondering how I was gonna leave him behind."

Rico remembered that moment when he'd fallen in love with Clopper at the animal shelter. It was a good one.

And then Adam made up his bed and Rico lay down on his surprisingly comfortable couch and fell asleep.

He woke up with a five-pound furry weight purring on his throat, and Adam calling to him over the back of the couch.

"Hm?" Oh, yawn, stretch, and be *very* grateful for those two ibuprofen, because otherwise he'd probably have a doozy of a headache. Rico wondered how Adam would know about that, and then didn't. Adam would know.

"You need to get up," Adam said, peering down at him, Finn over his shoulder. In the daylight, Adam looked dark and dangerous. Rico and Adam both had skin that was Mexican brown, but Adam's time in the military had burnt his face a little darker. He had a sharp nose, hard jaw, and big liquid brown eyes—as well as visible neck tattoos. Finn, his pale boyfriend with the strawberry-blond hair and ginormous blue eyes, looked waifish and winsome next to hardass Adam, but Rico was sort of glad for him. Finn looked like he would understand who Adam *really* was, and not think the dangerous soldier who had grown up around the terrified boy was the real Adam at all.

"Whyfor?" Rico asked, blinking. "And what the fuck is this thing on my throat?"

Adam scooped up the fuzzy thing, then shifted it back about six inches to Rico's stomach, where it regarded Rico from a pair of somber gold eyes.

"Rico, Jake. Jake, Rico. Rico, this is your cat. You told me to pick one after Gonzo died and I did. He's all your fault. Anyway, we're taking Clopper out for his morning dump. You're getting up and showering so my boyfriend doesn't have to see you naked, 'cause I don't like competition."

"Nice. I could shower after you leave for work."

"Not if you're coming with us," Adam said, his tone brooking no bullshit. "Finn's dropping me off at work, and you're bringing your laptop. You can hang out in his parents' deli and surf for a job—they got Wi-Fi, and it's a good spring day."

Rico blinked and wrapped his arm around Jake the cat, who drooled on him in retaliation. "I was gonna—"

"Wallow," Adam said bluntly. "You were gonna hang out, pet the cat, and wish you were dead. Then you were gonna call your moms and not come out, and that woulda made you feel worse. Then you were gonna eat all the soup, all the bread, and most of the butter, not to mention the cookies we got in the freezer—"

"Cookies?" Rico said hopefully.

"I work in a candy store," Adam wheedled. "Get your ass up and dressed and I'll get you some chocolate truffles that'll give you a boner."

Rico glared at him. "That's a lie. There's no such thing."

"As a boner? I beg to differ." Adam smirked, so playful and so earnest that Rico couldn't help it.

"Okay, fine. I'll get up and shower and dress and go sleep sitting down in a café—"

"You can sleep upstairs from the café," Finn said, surprising him. "It's supposed to be my apartment, but it's only got a single bed. Dad's been using it as an office since me and Adam started sleeping here...." Finn grimaced. "I, uh... I mean, you probably want your bed back...."

Jake the cat purred comfortingly on Rico's stomach, and Rico thought about how different this morning would have gone if Adam hadn't been here with Finn and his bright and shiny new life and the hope that Finn seemed to have given him.

"Naw," he said, thinking, *Hey, not like I'm gonna be doing anything hinky here anyway.* "If you guys don't mind a roommate, I don't mind the couch."

"Great!" Finn smiled, and Rico wondered why Adam didn't wear sunglasses all day. "C'mon, Adam—let's let him get ready!"

And like that, Adam snapped the lead on Clopper's halter and Finn grabbed the shit-sacks (Finn's word) and they went running out into the early spring day.

Leaving Rico with maybe a twenty-minute window to not be naked and embarrassed when they got back. He was used to his building in New York now, where if he was lucky, the water lasted long enough for him to soap the half inch of his hair that had grown out. He was out in five, freshly shaved in ten, and had dressed and started the coffee before Adam and Finn came back in, smelling like incipient warmth and exertion, and bickering companionably.

"He will not," Adam said as they came through the door. "He doesn't know me—"

"From Adam!" Finn cracked.

Adam's grunt sounded hard put-upon. "That's right, Finn. The guy don't know me from Adam—"

"He's hit on you like twelve times—"

"Like once—"

"Twice—I was there the second time, remember?"

Adam looked up at Finn blankly. "He wasn't hitting on me then," he said, completely sincere. "He was giving me a job, remember?"

Finn gaped back, flailing his hands and sputtering. "I... don't you... holy jebus mother trucking fucker! He's your *boss*, Adam. I mean, he gives you small jobs and takes a percentage and... he *knows* you. That makes him a contact!" He looked over to the counter to Rico, who stood bemused, eating a bowl of instant oatmeal, and shook his head. "Nothing. He knows *nothing*."

And then he turned around and stalked off.

And then he turned, stomped back into the front room, and scowled.

"But you *do* know how to distract me. You *should* ask Derek if he's got a job for Rico, 'cause when he's not picking up on you, he's not a bad guy!"

Adam sighed and scowled back obstinately, like Clopper did when Rico was trying to get him to go anywhere Clopper didn't want to go first.

"I don't want to ask him that, 'cause that would be taking advantage," he said, sounding aggrieved. "The guy hires me to do artwork for him and his clients—and he can't possibly need that much artwork—"

"Hence the picking up!"

Adam rolled his eyes when Finn's voice trilled at the end of that last word. "It's pity, Finn, okay? When he first gave me a job, I could barely afford dog food. He's made me a part of his network, but I don't want to take advantage of his... pity... to ask him if he needs a marketing guy for his firm—"

"Which he does, if you talked to *any* of his employees when you went into his office!"

Adam gaped at him. "Oh," he said, sounding flummoxed. "But... you know... taking advant—"

"It's called *networking*!" Finn wailed, obviously completely out of patience. He gestured to Rico and then back to Adam. "*You* talk to him. He thinks you walk on water. Get him to network a job for you, Rico!"

And then all of that energy and enthusiasm stalked into the bathroom and turned on the shower.

"There's no towels in there," Rico said, knowing his eyes had gotten big.

Adam swore, a pained grimace on his face. "I'll take him a clean one and some underwear. He's a little...."

"Excited," Rico supplied, trying to keep his smile in check while Adam flailed for words.

"Finn. He's just very, very Finn," Adam said, nodding like that explained the secrets of the universe. "Do you have, like, a business card or something? 'Cause...." Adam flailed his hands in a very un-Adam-like gesture.

"Relentless," Rico said, understanding.

Adam gave him a droll look. "Cousin, you got no idea. Here—I'm going to nuke some oatmeal and go get him his clothes. As usual, he spent forever on the john this morning, and now we're running late."

Rico couldn't help it. He started to laugh behind his hand. For a minute he thought Adam was going to be mad, or, worse, would look at him laughing and assume he was laughing for all the wrong reasons, much like the kids in high school had done, because Adam had *not* been the most social guy back then.

But Adam just gave him a sour look and started to thrash around the kitchen, pulling out bowls Rico did not remember having and starting breakfast for him and his boyfriend.

When the microwave was whirring away, Adam looked over his shoulder and shook his head. "No idea," he muttered and strode purposefully toward the bedroom like he had a mission.

Rico kept laughing softly because in their entire lives, he didn't think he'd ever seen Adam happy.

It just gave him heart, that was all. He didn't even remember the job until later.

LATER WAS really only an hour later, but it felt a lot longer.

They drove in Finn's car, an old Dodge minivan, and Rico made a pained sound as he got stashed in the middle seat.

"Did I or did I not leave you the Crown Vic?" Rico asked, aggrieved. Yeah, it was a cop's car—or it would be, if the cops drove their Crown Victorias in burgundy—but he'd gotten it cheap when he was right out of college. He'd always felt invincible in that car.

Adam looked abashedly at him from the passenger's seat. "Uhm, you know, Rico, when I got here, I mean—"

"He could barely afford food," Finn said bluntly. "He's taken it out a few times since Darrin made him a manager, but Rico, that car eats gas like gumdrops, you know that, right?"

Rico grunted. "Sorry, man—I didn't think—"

Adam shrugged, looking straight ahead as Finn brought them to J Street and turned right. "It wasn't a big deal—just meant I got to know the bus schedule real good for a while."

Finn shook his head and rolled his eyes. "Oh my *God*. He was, like, running to Old Sac and back every day. *Running*. And you should see what he was eating—"

"Finn, I love you, but please don't," Adam said simply. No smile, no banter, and Finn subsided, and Rico was left feeling like he'd never seen himself *or* Adam before.

"You didn't say anything," he said softly. "I knew things were tight, but you never said—"

"Rico, I love you, but please don't," Adam repeated, his voice a little harder this time.

Rico grunted into the silence. "So what *are* we supposed to be talking about?" he asked irritably.

"About whether or not Finn is ready for his finals this semester." Adam sent Finn a sly sideways glance, and two pink crescents appeared on Finn's cheeks.

"I take it that's a no," Rico said dryly, and they spent the next ten minutes of commute giving Finn a hard time about falling behind in his schoolwork because he'd fallen victim to a new video game and too much Red Bull.

"Classic rookie move!" Rico crowed. "That's why you don't buy the game until *after* you take your finals."

"My stupid brother," Finn grumbled. "He's *out* of school, and he's all, 'Love stinks, little bro, come play this game with me and make me forget my troubles.'"

Adam hooted. "Your sister will *not* forgive him for that!"

Finn shook his head. "Mari threatened to wax his back while he slept. Peter's got more hair on his back than most guys have on their chests—it's like, if he wants to attract a girl, he needs to wax that thing voluntarily."

"Oh my God!" Rico gasped between pants of laughter. "Your family is *really* fuckin' close!"

Finn rolled his eyes and came to a stop on Front Street, with the river to his left and the boardwalk on his right, the cobblestones rough under the wheels of the minivan. "Yeah, well, you'll meet them yourself after finals. I'll have Peter wax his back for the occasion."

"Wait, what?" Rico said hurriedly, because Adam had already kissed Finn briefly on the cheek and thrown open Rico's door.

"Hurry and get to class," Adam instructed. "You're gonna be late as it is."

"Yeah, okay—you're off at six?"

Adam nodded as Rico extricated himself from the minivan with his briefcase and charged laptop in tow.

"Yeah," Adam confirmed to Finn, slamming the door and talking through the window. "But text me when you're out—if Rico wants to go home then, we'll let him go home."

"Yeah. Make sure you go introduce him to my dad, okay?"

Adam nodded, looking stoic and brave. Well, dealing with parents probably wouldn't be Adam's strong suit. Dealing with *Finn's* parents could probably put *anybody* off their feed. "Kk—drive safe. Good luck on your finals, baby."

Finn nodded and winked, then drove away. Adam watched him go, a fond expression on his face. "Yeah—he's real smart. He doesn't really need any luck. He's fine on his own."

Rico grunted. "Money, Adam. You didn't have any money in December."

"I thought we weren't talking about this."

"I mean, I knew you needed a job and a place, but I thought, you know, gas money, right?"

"Wasn't a great time." Adam bumped his shoulder to get his attention and then crossed the street, making sure Rico was at his heels. "Come meet Candy Heaven," he said, trotting up the stairs from the cobblestone street to the boardwalk. "They made it a better time."

The sign hanging in front of the eight-foot wood-framed doorway was blue with a rainbow pathway and the words Candy Heaven on the front.

The french doors were already open, and Adam walked in, pulling a brown apron from his pocket and putting it on over his button-down shirt and jeans.

"Hey, boss!" he called, cutting through the store to the other entrance, where the cash registers were. "Darrin, I'd like you to meet—"

"Hello," said the *very* tall man at the register. He looked at Rico with the sort of vague recognition Rico's college professors used to show him when he had them for a second class. "I know you."

Adam grimaced. "Yeah, uhm, this is my cousin, Rico. I was gonna take him by River Burger and do the intros to Finn's dad and—"

"Yes, of course. He won't be there long. The man who's looking for him will be in… uhm, in about two hours at the most, I think."

"Oh God," Adam muttered. "Yeah. Okay. You say so."

Rico looked at Adam and then back at his boss. The owner of Candy Heaven had long, layer-cut dyed brown hair and wore a flowing tie-dyed tunic over his jeans and cowboy boots. He sported a pair of dangly earrings with series of concentric circles and rainbows in the center of the smallest circles, and the rather smug smile of someone who knew shit that Rico did not.

"Have we met?" Rico asked suspiciously. "You don't look at all famil—"

Darrin rolled his eyes, reached under the register, and pulled out a small plastic container of chocolate-covered… what were those?

"Chocolate-covered bug?" Darrin asked bluntly.

Rico recoiled. "Hell to the no?"

"Rico, take the bug," Darrin instructed. "Chew it, swallow it, get it down. It'll be weird and crunchy, but in the end, all you'll remember is spiced chocolate."

For a moment all Rico could do was gape, and this tall guy with the tie-dyed shirt used chopsticks to pop a chocolate-covered cricket in his mouth, and he had no choice but to chew.

It was weird and it was crunchy, and he swallowed it and tasted spiced chocolate. He swallowed again to get the memory of chewing on exoskeleton out of his teeth, and this time only the spiced chocolate remained.

"Who *are* you?" he asked, a little bit terrified.

"I'm Adam's boss. I'm special."

"You're telling me!"

"Yes, I *am* telling you. You should listen to me. I'm special. And this icky feeling in your heart? It's not going to last long. He was sweet, Rico, but he wasn't the end of the world. Not *your* world, anyway."

Rico's eyes bugged out so hard his vision blurred. "I... uh... wha...."

Adam grunted. "C'mon, Rico. You can recover on the way to River Burger. Thanks a lot, boss. You blew his teeny-tiny brain."

Darrin looked Rico up and down. "Yeah, I would have thought he would have been the smarter of the two of you. Apparently not."

Adam bristled. "Rico's plenty smart—he got in real late last night. Let's get him some more coffee and some time in the café and he'll be more coherent."

Adam hustled him out of the store while Rico still sputtered for breath. "You promise chocolate truffles that would give me a boner and your boss *feeds me a bug*?"

"Oh hell," Adam muttered. "Here. Stay right here." He parked Rico on the bench outside the door and trotted back inside.

"You are *not* feeding him those chocolates!" Darrin protested. "He's not ready for them, Adam. Do you *know* what's wrong with your cousin?"

"He got his heart broken," Adam replied obstinately. "And he needs something that will make him happy. I promised him your special truffles—"

"Two months," Darrin replied in a tone that brooked no argument. "Give him the ones on the right, the ones with coconut and almonds—he's not allergic, is he?"

"No."

"Then those. They're not what he wants, but they might be what he needs."

Adam's low, irritated growl actually warmed Rico to his toes. God, at least he was still the same Adam that Rico remembered from high school. "You are a piece of work, do you know that? I was trying to impress him—"

"Well, I bet he's *very* impressed. Hurry back, Adam. You have"—Rico could imagine the vague hand waving—"*networking* to do."

Oh *that* was it! Rico stood up, fully prepared to stomp back inside and *bully* the nice candymaker into telling him how in the holy hell he knew all this shit, when Adam scurried out, a little confection bag in his hand.

"How—but—I—"

Adam shook his head. "Don't ask," he muttered. "C'mon. After Darrin, Finn's dad should be a cakewalk."

Finn's dad turned out to be a nice middle-aged man with graying ginger hair and his son's sweet smile. Sure, Rico could sit down and use one of his boardwalk café tables to work. Yeah, no problem, if he got tired, Mr. Stewart would be *thrilled* to let him use the bed upstairs. Would Adam's cousin like a coffee? Some beignets? Absolutely—on the house!

Adam tried to protest, of course, but Finn's dad laughed directly in his face and sent him on his way with a hearty slap on the back and a reminder of some sort of get-together after finals.

Adam left, and Rico sat down at a table near the outside wall, unfolded his laptop, and got ready for some peace.

And was surprised when he got it—at least twenty minutes of it— while Finn's dad and a younger woman who looked a lot like Finn worked behind the counter. Together, they got breakfast sandwiches, hash browns, and coffee not only for people who were shopping in the Old Sacramento tourist trap but for people who had come through the tunnel from K Street before they started their office jobs.

Rico spent the time finding Wi-Fi and hitting up the want ads and headhunters in the area, looking for some job leads. Until he'd taken his plane tickets out for the trip home, he hadn't realized Old Man Kellerman had also sent him some top-flight references—and the inclusion of those three letters on company letterhead sent an unmistakable message. Kellerman wouldn't keep him from getting another job—as long as it was elsewhere.

Which, as Rico breathed in the flowers from the open green areas across the street (and exhaust from the freeway overhead) on what was an admittedly beautiful mild spring day in Sacramento, was actually both generous *and* smart.

Rico was on the other side of the country, and he wasn't desperate. He *could* get another job. Why would he make trouble for Ezra and Kellerman's Fine Fabrics if he wasn't trapped like a rat in a cage?

So he got his résumé in order and started looking for likely fits and job interviews, and was actually really pleased when Finn's dad came and sat down across from him, offering a large mocha and beignets.

"I'm going to have to take over dog-walking duty," Rico laughed after biting into a beignet. "Your family is trying to make me fat and you barely even know me."

Mr. Stewart laughed, the lines at his eyes crinkling, which meant he did that a lot. "Yeah, but we know Adam, and he's a top-notch guy. He can't say enough good things about you, so, you know, welcome to the family."

Rico's breath caught and a sudden ache opened up in his chest, like an infection had been festering there and he hadn't known until just now. "Thanks," he said quietly. "That's... that's really nice of you."

"I, uhm, take it this isn't the sort of welcome you'd expect from your own family?"

Rico looked at this nice man and thought of his own father, who worked long days and came home at eight at night in suit and tie and read the paper until nine. His mother waited on him—brought him dinner, sat at the table quietly, waiting for him to feed her crumbs of conversation—and Rico tiptoed by the kitchen, hoping the old man would ignore him completely, much like he'd done when Rico was a child.

His mother, Lydia, had eaten in the kitchen with Rico when he was a kid, which sounded cozy, like it should have been the two of them, and often it was. Except Rico had spent most of his time begging her to let Adam come over, and she'd told him no, because Adam wasn't their family's type of relative.

Rico had gotten to be a teenager and realized that his father didn't approve of Adam because Adam's mother was a fuckup.

Rico couldn't argue with that—Adam's mom wasn't the nicest of people. Rico had heard that woman tear down Adam's soul since he'd been a little kid, and he'd heard their grandmother do the same thing.

But that didn't mean Adam shouldn't have been able to eat in their kitchen. Although just because Rico's father said he couldn't didn't mean Rico hadn't snuck him food in the garage.

"Mine and Adam's family—we, uhm, don't do warm," he said, thinking it was an understatement. "I think Finn must feel like a miracle to him."

Mr. Stewart's face lit up, and Rico wondered if it did that for all his children or just Finn. "Yeah, well, Finn is special. Of course, all my kids are special—but it's nice to hear he's appreciated. So, we're having this big family shindig in about two weeks—Adam's going to bring you, of course. We're kicking off a new location, right? A franchise? My older two sons are going to run it. They actually *had* office jobs, and one of them has a law degree, but it was like they ran out into the world and then came back and said, 'Waah, waah, we miss our family!' so whateryagonnado?"

Rico laughed, because how could you not? He could totally see how sons might want to come back to this particular father. "I guess you're going to open another business. That's awesome!"

"Yeah, right? We're looking into advertising right now—"

"I could help!" Rico said, jumping in with both feet. Then he blushed, because, hello, desperate. "I mean, I'm in marketing—I've got my degree. I'm looking for a job here in the city. I could, uhm…."

"Great!" Finn's dad held out his hand. "It's a deal. Come up with a fee that works for you; we'll engage your services."

Rico gaped. "You haven't even seen my portfolio!"

"Well, yeah. But you're family! Just tell me you'll use Adam to do your art design—we got him a computer so he can do graphics as well as hand drawn, and we like his work too. This way we can, you know, keep it in the family, okay?"

"But—I mean, I need a budget and—"

Mr. Stewart looked embarrassed. "Oh—yeah. See? This is why I need Finn. He's better with this stuff than I am. I'll—"

"Dad!" The woman who looked just like Finn was waving frantically as a line of customers backed up behind the counter, and Finn's father (who must have a first name!) smiled apologetically and ran up to help her, leaving Rico gaping like a fish.

But gaping like a fish for too long would have let his beignets get cold and his chocolate get melty. He couldn't let that happen, so he grounded himself with coffee, fat, and sugar, and got back to work. After he'd sent his résumé out to a couple of places, he started doing some research for how to market one small café franchise and about how many billable hours that would take. He was pretty sure he could maintain one modest client and find himself a slightly larger job at the same time.

HE WORKED steadily for another two hours, looking up occasionally to thank Mr. Stewart profusely for the refills on coffee and, once, to ask if he could use the restroom. When he got back, the woman who looked like Finn was sitting in his place, and across from her was a guy in a suit. The girl got up as soon as he drew near.

"Hope you don't mind—Dad got worried about your computer, and it was break time."

Rico smiled at her uncertainly. "Uhm, thank you, uhm—"

"Mari. I'm an insufferable busybody." She grinned pertly, and her resemblance to Finn intensified.

"And this is, uhm...." He gestured vaguely to the sandy-haired stranger in the other seat. The man had blue eyes, an oval face, a flirty little nose, and lips that leaned when he smiled.

The man stood, his tailored gray suit falling into neat lines around his trim form. "I'm Derek Huston," he said as he extended his hand. "Adam sent me your way."

Rico narrowed his eyes, trying to wrap his head around this. "Adam *knows* you?"

Derek looked affronted. "Well, not *biblically*—his boyfriend would *kill* me. But he's done some artwork for me—in fact, I keep him on retainer. He's an awesome artist." Derek's freckled nose wrinkled. "He's a *horrible* businessman, but I guess that's what Finn is for."

Rico took his hand and shook it briefly. "Yeah, well, I'm glad he's got Finn. Here." He gestured to the chair. "Sit down." He turned to Mari. "Uhm—"

"I'm outta here. I was only supposed to hold your spot until you got back." She bounced away, and Rico watched her go, assailed by a pervasive sense of unreality.

"She's married," Derek said mildly, and Rico shot him a look of annoyance.

"I'm gay. I just...." He shook his head, not wanting to dump his business on a stranger. "It's been sort of a weird week. Finn's family is throwing me for a loop."

Derek was looking at him in a combination of surprise and... interest? Whatever it was, it made Rico's face heat, and he took inordinate pains finishing his coffee and eating the last bite of his beignet.

"So, uhm," he asked after an uncomfortable moment, "you were here looking for something?"

"Your cousin says you're in advertising."

"Marketing—there's a difference. But yeah. Got the degree in marketing, spent some years writing ad copy, just left an internship as a marketing director out in New York. Were you looking for someone like that?"

Derek nodded soberly. "I'm actually looking for *exactly* someone like that. But not for me, per se. Do you want to hear?"

"Yeah. Hit me with it—but whatever I do, I promised Finn's family I'd help them with a campaign for their new franchise, so I need some time for that."

That adorable all-American boy face lit up, and Derek said, "Actually, that makes you the employee I've been looking for all my life. Now here's what I need you for...."

Rico leaned forward and listened, asking pertinent questions, and when he was done, he felt a reluctant admiration for this brash, compact businessman who would walk three blocks just to have a cup of coffee with someone's cousin.

Derek Huston had a *vision.*

He ran a sort of consulting tank of various talents—from Adam, who worked as a graphic artist, to Miguel, an IT professional, to Stan, a gardener, and Maureen, an electrician, and Ted, a lawyer, and so on. His vision was to be the small business's best friend. He paid everybody a modest retainer and provided insurance and proof of employment and other employee benefits, and in return he got a percentage when he lined them up with gigs. Derek's talent was taking small businesses to the next level—by giving small businessmen access to high-end services that they might not normally have on a limited budget. Finn's dad couldn't really afford Rico—Rico had known that when he'd offered his services. He planned to work for a low fee per hour, and Rico wouldn't short his employer for the world. So if Finn's dad had gone to Derek's firm, the Shopkeeper's Friend, first, then Derek would have gotten a budget and given Rico the job—and Rico would have done it within the budget. The effect would have been the same—Finn's dad got a top-notch professional—but through the business, Finn's dad was protected, and because Derek was also drawing a fee from other clients who had bigger jobs and deeper pockets, Rico had a steady paycheck if Mr. Stewart decided to use another marketing exec.

When Derek was done, Rico found he liked this idea. He'd long since folded his laptop and was leaning on it, listening intently. "So I'd be my own boss," he said thoughtfully. "And I could take companies up a level. So, like, premium work. None of that elitist bullshit, right?"

Because *God*, Kellerman's high-handedness had rankled. Four months of kissing the old man's ass, forced to walk on his fellow interns if he wanted even a crumb of approval or a hint that the job would last, and Kellerman had tossed Rico aside like a dirty come-rag?

Even if Rico hadn't been heartbroken, he'd be pissed.

"No," Derek said, looking pleased. "See...." Derek looked abashed, and Rico cocked his head. For the past half hour, the man had been nothing but self-assured and confident and no-nonsense. But now? In this moment? He almost looked shy.

"See," Derek repeated, "the thing is, my dad ran a hardware store in Woodland for thirty years. You know where Woodland is?"

Rico nodded. "Yeah, I went to school at Stanford, lived here for a few years after. I know where it is."

Derek nodded like he was reassured. "So you know Woodland— it's like—"

"Pretty fuckin' small," Rico said with a smile.

"Right? So anyway, Dad ran a hardware store that his dad left him, and my older brother and soon-to-be brother-in-law are running it now. So this place—my family does the *best* carpentry, you know? We're great workers, and this hardware store had all these special woodworking tools that only hard-core galoots—you know what that is?"

At Rico's bemused negative head shake, Derek went on.

"A galoot is a woodworker who likes old tools, who hunts them down and finds them special. Anyway, my dad and now my brother and the in-law—they spend their days off hunting down old lathes and shit that nobody's heard of, so they've got this really premium stuff. And they were *going out of business* because nobody knew. So the first thing I did as I was going through business school was hook them up with a buddy who wanted to build a portfolio and was in marketing. He did this small marketing job for them, took just enough of a fee to buy our dorm a keg, and my family's business, it doesn't have to go under anymore. And it hits me. Sometimes the little guy just needs *help*. Just, you know, five hours of a personal assistant, a part-time marketer—but finding someone reliable sucks, and making sure you're not getting bilked sucks. I thought, *I* could do this, be that guy who matched people together and made it painless."

He smiled when he was done like he'd just said something really personal. Rico guessed that he had.

"That's awesome," he said, meaning it. "It's...." He grimaced, thinking about Kellerman and his security goons. "It makes business feel really human. I haven't thought of it like that in a long time."

Derek looked up and waved to Mari, who was filling up coffee cups around the café, and she smiled and got him a cup and then efficiently filled it while he talked. "What *do* you think about it? I mean, why marketing? Why advertising?"

Rico swallowed. He hated telling this story. But then, Derek was looking at him so hopefully, and it had been such a long time since he'd thought about what he did for a living and why.

"See," he said thoughtfully, letting Mari fill his cup too, "it sort of all comes back to Adam. When he was a kid…." Rico swallowed. "Let's just say his mom and our grandma weren't going for Parents of the Year. And sometimes it seemed like all day, every day, they just yelled about what a shitty kid he was and how it was the other one's fault. And he just…." Rico hated this. God, it felt like a violation, the thought of Adam, big brown eyes swollen with tears, hiding under the bed with a pillow and Rico's teddy bear because his own mom wouldn't have brought him one. "It wasn't fair," he said roughly. "And I thought that they just got it wrong. You know, nobody *told* them what a good boy he was, so somebody had to tell him. And he could always draw. So he'd draw a good boy with a halo, folding clothes, doing dishes, all the stuff he tried to help with but got yelled at for doing wrong, and then I'd write, 'This is Adam, working. He's a good worker.'"

"Did it help?" Derek asked seriously.

"Have you met Adam?" Rico asked back. He remembered his mom putting the pictures up on the refrigerator at their home, until his father got home and threw them away because they interfered with the décor in the kitchen.

Derek grimaced. "Yeah, uhm, he's sort of guarded, isn't he?"

"It's how he walked away—right outta their lives and into Iraq. I think he was relieved. Anyway, so I always thought of marketing as telling the truth, but telling it *louder*. Making sure the people who needed to hear got the message."

"So, not lying or backstabbing or smear campaigning?" he asked soberly, like it mattered.

"I swear," Rico said, because after Kellerman trying to undercut his competitors to the extent of laying off his own people, Rico had done enough of that. "That is *not* what I'm in for."

And then Derek did a terrible thing. All of that confidence, all of that goodwill, all of that force of moving forward—it all got balled up and thrown into Derek's best smile.

He was *beautiful.*

"Oh my God," Rico whispered to himself.

Derek didn't hear him. He pulled out a business card and wrote a number on the top. "That there is my personal extension, and there's my cell phone. I just got your card from Adam—if you don't hear from me by next Monday, call me up. I want you to come in, do the orientation, and sign some papers and get started with the retainer and the bennies. You know Adam, but he's not my only artist; I've got a few others. He appears to have no ego whatsoever, so it shouldn't be a problem if you need someone else for artwork—we've got a portfolio if you need it. In fact, I need to get you a catalog of the services and employees so you can refer back to us if you need to. Half our business comes from, like, the electrician walking in to rewire the place and saying, 'Hey, your plants are dead, do you need someone for that?', so it's important, you know?"

Rico nodded. "So that's it? I got the job? Don't you need to see my résumé?"

"You went to Stanford, you worked in advertising for a while, and you just got back from a failed love affair in New York—"

"Wait," Rico snapped, voice hard. "How did you know that?"

A little smile flickered at the corner of Derek's lips. "'Cause Darrin told me—"

"How did he know?"

Derek shook his head. "That's not what matters, you know that, right?"

Rico rubbed his chest, feeling that miserable ache returning when he'd almost managed to forget it all morning. "Yeah, so what matters?"

Derek leaned forward, looking very sober. "What matters is that... damn. You are one of the most attractive men I've ever seen in my life. And I'm going to try really hard not to make you uncomfortable with that, but I thought it needed to be said. And I'm not going to put any pressure on you. I've had my heart broken, and it sucks. But... you know." He looked away, and that shy man who had talked about his family surfaced for a moment. Rico got the impression Derek didn't let that guy out a lot. "When you're ready? You just let me know, okay? 'Cause if you... if you even think I'm cute, I'll be so all over that."

"And if I don't, ever?" Because hello, sexual harassment.

Derek managed to look sheepish. "Well, no harm, no foul. Just...
you know. If, say, you wake up one night and go, 'Holy wow! I'm
ready to date again and that Derek guy I work for might be receptive!'
Yes. Yes, I am. Say the word."

Rico grimaced. "That's sweet," he said, pretty sure no
relationship would be on the table forever. "But right now I'm planning
on being single for a very long time."

Derek laughed, a growly, happy sort of sound that did confusing
things to Rico's stomach. "Darrin said that's what Adam planned. Adam
needed Finn more than any man needed anyone in the history of ever."

"I don't need anyone," Rico said stubbornly, and Derek laughed
more and louder.

"It's *so* cute that you think that," he said, looking sincerely joyful.
Then he sobered. "We all need someone, Rico. I mean, you have your
cousin and his new family, and that's awesome. But people want to
find someone to let in their hearts. Give it a little while, you may find
I'm that guy."

Rico scowled. "For all you know I am a *complete* asshole, you
realize that, right?"

"Oh my God—you and Adam, I could swear you were twins. If
you don't hear from me by Monday, that means I got drunk at my
sister's wedding and can't move. Wake my lazy ass up and remind
me." He stood and offered a hand.

Rico took his hand again, but this time Derek squeezed a little
tighter, lingered just a moment, and rubbed the back of his hand with
his thumb.

"I promise, no harassment," he said softly. "I meant it when I said
you have space and choice and no creepy boss man groping you. That's
not the business I want to run. But don't ever think I'm backing off
because I'm not interested. I'm just waiting until you know if you are."

And then he released Rico's hand, dropped a couple of bills on
the table, and sauntered off, doing everything but whistling.

Rico sank down into his chair, looking at the sharp, clean lines on
the front of the business card and Derek's numbers on the back.

Damn.

Rico really sort of wanted to work with that man.

The New Normal

JET LAG/TIME difference smacked him in the face about an hour later, and he was *just* about to impose on this family of complete strangers for the promised apartment upstairs when Finn's minivan careened around the corner, Finn at the helm.

Rico stood up, bussed his table a little, and was ready when Finn tapped on the horn.

"Uhm," he said, looking around, but Mari and Mr. Stewart were busy working what had turned into the lunch rush. Mari gave him a distracted wave, so he left more money on the table and trotted across the boardwalk and down the stairs to hop into Finn's minivan.

"Did you get lunch?" Finn asked without even a preamble.

"Uh, no. Still sort of floating in coffee."

Finn nodded. "Yeah, I get that. You lose time when you're trying to do your homework there—at least I do. Anyway, I'll take you home, you can eat lunch and crash, and then Adam and I will bring home dinner tonight."

"Where are you going?" Rico asked through a yawn.

"Dad needs me there to help in the afternoon. Mari was supposed to do it, but I guess she got a call about her kid being sick at day care, so, you know, we're doing this now."

Rico laughed a little, feeling helpless. "Is your life always this... I don't know—"

"Tide of chaos washing ashore on the beach of what the fuck? Yeah. But we're used to it, you know? Clopper won't need walking until after six, so you can even sleep in the bed if it'll be better for your back. Apparently Darrin told Adam that once you talked to Huston, you'd be all done at the café."

"And you *believed* him?" Rico asked, baffled. "How could he possibly know that's true?"

"Because he's *Darrin!*" Finn said, rolling his eyes without shame. "You know... didn't Adam tell you about Darrin?"

Rico yawned. "No, and he didn't tell me about Derek either. Have you *met* Adam?"

Finn laughed. "I hear you. I'm lucky he told you about me."

"I hear you."

Silence.

"And you two have a little bit in common," Finn said, exasperation thick in his voice.

"Besides the brown eyes?" Rico said, only half kidding, and Finn cut a left-hand turn that practically smushed Rico against the window.

"And other fun heritage," Finn grunted. He straightened the car and then screeched to a halt in front of a crosswalk.

"And brown shorts," Rico muttered, wondering how Adam had survived this long.

"Very funny. I'm saying."

"Saying what?"

"Your family—doesn't sound particularly warm."

Rico made an indeterminate sound in his throat. Yeah, that was actually understating things, but Rico had been schooled not to talk about your family to people outside of it.

"Like I said," Finn responded dryly.

Rico yawned—not because he was trying to be funny but because he'd gotten off a plane thirteen hours earlier and had turned his life upside down in less than a week. "I'll brain human contact tomorrow," he mumbled through his yawn. "Today I'm just going to sleep and wake up to my rebooted life."

"Yeah, okay. Sorry about that. I just really need to see you happy, if that's okay."

"Why?" Rico asked as Finn pulled a hairy U-turn to end up right in front of the Victorian apartments. "Why does Rico need to be happy?"

"So Adam can believe it happens. He *reveres* you."

"He shouldn't. He was always okay on his own." Finn opened his mouth again, but Rico was through. "No brain, remember? Thanks for the ride, Finn—you and Adam, you've got this considerate relative thing down."

"Well, you're the one letting us crash at your place."

Rico nodded, and… apparently really *did* lose what was left of his brain. "Uhm, you two… don't go looking for another place right away, okay? I, uhm…." Oh God. They were coming home that evening with dinner. They'd gotten him a job and carted him around the city and introduced him to nice people who could make beignets.

Finn nodded like he'd finished his sentence. "Yeah, no. Roommates. It's good. We'll make it work."

"Good. You guys keep the bed, okay?"

"Well, it's actually our bed," Finn said, and Rico blinked, because he hadn't seen the bedroom yet. "We put yours in storage. We were sort of gathering furniture for when we move out, you know? But it works out good, because there's a chest of drawers under the television, and you can use that when you unpack."

"Oh God. Head hurts. Brain blown." He hadn't noticed *any* of that the night before. He'd been exhausted and heartbroken and just *so* willing to sit and let Adam feed him soup and coffee.

"So don't think about it," Finn said, putting the car in park and popping Rico's lock. "Go inside, strip to your skivvies, and crash."

From anyone else, Rico would have thought that was a come-on, but not from Finn. In fact, he sounded a *lot* like his dad. "Gotcha," he said. "Now *that* I can brain."

He'd worn slacks and a polo shirt to sit in the café, the creases from his luggage just barely shaken out. After walking through the door and checking on Clopper, then taking a leak—Lord, that had been a lot of coffee—he barely remembered to lay his clothes neatly on top of his suitcases before crawling between the sheets on the couch and passing out.

HE WOKE up to Finn and Adam walking through the door, talking intimately about something that made Finn giggle.

They had takeout bags with them, and as Rico stretched and then threw on a T-shirt and some cotton sleep shorts, they turned on the kitchen light and started to set the table and open the containers, still talking. Occasionally they stopped and touched—Adam's hand on Finn's hip, Finn's hand on Adam's back. The kitchen was amazingly small—two counters with about four feet of space in between—and once, when they had to pass each other, Finn stopped, hugged Adam, and swung him around so he was on the other side, near the stove. Adam laughed and fetched the cloth napkins (cloth napkins?) from the drawer and then hugged Finn and swung him back around to get to the table.

By the time Rico was decent—and turning on the living room light—dinner had been served.

"Do I need to dress better?" he asked, only half kidding. The plates matched, and they had cloth napkins and placemats, and cups for milk. He'd eaten so much takeout when he'd been working in advertising that the only dishes he'd had were of the plastic variety.

"Are you kidding? That's gonna be us as soon as we eat," Finn told him, and then they sat down at the table and started dishing out the food.

Rico sat in the seat to Finn's left so as not to get elbowed and took stock. They had lettuce, tomatoes, chopped red onions, sliced almonds, blue cheese, grilled mushrooms, grilled onions, bacon crumbles, bacon pieces, a big stack of hamburger patties, salad mix, and a bottle of ranch and a bottle of Italian dressing. There was also a bag of wheat bread and some ketchup.

"What are we eating?" he asked, genuinely curious.

"Free food," said Adam. He was cutting up a substack of hamburger patties and scattering the pieces over a pile of lettuce. As Rico watched, he added pretty much everything else on the table, then poured ranch dressing over it and dug in. Finn was apparently a traditionalist. He stacked two patties between two slices of bread, added lettuce, tomatoes, mushrooms, and onions, poured some ketchup, and ate it like a sandwich.

Rico used the salad fixings on a pile of lettuce, and the hamburger fixings on a slice of beef on bread, and kept *his* meal in discrete piles like a human being.

"Hey, Adam," Finn said, chewing on his lettuce and tomato burger.

"Mm?" Adam was plowing through his salad with a single-minded intensity that bespoke a long day.

"What do you think? Rico's eating a salad *and* a sandwich."

"So?"

"What does that say about his personality?"

Adam looked up at Rico's food and then at Finn's plate. "It means he's going to spend less time in the bathroom tomorrow. Eat more vegetables, Finn. I'm begging you."

Finn rolled his eyes—and picked up a tomato, raw, and ate it. "I mean, your meal bespeaks an integrated life." Finn nodded, wide-eyed, like this made total sense.

"And yours says you eat like a twelve-year-old."

Finn nodded again. "See? What does Rico's say about him?"

Rico took a bite from his hamburger and closed his eyes in bliss. The mushrooms and onions had been grilled to *perfection*, and the meat wasn't just a frozen patty—it had been seasoned with something secret and sexy and amazing.

Adam grunted. "It says he knows a good thing when he sees it. Now leave the man alone and let him eat."

Rico smiled shyly at his cousin over his burger. Adam always spoke the best kind of sense.

THEY FOUND a kind of balance.

The next day, Rico's boxes were delivered, and he spent a couple of days going through his stuff to try to figure out what to keep at the apartment and what to put in the storage facility, which was less than a mile away.

Turned out Adam and Finn had so little, they had a surprising amount of room for him in his own apartment.

While Clopper danced around his feet, Rico wiggled into their personal space. His suits went in their closet, because both of them lived in jeans, khakis, and T-shirts, so there was room to spare. His underwear and casual clothes went in the nice antique dresser under the television. Adam had apparently refinished it, along with some antique frames filled with his own artwork, in his spare time.

"He says he feels stupid with his own stuff on the walls," Finn confided as he helped with the great "shit shift" as they were calling it. "I keep telling him I don't have anything else we can put up there, but the truth is, I just like looking at it."

Rico had to agree. It *was* good to look at. Adam liked all sorts of different styles, and he was still playing with them as his fancy dictated. Rico liked the pen-and-ink drawings colored with pastels the best, but the watercolors came a close second.

And it sure as shit beat the blank walls Rico had left him with.

In the end, all they needed to buy was a long, low dresser that doubled as a coffee table and a twin-size mattress pad and new pillows so Rico didn't dig a hole in the couch with his ass as he slept. During the day he put the bedding in the top of the "coffee table," and in the evenings they could watch movies or play video games together on the couch. The video game set was Finn's, and as Rico and Adam engaged in duels to the death on *Assassin's Creed* and Finn and Clopper cheered them on, Rico had to wonder what had been wrong with him that he'd never invested in a game system of his own.

Sunday night, after they'd finished moving him in and eating dinner—Finn had made what he named "fake fish salad," which had worked well in the rising heat of late April—they were doing the video-game thing when Derek called.

Rico trashed his character when the phone rang from the charger, and as Adam and Finn called after him, "Hey, dude, what the hell?" he felt an absurd surge of excitement in his chest and wondered why he'd done that. "I, uh, think it's the boss," he apologized, trying not to run for the phone like a teenager. "Hello?"

"Hi, Ricardo Gonzalves-Macias?" Derek slurred playfully into the phone.

Rico looked at Adam and pointed to the bedroom, then got the wave-away as permission. It figured—they'd had sex a couple of times in the past five days, but Rico got the feeling that all the magic was between the two of them and didn't involve monkeys on the ceiling or a giant ice-squirting Splorch! There was no reason a friend couldn't go sit on their bed.

"Yeah, this is Rico. Derek?" Because he'd promised to be drunk at his sister's wedding, and it sounded like he very much was.

"Yup. Told ya I'd be hammered. But I really wanted you to know I was serious. But I've been up to my balls… uhm, eyeballs in wedding for the last five days. But I really wanted you to know I was serious."

Rico had to laugh. He sounded so… serious. "Yeah, I hear you. I've got your address. I'll be there tomorrow."

"Oh." Derek sounded disappointed. "That was easy. I thought I'd have to do more talking."

"Well, it's just a job, Mr. Huston. It's not an, er, marriage."

Derek's laugh over the phone sounded low and dirty. "Oh, so you *are* going to be a challenge."

"A challenge implies success," Rico replied primly, leaning against the doorframe of the bedroom. Finn must have brought in his own comforter—this one was blue and purple. Not exactly Adam's colors, but they went nicely with the watercolor of the river as seen from Front Street that Adam had put up on the adjacent wall. "I really don't think you can get your hopes up."

Oh, that laugh. Didn't get worse the second time around. "Are you talking to me from a darkened room? You've got dark-bedroom voice."

Rico's eyes widened and he searched for the switch, almost forgetting it was on the wall right behind him.

"No!" he said hurriedly as the lamp switched on. "What the...." He looked up to where the ceiling fan used to be and saw that the lights had been rewired. Now, apparently, he had two end-table lamps instead.

The effect was disconcertingly intimate, in spite of the light.

"Something wrong?" Derek asked, amused.

"No, just my cousin improved the holy shit out of my apartment when I was gone. It's confusing." He sat down on the bed and realized it really *wasn't* his bed. The mattress was a little softer, a little more welcoming, and that comforter was *really* sweet—nice thread count, really fluffy.

"Your apartment was a dump when you lived there?" Huston sounded suddenly alert, like this mattered.

"Not a dump," Rico admitted, still looking around. "Just... just not personal. Adam and Finn made it personal."

"Oh, well, you'll miss them when you kick them out."

"Not kicking them out," Rico told him. Adam had added a pegboard for what must have been Finn's hats—there were goofy fleece ones, and a few souvenir baseball hats, and a giant Day-Glo squid hat from an amusement park.

There was color here, when he'd left four white walls. He'd had dinner *at the table* for three out of the past five days. His dog was here, and from what Rico could see, the big doofus loved Adam more than he loved Rico. And the cat was here (literally *right here* sleeping on the pillow next to Rico's hand), and while Jake did not seem to have any loyalties, per se, he didn't mind sleeping on Rico's neck during TV time or on Finn and Adam's faces at night.

"You got a big house or something?" Derek asked. It sounded like a "getting to know you" question, not a flippant one.

Rico petted the cat and watched him purr motorboat-drool across the pillow. "I've got a tiny apartment, but Adam was watching it when I was out of town."

"So...."

"So I got back early, and him and Finn have, like, a family here." Rico swallowed. He didn't want to say, *Like the family Adam and I never had*, but that was exactly what he'd been thinking. "It's nice," he finished simply.

"You and Adam not get a lot of that?" Derek asked, the pleasant looseness fading from his voice. He suddenly sounded like a man in a dark room too.

"We got each other," Rico said, not wanting to talk about it. "What time do you want me there tomorrow?"

"I want you here tonight," Derek said, his voice brightening to the standard flirt.

"Yeah, but I just finished unpacking and I'm not putting on a suit at seven o'clock Sunday night."

"That's a shame," Derek said, and Rico could hear the smirk in his voice. "But who says you gotta put a suit on?"

"You want me to come naked?" Rico asked, suddenly wary and a little bit confused.

"You never heard of shorts and a T-shirt to come have a beer on a guy's couch?" Derek half laughed.

"That sounds a little, uh, informal," Rico hedged.

"Well, unless I'm at work, I can be an informal guy." He was back to teasing, and Rico felt comfortable with that. "I like going… casual." He put some playful flirtation into the word, but Rico couldn't respond.

Instead he remembered the pristine refrigerator, the strictures on his grades, the claustrophobia of not being able to talk, run, or breathe after his father got home.

The implicit knowledge that he had to be perfect to be loved, otherwise he'd end up like Adam, under the bed, hearing people curse his name.

"I.…" Oh man. This conversation was suddenly *just* as personal as Derek had planned for it to be. "Adam and I were used to… uh, heavy-duty social limits." He chose his words carefully, because he didn't want to get into the cold silences, or Adam crying under the bed. "We're, uh, sort of testing them now."

"Huh."

"Huh what?"

"That's interesting. You and your cousin are testing your limits by having family time and rooming together and being all… happy and warm. That says… interesting things about what your life was like before."

Rico groaned. "Look, when did you want me there tomorrow?"

"That depends on when we get off the phone tonight," Derek responded pertly.

"Don't you have a wedding or something?"

"Nope. Wedding all done this morning. Sister on honeymoon with a doofus who deserves way better than her but pretends he can't pick his own ass without her help, caterers have left and filled my parents' freezer with a trucking fuckload of uneaten barbecue because Renee can't estimate for shit, and entire family—including extended family, mind you—have helped clean up the mess left when you hold a wedding decorated with acres of fucking crepe paper on a wind plain."

Rico couldn't help it. He laughed. "Sounds like... a fucking disaster."

"Hence, alcohol," Derek agreed, but he sounded happy too.

"So, your new brother-in-law—does he have a backup plan for pretend ass-picking, or is he going to be a boil on your family's for a while?"

"Well, he was going to be an actuary, but now he's helping my dad and my brother at the store. I'll get to hear my dad bitch about him for the rest of my life."

Rico laughed. "He must be a friend."

"Yeah—he is. And my sister doesn't deserve him."

"Hence alcohol?"

"It's not a broken heart," Derek said, sounding 100 percent sober. "It's just... well, Renee isn't my favorite relative. Hale was in my top-ten friends."

Rico had to laugh there. "Understood. Who *is* your favorite relative?"

"Everyone *but* Renee," Derek said promptly.

Rico laughed more. "Explain that!"

"Okay, I will," Derek said, and now he'd gone from sober to wily. "But when I'm done, you have to answer me one question."

"What question?"

"I'll decide when I get to it."

"That's—"

"C'mon, Rico—I'm not gonna tongue you from the phone, okay? I tell you happy family story, you answer me a question. That easy."

"Shoot."

"My sister Renee is the biggest frickin' airhead on the *planet*. And not in the 'Oh crap, I lost my keys for the five-hundredth time' way, because my little brother Kevin does that all the time, but he means well; and not in the way of 'oh hell, did you really say that,' because *that's* my older brother Dillon's territory."

"So in what way—"

"Is she an airhead? As in, she spent hours—and I mean frickin' *hours*—on this wedding, picking the right centerpieces, right? And the right color crepe paper, and the right color flowers, and the perfect antique railroad lamps for this outdoor wedding. But in all that picking, not once did she think about who was going to dish the food or the cake or play the music, or even about hiring a sound system, so, this wedding that she's been planning for like the last six months? Happened this morning because her *entire family* ran in to pick up the slack. So she's shortsighted and inconsiderate, and she pisses me off, and *that's* why she's an airhead."

Rico found he was laughing in earnest. "Wow, uhm, Derek, tell me how you *really* feel!"

Derek grunted. "I feel *irritated* because it was a hardship on my parents and she took advantage of me. So there you go. Now you know something about me."

"Your family means a lot to you."

"Yes, yes, it does. Even when they piss me off and I am forced to ramble drunkenly on the guy I was trying to impress."

"I'm no one to impress," Rico said softly. God, he hadn't *begged* Adam and Finn to stay, but then he hadn't had to. Here he was, twenty-eight years old and just now figuring out what living with a *real* family was like.

And what recovering from a *real* broken heart was like.

It was a sobering realization, here in the intimate lighting of what used to be his bedroom.

"Well, you impressed the hell out of me."

Rico swallowed, suddenly wanting to fall into his joyous flirting like he'd fallen into Ezra Kellerman's eyes.

Except unlike *that* fall, he knew where this fall ended.

"Did you have something you wanted to ask me?" he asked, his voice sounding small and stony, even to his own ears.

"Yeah," Derek said huskily. "Lots of things I wanted to ask you. But we'll take it one thing at a time."

"You're making a lot of assumptions about how much we'll be—"

"Rico, I'm not flirting now. I'm just genuinely curious, because I've known your cousin for months now, and I met you on Thursday, and I just want to know."

Oh awesome.

"Fire away."

"If you could describe your family in one word, what would it be?"

Rico thought about it. Thought about Adam under the bed, and his own mother, afraid to violate the rules of the house carved in blood, stone, or water. Thought about his grandmother, who could shriek about how her favorite children could do no wrong and her least favorite child (Adam's mother) could do no right.

Thought about Adam hauled out of Easter dinner by the ear and having the door shut in his face.

"Bitter," he said.

"Yeah," Derek said softly. "I got that impression. You know what?"

"What?"

"I go to that store where your cousin works like three times a month. Do you know why?"

"You're missing out on the joyride of early diabetes?" Because that store—yikes! Once a year, and Rico would have an ass that bounced off walls.

"'Cause everyone—from the employees to the owner to the sugar in the barrels—is sweet. I think you're going to do really well here, Rico. I hope you give us a real taste."

Rico swallowed, suddenly wanting a lemon drop or a chocolate boner truffle with ferocity. "Thanks, boss," he said, licking his lips. "What time am I showing up?"

"Ten. We can get you the orientation, and then you, me, and Miguel can go out for lunch."

"Who's Miguel?"

"My IT professional and business intern. He's a nice kid, but he's going to be starting his own business in a month up in Roseville. Free lunches and lots of informal in-servicing for the guy so he gets a good start."

"That's nice of you, boss," Rico said, meaning it. "Just don't...." Oh God. He was going to say, *Just don't give him the boot if he sleeps with your family*, but suddenly he couldn't talk about that. "Just don't spoil him with kindness, right?"

Derek snorted. "Not possible. Especially not this kid. This kid's like your cousin. Drinks it in and gives it back in spades."

"Oh." Rico had nothing to say to that. "So, uhm, tomorrow. Ten o'clock, at the address on your card."

"Yup."

"I can do that."

"See you then."

Rico hit End Call and flopped sideways on the bed so he could pet the drooling adolescent cat on Finn's pillow.

"Don't look at me like that," he mumbled to the cat, who was looking at the back of its eyelids, mostly. "He's nice, but seriously, another workplace romance?"

But Derek had promised to draw up a contract that would keep his interest professional and not interfere with Rico's job. He'd stated flat-out that Rico could get him to stop by saying no.

And Rico didn't want to say no.

Because it felt good to have someone interested in him. It was flattering to have a good-looking guy like Derek Huston call him up and talk to him about personal stuff in the guise of setting up an orientation.

The last thing Rico had seen of Ezra had been the good-bye in his face as he'd handed over the blackmail papers that would set Rico free. And here Derek was, promising to back off if Rico asked and making himself human and accessible and...

Kind.

God, what sort of kindness had Rico and Adam known?

Rico stroked Jake's ears, scratching behind them, and smoothed his wet, drool-coated whiskers back. That's why he'd gotten animals after he'd settled in—Jake was, after all, Cat 2.0, the reboot, after the late unlamented Gonzo. That was all he had—no pictures, no decorations, hand-me-down Ikea furniture—but a dog and a cat, because if he fed them and petted them and took care of their crap, they would love him back ad infinitum.

He needed to remember that. Jake would love him no matter what.

The same could not be said for Derek Huston.

Working for the Man

ADAM NEEDED to go in and get a check from a job he'd finished two weeks before, but he didn't let Rico drive the Crown Vic the five blocks to Derek's neat little office building in the top of another set of converted Victorian houses.

"But," Rico protested as Adam put on his khakis and a button-down shirt. Rico himself was in his best suit and a tie. "We can't just... *walk the dog* to this guy's office and pick up your check."

"He works less than half a mile away, Rico. The dog needs to dump, Finn's already at school—you told me you walked all the time in New York."

Rico grunted, put out but finding it difficult to explain. "But... but I *like* the car," he said plaintively. "Why can't I drive my car?"

"Carbon emissions, global warming, saving for a mortgage—any of that ringing a bell?"

Rico grunted. "But when *can* I drive my car?"

"I don't know—when you take me and Finn on a road trip to San Francisco on account of us being *outstanding* family members."

Rico perked up. "Hey—I mean, I've got a job, right?"

"Well, you're still doing that thing for Finn's dad. And seriously, you weren't hurting in the money department before, right?"

Rico grunted. In fact, he could probably live off his savings for a year, even without Finn and Adam helping with rent. "You know... just don't like to...."

"Man, I heard your dad at family gatherings same as you heard my mom. That man didn't have a dime he didn't want to strangle or disinfect. I hear you. But I'm saying, it doesn't have to be Finn and me, but a trip somewhere, in your precious car, before Sacramento remembers who it is again and tries to cook us fucking dead."

Adam had a point—there was *spring* in the valley, and that didn't happen often.

"There's an exhibition game in San Francisco in a couple of weeks."

Adam grinned. "*That's* what I'm talking about." The grin faded, and he clipped the lead around Clopper's neck. "Uh, how much? I mean, I've got money now, but I need to make sure—"

"Like you said," Rico told him, straightening his best spring suit coat and twitching the collar, "my treat. I'm tired of Windexing dimes."

The walk to Huston's office really was embarrassingly short. Three Victorian houses had been converted, then joined together with walkways on the second and third levels. A reception area had been built on, complete with elevator, and Adam took Clopper on the elevator because the dog seemed to love it. He sat down and slowly wagged his tail, looking toward the doors with a lolling tongue, like he anticipated free dog chow at the end when the doors opened.

"What in the hell?" Rico asked, shifting his briefcase to his other hand. He wanted to have a hand free in case whatever the dog was hoping for on the other side of the doors actually materialized.

"Well, one day Derek—"

The doors opened and there was the man himself, crouching down at Clopper's level and offering him a white-chocolate dog treat.

"He *bribed* my *dog*?" Rico said, scandalized. "Oh my God!"

Derek stood up and laughed, brushing his hand off on the seat of his nice gray suit before reaching out to shake Adam's hand and then Rico's.

"You can hear that dog breathing from two blocks away," Derek said, grinning. "I *love* dogs—my parents have five of them. I just got my house finished to where I could get a dog, but I haven't gotten around to it yet."

"He's been mackin' on your dog," Adam said tersely. "How they hangin', Derek?"

"Low and inside, Adam."

Adam grinned and looked at Rico triumphantly. "See? Even Derek thinks baseball's a good idea! Does Janine have my check?"

"Yeah—there's a bonus there because you finished early—"

Adam looked horrified. "No—no, that's not why I—"

"Yeah," Derek said, his voice taking on the long-suffering tone of someone who'd had this conversation before. "But you did good work before the deadline. So the client paid you extra. It's what people do."

"I was just trying to get done before Easter," Adam muttered. "I didn't want to spend Easter Sunday—"

"Did you and Finn have a nice time at his parents' house?" Derek asked kindly, winking at Rico.

Adam shook his head and narrowed his eyes. "Yeah. Sure. They're trying to make me fat. Let me go find Janine. Thanks, Derek." And then he stomped off, muttering to himself, Rico's dog in tow.

Rico couldn't stop the smile twisting his lips.

"He's a tough nut," he said fondly. "It's good to see you've cracked him."

Derek grunted. "You think that's cracked? That's barely softened. God, we had to pull Finn in here to get him to sign a decent contract." Derek shook his head and turned, taking in Rico's best spring suit and his dazzling emerald green tie.

"Nice," he purred, and then he made the once-around gesture with his finger.

Rico rolled his eyes, but the suit had been one of his last purchases before he'd left New York, and he was sort of proud of it. He held his briefcase out at his side and did a smart little pivot, his dress shoes sliding easily on the short pile of the carpeting.

Derek laughed and clapped his hands. "Very nice," he said, and then, to Rico's amusement, he did the same.

His trim form was *very* nicely accentuated in something Hugo Boss, gray linen, with a melon-colored tie. Rico obliged him by clapping.

"So, that's something we have in common," Derek said, eyes twinkling.

"We're both clothes whores? Call the news." But it was hard not to look appreciatively at Derek—the suit fit him well. And one of the things that had first turned Rico's key about Ezra—and had first made him let his guard down, when it had been cranked up tightly from pretty much the moment he had been born—was seeing Ezra, sleeves rolled up to his elbows, tie undone, hair rumpled, as they'd been up late working on a campaign.

"Hey, we're almost the same size. You're nice to me, I might let you borrow my suit!"

Rico laughed. God, the incorrigible flirt was back with a vengeance. "Well, I got my own, but that's sweet. Are we going to do this orientation thing?"

Derek suddenly sobered, the flirt gone. "Okay. Yeah. But I need you to be sure."

"Sure?" Rico frowned. "Yeah. It's a good setup. I approve. Why you gotta ask again?"

"'Cause I want you to know your own mind going in," Derek said, and for a moment his face was unreadable, the face of the seasoned business negotiator.

And because he wasn't laughing or flirting, Rico suddenly understood that he was talking about exactly that. "If I don't like something, I can walk away," he said, throat dry. "You haven't twisted my arm."

Derek nodded. "Good. Because all… all kidding aside, I *did* take a look at your résumé and the portfolio you sent me, and you really are big time for my little business. If you're not here for the guy in the suit, I'm wondering what you're here for?"

Adam appeared on the other side of the glass door he'd disappeared through, tugging on Clopper's lead with exasperation. For his part, Clopper was chewing more of those white-chocolate-dipped dog treats—and Rico could tell that because big bits of them were coming out of his giant maw as he gobbled.

"I'm here to work somewhere I feel good about," he said seriously. "And because my cousin vouches for you. And you've apparently bribed my dog."

Derek's customary smile threatened to return. "Well, I'm not going to quit bribing your dog."

"Rico, you gotta make them stop!" Adam complained as Clopper dragged him out on the walkway. "And Jesus, you two, stop flirting and get in there. You're *talking* in front of the *elevator*. It's like you're little kids or something."

The elevator opened at that moment, and they had to move out of the way so the person inside could get out and let Adam in.

A young Hispanic man with straight black hair cut with feathered bangs came out, pausing to pet Clopper on the head. "How you doing, Adam?" the guy asked. "You still working for Darrin?"

"Yeah, Miguel. It's getting busy again, but Darrin says the right employee hasn't showed up yet."

Miguel shook his head. "Well, the last person he was waiting for was you, so I'd have faith. Whoever it is will be right for *someone*."

"Yeah, well, I think he had a dream about my cousin, so maybe *he's* right for someone," Adam said sourly. He smiled, though, and waved as he tugged Clopper into the elevator and away from the young man's attention.

The elevator doors closed and Miguel stayed there for a moment, gazing wistfully at his shiny reflection, before turning back around to Rico and Derek.

"You didn't ask about Finn," Derek observed mildly.

"Give it time," Miguel replied, equally mildly. "I've finally realized his nose is crooked and the tattoo on the neck was a bad idea." He swung to Rico, regarding him with thick-lashed brown eyes, a standard smile of greeting on full lips. His eyes widened like he recognized someone. "Oh for crap's sake. You have *got* to be Rico."

Rico sighed and extended his hand. "And you have *got* to be getting over my cousin."

"I never stood a chance," Miguel said philosophically. "Derek didn't either."

Derek rolled his eyes. "I asked him to dinner. He said his boyfriend would object. I got nothing on Miguel's level of unrequitedness."

Miguel groaned. "It's stupid. He worked at Candy Heaven for a week and *still* didn't know my name."

Rico smiled at him as Derek opened the glass door to the offices to let them pass. "That's Adam," he said, telling God's honest truth. "He's pretty sure most people will reject him, so he doesn't let them register unless they're aggressively nice."

"It comes off as badassery," Miguel said, self-deprecation in every syllable. "And it's deadly attractive."

"I guess, if I'm the only guy here who isn't pining after him!" Rico said sourly. They walked into a white-carpeted waiting area with oxblood corduroy couches and antique end tables. A pretty receptionist wearing a black suit and pristine white shell underneath it waved at them and then went back to something she was doing on the computer in front of her. She had three bowls on top of the shelf surrounding her desk—one with mints, one with chocolate, and one with the dog treats Derek had given Clopper. Rico would like to bet that Clopper wasn't Derek's only doggy visitor—or the only person to take advantage of Derek's goodwill, either. The end tables sported a copy of almost every craft magazine known to man, from *Quilting* to *Knitting* to *Gardener's Weekly* to *Woodworker's Digest*, and Rico wondered who in Derek's family sold magazine subscriptions.

Miguel waved to both of them casually, saying, "Meeting in your office, Derek?"

"Yeah," Derek said. "Take fifteen, check out your schedule. We'll orient Rico here and all go out to lunch, deal?"

"Deal."

Miguel disappeared down the hall and to the left, and Derek ushered Rico down to the very end of the hall, where the boss's desk sat in regal silence.

"Hope, do me a favor and send my messages to my computer, yeah?"

"No worries, Mr. Huston—already done!" Hope sang, and then Derek reached around Rico and closed the door.

Rico stopped for a moment, arrested by the warmth of his body and his smell—Polo? Obsession for Men? Rico had never been good at that game, but that didn't mean he hadn't liked to smell Ezra's neck and guess. Now, just as strongly, he wanted to smell Derek's neck, and that urge sent him stepping sideways, away from Derek's body, while he looked around.

"Your furniture is top-notch," he said, making conversation and truly admiring as well. He saw nothing standard, nothing Ikea—Queen Anne chairs with embroidered seats and sturdy legs were ranged around a heavy-duty oak desk with scars around the front and the sides to testify that it had survived the business wars.

Behind the desk sat a classic ergonomically designed computer chair, but Derek's guests were supposed to feel like this was a comfortable visit and not a down-and-dirty deal, and Rico appreciated that.

"Thanks. Family of woodworkers, remember?" And then, before Rico could respond, "And I didn't have a crush on your cousin. I asked him out, he said no, and then I saw him with Finn. You don't get in the way of that sort of thing. It's bad karma."

Rico let out a breath. "Is the gay community in Sacramento really that small?" he asked almost dryly. "I mean, I've been back and gay for five minutes and the whole world's in love with Adam."

"I was *never*—"

"I know." Rico sent him a crooked smile. "I was trying to joke about it. I don't know what to say."

"How about tell me why you lived here for six years and don't know what the community is like?"

Derek had a big window surrounded by spring green drapes, with blinds to keep out what would probably be brutal afternoon sun. Rico stepped over and raised the blinds, delighted to see a view of the tree-shrouded street. "I didn't come out until I went to New York," he said. "What did Miguel say, fifteen—"

"Why not?" Derek asked, leaning against the front of his desk and crossing his arms.

"You're out to your family?"

"Yeah."

"They throw you a parade?"

"They didn't disown me, and only my mom's sister stopped talking to me. Mom doesn't like her much anyw—"

"Did you see that scar on Adam's forehead?"

Derek's defensiveness dropped a little. "Yeah."

"Our grandmother slammed the door in his face before he had a chance to take that final step out of her life. Broke his nose too. Made it through two tours in the Middle East unscathed, but that bitch split open his forehead and broke his nose. I came out to myself in New York. Adam's the only family I've talked to about it. Isn't there some sort of code about not telling people unless you want them to know?"

"I didn't see the bylaws. I'm sorry about—"

Rico swallowed. This man could make business personal like no one he'd ever met, not even Ezra. "Can we sign contracts today?" he asked, voice broken and a little desperate. "And talk about nothing except the job? And maybe where we eat for lunch?"

"Yeah," Derek said softly. "Sure. I hear you. Just business today."

"Thanks," Rico said, relieved on so many levels. For starters, he'd just said his first no—and Derek had done just what he'd promised.

It sort of made Rico want to confide in him—but not today.

TWO HOURS later Rico had signed all the contracts, double-checking to see the language Derek had promised was there, and then he'd gone through the orientation binders Derek provided.

He liked the business more by the passing minute.

Miguel had come in and quietly and competently led him through the steps of securing a job on his own if he wanted, and the pros and cons—mostly pros—of referring a potential client to Derek's business.

"Derek protects the client too," Miguel said earnestly. "But generally his lawyers—he's got two of them—keep everything clean and legal. And I've seen him go after people trying to welsh on a deal a couple of times—he's relentless. If his people do the job, he goes to the mat for them."

"That's good to know," Rico said, feeling better and better about this deal as they went on. "My last boss, not so much."

"What was it like?" Miguel asked, stars in his eyes. "Working in New York?"

Rico smiled, remembering that *he'd* felt the same way less than a year ago. "You know how you look outside that window and you look down on all those trees?"

"Yeah?"

"Not so much."

Miguel thought about it. "How'd that feel?"

"I really missed the sky." But he would have been willing to stay there, chafing under Kellerman's boots and eating the old guy's shit, if only for Ezra. Now he asked himself, when would that have started to pall? When would he have needed to break out of there because being trapped in that job was almost as bad as being trapped in the closet, and he finally wanted to know what it felt like to be all the way free?

"Yeah," Miguel said, face falling. "I've visited before. I'm not sure I could live there."

"I thought I wanted to," Rico told him, gaze straying to the window again. "But you know? It's been a good five days back."

Miguel nodded. "I'll say, if you landed in Derek's lap."

Rico looked at him, young and bright-eyed and a little bit… unseasoned, maybe, for what he thought Derek might want in a partner. He had to ask. "So, you and Derek…."

Miguel shook his head. "No. No! That would be taking advantage," Miguel said earnestly. "That's not something Mr. Huston does."

Rico felt his lips twist in an unfamiliar smile. "You'd be surprised," he said.

"Yeah, but if he's hitting on you, you know he's in earnest," Miguel told him. "Otherwise I might have blown him in the first week just out of sympathy. You've got to admit. He's pretty cute."

Rico grinned, because *Miguel* was pretty cute. "Cute would not be my word," he mused. "Not for Derek."

Miguel shot him a look and rolled his eyes. "Oh *man.*"

"What?"

"I've got to *leave,* and I would *love* to see you two dance!"

"How do you even know we'll—"

Miguel shrugged. "Because I haven't seen him date, really. If he's hitting on you, Rico, he means it." Suddenly Miguel got really serious. "You'll be nice if you let him down, right? I mean… he's a good guy."

Rico wanted to pat him on the head. He refrained. "I promise to be nice in my rejection."

Miguel grinned again, popping a dimple, and Rico shook his head. Yeah, this kid wouldn't be Derek material.

But apparently Rico was.

The Big Dodge

THE REST of the orientation went smoothly, and lunch was… pleasant.

Derek didn't hit on Rico with Miguel there, and without sex on the table (or under the table, or permeating his clothes or his smile or his hair, because *damn*, looking at Derek and his all-American-boy smile did *not* get harder), they could banter about books or music or anything at all. Miguel and Rico discussed the merits and demerits of Mexican soap operas—Rico's grandmother loved them, which was why Rico despised them, and Miguel's grandmother loved them, which was why Miguel adored them, and after some lively chatter about that, Derek interrupted them, laughing.

"Well, guys, it sounds like it's not the television show, it's the grandmother!"

They'd laughed, and Rico was sort of proud of how he'd relegated that unpleasant part of his life to lunch conversation—right up until, as though summoned by the words themselves, his phone rang, and it was family.

"Oh hell," he muttered, looking at his phone. "It's my mother."

They were eating outside in a little café about two blocks from Derek's office suite. Rico stood up and excused himself as he answered the call, and then he walked around the corner to the shady side of the red-boarded building.

"Hey, *Mami*," he said resignedly. "Sorry I didn't call last week. Things got busy."

"Too busy to call, Rico?" His mother never yelled. She just got "disappointed," and there was no fighting that.

"Well, my internship ended unexpectedly. I'm actually back in Sacramento, having lunch with my new boss."

"Your internship ended?" His mother turned and spoke a rapid spate of Spanish at someone, repeating the news, and oh good, Rico's grandmother knew now.

"Yeah, *Mami*, it's all over now. I'll, uh, talk to you later this week, okay?"

"But Rico, where are you staying? Didn't you let your—" There was a disdainful pause. "—*cousin* take care of your animals? Did you just kick him out on his ear?"

"No," he said shortly. "He's still there with his boyfriend, and I'm sleeping on the couch. I asked them to stay. They're good people."

Rico recoiled as the eruption of Spanish poured through the phone. Another voice added to the cacophony, and he gave up trying to follow the words—his Spanish was pretty rusty since he'd moved out of the house—and just settled down to wait until she was calm enough to speak English.

"Rico!" she said finally. "Your grandmother doesn't like this *at all*—"

Something in Rico snapped. He wasn't even aware it was stretched tight, but apparently it had been ready to go at any minute. "I don't care what she likes, *Mami*. I went away to New York, and I got to be someone else, and you know what? I *liked* that person. He was pretty brave. So I'm not coming back to be who she wants or who you want anymore, okay?"

"But your cousin! Rico, he's—"

"He's gay. And you know what? So am I."

Rico hit End Call, took three deep breaths, and went back to lunch.

Derek had ordered a chocolate-chip cookie with ice cream on top—and three spoons. When Rico approached, Derek looked up and raised his eyebrows boyishly, unaware that Rico had just done this spectacular, brave, terrifying thing in the span of a two-minute conversation, and Rico grinned back.

God. He really wanted a bite of that cookie.

BY THE end of the week, he'd decided the cookie was worth it. He'd picked up a job almost immediately—Derek hadn't been kidding about Rico being the employee he'd been waiting for—and between that gig and working a modest campaign for Finn's dad, Rico was pretty busy.

Derek *did* behave at work. Rico had a cubicle and a desk where he could work, but he wasn't required to be there, as long as he could show time spent. He did most of his work there anyway, because the computer was more powerful and he had more space. When he'd lived alone, he set it all up on the kitchen table, but Adam had been using that to do *his* work, and Finn had been doing homework there all week. It wasn't a hardship, really.

Rico wasn't the only one who took advantage of the offices, and the people Derek hired were motivated and, usually, happy. He liked that. There'd always been tension at Kellerman's, because the whole marketing department had been pitted against each other like gladiators.

Derek swung by once a day, checked to see people's progress, and had actual *conversations* with them. When the outside people—landscapers, electricians, IT people—came in to collect their checks, they usually had conversations with Derek as well. He made them take pictures of their accomplishments, and Hope spent much of her time assembling online and paper portfolios. *Nobody* who worked for Derek got away with not having work to be proud of.

The energy was refreshing—Rico liked it.

And Derek flirted, yes, but not uncomfortably so. He wiggled his eyebrows and laughed and spent an awful lot of energy widening his baby blues at Rico and trying to get Rico to laugh back.

Rico was finding it easier to do. And the image of Ezra's blue eyes became less and less prevalent every time.

Of course, in the meantime, he was dodging his mother's calls like a shoplifter dodged a mall cop.

Friday night found him sitting in the stuffed chair, his tablet on his lap as he put the finishing touches on the work for Mr. Stewart, while Adam and Finn slept on opposite sides of the couch. Adam had been working his own extra gig on top of his full-time job at the candy store, and Finn had been writing papers all week. Right now Adam had his arms crossed and his face turned into the side of the couch like he was hiding. Finn sprawled, legs on top of Adam's thighs, head leaning back against the armrest, snoring loudly. Clopper finished the picture by sitting on the ground with his head on the little space of cushion next to Adam's ass. The dog had been run off his own ass by the levee that afternoon after Adam had gotten off work, and he, too, was asleep.

Rico took a moment from his work to switch his tablet to camera and take a picture. Chuckling, he made it his wallpaper—because hey, who *wouldn't* get a laugh out of that—and he had just gone back to work when Adam grunted and shifted.

"Mudderfuckinsnowziitkerist," he muttered. He picked up his phone and squinted at the readout, then turned his head and glared at Rico.

"You been dodging your moms all week?" he asked grouchily.

Rico grimaced. "Yeah, why?"

"Whydoyathink, genius?" Adam hit Connect. "Hi, Aunt Lydia. No, he's not here. He's out. I dunno. A Broadway revue? I don't know if that's where gay people go. It's not where *I* go. I go to the fuckin' baseball game. No, Aunt Lydia, I'm not being a smartass, I'm being a tired ass."

Finn choked on a snore and flailed around, clocking Clopper on the head and setting the big dog barking.

"Whozat?" he asked when he'd recovered.

Adam grunted. "Rico's moms."

"What's she doing on the phone with *you?*" Finn asked, bristling. Rico didn't blame him.

"Trying to figure out where Rico is," Adam answered patiently.

"Well, he's right—"

Adam tried gamely to stop his mouth with one stockinged foot. Finn dodged neatly, slapped him on the toes, and said, "Never mind, I get it."

"What was that, Aunt Lydia? No, that wasn't Rico. Rico's hiding from you like the bloody coward he is. That was my boyfriend, who would rather cook you all up as barbecue than have you talk to me. Why? Because you were mean to me. Yeah, no. I'm not going to get into what a shitty little kid I was. Here. I'm hanging up now. You want to talk to your kid, maybe don't be such a fucking bitch and he'll want to talk to you."

Adam hit End Call, but as he swung his legs up and around the couch, the phone started buzzing again.

"Rico?" Adam said plaintively, and Rico held out his hands.

Adam threw the phone and he caught it neatly.

"Yeah, I hear ya." Poor Adam—he'd been dealing with her all week. It was time for Rico to pony up.

"Dude, you don't even have to talk to her, but find a way to block her number, okay? Man, my moms don't *have* my number—I don't know how *your* moms got it."

"I gave it to her when you were coming to watch the apartment." Rico sighed. He'd had some misguided notion that family was family then. The longer he lived in fear of dealing with his family about the

Rico he'd discovered in New York versus the Rico he found himself to be here, the more votes he cast to keep Adam as his family and jettison the rest of them.

"Yeah, well—"

"Bed," Finn demanded, tugging at his hand. "My phone's set. I need to touch chest or something to make up for your stinky feet."

Adam grunted. "Yeah, all right."

They toddled off to bed, Finn dragging Adam by the hand. The cat, who had been lying on the couch, hopped off with a thump and padded after them, but the dog stayed, looking at Rico dolefully.

Rico sighed and moved to the couch, and the dog moved his chin from the couch cushion to Rico's lap and fell back asleep.

Adam's phone continued to buzz angrily, and finally, on the third round, Rico picked it up.

"Yeah, *Mami*, I'm here."

The injured silence on the other end spoke volumes.

"You couldn't talk to me? You had to let me talk to your... *cousin* instead?"

"You know, the fact that you are that evil toward *him* could be one of the reasons *I* don't want to talk to you, do you understand that?"

"He's a bad boy, Rico—he's always been a bad boy. Your grandma says he's the one who made you gay, and I think you need to ask him to leave."

Rico grunted. God, it felt like his whole life he'd been avoiding this conversation. Well, maybe it would be like a really painful bowel movement. Once it was over, he'd feel better and he could flush the stink away. Finn seemed to be the master of this philosophy—maybe Rico could ask him first.

Or maybe Rico could man up and take his own karmic dump.

Yeah, probably that last one.

"*Mami*, when I was nine, Adam was hiding under the bed one day, and I snuck him some lunch. He ate it there, under the bed, and I snuck back into the kitchen for cookies. On my way back, I saw Abuela watching soap operas. I saw the girls in their pretty dresses, and then a boy.... He was tan, and he had blue eyes, and I thought he was so beautiful. I made a noise, and Abuela turned around and said, 'Eh, Rico, the girls are pretty, no?' and I said, 'The boys are way prettier.'"

His mother's breath caught. She might have remembered that day, but not why.

"Abuela spanked me until I couldn't sit down and then told you that Adam made me say something bad. You thought it was a bad word, but all I did was tell the truth—that the boys were prettier. It wasn't Adam. I didn't know about Adam until Easter, same as you did, because he was so afraid he didn't tell any of us. But me, I knew about. I had all these girls in high school and college and I didn't love any of them. After college I grew up, because that wasn't nice, you know? To use people because you couldn't be honest with yourself. So I had *nobody*. I had *nobody* after school. I didn't have anybody until I went to New York. And it didn't work out. But I can't do that anymore. I can't go back to having nobody or the wrong body. So you tell Abuela she's a real bitch, and both Adam and I think so. Tell her that Adam's a better person than she could ever be.

"And then you decide if you want me to be your son, okay?"

He hit End Call and sat still for a moment, breathing hard, while Clopper methodically licked his knee. He'd come out. To his mother. For real. There could be no misunderstanding now, no going back and saying it was a joke because he was mad. What he'd just said? That was irrevocable. A part of him wanted to jump up and down and wield the cell phone in unholy triumph.

Most of him was just sort of shell-shocked.

He'd been dreading that moment his entire life, and now he'd done it. And... oh God. His mother would tell his father and....

And so what?

How often did his father talk to him anyway?

But that didn't stop his hands from shaking in Clopper's fur, and Clopper turned his big broad tongue to Rico's palms. Heartened in spite of himself, Rico started to fondle the silver-gray ears, thinking about the ungainly mixed-breed puppy he'd rescued three years earlier.

Something about that dog... he'd been found in a puppy mill, one of the few surviving animals after a parvo outbreak, and he'd just been so ready to be loved.

Rico had loved him unconditionally, and Clopper returned the favor. For some reason the dog reminded Rico of someone, but Rico had never been able to figure out who.

He was just about to get it—almost had it in his mind—when a phone rang again, this time his.

It was Derek.

"This is Rico," he said, knowing he sounded a little loopy, like he'd been caught sleeping. More like meditating in a quiet room, with only a muted baseball game for company.

"Wow—how *do* you get bedroom voice at eight at night?" Derek marveled.

Rico's smile took him by surprise. "Derek—man, good to hear from you."

"Really? Wow. That's the best greeting I've gotten yet!" Suspicion crept into Derek's voice. "Who died?"

"Nobody," Rico replied, "but I did just come out to my mother."

"Wow," Derek said, sounding as stunned as Rico felt. "Really?"

"Yeah. Surprised me too."

"Why… why now?" Derek's voice rose and fell like they were still bantering, and that made it better. Keep it light, keep it flirty— make it not the end of the world.

"Because I came back to California, but I didn't want to come back into the closet," Rico said, and this was true. "And because damn, I really wish my family would get off Adam's back."

"So what are you doing to celebrate?" Derek asked. "Champagne? Caviar? Clubbing?"

Rico grunted and looked at the tablet he'd set aside. "Finishing my work for Mr. Stewart?" he suggested.

"What, you don't believe in celebration?" Derek jibed. "What would I have to do to get you on the dance floor?"

"A lot of fast-talking *before* eight o'clock at night," Rico returned. "Why were you calling?"

"Well, since I'm not going to see you dance—*tonight*—maybe we can go do something tomorrow. I happen to have tickets to the River Cats' spring training and exhibition game. It's not the Giants, I know, but, you know, first date. Thought I'd start modest."

Rico laughed. "So, River Cats practice? That *is* modest—"

"What else were you going to do?" Derek wheedled. "C'mon… I happen to know Adam and Finn both work—you can't hide in their skirts forever."

"I've been back for a week and a half!" Rico defended. "I got me a new job, a new pain in the ass—that's you, by the way—and I came out to my mother. Dude, I'm calling it a win and going to bed. In an hour."

Derek's low laughter rippled up his spine, and for the first time—
literally the first time—since he left New York, Rico wasn't haunted by
Ezra Kellerman's fathomless blue eyes even a little.

"So, River Cats game? I can't molest you there. Mostly I can just
ply you with beer and belittle your choice of first basemen."

"That's cute that you think I know baseball that well."

Derek sounded scandalized. "You *will!*" he gasped. "When I'm
finished with you, you'll be—" Suddenly his voice dropped and a filthy
laugh echoed over the phone. "Heh heh heh… thoroughly debauched."

Rico laughed in spite of himself. "You just keep hoping. But I'm
good for some beer and some sun and some company," he said, his
chest growing lighter with every word. "You promise to keep your
hands off my ass and it's a deal."

"Oh my God!" Derek whooped. "That was *way* easier than I
planned!"

Rico had an uncomfortable image of Derek jumping up and down
in his underwear. He'd have a six-pack—he worked out after he left the
office every day; Rico had seen him carrying his gym bag. And sandy
brown hair, probably, on his chest and his happy trail, probably to the
waistband of boxers.

Yeah.

Boxers.

Derek would wear white cotton boxers.

And he'd have a tan.

"You, uhm, planned more?" Rico asked, just to get that image of
Derek frolicking in his underwear of choice clear of his dizzy brain.

"Well, I've got you on the phone—I can talk for at *least* another
half an hour. Can you?"

Clopper whined, and Rico realized that Finn and Adam had been
so wiped they'd actually left the dog walking to him. It was the first
time he'd gotten to walk his dog since he'd arrived home.

"Yeah. Yeah—I'll be taking the dog out for a walk, do you mind?"

"No, not at all. Tell me about your neighborhood while you're
out. It'll be… sexy."

"My neighborhood is *so* not sexy," Rico said, sliding on his
sneakers and finding Clopper's lead. Adam hung it neatly from the
hook on the wall. Finn dropped it wherever he was standing when he
unlatched it. Oh, there it was, under the table!

"There's not a lot of sexy neighborhoods near where you live," Derek agreed.

"Wait a second." Rico grunted while he juggled the phone and snicked the lead on the dog's collar. He stood up, huffed, and then said, "How do you know where I live?" before heading out the front door.

"Worried I'll stalk you?" Derek teased.

"Yes. You've already announced your plan to hit on me—haven't you heard of escalation?"

"Hey, you agreed to go out with me. Haven't you heard that no means no?"

Rico had to chuckle. Derek was audacious and fun—and not threatening in the least. "I'm going to a baseball game. I guarantee the only ones getting to home are the players."

"Ouch! I am miffed, sir, miffed, I tell you, that you would think I could be had on the first date."

Rico paused at the bottom of his apartment steps, suddenly curious. "You can't?"

"No," Derek said, just as suddenly serious. "I'm actually—I mean, for a gay man in the city—sort of an old-fashioned guy. I mean… no cheating, no one-offs. Not even when I was younger. I just…."

"Wanted what your parents had," Rico said, but he didn't say it mockingly. If he'd had a functional family, he would have wanted what they had too.

"Well, yeah! I mean, when you meet my parents, you will too."

"Yikes!" Clopper took off at a good clip to the left, and Rico followed, because hey, it was his dump!

"Yikes what? Meet a mugger?"

"Are there muggers in this day and age?"

"There's theft everywhere."

"Yeah, well, my cousin puts out packages for the homeless on all the dumpsters in our area once a month. Sandwiches, clean socks, toothbrushes, that sort of thing. I think that buys me karma." Rico hadn't figured out what he was doing until the day before, when Adam had been making the packages, and he'd been…

Touched. Terribly touched.

As he passed the dumpsters that had been set out for trash collection that morning and not dragged back in yet, he saw that nine out of the ten packages had been picked up. As he looked at the one about a block away, a man wearing rags and pushing a shopping cart picked up the last one, looked left and then right and clutched the bag to his chest before he grabbed his cart and ran away, pushing as fast as he could.

"Okay, two things," Derek said, unaware of the little drama Rico had just seen.

"Yeah, hit me."

"One, why did you say 'Yikes'?"

"Why would you think I'm meeting your parents?"

"Oh," Derek said softly. "I was hoping. Well, that and planning. Finn's parents asked me and mine to their big shindig opening. Some of my people did decorating work in the new store. I was going to go, and I figured you would be too."

"Oh." Rico hadn't thought about that. In fact, if anyone had asked him, he would have assumed that Derek—the boss of the company—would have blown off the invitation, and probably wouldn't have mentioned it to his parents.

But then, that was what Kellerman would have done. Or Ezra.

"Oh what?" Rico heard genuine curiosity.

"I'd... I don't know. Hadn't assumed I'd be going. But yeah. I guess I'll meet them there."

"You thought I was going way too fast."

"Yeah." Clopper walked up to a crosswalk post, sniffed to see who'd been there, and then peed to introduce himself. When he was done, he looked from Rico to the post and then back again, and Rico took the hint and pushed the button.

"Well, now that I know how deep your fear of commitment runs...."

"It... it hasn't been long enough," Rico said. The mild spring night smelled like willow and eucalyptus trees and the nearby river. Pleasant—familiar—but not the concrete jungle of New York. Rico had been looking forward to walking through Central Park in the spring, but he'd never made it.

Well, Sacramento in the spring wasn't bad. True, it only lasted about a week, but it wasn't bad.

The silence on the other end of the line hung heavy, though, and for a moment, Rico thought Derek might be having second thoughts about the next day.

Turned out he was only gauging his prey.

"So, tell me what I'm fighting here," Derek said after a fraught moment. "What sort of damage did he do?"

"Nothing horrible," Rico confessed, realizing he had to say this out loud to believe it. "Just... just, you know. The boss's kid. He'd been around the walk-in closet; I mostly just knew the cupboard under the stairs. I just, you know. Thought when the time came, he'd fight for me."

"Not so much?" Derek asked softly.

"I think he forced his dad to write me a good letter of rec, so that's something."

"That was probably a lot." It was so kindly said that Rico had to remind himself that this was the guy who wanted to replace Ezra.

"Well, his dad wasn't a prince," Rico murmured. Clopper trotted along past the reconditioned Victorian houses—and past some not so reconditioned ones with sagging porches and peeling paint. In the background a siren wailed, not too close—just close enough to give ambiance.

"Yeah, well, it's hard to be yourself when the people who are supposed to love you aren't behind that person you're trying to be."

Rico grunted, and in the silence over the phone, he heard a siren wail.

Wait a minute.

"Where do you *live*?" he asked, and Derek's throaty laughter told him his guess had been on point.

"About two blocks away from the offices. You're on your way there, right?"

Rico looked around and realized that yes, he was wandering that way. "So how did you know where I lived?"

"I'm your boss, I have your address, and I know the area. Are you impressed with me?"

Without meaning to, Rico relegated Ezra to the back of his mind, where the azure of his eyes faded. "No. You're way too impressed with yourself for me to make any difference."

Derek's throaty laughter followed him—with more conversation, of course—around the block as he finished his walk.

When he got to the foot of the stairs of his own building, he paused.

"So, uhm, signing off now." Unaccountably, he blushed. "I'll, uhm, see you tomorrow. What time?"

"Eleven thirty. We can go get something healthy before we fill up with dogs and beer."

Rico smiled. Derek had ordered chicken and sprouts on whole wheat when they'd gone out to lunch. He really was as wholesome as he looked. "Yeah, okay," he answered. "I'll, uhm—"

"Rico?"

"Yeah?"

"You, uhm, like the way I look?"

Rico grinned and patted Clopper's head as he tried valiantly to run up the stairs. "Yeah. Nothin' wrong with the way you look. You know that."

"But I like that you look at me. I like to look at you too."

Rico was stuck, tongue-tied, for three or four breaths. "Uhm, I don't know what to say to that."

"Say you'll look at me tomorrow the same way you're thinking about me now."

"Yeah," Rico whispered, mesmerized by his voice, by his confidence, by the humor and kindness that had permeated their conversation. "I can do that."

"Good. Night, Ricardo. It's been a good convo."

"Backatcha."

"Night."

Derek hung up, and Rico stood at the steps, trying to catch his breath. Clopper nosed his hand, and he took the first step up and then turned to look out into the night.

It was like the sky was a special shade of purple and orange for the sunset in Sacramento. It might not have been better than the colors in New York, but Rico felt like those colors were *his* colors. They were made for him here, when he'd always just been visiting in Manhattan.

How was it he was going to go sleep on the couch of an apartment he'd never made his, but he'd never felt so much like he was home?

Take Me Out

"YOU THINK?" Rico asked after carefully tucking his polo shirt into his slacks and spinning around with his arms out.

Finn's eyes were like a cartoon character's, they were so big. "Uhm...."

"Fine, fine, fine," Rico muttered. He stripped off his polo shirt and folded it back into the dresser.

"The pants too," Finn instructed, arms crossed in front of him.

Rico looked over his shoulder. "Aren't you being a little per—"

"You asked for my help," he said, strawberry brows arched over his blue eyes. His mouth was drawn into a little pout, and Rico wondered for the umpteenth time whether this kid dropped out of a basket full of chocolate bunnies from the clouds.

"I did, but—"

"Are you going to work, Rico?"

"Uhm, no, but—"

"Why would you want to put that kind of distance between yourself and the guy buying you hot dogs?"

Rico stopped, just dead stopped, there in his boxers, his slacks pooled at his feet, while he stared at his cousin's boyfriend. "What?"

"It's fuckin' California!" Finn said, gesturing. "Jesus, Rico—you're going to a baseball game! What would you wear to a baseball game with Adam?"

Rico scowled and started going through his drawers. It was on the tip of his tongue to say that he and Derek needed all the distance between them they could get because Ezra was still looming between them like a big fucking shadow. But he didn't. He'd agreed to this date and he'd stick by it.

He rooted some more and came out with a pair of slim gray poly shorts that he'd just bought in New York because the new spring collection was out and Ezra had taken him to shop for leisure wear. He didn't stop to watch Finn's reaction—he was on a roll. He rifled through his drawers some more and came back with a gray shirt with pinstripe black checks on it. He slipped them on quickly and held his arms out to Finn in triumph, expecting praise.

Finn's horror appeared to know no bounds. "Oh my God. Oh my God." He reached into his pocket, took a picture, and sent it, presumably to Adam.

"What's wrong with this outfit?" Rico asked, at his wits' end.

"Nothing—if you're a fifty-year-old father with Nordic ancestry," Finn said. He stopped waving his arms for a moment. "In fact, you should give it to *my* father! But... God, Rico. You're *Mexican*. Do you know what that *means*?"

"You have to celebrate the Day of the Dead and you can't burp after dinner without your grandmother lighting a candle for your sins?"

"Your grandmother's going to hell—the bad one where nobody remembers you, just so you know. But *no*, it means you can wear *color*, dammit! Blues, reds, greens—hell, I'd settle for a decent brown! You put that gray next to your skin and you look *dead*!"

Ezra had *loved* this outfit. For a moment Rico defended his old lover while he fought betrayal. "You're exaggerating. It can't look that—"

Finn's phone dinged. Finn read it and grinned like a little kid, vindicated. He held it out to Rico, and Rico had to look twice to figure out who the green guy was.

"Oh God—"

"No, read the caption," Finn instructed.

"Tell him he looks fucking dead. Darrin said to put him in my khaki shorts, white tank top, and the dark blue button-up with the bright green slashes on the side."

Rico raised his eyebrows. "He's just going to *dress* me—Darrin doesn't even know m—"

Finn had already disappeared, and Rico grunted, setting down the phone and taking off the offending silver-gray clothes. One of Adam's paintings sat in the right corner of the shot, behind Rico's shoulder, and the color on the phone was dead-on, which meant that Rico really *did* look dead. He'd wanted to look put together and not slutty—dead was definitely overkill.

Finn came back into the living room with Adam's clothes over his arm.

"Aren't you supposed to be at work?" Rico asked, because that had been the plan, right?

"Yeah—I'm asking your date for a ride in. I hope that's okay."

Rico blinked. "You're wha—?"

And at that moment they heard the knock at the door. Finn gestured to the clothes on the couch and waved his hand, shooing Rico to the bedroom while the dog went apeshit all over the apartment, begging to eat the stranger on the other side of the door.

Rico dodged into the bedroom just as Finn greeted Derek, and he dressed in record speed, praying liked he'd *never* prayed about a date before that the family member who'd opened the door wasn't embarrassing the holy hell out of him.

He took a moment to check himself out in the mirror as he was turning away, and he had to stop a little longer. First he messed with the hair, cut ruthlessly short to help style it as it grew out of being shaved. Yup. Black, straight, and gelled—not going anywhere. Then he straightened the collar of the bold blue shirt and made sure the tank was tucked in underneath. Adam's shorts fit him surprisingly well, given that Adam was about four inches taller—probably because Adam was all lean strength and Rico was built a little stockier. The ribbed tank was snug—but then it was meant to be—and the bowling-style shirt actually looked really good with Rico's caramel skin.

Well, Finn probably *couldn't* wear clothes like this, Rico had to concede. With his hair and eyes, it would look garish and clashy—but that didn't mean he didn't appreciate them on.

Rico was just patting down his ass for the familiar lump of his wallet and his phone when Finn shouted, "Rico, I fished your wallet and shit out of the corpse shorts! Stop looking under the bed for it!"

"Oh God," Rico muttered, and then he petted Jake the comatose cat twice for luck and ran out to the front room.

Finn was wandering around the living room, picking up Rico's clothes and folding them to put them away, which was so generous that for a second it made Rico's throat catch. God, he was a nice kid. Then Rico heard what he was actually *saying* to Derek, and wanted to build a life-size gerbil cage so they could lock Finn in it.

"Yeah, he must have been really nervous. He's been trying to find decent clothes *forever*. I appreciate you giving me a ride back to Old Sac—I don't mind if you just drop me off before you go over the bridge to the field. Adam didn't want Rico alone before the big date. Yeah—oh, hey, Rico!"

Rico stood there, looking at Derek and feeling stupid.

Derek knew what looked good.

A River Cats jersey and denim shorts. That was all. But the confidence he wore it with? *That* was dazzling.

However, when he saw Rico, he straightened and gave a low whistle. "Don't you look nice," he said, voice low and suggestive.

Rico had to fight not to go get the "corpse shorts" and throw them on.

"Uhm." That was it. Brain blown. Conversation over. It was going to be the worst date in history.

"Darrin helped us pick it out," Finn said proudly, shoving the last of Rico's clothes in his dresser.

"Darrin?" Derek pulled his alarmingly intense blue-eyed gaze from Rico and back to Finn, and Rico felt like he could breathe again.

"Yeah—he's got a thing for Rico."

Rico's eyes widened, and Derek's must have too, because Finn wrinkled his nose at both of them and shook his head.

"No, no, not like that. Like he had a thing for Adam—wants to give him advice and stuff. He keeps telling Adam to bring him by the store so he can... what was it? Oh yeah. 'Assess the damage.'"

"I had no idea," Rico said, bemused.

"Yeah, Adam keeps telling him to keep his big nose out of your business." Finn started to pet Clopper, who was looking at them balefully, as though he knew he was about to be left alone again. "We'll be back, Clopper. Don't worry. I've got a short shift, Adam's off in four hours—we'll take you to the river and let you run until you pass out." Clopper licked him on the face, and Finn laughed and scratched him behind the ears some more.

For a minute Rico wanted to look away from the intimate moment between some other guy and his *own dog*, but then Derek came over and started petting Clopper, and Rico couldn't have looked away if robots had started humping in the kitchen.

Derek had long-fingered hands—elegant, not like a woodworker but like the businessman he'd made himself into—and they slid into the ruff of muscle and smooth-furred skin at Clopper's neck with fluid ease as Derek gave him a thorough rubdown, complete with over-the-top praise like "How's my beautiful boy? You gonna stay here and be an angel while your daddies all go and party? Don't you worry, Uncle Derek's gonna bring you *the best* treats! Oh yes he is! You'll get fat and then we'll take you running and it will be *glorious*!"

Nonsense, all of it, but Rico's slutty dog, who apparently could be had for a bowl of food and a fondle? Ate that shit up.

By the time Derek stood up and said, "Okay, all, are we ready to go?" Finn was at the door, jiggling his house keys in his pocket, the dog was sprawled on the floor, sated with the ecstasy of all the attention, and Rico could barely walk for the hard-on.

Something about watching a man in a T-shirt get friendly with his dog—Rico had no idea it would be sexy, but as Derek's muscles worked and his friendly ease of command just *ordered* the dog to be happy and asleep, everything in Rico's body from his toes to his nose to all points in between was happy and tingling and ready to be rubbed, scratched, and fawned over just like the damned dog.

Derek turned to Rico, a goofy, dog-loving grin on his face, and Rico just stood there, fully clothed and fully aroused, his mouth parted a little as he tried to get his whole perspective under control.

"Oh," Derek said, his expression changing entirely. "Liked that, did you?"

"Uhm...." The whole date might have died right there as Rico's word brain blew up one more time, but Finn got impatient.

"Uh, guys," he said, one hand on the door, "as much as pet care could count as foreplay, I really gotta get to work."

Both of them shook themselves—much like Clopper, actually— and turned to Finn at the same time before filing docilely out of the apartment and down the stairs.

At the bottom of the stairs, Derek's chariot awaited, cherry red exterior, white upholstery, top down in the spring sunshine.

For a moment Rico was appalled. "You left the top down? In *this* neighborhood?"

But Derek just laughed. "My God, you worry a lot. Get in—but let Finn in the back fi—"

"Woo-hoo!" Finn whooped, vaulting over the side of the car for a sweet butt-landing in the back. "Now Derek, *this* is a car!"

"You don't like the Crown Vic?" Rico asked, absurdly hurt for his baby.

"In the winter? Yes. The black interior works. But on a day like today?" Finn laced his fingers behind his head and grinned. "To Old Sac, Jeeves! And step on it!"

Derek chuckled and Rico rolled his eyes.

"You know, you're sort of a demanding little shit," Rico told him affectionately, and Finn leered.

"Yeah, I know—Adam says so too!"

Both Derek and Rico groaned.

"No!" Derek howled. "I *do not* want to hear about your sex lives. No, no, no, no—"

"Dude," Rico agreed. "I'm sayin'—man, the only way the roomies thing works is if we pretend it doesn't happen."

Finn smirked, his little Cupid's bow mouth pursing in an evil line. "Oh, it happens. Chew on *that*, both of you."

Derek shuddered and started the car in an attempt to flee the vision of Finn and Adam naked together.

"I don't know what *you're* so grossed out over," Rico said over the purr of the engine and the sudden whirr of the wind. "I mean, he's *my* cousin."

Derek's mouth curved up at the side, and he shot a smoldering glance at Rico as he stopped at the intersection. "Not grossed out," he growled soft enough that Finn couldn't hear him.

Rico blushed. Turned on. Oh God. Yeah. Without the cousins thing, the vision was probably shameless porn.

"Oh," Rico said, looking away. For the fifteen minutes it took to get to Old Sac, Rico looked studiously out the window, watching the tree-lined streets in Sacramento stretch luxuriously in the spring sunshine. By the time Derek turned on the cobblestone walk of Front Street, the weather and the smell of green and river had relaxed Rico enough for him to lean back and enjoy the ride a little.

And then he saw that instead of pausing in front of the boardwalk, Derek was finding a place to park.

"But... where... I thought...."

"Well, I wanted to eat at California Fats!" Derek said brightly. "'Cause, you know. Salads. But first I thought we'd stop in and see what kind of candy you liked."

Rico gaped at him while Finn hit the seat back repeatedly with his knee. "Rico, I can't vault out of the back, 'cause then I'd have to stand on top of the leather, and that would be a crime, and we like Derek."

Rico got dumbly out of the car, and Finn hopped out, waved at the two of them happily, and sprinted toward River Burger. Then Rico turned his attention back to Derek, who was smiling gently and gesturing with his shoulder.

"Come on," he said playfully. "Who doesn't like candy?"

"The last time I was here, Darrin fed me a cricket," Rico said darkly.

Derek laughed. "Yeah, he's done that to me too. But see, I think he only does that to people who don't know what they really want."

Rico stopped and squinted at him. "But I knew what I really wanted. I wanted the chocolate truffle—that's my favorite!"

Derek rolled his eyes and tugged at Rico's hand. "Yeah, but those are for special occasions. What's your everyday candy, the kind that you could have one a day after lunch and go, 'That's it. Need for sweet over.'"

"Chocolate truffles," Rico said obstinately.

"You don't eat chocolate truffles every day!" Derek argued. "If you did, you'd be really fat."

"And you wouldn't be hitting shamelessly on me."

"You think your ass was what got my attention?" Derek snorted. "Because seriously, I beg to differ. You could have a massive muffin top, love handles for six, and multiple chins, and I *still* would have noticed your eyes."

"My eyes?" Oh God. Was Rico really that weak? Such an old line, but it got him, oh yes it did.

"Yeah." Derek quirked up a corner of his mouth. "Like chocolate truffles."

Rico's mind flailed, and he didn't find purchase until they got inside the candy store.

"Oh my, look what the dog dragged in," Darrin said as they came in. He eyed them both, responding to Rico's anemic wave with an arched eyebrow. "What can I do you for, boys—or are you here to see Adam?"

"Just trying to get Rico his favorite candy that's *not* truffles," Derek said, grinning cheekily. "Something that will sit through a baseball game and not melt."

"Hard candy is thataway"—Darrin gestured—"but I already know what he wants."

"If you give him the lemon sour, it'll kill him," Adam said, coming down from the high wooden loft.

"Rico doesn't get the lemon sour," Darrin said pleasantly. "He's more a cherry kind of guy."

Adam studied Rico like they hadn't been eating oatmeal together since they were both in diapers. "Yeah, okay. What's Derek? Spearmint?" Then, before Darrin could answer, Adam said, "No. Apple mint. Yeah, Derek? Apple mint—the candy sticks are right there along the side."

Derek grimaced. "Close, Adam, but no cigar. Root beer."

Adam groaned. "*Dammit.*"

"But it's still in the candy stick area." Derek gestured. "So I'd say you're getting as good as the boss."

"He is my assistant manager," Darrin said mildly. "Now go get Derek his root beer candy sticks, and get your cousin his wild cherry."

Adam wrinkled his nose and trod lightly over the dark wood of the sanded boards. He reached above the barrels lined up at the Front Street door and pulled out two boxes, one with dark red sugar sticks wrapped in cellophane and the other with dark brown.

"Yeah, well, Derek won't let me get the boner truffle," Rico accused, and Derek winked at him.

"I'd rather see if we don't need one of those," Derek said smugly.

Rico allowed his gaze to rake over Derek critically. "Conceited much?" he asked before checking out the candy he was apparently specially suited for. Each stick had a label talking about how the candy stick was a classic candy product and how the company made the same product that used to be found in general stores everywhere, and as Rico grabbed a few, he got one of those flashback moments—one that took him back to being a little kid.

Adam grunted next to him. "That sounds like sugar shock waiting to happen."

"Rico's not that sweet," Derek said smartly, taking three of the root beer sticks.

Adam shook his head and looked at Darrin. "My treat," he said gruffly, and Darrin nodded promptly, ringing it up.

"Wait, no—" Derek protested, while Rico said, "Adam, we didn't—"

Adam shook his head and pulled a small brown bag out of his back pocket. "Have a sweet day," he ordered, putting the candy in the bag. "Now go eat lunch. You're making me remember something about a Giants game, you assholes, and I don't want to dream about a day off if I don't got one."

"Yeah, well, Giants game still on the table," Rico said, clasping hands with Adam and bringing him in for the chest bump.

"Damned straight. Now go the fuck away."

"Of course," Derek conceded, taking the bag from him. "I hear you. Going. Thanks, Darrin!"

Darrin did the finger-wave thing at them. "Have a sweet day!" he chimed. "Rico? Not tonight, but soon."

Derek pulled him out of the store and onto Front Street before Rico could ask what that meant.

"God," he muttered, trotting next to Derek as they crossed the street. "I don't even know how he works there. I mean that place is so surreal, and Adam is so... *Adam*."

Derek laughed slightly. "Yeah, Adam is something. Was he that plainspoken as a little kid?"

Rico swallowed a lump in his throat. "No, that's just what you get when you survive the shit he's survived. I... I wish I could be strong like Adam."

"Yeah?" Derek paused as they came up the stairs of the next boardwalk. "Why?"

Rico shook his head, unwilling to put it into words.

"No," Derek said, taking his hand and pulling him down to one of the wooden benches set every so often down the boardwalk. He pulled out a cherry candy stick and handed it over. "Here. Let's eat our candy first. Then, when our insulin levels drop dangerously, we can go have some veggies and protein."

"I'm still waiting for this mysterious baseball game," Rico said suspiciously.

"Well, the training is going on all day, but the game starts in a few hours. So, you know—we got time." Meticulously, Derek shoved the cellophane wrapper down his root beer candy stick and popped it in his mouth, pulled it slowly out, and grinned like a little boy. "So, tell me."

Rico followed his example, shoving the cellophane down and then licking from the cellophane to the tip. He caught Derek's avid look and his face heated again. "That's why," he said after he swallowed the cherry flavor down.

"What's why?" Derek asked, just as quietly.

"'Cause he got his heart broke again and again, and he still managed to pop up. It's brave. I'm... God, I want to be brave for you."

And he did.

Companion, boss—Rico just *liked* Derek so much, and with Derek's mischievous grin and the way his eyes crinkled, Rico *yearned* to kiss him, taste the root beer in his mouth, lick the bit of sugar off the corner of his lips.

But he couldn't. Because when he closed his eyes, he saw Ezra back in his blue spring-weight jacket, the bodyguard at his side.

He saw the good-bye in Ezra's eyes as he put the envelope of lies in his hand.

He remembered Christmas morning, when he'd woken up in another man's bed for the first time and had dared to dream that he'd be out and proud and fuck the rest of the world, just like Adam. And how he'd sat at the Kellermans' table during Passover, had wine poured in his name as the Stranger, and how Ezra hadn't looked at him once the entire evening.

How, even before Ezra and his father had burst into that meeting, he'd known, somehow *known*, that if Ezra had to choose between his father and Rico, he'd choose his father every time.

Or even just the one time.

The important time.

"No need to be brave today," Derek said and sucked on his candy again. But without the crinkle at his eyes and the mischievous grin, it didn't look sexual at all.

"No?" Rico asked hopefully.

"Naw. No bravery. We're going out to lunch and watching a game. Bravery can come later."

Rico smiled. The sun was warming Derek's hair, bringing out the gold that couldn't be seen inside the office, showing his age, which wasn't youthful, like Ezra, but in his early thirties. Derek smiled back, the root beer candy halfway in his mouth, the cellophane-wrapped end hanging out.

"No bravery is fine," Rico said quietly. "'Cause I'm feeling too lazy to conquer the world."

Derek nodded, eyes half closing against the weight of the sun. "That's the spirit. Nothing has to shake the world today."

"But someday," Rico found himself promising rashly.

Derek's smile widened, and although his eyes remained hooded, that smile looked dangerous, like a lion's smile as he lies in the sun, dreaming of meat. "I'll hold you to that," he promised back.

They didn't say much more as they finished off their candy, lost in thoughts of sun and meat.

FOOD, COMPANY, baseball—and sunblock, Derek didn't even forget sunblock. How could it get any better?

They left the car parked in front of the boardwalk after lunch (since they'd been lucky enough to get a nonmetered spot) and walked over the bridge to Raley Field. Rico paused for a moment right over the river and looked out over the *Delta King*, the riverboat that housed a restaurant and a hotel. Classically white, a riverboat with a giant paddle wheel, it was as iconic to the riverfront as the bridge he was standing on.

The heat of the spring sun baked into them for a moment, and Rico shaded his eyes and lifted his face to the wind.

"You forget," he said after a minute. "It's so small. When I lived here, it was the center of the universe. I got to Manhattan and realized how small this city is, and now that I'm back—"

"You think it's small time and can't wait to get back?" Derek asked, something sharp and edgy under his voice—almost defensive, really.

"No," Rico said honestly. "Not at all. I think… I think it fits me."

The lines around Derek's jaw relaxed, and he turned to Rico with a smile that almost glowed. "Good," he said softly. "Let's go buy us some hats."

He started walking across the bridge again, and Rico had to struggle to catch up. "Some hats?"

"Yeah—I forgot my baseball cap, and you're still getting pink. We need some hats."

"That's… uhm, abrupt."

Derek shrugged, his movements overcasual. "Yeah, but, uhm, I was going to kiss you, and no matter how much we like it here, this isn't a great city for that."

Rico swallowed and remembered that moment with the wind in Derek's sandy hair and the almost shy way his lips curved up into a smile. "That's too bad," he said, voice rasping in his throat. "I, uhm, would have kissed you back."

Derek looked at him, nibbling his lower lip like a teenager. "Good. I'll have to remember that when I take you home."

The practice was almost over when they arrived, but they did get to see the players gather near the rail to sign balls for kids before they got called in to put on their uniforms. During the wait they listened to live music, saw performances by local school dance teams, and enjoyed—lived through—a mass choir presentation by the Northern California Honor Choir. Derek bought them hats from the team store almost as soon as they arrived, and then hauled Rico to the beer garden, where they debated light beer and lager and looked out at the proceedings with gentle humor.

"Oh," Rico said, wincing when the honor choir soloist missed her high note. "Oh no. She's not going to recover from that."

They both sat on tenterhooks as the song went to another high place, and this time she took a deep breath and locked her hands over her tightened midriff and hit that out of the park.

Rico and Derek participated in the gentle swell of applause that rolled out in support.

"You didn't think she could make it," Derek said, something about his blue eyes serious.

"It's hard to recover from a screwup," Rico confessed, peeling the wrapper from the front of the bottle absently.

"Is that what you think New York was?"

Rico looked up at him quickly. His blue eyes were kind, yes, but intent. "It was…." Rico smiled. "A learning experience," he said at last. "One I think I'm still learning from."

"Hm." Derek tipped back his beer and finished it off, then held out his hand for Rico's. "One more?"

Rico shook his head. "Giant water," he said honestly. The sunshine and the fresh air made him not want to be buzzed and sleepy.

"Yeah, me too. I'll be back."

He got back and they talked of other things, the time passing as quickly as it had during lunch. When the two teams came out to play, they weren't buzzed in the least, and moving to their seats proved a good opportunity to stretch their legs.

The River Cats beat the Tacoma Rainiers 3-2, with two runs in the bottom of the ninth inning, and by the time the game wrapped, the sky had turned a deep spring purple and Rico was wishing he'd brought a sweatshirt. They were on their way out when Derek claimed to be running to the bathroom.

He came back with two zip-up hoodies in River Cats maroon, and Rico took one in embarrassment. "That's sweet," he said. "Did you want this ba—"

Derek shook his head and smiled that same curiously shy smile he'd shown on the bridge. "It… it was just a really nice date," he said, looking off to the side as they went back over the bridge. The breeze coming off the water cut a little sharper, and Rico huddled into his new sweatshirt, grateful. Accidentally on purpose, he bumped Derek's hand.

Derek uncurled his fingers and Rico slid his palm forward, twining their fingers and squeezing. Derek didn't look at him, but the corner of his mouth peeped up in a little smile.

"Yeah," he said. "Yeah, it was."

Derek drove him back to the apartment with the top on the car rolled down. The breeze carried in the good and the bad—the grease from the back decks of the barbecue joints, the spilled beer from the pub walk, and the eucalyptus, willow, and running water of the riverfront. Some of it was lovely, and some of it was fetid, but all of it was the city, and Rico leaned his head back and let the smells roll over him.

Derek pulled to a stop, and Rico opened his eyes and looked up. The light pollution obscured the stars, but the sky was deep enough he felt like he could look into it for years.

"Pretty," Derek murmured.

Rico turned to look at him. "Surprising," he said softly.

Derek met his eyes. "In what way?"

"You think it's all murky and mysterious and broods over everything, and it's really... very simple."

That pleased, shy smile played with Derek's mouth, and he looked away. "Is that bad?" he asked, sounding so wistful Rico forgot his broken heart and his healing space for a moment.

"No."

Derek met his eyes and leaned forward, then paused to see if Rico was ready to meet him.

Rico was.

Their mouths met, and Rico closed his eyes and fell into the kiss like he'd been thinking of falling into the sky.

Except the kiss was all comfort. Derek held him in place with firm fingers on his chin, and Rico gave himself over to the direction, opening his mouth to Derek's kindness and his urge to give something to Rico that Rico was desperate to take.

Warm and soft, insistent, growing harder, more, until Rico moaned and unsnapped his seat belt, throwing himself practically in Derek's lap in an effort to get closer.

Derek unhooked his own seat belt and swung Rico's leg over his so Rico straddled him, and shoved his hands under Rico's shirts until he touched skin.

Rico groaned softly into Derek's mouth, shaking with the joy of being touched. "Ooh...."

Derek pressed his fingers into Rico's shoulders, and Rico kneaded Derek's chest through his sweatshirt. He whimpered in his throat, wanting more.

"What?" Derek whispered against his throat.

"Skin," he said, tugging at the sweatshirt.

"Shh...." Derek used surprising wiry strength to pull Rico against him. "Slow."

Oh, the hollow between his neck and shoulders was warm and smelled like sweat and sunshine, a little like beer, and a little like faded aftershave. Rico pulled that smell into his lungs, let it permeate his cells, let it ground him. Turned his head, lipped at the side of Derek's neck, then swiped his tongue along the crease of neck and shoulder.

Listened as Derek's "oolf" of arousal vibrated his entire body under Rico's spread legs.

For a moment the position was unbearable. Rico's erection pressed against his waistband, but nothing put any pressure, any friction, any care, on the parts of him that needed friction or care the most. Then Derek slid his hands down under clothing and cupped ass.

Rico collapsed forward, and oh God, their fronts mashed together, and if he canted his hips just *so*, and Derek spread his cheeks and grazed him where he was tender—

"Shh," Derek whispered.

Rico turned his head to tell him that he couldn't, that he needed, that he wanted a hand or a mouth and skin on skin. Derek captured his mouth again, deepened the kiss, and then slid his hands forward and unzipped Rico's fly.

Rico gasped inside Derek's mouth, but Derek didn't stop the kiss. He closed his hand around Rico through his boxers, and Rico groaned, rocking his hips forward rhythmically, until he threw his head back, undone by the intensity.

And opened his eyes and saw the night sky, a few brave stars fighting the city lights.

And realized he was getting a hand job in the front of a Dodge Charger.

And stared at Derek in surprise.

Derek grinned evilly and cupped his neck with the hand *not* stroking his cock. Roughly, he thrust his thumb into Rico's mouth and commanded him to "Suck!"

The thumb in his mouth was both a gag and a filthy reminder of the thing Rico really wanted to suck, and the hand down his pants moved expertly, squeezing, sliding in his precome, tagging his balls.

God. So blatant, so carnal, so unapologetic. No fear of discovery for Derek, just joy.

"Someday," Derek whispered, "you're gonna be sucking my cock."

The words were all he needed. Rico closed his eyes, pulled hard on the thumb in his mouth, spasmed from his knees to his armpits, and came.

He lowered his head to Derek's shoulder, opened his mouth, and groaned.

Derek wrapped his arms around Rico's back and held on, just held him, until the shudders vibrated through his body and ceased.

Their panting echoed in their ears for a moment, and they were alone in the world. Then Rico heard the woman across the corridor from his apartment swearing at her cat and the guy above her cheering for the Giants on television.

"Oh God," Rico said numbly.

"Yeah, we did that." Derek's eyes were half closed and he looked more smug than Adam's comatose cat.

"Oh God."

"Hey, I was going to be a gentleman." Derek smirked.

Rico closed his eyes against Derek's shoulder. "I can't believe we did that."

"I noticed."

Oh no. Rico had come, but…. "Did you? Could you?" Helplessly Rico thrust his hips forward, and Derek's erection pressed back.

"I did not," Derek breathed. "But I think you're too embarrassed to go down on me in the car now, so maybe another time."

Rico was suddenly *starving* for him. He moved frantically, shaking hands to Derek's belt, imagining the touch, the silk of another man's cock, the salt and sweet of precome—

Derek closed his hands over Rico's, and Rico whined, a terrifyingly needy sound, from the back of his throat. "But—"

Derek's open-mouthed kiss calmed him. "But you're not ready yet," Derek said when he'd gone pliant again. "This was a *spectacular* first date. Wanna do it again?"

Rico nodded, the shaft of disappointment painful in his chest. "Yeah," he said. "But—"

"You'll tell me."

A panicked laugh welled up. With Ezra it had been a sudden fall into love and a float into sex. This was a pitch off a sharp cliff, and now Derek was holding him back by the scruff of the neck when he wanted to fly.

Was terrified to fly.

"I'm usually the grown-up," Rico said softly, swinging his leg up and around so he could sit back in his seat. It was a little awkward, made less so by the open roof, and when he was in place, he leaned his head back against the seat and tried to get his head straight.

His come was already sticking his underwear to his pubic hair. That was actually a novel thing for Rico. All things considered, he figured teenagers could keep it. He wanted adult sex, in the bed and everything.

"Yeah?" Derek reached around his shoulder and brought him in close, until Rico snugged tightly against his chest.

"I... I mean, I had no idea how easy I was," Rico muttered, a little embarrassed.

"You know, uhm, when I was in college, I had what I thought was going to be my be-all, end-all relationship."

Rico looked at him, surprised. "Yeah? How did the end-all part happen?"

Derek sighed and stretched his legs out against the floorboards, making himself comfy. "Well, you know. College romance—you had them, right?"

"Not really," Rico said, remembering his words to his mom. "By my second year, I... I was tired of lying. But I wasn't ready to come out, you know?"

Derek adjusted his position and looked into Rico's face, his silhouette blocking out the sky. "So... between college and New York?"

Rico hid his face against Derek's brand-new maroon sweatshirt. "Oh Lord. Yeah. It was, like, seven years of me and my fist and Internet porn." God. He hadn't even told *Adam* that. His *mother* probably hadn't fathomed the extent of his loneliness.

"Wow," Derek said, shuddering. "That makes my stupid college breakup look downright *tame*, you know that?"

Rico chuckled weakly, the comedown from the frantic kiss, the almost-sex in public making him feel vulnerable and sad. "Tell me anyway," he practically begged. "You're sort of... godlike right now. I want to hear about you being human."

Derek laughed dryly and tilted his face back to the sky. "Oh, I was very human. I *cheated*, Rico."

Rico didn't gasp, but he did sort of wake up. "*You?*" Because Derek... Derek was scrupulously honest. Derek ran a clean ship. Derek corrected the person behind the counter when they gave him the wrong change. Derek was so... *wholesome.*

"Yeah." Derek laughed humorlessly. "I... you ever do something you regret?"

"Yeah," Rico rasped. "I let... I let Adam get thrown out of the house on Easter Sunday, and I didn't speak up for him. Didn't come out like he did. Just let everyone think he was a monster, and didn't say I was the same sort of monster."

"Yeah," Derek said, kissing his temple. "The closet does shitty things to us, Rico. Sometimes you can't act like you walk in the sun when you're in the closet. See, I wasn't out to my parents yet either. And Mom was talking girlfriends, and I just... just... had Alec at college, and let Mom push Rhonda at me when I went home. And Rhonda was all for it. She wasn't serious, but she was willing, and... I just had this sort of weird double life. But...." Derek shook his head. "But one day during our last spring break, Alec came up from San Francisco to surprise me, and the whole thing just sort of fell apart."

Rico yearned for water. For coffee. For something to do with his hands.

"That must have *sucked*," he said. "For everybody."

"Yeah," Derek said. "Rhonda was hurt but not too devastated. I think we both knew it wasn't going anywhere. But Alec—God." Derek shuddered. "He was... he was destroyed. I *never* want to hurt anybody like that again."

"He just... just walked out?" Rico asked. "I mean... I mean, I get it. I get why you did what you did. They couldn't forgive you eventually?"

Derek shrugged, and his voice sounded rough and cracked. "Eventually. I mean, Alec and I went back to living together in our dorm and my parents spent the next year coming around. For the most part, they were pretty great, actually. They'd ask, 'Uhm, you're *sure?*' but they didn't pull me out of school or threaten me with anything. They didn't call me names, and they never said they wouldn't love me. They weren't thrilled about what I'd done with Rhonda—but Mom even said they were sorry if I felt pressured into it. Rhonda still calls me every now and then—she runs her own drapery business, and she's a client *and* an employee, so I guess we're good."

"What about Alec?" Rico asked, because this was the important one.

Derek's shrug hid nothing. "We tried. We got back some of our original relationship, but… but not enough to trust. Not enough to plan for a forever. The next time, *he* cheated—with a boy this time—and we both… just looked at each other when I walked in on them. I said, 'I did this. I broke us beyond repair. I'm so sorry.' And then I packed my stuff and moved out of that dorm and into another one. I hear they're still together, and it's been ten years, so maybe I did him a favor, you know?"

"No," Rico said. "No. I'm… why are you telling me all this?"

Derek turned toward him again and brushed his cheek with careful fingertips. "Because I always swore after that to take my life with nothing but straightforwardness and honesty. And I *hurt* after Alec. All of it—the two betrayals, the 'could have beens,' the 'I can't fix this.' My mind may have thought I was ready—hell, my body was made of 'Go!'—but my heart.…"

Straightforward and honest.

Rico closed his eyes and thought of Ezra, of the ways their hands had shaken Christmas Eve, when Rico had been missing a family to celebrate with and Ezra had been desperate, so desperate, to please.

"Still hurts," Rico whispered honestly. "It's getting better, but it still hurts."

Derek kissed him gently on the top of the head. "I'd rather not be just the rebound guy," he said. "I—I mean, I maybe came on too strong at the beginning. But God, I wanted you. Still do." He straightened, shaking Rico off his shoulder, and then leaned across Rico's body and manually unlocked his door.

"But get out?" Rico asked, understanding.

"I want you when you're whole," Derek said, and for a moment, there in the cooling air and the starlight, Rico caught a hint of vulnerability.

For all his assurance, all that he had apparently learned from his past relationships, Derek was afraid of being hurt.

"So," Rico asked, trying not to be hurt too, "this was… what? An experiment to see if I was ready?"

"A first date," Derek said, teeth glinting a little in the darkness. "We'll have a second sometime next week, if you like. And then a third. And then as many as we want to keep going on."

"But…?"

Derek cupped his chin and brought him in for one last hot kiss. "But no sex until you're ready," Derek told him. "You tell me."

Rico looked him square in the eye and nodded. "You're a really good man."

"So are you."

One more kiss—one—and then Rico pushed himself out of the car, sticky-clammy underwear and all.

Quietly he walked up the stairs and into the darkened apartment.

Adam was sitting on the corner of the couch, working the remote and watching baseball on one channel and an old Vin Diesel movie on the other, while Finn was curled up asleep, his head in Adam's lap.

The dog was asleep on his bag in the corner—on his back, all four paws flopping shamelessly on his tummy. The cat was half on the couch, half on Adam's shoulder, drooling.

"How was your date?" Adam asked softly.

"Enlightening," Rico said, reaching into the dresser under the TV to grab underwear and some sleep shorts. "What did you do to my dog?"

"Ran him off his ass. Tomorrow is a day off and we want to sleep in." Adam saw what was in Rico's hand and his eyes narrowed. "That bastard slept with you on the first date? I'll kill him."

"No," Rico hedged. "Spilled something on my pants. Clammy balls."

"You're a shitty liar—just tell me you creamed your jeans and get it over with."

Rico made a noncommittal noise and then despised himself a little, because he liked to think he was more enlightened than that. Rico didn't grunt—he communicated. "Fine. He got me off and then told me it was too early to have sex. And now I feel embarrassed *and* sort of more horny. Have we been honest enough for you?"

Adam shrugged. "Yeah. At least now I don't hate our boss. That sounds like an okay move."

"Glad it meets your approval," Rico said dryly, heading for the bathroom. "You staying up?"

"Yeah—taped the game *and* the show. You want in on this action?"

"You know it. But maybe more the show. I'm over baseball for the day."

Adam sighed. "Yeah, they lost this game anyway. Take your shower and bring me a soda when you're out."

"Yeah. Will do."

Rico got into the shower and let the water sluice down, rinsing away the day and the beer and the almost-sex and the disappointment and the humbling realization that Derek was right about all of it.

As he got out and was toweling off, he remembered something.

"Now remember," Ezra said, *looking like an earnest child trying to keep a secret, "we can't tell anyone or you'll lose your job. And we have to pretend at work, right?"*

Rico had laughed and kissed his bare shoulder as they'd lain in bed watching the Christmas snow through the big bay window from his apartment.

"Not a problem," he said. *"No one to talk to anyway."*

And the next day at work, it felt like none of it had happened.

Adam was waiting in the living room, remote in his hand, thinking that at least their boss wasn't a pushy bastard who would take advantage of Rico's virtue.

He'd told someone.

It had happened.

That made it better than any other sex he'd had ever.

The Dark Fates

FINN'S PARENTS threw one hell of a party.

After weeks of movies and meeting for dinner, as well as a mosquito-bitten Saturday spent hiking up in Auburn, the grand opening fete seemed natural and easy. Just an outing with Rico's not-so-serious boyfriend and his cousin's pretty serious if playful in-laws—nothing to see here, folks.

Held in the picnic area of Reichmuth Park, catered by River Burger itself, and replete with balloons and streamers and free hot dogs for any and all who came by, the opening celebration of the new store really was a place for families.

After enduring another critical wardrobe assessment from Finn, Rico wore a pair of Adam's denim shorts and one of the bright blue River Burger T-shirts Finn had snagged from his father. The caveat, of course, was that he had to help man the barbecue, keep the chips, condiments, and drinks stacked, and help any and all lost children find their way to their parents.

That last one he had to do on more than one occasion, because Finn's dad had asked them to bring Clopper, and the big moo just attracted attention.

Of course, Derek was playing with him too. *Derek* was wearing a purple T-shirt from a local soccer team he supported, as well as khaki cargo shorts and a baseball hat, and *he* was under no such obligations to help with picnic duty.

No. All Derek had to do was be Derek—adorable, flirty, and in charge. Derek was the one who saved Rico from his time on the grill by insisting he'd be a ringer in the softball game. He wasn't wrong, actually, but Rico blushed that he'd remember about Rico playing ball in college.

If they hadn't been playing against Candy Heaven—who had Adam on their team—they might have stood a chance.

As it was, the fourth time Adam hit a ball over the fence on cleanup, Derek jogged after it good-naturedly while Rico looked at Finn's dad with a shrug.

"It's only the third inning!" Finn's dad argued, holding his foot on the bag as the third player trotted home.

"It's 18-2, Dad!" Finn's older brother Peter complained. "Why didn't you snag him for *our* team?"

"Because I have five children!" Mr. Stewart whined back. Adam didn't even smile as he trotted in hard on the heels of a girl with a skunk stripe in her hair, whose kid was cheering from the stands. Clopper knew this kid—he hadn't left the boy's side since the game had begun. "And two other sons-in-law!" he laughed, swatting Adam on the backside with his glove as he passed.

Adam cracked a smile, and a part of Rico melted a little in relief. He'd been so grim when he played, like he owed it to the world not to screw up. Rico had known, though—Adam had always been the better athlete. But it took money and involved parents to participate in high school sports, and Adam had neither. So Rico had gone to college on a partial sports scholarship, and Adam had gone into the military. Watching Adam's shy little smile, Rico wondered sometimes why Adam didn't just explode into pain and bitterness.

And then Finn—who was playing first base—broke family ranks and trotted at Adam with flailing arms. "Adam, Dad says we can quit! You won!"

Adam gaped at him for a moment, but he recovered himself enough to be braced and ready when Finn leaped into his arms and wrapped long legs around his waist. Finn locked lips with him in a kiss that made everyone on the field feel superfluous. At the signal, Derek came trotting in from left field, and together they ran for the bleachers.

"Oh thank God for Finn," he laughed. "There's nothing like invoking the Daddy, Daddy Mercy Rule to keep the rest of us from dropping dead on the field."

"Was that what that was?" Rico asked, bemused. The one thing— the *one* thing—his father had ever come to see was Rico's sporting events. Once Rico had broken his finger in fourth grade and he'd yelled at Rico—voice thundering until Rico had been in tears—all the way to the hospital. *Any idiot knows you don't keep your finger out of the glove.* It was showboating and tacky, and Rico deserved the pain, and he deserved not to play.

"Yeah," Derek said, grinning. "Didn't you ever use that one?"

"No," Rico said, keeping his smile in place. "Never occurred to me." His father, and that suddenly tapped rage, and the stony silences in between. No mercy there. As they moved to the infield, accepting the good-natured ribbing from the other employees at Candy Heaven, Rico had a flash of perspective, that *that* was why working at Kellerman's had seemed natural.

Derek muttered something under his breath, and Rico turned to him, pulling himself completely in the moment.

"What? What's wrong?"

"Nothing," Derek said with a gentle smile. "Nothing—later." He nodded toward the stands and waved. Two people who looked like they'd stepped out of a flier for Middle America waved back wildly, and Rico stared.

"Oh crap."

"Don't let them scare you, Rico—they're only middle-aged people who have spawned and nurtured children."

"Derek, they're *your parents*!"

"They'll love you! C'mon!"

"But Derek...."

It was no use. Derek had jogged the remaining distance across the field and was making his way through the bull pen. Rico had no time to protest that they'd only been dating for a couple of weeks or that their kisses were driving him crazy. He most certainly didn't have time to say he wasn't good with parents—he'd never met any as a boyfriend, actually—and that his own weren't great examples.

There was only time, really, to follow Derek while dusting his shorts off with his glove and trying to smooth his growing hair back with his hand.

"Rico!" Derek called over his shoulder. "Come say hi!"

Oh Lord.

"Oh, this is Rico?" Derek's mom was small and roundish. She'd let what had probably been blonde hair go silver and cut it into a short, practical cap of curls, but nothing could age the blue of her eyes, which were just like Derek's. "Oh, honey, he's handsome. You said he was good-looking, but you've said that before."

The man next to her—fit, in his early sixties, perhaps, with thinning gray hair and a long-jawed face—nodded apologetically. "What was his name? Cameron? Derek, I'm not a great judge of these things, but, uhm...."

"Butt-face," said Derek's mom.

Derek's mouth fell open, and then he winced and closed his eyes. "Uhm, Mom?"

"No? That isn't the term?"

"No, it's… well, it's a horrible term, and it's for women, and it's 'butter face.' But don't use it. Don't ever use it."

"But your brother uses it all the time!"

Derek's voice pitched to that of a scandalized twelve-year-old. "Well, make him stop! Oh my God! He's thirty-five years old! He can't afford to be an asshole like that—he's your only chance for grandchildren."

"There's always Kevin! And what about your sister?" his mom asked, seeming genuinely surprised. "She just got married."

"She should *never* be allowed to propagate," Derek said darkly, and his mom just laughed.

"So, Rico, we saw you make some beautiful catches—Derek said you played ball in college?"

Adam was passing by at that point, and he looked up. "Yeah, he was real good. Good game, Rico!" Then Finn grabbed Adam's arm and tugged him up to the grill, where apparently things were getting dire, because a crowd of kids with dirty cheeks and worse hands looked with doleful expressions at the hot dog plate.

"The hell of it is, he means that," Rico said dryly to Derek.

Derek rolled his eyes and laughed. "That's Rico's cousin—"

"The boy who should go pro?" Derek's father asked. "He's good—damn good. Did he play in college too?"

"No, he went into the military," Rico said, trying not to sigh. "But I don't think he'd be happy playing organized sports, really. Adam's sort of his own guy."

Derek snorted softly and they all saw Finn's dad gesturing toward Rico, fading ginger hair peeking out from under his ball cap, apron stained with everything from ketchup to coleslaw. "So hey, Rico's got to man the grill, but come meet the Stewarts—they threw this shindig. We'll drag him away when we're ready to eat, okay?"

"Nice to meet you, Mr. and Mrs. Huston," Rico said formally, and Derek's mother didn't let him down.

"Oh, call me Sylvie, and this is Edgar."

Rico shook hands with them both and then nodded at Derek as he was leaving. The whole time he was thinking that his mother, should she ever have met one of his friends, would have insisted on Mrs. Gonzalves-Macias.

His father would have insisted on Mr. Gonzalves, and not tolerated any mistakes.

And Adam's mother would have screamed "Faggot!" and had her current boyfriend beat the friend off the property.

So Derek's parents might have been a little out of touch, but they were better than the alternatives. Rico would know.

FINALLY EVERY available hot dog and hamburger had been grilled and Rico and Adam sat down with what amounted to their prospective in-laws.

Rico caught glimpses of Adam every now and then, regarding everyone with big eyes and with the corners of his mouth only slightly turned up.

Nobody seemed to expect too much more from him, though, and Finn's family talked animatedly around him.

Lucky bastard.

Rico himself was in the hands of a master inquisitor, and she had marshmallow cheeks and twinkling blue eyes.

"So, Rico, you're in sales and marketing. Derek tells us you're just back from New York?"

Okay. Softball. "Yes, ma'am. I had an internship in the marketing department for a fabric company. The position ended a little early and I came home."

"So how long did you live in Sacramento?"

Rico swallowed, thinking about his white-walled apartment and how Finn and Adam had added more color to it in four months than he had the entire time before that.

"About six years." The shadows were growing longer, and there was just enough chill in the air to make him wish for the hoodie Derek had bought for him, which he'd left in the car. Or Derek's arm around his shoulder, which he was painfully aware he hadn't earned yet.

"Are you going to stay in the area now?"

Sitting there in the park, you could smell the newly mown hay of some of the outlying areas, the mustard flowers that ran riot for this exact two-week period, and even the river smell from the delta and feeder streams and sloughs that marked the area. The orange and purple of the sunset was tinted amber here in a way that he had seen nowhere else he'd lived—not the Bay Area, not SoCal where he'd grown up, not New York.

Suddenly the pit of his stomach ached to call this place home.

"Yes, ma'am," he said thoughtfully. "I... I mean, my whole life was up in the air until I took that internship. Once I got back here, I realized that however things fell out, I wanted to land here."

Sylvie smiled, pushing the apples of her cheeks up under her eyes, and he thought that Derek got that expression from her too. "You should come visit our place in Woodland," she said enthusiastically. "Before it gets too hot in the summer. We used to have about ten acres of farmland around it, and I farmed that while Edgar was running the hardware store, but when the kids all hit college, we sold that land off for a *fortune* to the university, and now they use it for experimental farming."

"Yeah?" he asked, curious. "What do they farm?"

"Well, from what we can tell, they're working on advanced crop rotation, to see exactly how much of what kind of nutrient each crop pulls out. So they grow *everything*. Sweet potatoes, regular potatoes, okra, sunflowers—it just matters what experiment they're doing." She laughed delightedly. "The best part is that after every harvest, they offer us some of the produce they don't need for testing. It's a lot like running the farm, except without all the work."

Rico laughed, liking her very much. "So what do you do with all of that time?"

Derek's snort of disgust vibrated his slightly sweaty body against Rico's arm. "They *garden!*" he said, outraged as only a happy child could be by happy parents. "Garden. My whole childhood I heard Mom complaining about the harvesting and the weeding and the planting and the stupid combine—every summer it was a choice, right? You can go work the farm or you can go help Dad in the hardware store. And as soon as we hit college, they sell the lot of it and start *gardening*."

"Flowers, Derek," his mother said mildly. "There's a difference."

Rico laughed harder, *loving* the way Derek's cheeks flushed and the way these two seemingly mild people could reduce his Captain of the Universe boss to a flustered little kid.

"Yeah, well, I can think of worse things," Rico said, grinning. His eyes were full of Derek in that moment, and in a sudden breath,

Derek's eyes widened back, and he knew it. The moment lengthened, stretched, until Derek's father ran it over with a clumsy segue, which probably meant it was getting uncomfortable.

"So, Rico, has he talked in his sleep yet?"

Derek's cheeks pinkened in mortification, and Rico knew his did the same.

"Uhm, no, you guys, we're not, uhm," Derek said at the same time Rico said, "Uhm, we haven't, I mean, we just started to, uh…."

Derek's mother turned to his father and smacked him on the back of the head. "Edgar, what in the hell were you thinking?"

Edgar looked down into his plate, which had been cleaned of hot dogs and potato salad for about ten minutes. "Sorry, Sylvie," he mumbled.

"I *told* you not to ask until Derek couldn't hear."

Derek buried his face in his hands.

LATER, NEITHER of them could remember how they got away from the dinner table. Rico had vague memories of Sylvie shooing them to "go walk off dinner," but that was just a guess. It was one of those moments of complete and total humiliation that seemed to jump time, and as they ambled away from the noisy group of Stewarts and friends cleaning up from the barbecue, Rico couldn't apologize fast enough.

"Man, I'm so sorry—I—"

"*You're* sorry?" Derek snorted. "I'm the one with the parents."

"Yeah, but your parents are awesome, but, you know, it's been a couple of weeks, and probably everyone assumes we're sleeping together, and I didn't think about how you'd explain that—"

Derek shook his head and turned, grabbing Rico's hand in the cooling twilight. "We're doing fine," he said, his usual smile wiping away some of the embarrassment. "Yeah, I've had relationships that have lasted as long as it's taken us to get *back* to third base, but you know what?"

Oh Lord. "What?"

"I couldn't talk to those men for hours. None of them wanted to ride in my car the way you do. Those guys? They didn't go out for a baseball game and a beer, and they didn't play on a losing softball team, okay?" Derek brought Rico's knuckles to his lips and then laced their fingers together as he lowered their hands. "We're doing fi—"

Rico kissed him. Oh God. He was so earnest. So much a product of his happy parents. So very, very kind. And *damn*, he was cute. Rico wanted to devour all of that, to fill his soul with it, to be able to just laugh and smile that easily about what seemed to be the most embarrassing of things.

And the feel of his mouth under Rico's was... *amazing*. It transcended hot dogs and soda, even transcended hot and wet. Derek tasted like dust and joy and baseball and *Derek*, and Rico let go of his hand so he could cup both cheeks and plunder and taste and taste and plunder some more.

Derek groaned and pulled back, and their bodies plastered together obscenely close in the middle of a public park in the lowering evening, and Rico's aching erection gave an impatient throb in his Under Armour.

"Oh God," Derek panted. "Where did that come from?"

Rico tried to catch his breath and remember that they were waiting for *him* to recover after all. "I don't know," he breathed. "I just wanted you to know...."

"Know what?" Derek asked, suddenly serious.

Rico smiled slightly and tried not to just haul him into the jungle gyms and make like rutting monkeys. "Know that *someday*, probably soon, I'm gonna see if you talk in your sleep."

Derek's chuckles shook them both, and they pulled apart and started their amble back to the party. Derek bumped his shoulder, though, and Rico found himself being steered to the swing set instead.

"Aren't we a little—"

"Just swing," Derek said, looking far too serious for such a playful request.

Rico sank into the black vinyl swing anyway and pushed off, appreciating the stretch and heave his body had to do to move the swing in its smooth arc. "Swinging, sir!"

"Yeah, obedience is appreciated in an employee," Derek shot back, but he was doing his own push and stretch and heave, and together they swooped up into the purple sky and dove back toward the cooling earth.

Damn, it was fun.

Rico pushed up higher, and higher, and faster, laughing like a little kid—laughing like Derek—until he became aware that Derek had stopped his swing and was just watching as Rico played like a grade-schooler.

Rico couldn't help it, though. He pumped through the air a few more times and then glided to a stop, feet skidding in the safety bark underneath the playground equipment. "Why'd you stop?" he asked breathlessly.

Derek shook his head. "I just…. Never mind. C'mon. Let's go back." He shoved up off the swing and Rico followed.

Without light, Rico couldn't see much about his expression, but something obviously troubled Derek—that much was obvious.

"No, seriously—Derek—" Rico caught his shoulder, swinging him around so they were facing each other. "Not that I'm complaining, but what gives?"

Derek shook his head and shrugged. "I was being stupid," he said. "I'm sorry. I get this… Don Quixote thing sometimes."

"No, c'mon." Rico studied him, unsure of what was wrong. "It's been a great day."

Derek nodded and kissed him on the forehead. "Yeah. It has. I want a lot more like it. I want them with you."

Rico's smile made a quick return and then retreated again. "Then what—"

Derek bit his lip. "I just… I get the feeling you and Adam—you didn't have much of that when you were kids. I just… I wanted to give it to you, that was all."

Rico's breath caught. It was so simple, and so very profound, and so generous, and so…

Impossible.

"That's…." And now he smiled, for once a little older and a little wiser. "That's really sweet, Derek. You know that? But maybe we just work on a happy now, okay?" He shrugged. "A happy then isn't really going to happen."

Derek kissed his cheek. "I can only wish."

"You've got the best heart for that."

This time the kiss hit his lips—but they kept it under control. When it ended, they regarded each other soberly. The sodium lights had just come on, and Finn's and Derek's families were standing around, talking in that lingering way people had when they didn't want a good moment to end.

"Let's go join them," Derek said, the grown-up once more.

They walked back holding hands.

BUT THE words "happy now" haunted Rico, and as they sat in the car talking that night—which had become their habit when Derek drove him home—he couldn't help but think about Derek's easy smile, that core of sweetness, the hidden vulnerability that he kept so skillfully masked.

Derek was in the middle of a rant about the one thing that ever seemed to piss him off—the Los Angeles Dodgers—when Rico turned to him suddenly, brushing his temple with fingertips that suddenly trembled.

"What?" Derek asked, surprised.

"Just… you know. I'm happy *now*."

Derek smiled, turned his head and kissed his fingers. "Yeah?"

"Yeah."

"So, uhm, you want to schedule a sleepover? Like grown-ups?"

"I should get tested," Rico said with a swallow. He and Ezra hadn't used protection. They had seemed so… permanent. So innocent. Stupidest thing he'd ever done, he acknowledged now, but Derek didn't judge.

"You do that," Derek said soberly. "I get tested twice a year. Haven't had a relationship since my last window."

Rico nodded and then laughed at himself. "You're very smart."

"Tell me about him," Derek asked abruptly.

Silence fell for a moment. Really? "Doesn't this violate some sort of—"

"Let's just say I want to know my competition," Derek said, sounding casual. Rico had a feeling—an uncomfortable feeling—that he felt anything but.

"Okay. See, when I first started working for Old Man Kellerman, I thought, 'So this guy's the mentor I've been looking for all my life!' He was ruthless, he was cutthroat, and he didn't let anything get in the way of his business. I still had all my old man's bullshit ringing in my head about giving no quarter, not being soft, and I'd sucked at that, you know? I mean, I'd worked for five years at a little ad agency, and yeah, I made money, but I didn't get a lot of recognition. I was working with the owner's family and they weren't *awesome* at the job, and finally, I was working for someone who could get it done, right?"

Holy God. Just talking about it made Rico realize how stunted his life had been. His father was like, the *anti*-Derek, and working for Derek was the most dynamic, exciting thing he'd ever done.

"I know the type," Derek said darkly.

"Yeah, well, I didn't. I mean, I *thought* I did, but I hadn't realized, you know? And then Ezra and I started working together, and… he was like… like this gorgeous, exotic flower, and his father was Old Man Winter. And he sort of bloomed whenever I walked by. And *God*, isn't that powerful? To just be the reason someone blooms? But… I mean, I didn't get it, but I do now. This last month, really." Rico's face heated. "Working for you. Living with Finn and Adam. You all are… your whole selves were completely realized, and then the other person just made you better. But you were flowers already, you know? You—straightforward, honest. Even when you fucked up, that part of you was still there. Adam—strong, kind. He *was* that flower before he found Finn. Finn just saw it first. And Finn—an act of fuckin' God couldn't make that kid any more or any less than he already is. So Ezra—he needed to get out from his old man without me. Or at least have the strength to do it when I was there. But he didn't."

"Did you ask?" Derek asked gently.

Rico swallowed hard, his eyes burning. "Yeah," he whispered. "Kellerman was throwing me out of his office in front of the whole fucking world, and I said, 'Come with me,' and Ezra said, 'Just go.' And he came to give me my plane tickets—my payoff, really, for getting the fuck out of there immediately—and I said, 'Come with me,' and he… well, he was hustled out by his bodyguard, but he didn't fight it. He's a grown man. He makes business trips, he has his own bank account and a degree, same as me. That's twice I told him 'Come with me,' and twice he walked away."

Derek nodded. "I should make you ask him a third time," he said, mouth twisting. "You know, like the fairy tales? But I won't."

Rico nodded. "I appreciate that," he said weakly. "I, uhm, don't think I'd offer it right now. I… I mean, I get it. I wasn't out of the closet either—not to my mom and dad. But I was going to. When my internship was over and it looked like I had a job and a future all mapped out rosy fine? But I came out, and my mom gave me a chance to back out of it, and I told her I meant it. And Ezra had the same chance, and he went back in."

"Why didn't you go back in?" Derek asked. "Why is that?"

Rico smiled a little. "'Cause… 'cause Adam's happy. And 'cause you and Miguel, you're good people to hang out with. Even if you and me don't… you know. If we didn't." He blushed. "If we weren't gonna…." And more blushing. "I mean, good people. I can't… you can't shit on that, you know? My parents, they followed all the rules, but they were like Kellerman. Old Man Winter had nothing on 'em."

Rico turned his head and breathed deeply through the open window. "I really fucking love the spring and the summer. Even the autumns here, where it doesn't get cold until goddamned November. I don't need snow to be complete, you know what I'm saying?"

Derek captured his mouth, surrounded him with warmth, and just when Rico started to think he'd melt, Derek pulled away. "I've got a pretty good idea," he murmured throatily. He slid his fingers up along the base of Rico's skull, and his fingers, massaging through Rico's hair, were the best reason yet to grow it long.

The kiss went on, and on, growing urgent, because they were both horny, but restrained, because they were grown-ups this time, and they knew what they wanted, and the best part about being a grown-up was that you got to wait for when it was good.

They pulled away, and Derek breathed in the hollow of Rico's ear. "Get tested tomorrow," he murmured. "Friday night, I think maybe you and me are going to watch movies at my place, you good with that?"

Rico moaned a little, because... oh God. His cock ached and his skin tingled, too tight on his muscles, and his muscles vibrated, too tight on his bones. "I want you *so* damned bad," he muttered. "You know I can't get off, right? I *sleep on the couch*. I can't even beat off in the shower because there's three guys trying to take a dump in the morning."

Derek chuckled, the sound filthy and evil. "This morning I imagined your mouth on my cock," he said, shocking Rico badly. "And I licked my palm and stroked myself and came all over my fist."

Rico moaned again and then reached into his pants and tried to adjust his aching erection for just a little comfort, a little ease.

"Are you jerking off?" Derek asked, surprised.

"No," Rico panted, undulating into his hand because dammit, it was *there*. "I'm just trying to make ro—"

Derek cut off his blatant lie with a blatantly carnal kiss.

And then he removed Rico's hand and replaced it with his own.

Rico returned the favor this time, and it was awkward, because for all their talk of being grown-ups, hello, they were making out in the goddamned car *again*, but this time he circled Derek's cock with his own fingers and had the exquisite pleasure of Derek groaning into his mouth.

And then it was fast and dirty, a race, the pressure of Derek's roughened hand on him, the silk and slick precome of Derek's drooling cock in Rico's hand.

They bucked, and ground, and Rico couldn't tell which one of them came first, because the hot spill of Derek's spend on the backs of his fingers was as glorious as the starburst of orgasm behind his eyes.

When breathing became a thing again, Derek groaned in the not-sexy "oh crap!" sort of way.

"What?" Rico asked, trying to see straight. "You're professing your profound gratitude that I live in sort of a shitty neighborhood?"

"No," Derek rasped. "I'm expressing my profound disgust at having to go home with jizz in my shorts."

Rico laughed shortly. "Welcome to the party, pal."

Derek wiped his hand off on the inside of his shirt and laced his fingers with Rico's in the dark. Derek's hand was a little moist, and a little hot, and shaking just the slightest bit. "Sleepover," he said, trying to convince himself. "I'll come get you Friday night. Grown-ups. Real. We're making this real."

Rico brought Derek's hand to his mouth and turned his palm, lipping it gently, nuzzling it, licking the salt part of the center. "It's very real," he assured him, not sure why he felt the need to. This man… was a good son, a good brother, a really awesome boss. He was a person—a hot person with muscular shoulders and an almost smooth chest and pretty blue eyes and laugh lines that crinkled in the corners of what had once been a freckled face—but all of that *appeal* made up the least of his personhood.

He wasn't a dream, or an image, or yearning under a snow-lit black sky.

Derek was *real*. And everything he'd done in Rico's life so far had been made of the sort of kindness Rico had only dreamed about.

Derek's whimper was real too. "Don't tease me," he half laughed, half begged. "Don't promise if you don't mean it."

"I promise."

He meant it. It would come true.

THE NEXT week was *busy*. Rico finished his strategy for Finn's dad and then began to implement it because he wanted to see it work now that the place was open for business and they could stream customers there. He caught two more clients from Derek and then sat down to figure out if he could devote all his time to just those clients and give them their absolute money's worth.

Derek approved enough to kiss Rico behind closed doors, just once, and not carnally at all.

The kiss almost exploded all over Derek's desk, and Rico practically ran backward and leaned against the window treatment, panting badly and adjusting himself in his pants.

"Jesus, we're horny," he said, trying to make the moment light.

Derek was still seated, head buried in the crook of one elbow while he fixed himself with his other hand. "Ten years—*ten years* and I've never hit on an employee. Now I know. *Now* I fucking know."

"Never?" Rico asked, trying to distract himself from the taste of Derek's mouth *still on his tongue.*

Derek looked up from his arm with something like desperation. "I hit on Adam, and he was cute. But God, Rico, I saw you sitting there in the sunshine, and you were.... *God*, you were... and then I talked to you, and you were *fun* and smart, and you wanted to do your job with a good heart, and—"

Rico realized that Derek needed him. Just seriously *needed* him.

He ventured across the office and leaned over the desk, kissed Derek on the top of the head, and stroked the backs of his hands. "I didn't know that," he said quietly. "You... you've got all this confidence, Derek. It's hard to know where the confidence stops and the guy begins."

"Well, right now he's beginning to dread watching you walk through the door," Derek half laughed. "You *swear* there will be a sleepover?"

"Yeah," Rico said with a gentle smile before nuzzling Derek's temple. *Please tell me there's Christmas, please?* "I promise. You and me are moving to the next level. And we'll stay in bed on that level for at least three days."

"And there's no one else," Derek said, looking up and meeting his eyes.

Rico swallowed. No Ezra in his heart anymore. It was a scary thing to think about.

"No one else," he promised. *Please let me be telling the truth. I don't ever want to hurt this guy. That would be the worst thing I've ever done.*

Derek nodded and sat up straight and organized the stuff on his desk with a meticulousness he usually avoided. "Okay," he said, pretending he hadn't completely lost his composure. "We'll plan on that. I'll come get you at seven tomorrow."

Rico nodded, his heart beating about a thousand times a minute. "Yeah," he said roughly. "I'll tell Finn and Adam they can have all the monkey sex they want."

Derek shook his head in disgust. "You know, I really don't think our sex life and your cousin's sex life should be so closely related, you think?"

Rico shrugged. "Yeah, well, they're usually pretty quiet. I like to think sometimes Adam lets loose too."

Derek grimaced. "I forget. I shouldn't, but I do. Your cousin... he's, like, proof, right?"

"That the walking wounded can still fight? Yeah."

Derek nodded. "Okay, then. We'll think good thoughts for him. But *not* on our weekend."

"Deal."

FINN AND Adam were going out Friday night too. Finn wanted to take Adam dancing, complete with a new shirt, something eggplant purple and tight across Adam's impressive chest, as well as pants that Rico wasn't sure would allow Adam to breathe.

Finn wore cutoff jeans and a fishnet tank top, because hello, it was ninety degrees outside, and he spent a good half an hour convincing Adam that, no, he did *not* look like a rejected seventies porn star, before Adam looked at the clock and said, "Fuck, it's almost seven. Let's get the fuck out of here so we can get back and shower before ten."

"Does something turn into a pumpkin I don't know about?" Finn asked facetiously.

"Yeah, my...." Adam looked at Rico and blushed. "Never mind. I just don't foresee this being something I want to do for hours on end."

Finn rolled his eyes at Rico. "Yeah. Mr. Try New Things he is *not*. Have a good time, Rico. When we gonna see you?"

Rico shrugged. "Uhm, unless you need me to take care of Clopper, I was, uhm, thinking, Monday evening?"

Adam blinked, assimilated, and shrugged. "Yeah. Okay. Got condoms?"

"We both got tested," Rico said, smiling because Adam *would* ask that. "We're both clear."

"Fuckin' awesome. Don't forget lube."

"There's extra in the bathroom," Finn said helpfully, and then he waved a flirty little wiggle of his fingers. "Bye!"

Adam threw open the door and froze.

"Holy mother of bitch-screaming shit-fucking harpies," he snapped. Then he slammed the door and turned around, leaning on it like he was fending off zombie hordes outside ready to eat his brains.

"Adam?" Finn asked, concerned. "Adam, baby, who were those women?"

Adam looked at him from big brown eyes in a shock-white face. "Mothers. Everybody's fucking mother. God, Finn, do we have to go out there? Man, I fucking moved here to get the fuck away from them. Can we just… just hide under the bed until they go away?"

Outside, Rico heard three *very* familiar voices screaming in Spanish and a heavy fist on the door.

"Oh fuck," he muttered. "Adam, seriously?"

Adam nodded but didn't look at him. "I've got to… I've got to…."

Finn, on the other hand, ran to the bookshelf in the kitchen—the one where Adam kept his art supplies—and started to rummage around.

He came back with a charcoal drawing Rico couldn't quite make out, and then coaxed Adam to move aside, kissing him on the cheek and nuzzling his temple while Rico went over and tried to get the door handle so he could go outside and deal with his business.

Finn got there first.

They sort of slid Adam to the wall, where he was still staring, shocky and glassy-eyed at the ghosts of his past, when Finn shoved out the door and started screaming back at the women *in Spanish.*

That made Adam's eyes focus and widen. "Holy crap."

"He speaks it better than we do," Rico said in wonder.

"He never had reason to hate it," Adam said darkly. Then he stood and squared his shoulders. "Okay. I can't let him do this alone."

Rico shook his head. "I can't let you do it *period*. They're here to see me—fucking with you is just icing to them. Go, get your boy, and leave. They'll stay here and I can finish this."

Adam shook his head. "Naw. Strength in numbers. C'mon, man. Let's go do this." With that he pulled the door open and stepped outside.

Finn was still yelling—and surprisingly enough, the three women in the hallway of the walkup had stopped talking long enough to listen.

"You see this? This is what you tried to make him into," Finn shouted, his Spanish flawless. "You wanted him to be small and scared and nobody. But he's *everybody* to me. So you keep your nastiness and your venom away from our home, *qué*? We don't need you. We're *happy*, and not one of you has ever been happy in your entire miserable lives."

Adam calmed him down with hands on his shoulders and a whisper in his ear. Rico didn't hear what he said—he was busy facing the three tiny women who had caused so much chaos.

Adam's mother was the odd duck out. She wore her long graying hair pulled partially back, with the rest in a wavy mass falling to her shoulder blades. She'd dyed it, but not recently, and about an inch of gray showed, and her deeply lined face showed years of hard living. She was dressed in jeans that hugged tight to her over-generous hips and a tatty pink velour hoodie with a ragged row of sequins on the bottom.

She glared at Rico through two pounds of makeup like it was his fault she'd been hauled on a plane from San Diego to yell at her blood relatives, and Rico glared back. God, she'd been a bitch—*such* a bitch—to Adam.

She stood shoulder to shoulder with Rico's mom, who, although a few years older, looked about twenty years younger. Lydia Gonzalves-Macias wore sensible black pumps and an elegant, timeless black suit with a gold collared shirt under the suit jacket. It was the kind of thing she'd worn to work every weekday he could remember, and her hair— blown and gelled smooth—was up in an elegant chignon at her nape. She wore her makeup understated and her delicate hoop earrings in gold, and the look on her face was so decidedly neutral that Rico felt a wave of rage. Always the good girl, Rico's mother. Always the one who did the right thing, who toed the line between Rico's demanding father and frigid grandmother, never once standing up for anyone in their path.

In the center of the pyramid of hate stood the grand matriarch herself.

Helena Macias didn't *look* that imposing. She stood shorter than both of her daughters by a good four inches, and her own hair, long since gone gray, was styled in careful short curls around her lined face.

Her little black eyes glittered in the network of wrinkles and scowl lines like a snake's.

"Hola, harpies from hell," Rico called, feeling his jaw tighten. "Don't you have small children to frighten? Husbands to please? Dogs to euthanize?" Clopper was going *ape*shit in the house, and that last vicious dig at Adam's mother made her flinch. Yeah, he'd never forgiven that woman for putting down Adam's dog when he shipped out. If nothing else, as a man serving his country, Adam had deserved better.

"We're being serious, Rico—" his mother began, ignoring the digs at the three of them, but of course his grandmother interrupted.

"Stop this foolishness," she snapped. "You are no more gay than this one"—she spit in Adam's direction—"was a hero."

Finn leaped at her—a full-body leap—and Adam caught him around the middle before his hands made contact with Helena Macias's aristocratically boned face.

"*I'll fucking kill her!*" Finn snarled, and Adam gave Rico an agonized look before throwing Finn over his shoulder and opening the door behind Rico.

Of course, Clopper took the opportunity to make his escape, and Rico had to grab him by the collar as he lunged through the door for the three women.

Finally, *finally*, they took steps back, the two mothers going flat against the doorframe of the apartment across the hall and Grandma Macias ending up practically in their laps.

"Would you silence that fucking animal!" Adam's mother, Lucy, shouted. "Jesus, asshole, shut him up or I'll put him down!"

"You lay a hand on my dog, lady, I'll have you arrested," Rico snapped. "You three flew out from San Diego to do what? Yell at me? Threaten my dog? Piss Finn off so bad he practically commits battery? What in the *hell* are you doing here?"

"Your father doesn't like this, Ricardo," his mother said, making her voice strong. Well, yes, all of her clients thought she was strong. They had no idea she was just doing as she was told. "He says for you to stop this… this *gay* thing right now and come home, and we'll find a nice girl and—"

"And I won't sleep with her," Rico said, still pitching his voice above Clopper's. Jesus, the dog wouldn't shut up, and Rico didn't even want to make him. "So you either accept me as I am and let me come down for Thanksgiving and Christmas, or you don't, and I'll stay here and you can live back down south and we *never* have to see each other again."

"It's *him*," Grandma said, pointing her sharp little chin at the door. "*He* made you this way. I told you, Lydia, you let your boy lie down in trash, he'll pick up the stink!"

"Adam's the only family I care about!" Rico yelled.

"Rico!" his mother protested, and the hell of it was, she sounded truly wounded. Her eyes glittered with tears and her chin trembled.

"Dammit, *Mami*—you couldn't have come here yourself to talk to me? You had to bring *them*? Just once, couldn't you have been brave enough to want to love me for me?"

"Instead of what?" his mother demanded. "What *he* made you do?" The venom—and disgust—were unmistakable, and Rico fought the urge to vomit.

"That's *gross*," he snarled. "Oh God—no. He's my *brother*—"

"He's the little bastard *she* wouldn't give up for adoption," his grandmother pronounced, and Rico—God help him—almost let loose his death grip on Clopper's collar.

Suddenly Clopper calmed down, whining subserviently, and footsteps sounded on the stairwell.

"Jesus, Rico, what's wrong with Clopper? He doesn't bark like that at *anyone*!"

Derek took the last few stairs, his face open and pleasant, because he didn't expect to find a Mexican soap opera on Rico's front door. Rico could only be grateful the lady who lived across the way was either asleep or shopping, because she could have given Grandma Macias a run for her money as far as vicious old bats were concerned.

"Derek," Rico said, the relief in his voice a little pathetic. "Oh my God. *Derek*. I am *so* glad you're here."

He looked good. Loose jeans, a microfiber shirt—sort of casual dating at its best. But Rico could tell he'd just shaved, and probably just brushed his teeth, and maybe even changed his shirt a couple of times. He wanted this to be nice, and Rico had been... oh, God, he'd wanted to erase the memory of anyone else's touch on his skin.

"Yeah?" Derek put a calming hand on Clopper's head at the same time he leaned forward for a kiss.

Rico didn't even think twice. Just leaned in and touched lips with him, smiling in gratitude. In front of them, he heard three shocked gasps, and Derek's eyes widened as he pulled back.

"So, uhm, ladies? Are you related to Rico?" He smiled winningly at Rico's mother. "*You* look like you could be his sister, but I know he doesn't have one. Are you his mother?"

"Rico, who is this *bastardo*?" his mother asked in Spanish.

Rico flinched from the obscenity. "*Mami*," he said, continuing in Spanish, "either talk to him in English or—"

"Ma'am, I promise you, my parents are happily married and living in Woodland," Derek replied pleasantly in Spanish. "And I was *so* looking forward to meeting Rico's family. I think very highly of Rico, and of Adam, and I was hoping the apples hadn't fallen far from the trees." Derek narrowed his eyes. "I understand now that they were apparently catapulted to the other side of the state."

"*Mami*, this is Derek. He's my boyfriend. We were on our way out—and so were Finn and Adam. We'll be out in five minutes, and if you don't want to see any gay people holding hands or kissing, you three had better be the *holy fuck* away from my place."

"But Rico!" his mother complained.

Rico shook his head, thinking of Finn and Adam and Derek and how much he loved them all. "You can't be mean to these people, *Mami*. And if you can't be mean to them, you can't be mean to me. If you got something to say that's not mean, you come back and say it to me yourself." He glowered at his grandmother and Adam's mother. "You two—if you ever come here again, I'll let my dog loose on you. *Nobody* treats Adam that way. Not anymore."

With that, he reached behind him and hauled Clopper back inside, leaving Derek to slam the door in their faces.

As You Mean to Go On

THE MINUTE Rico let go, Clopper bounded for the bedroom, whining and scratching at the door when nobody opened it.

Rico and Derek sagged back against the front door in relief.

"That was…," Derek began delicately.

"Awful," Rico supplied, letting him off the hook. "Fucking awful. God. Adam. He had to carry Finn away. They were so awful, Finn almost jumped them. Can you imagine that?" His voice shook, and so did his hand as he wiped it over his mouth.

God. Family confrontations. He'd been the good boy his whole life so he didn't have to live with people being ugly to him. And he'd just *done* that.

Suddenly Derek's body warmed his space, and Derek embraced him, pushing him against the door in an effort to get closer to his skin.

Rico clung to him for a second for support, for care, realizing he might not have had the strength to do what he'd just done if he hadn't known he had people when it was over.

"Finn really attacked them?" Derek asked.

Rico nodded into his shoulder. "Grandma Macias spit at Adam. Finn lost his shit."

Derek let out a low whistle, and in the silence that followed, they could hear Finn sobbing through the bedroom door. "God. Poor Adam."

Rico looked up and smiled crookedly. "Poor *you*. You were pretty awesome, you know?" He pulled away, reluctant to leave Derek's heat. "Let me go check on them." He sighed, thinking about the suppressed excitement in the apartment ten minutes before. "They were going dancing—I'm thinking not so much now."

He walked down the quiet hall and rapped softly on the door. After a pause, Adam opened the door a crack, his face set in stoic lines. No, Adam wouldn't cry, not after that.

Clopper, seeing his opportunity, whined and pushed inside the bedroom, and Rico got a glimpse of Finn lying in the middle of the bed, face buried in a pillow.

"They gone?" Adam asked gruffly.

Rico shrugged. "If they're not when we leave, I'll call the cops myself," he said. "You guys don't need to talk to them again."

Adam squinted. "We?"

"Derek showed up. He was awesome. Apparently all the white people speak Spanish better than we do."

Adam grunted. "That's something I did not expect. So, you guys taking off?"

Rico swallowed, unhappy about just leaving it at that. "You know, Finn had the right of it," he said seriously. "They shouldn't have said those things about you. They should *never* have said those things about you. Those women—my mami included—they had no right to make you what was wrong with their lives. I'm almost glad Grandma kicked you out. They'll leave you alone now. I'd *pay* them to leave me alone."

For the first time, a crack appeared in Adam's stoic façade, and he threw a glance over his shoulder at Finn. "He, uhm... it hurts him when people aren't good to me," he said apologetically.

"It's okay if it hurts you too," Rico said. Maybe before they'd roomed together for a month, he would have felt self-conscious about the kiss he placed on his cousin's forehead, but he didn't, not now. "You're a good person. It should hurt when people are awful." Rico stepped back and looked down the hall to where Derek was watching compassionately.

"You go," Adam said softly. "Thanks, Rico. I'm sorry for you too. You've always been the good boy. You didn't deserve that."

He closed the door, and Rico was left staring at what used to be his bedroom door.

"You've always been the good boy too." He left then. Adam had Finn, and Derek was waiting.

GIVEN THE subdued mood when he grabbed his overnight bag and they got into the car, Rico was surprised Derek didn't just drive him to his mysterious house near his office.

Instead, he braved the Friday evening traffic to take him to Rick's Bakery, and Rico found himself sat down in front of a giant helping of tiramisu before he could even mention that they hadn't had dinner.

"Is this your way of saying the weekend's off?" he asked suspiciously when they were settled on the patio. The place had patisserie ambiance—white-painted wrought iron tables, pink napkins, a giant slice of chocolate cake in the window. It was the kind of place that made you crave carbs, and Rico was surprised that the man who ate chicken and sprouts every day for lunch would even know where it was.

Derek recoiled. "What? Oh no. *Hell* no. This is my way of saying sometimes you need your dessert before your dinner. This qualifies as one of those times."

Rico smiled at him, a line of tension between his shoulders and down his spine loosening. "So what's for dinner?" he asked, delicately cutting into his dessert and then taking a bite.

"Hamburgers," Derek said pragmatically. "I mixed the meat and the seasoning and left it in the fridge. I thought we could sort of build our own."

Rico let the dessert dissolve on his tongue while he shuddered in ecstasy. Oh great heavens, that hit the spot! "That sounds great," he said sincerely. "And I'm gonna really need the protein in about an hour." He opened his eyes reluctantly and moved his knee to brush Derek's. "But this was a nice idea. Thanks."

"So, you and Adam?" Derek asked, and Rico realized he might want a better explanation. Maybe *deserved* one.

"See, Grandma Macias watched us after school when we were growing up. Adam's mom had him out of wedlock, and… they were awful. They fought constantly about it, and Adam… God. He spent most of his time under the bed. Just this sensitive little kid—I mean, you can't tell now because he never talks, but he's got this heart…." Rico shook his head. "And my mom… well, she graduated from college and met a rich Mexican Catholic who never talked and thought children should be seen and not heard."

Derek sucked in a breath between his teeth. "Wow—that's the first time you've ever really talked about your father." He sounded a little stunned.

"Well, that could be the first time there was something to mention," Rico replied, hopefully with dignity.

"That's a lie by omission, Rico, and you know it," Derek told him, and for the first time since Rico had met him, he actually sounded a little hurt.

"What's wrong?" Rico took another bite of his dessert, hoping for another rush of joy that had eased some of the awfulness of the harpy tribunal he'd just kicked off his doorstep.

"Just...." Derek shook his head and bit his lip, looking away. "Just, I've heard more about your old boss than I have about your father. And... you just... I don't know. You never complain about your ex—"

"I thought that was bad form?" Rico said, looking up. He seemed to recall *that* much from dating.

"It is!" Derek assured him. "It's just... I don't know. I hope... you know... if we ever break up, I've made a bigger impression on you."

Rico's mouth fell open, and for a moment he seemed to see clear through Derek—and for the first *real* time, he saw that for all his confidence, Derek was just as susceptible to self-doubt as any other human being on the planet.

Maybe even more so.

"Derek, I... the way I feel about you is *nothing* like I felt for Ezra. I mean, Ezra was sweet, but he was.... God, he was transient, you know? Nothing about us—about *him*—was fully formed. He was looking for someone who could save him, and he wasn't ready to save himself. I...." Rico smiled. "God—do you *know* how happy I am to come to work each day? How happy I am to see you? You get such *joy* out of things. Playing softball, watching a game, petting my cousin's big stupid dog—"

"I thought it was yours!" Derek said, looking bemused.

"Yeah, well, the dog decided different. Anyway, you're just so much *bigger* than that. So much more real. God, Derek, how could you not know I feel so much more for you?"

Derek smiled crookedly. "Maybe because your dad was never there, and you don't know how to tell me?" he said, sounding uncharacteristically like a slightly lost child.

"Oh," Rico said softly, looking into those wild blue eyes. The lashes were a little spiky, and his lower lip was red from worrying. Rico reached out and eased it with his thumb. "Okay. So I can tell you now. You're really fucking important to me. You...." Rico smiled a little. "You sort of just blazed into my life, you know? I needed... I don't know... a star to follow, and you were just so bright. But you're human now. I think...." He blushed and looked away.

Derek captured his hand. "Think what?" he asked, the urgency in his voice giving him away.

"I think you're more beautiful that way," Rico confessed shyly.

He looked up, and Derek was biting his lip again, just as shy. "Yeah?"

"Oh yeah."

Derek nodded like he'd expected it all along, breaking the mood by clapping his hands in glee. "Oh yeah. I'm getting some tonight!"

Rico laughed and took another bite of tiramisu, then held it up for Derek to take a bite.

Derek did, his eyes sparkling as he savored and swallowed.

"You know what?" Rico said, smiling as the tension and the sadness melted away like sugar. "You might be right."

Rico's cell phone started buzzing then—it was his mother. He texted Adam to get in touch with him through Derek and turned his phone off, winking cannily at Derek as they stood up to leave.

"You sure you want to do that?" Derek asked, some of his confidence back in place. "What man in the twenty-first century wants to live without his cell phone?"

Rico's stomach rumbled, protesting the sugar overload, and he laughed. "A hungry man who doesn't want to talk to his mother!"

"Ooh—*sexeh*!"

God, Rico hoped so. He had to have *something* to offer after the debacle on his doorstep.

DEREK LIVED in a small brick house about two blocks from his office. It sat, out of place among all of the Victorians in various stages of refurbishment, squat and red and charming as a gingerbread domicile in a European country.

"That house is…."

"Hot as fuck in the summer," Derek supplied glumly. "The first thing I did was put misters on the front and back porches so a cross breeze would actually cool it down."

Rico grinned at him, a little relieved. "I was going to say too cute for words."

Apparently Derek had made use of his own gardening services—the neatly maintained brick flowerbeds along the walkway were planted with daisies, pansies, and tea roses, and the effect was cheerful and colorful at once.

Derek laughed. "Yeah, my mom—she saw those beds and decided she was absolutely not going to rest until I lived in the cottage of the three bears."

Oh, damn. Well, there went a whole other preconception. "So, did she do the decorating too?"

Derek led the way into the neatly swept alcove and opened the wooden front door with etched stained glass at the top. "Uhm, no," he murmured, stepping aside so Rico could go first. "I, uhm, did that."

Rico paused in the small foyer and looked around, whistling lowly. "Well done!"

Derek's choices were unapologetically male—low-pile berber carpeting and comfy leather furniture. The space was small, with low ceilings, but he'd made the best of it. He'd kept the walls crème colored but used dark wood frames around the picture windows and the sliding glass door leading to the small backyard. The effect was like stepping into a natural space of shadows and light. The brightness of early June lit up the green space of the backyard and what looked to be a small concrete patio, complete with barbecue and a picnic table.

Rico could even see flowers.

He half laughed. "This... this is *really* nice," he said. "You... damn."

He thought of his apartment, which he'd always considered crappy. Finn and Adam had made it into an appealing space, and Rico? Rico had drifted to New York, hoping someday he'd find a place.

Derek had made himself a place.

God, who wouldn't be impressed by that.

Derek shrugged as he shut the door behind them, looking pleased. Rico thought he might even be blushing. "Yeah. Well, my mom keeps reminding me that it needs color. I'd like to commission your cousin to make me something, but I'm afraid Finn might rip my balls out through my spleen."

Rico laughed, because Finn really was that jealous. "Not if you and me are a thing," he said. "You know, you could settle."

In the close space of the entryway, Rico could actually *smell* the warmth of the flush that rolled off Derek. "You think I'm settling?" he asked seriously.

Rico shrugged. "I mean, you did hit on Adam first."

"And then I met you," Derek said, moving into his space. "And I realized that you were the best guy for me. I mean, would you want me if I *hadn't* noticed Adam?"

Rico had to smile, and the feel of Derek's hands at his waist eased the little jumps of jealousy. "We look a lot alike," he admitted, because excluding the tattoos and the toughness and Adam's habitually taciturn expression, yes, they really did.

"You're the metro version," Derek said, eyes twinkling. He slid his hands under Rico's tight T-shirt, digging his fingers slightly into the muscles of his back. "And since I'm sort of the metro guy...."

Rico couldn't help it. His smile stretched his face and he leaned forward to press lips, to taste. Derek opened his mouth and Rico fell into him, groaning as Derek palmed his back, his shoulder blades, his shoulders, skin on skin, in the cool dark of the entryway.

The kiss grew hungrier, and Rico's overnight bag slid down from his shoulder and landed on the floor with a plop. He brought his hand up to cup Derek's neck, sliding the other hand around toward his backside. He squeezed, and Derek tensed, bucking his hips into Rico's.

There was no pulling away, no backing down, no stopping to think or banter or discuss. There was only Derek pushing him back against the entryway closet, grinding against the crease of his thigh through his cargo shorts.

"Want," Derek said gruffly. "Now."

"Yes," Rico breathed, and all of the irritating soul searching vaporized in the heat of Derek's hands on his skin.

Derek fumbled with Rico's fly and the cargo shorts dropped to the floor with his underwear, and Derek dropped to his knees right there on the thick entryway rug and took Rico into his mouth with a groan of hunger.

"Oh God—so fast!"

Derek pulled back and wrapped his fist around Rico's cock, looking up to meet Rico's eyes. "Fast. This time'll be fast," he promised, blue eyes deadly serious. "God...," he breathed, his gaze all for Rico's body. "So pretty." He closed his eyes and stuck out his tongue, rubbing the rough of it over the dripping cap.

Rico grunted roughly and pressed back, his head making a hollow thunk on the closet door. His world, which had been a complicated, slightly painful tangle just hours ago, had shrunk, simplified, down to Derek's hand around the base of his shaft and his tongue licking the ridge.

Oh God.

And his other hand cupping Rico's balls, distributing spit behind them, tickling his pucker. Rico widened his legs a little, then reached behind himself, grabbed his cheeks, and spread.

Derek's eyes widened and he suckled on the head—just the head—of Rico's cock. "You want it," he whispered roughly.

Rico nodded, squeezing his eyes closed. His stomach muscles fluttered as he clenched and released. He and Ezra had taken turns, gentle, always so sweet. But Derek *wanted*, and oh, God help him, Rico wanted Derek.

Specifically he wanted Derek to take him, fuck him roughly, own him. All of that blazing confidence, that brilliant excitement, pulsing inside Rico's body....

Derek squeezed and stroked, the pressure whirling in Rico's gut, his groin, and Rico groaned, spurting a brief burst of precome into the darkness of Derek's mouth.

Derek's tongue and throat worked, soft and stroking, teeth carefully shielded, as he swallowed.

He pulled back and spoke, his breath fanning Rico's engorged, sensitized head. "Turn around," he commanded. "Spread your legs."

Rico did, leaning his chest heavily against the door, expecting Derek to stand up and fumble with his jeans, but instead Derek spread him, one hand solidly on each cheek.

Breath fanned his crease for a moment, and Rico's chest shuddered in and out as he waited.

"You showered," Derek whispered against his buttcheek.

"Everywhere," Rico told him, because he'd been *dreaming* about this moment for more than a month, wondering what Derek would do with his body if they ever touched like this. He'd showered, rubbing the washcloth behind his balls, in his hole, in his creases, dreaming about Derek touching him.

And now Derek spread him wide and slicked his tongue gently between Rico's cheeks. He brushed Rico's entrance and Rico's whole body twitched.

Derek laughed, vibrating against his skin. "Like that?" he asked.

"Yes," Rico answered, willing to give him anything—willing to beg, after all this time.

He didn't have to beg.

Derek lapped at him, played with him, penetrated him, and Rico found himself whispering encouragement.

"Yes, yes, God, Derek, it's… oh God, need more…."

Derek's finger, just one, slid inside, and Rico clamped down on him hard. Derek pulled in a mouthful of Rico's flesh in response, and Rico pounded the closet door lightly, shaking with desire.

Derek pulled out and grabbed his hips, using them as leverage as he pulled himself slowly up, kissing Rico's spine and his ribs as he rose. He covered Rico's body with his own and undulated, a powerful stroke of his body on Rico's.

"You ready for this?" he asked in Rico's ear. "Up against the wall?"

"Quick," Rico begged.

Derek stayed close enough for Rico to feel him as he fumbled in his pocket and then with his belt. For a moment they separated, stepping out of their shoes and pants, shucking their shirts over their heads and letting them drop at their feet. Just that quickly Derek pressed him against the door again, his bare groin hard and prodding against Rico's buttcheek, the coolness of lubricant slick against Rico's skin.

"You ready, Rico?" Derek asked, breath hot in his ear.

Rico's hands were sweaty and shaking, braced against the door. "Derek," he said helplessly, thrusting his bottom backward, begging.

"Say it." Derek kissed his neck, licking, and Rico tilted his head to give him access.

"I want you to fuck me so bad," Rico admitted, knees so weak he almost worried he couldn't do this.

Derek reached down, grasping himself, and Rico felt the head of Derek's cock against his entrance. His eyes popped open.

"Oh God," he said, breath coming faster. "Derek—"

"Sh…." Derek wrapped his free hand around his chest. "We'll go slow."

Slow… so slow…. Derek pressed against him, stretching, stretching, and Rico's stomach trembled as he fought the urge to push against him and take him in, or clench against him, keeping him out. Derek licked his hair and his neck, and pinched his nipples. That last one did it, and Rico melted, relaxing, thrusting backward as his asshole gave way, let Derek in.

Both of them groaned as Derek's head popped inside, and Rico's body shook as he shoved back again, taking more in, more, more—oh God….

"Jesus, you're big," he gasped.

"All the better to fuck you with," Derek chuckled and then rocked back and forward, back and forward, a little bit pulling out, a little more thrusting in, again and again, his rhythm slow and sweet and...

Driving Rico crazy.

"Augh! Promises, promises," Rico moaned.

"Want more?" Derek teased, pinching his nipple.

"Of you? Oh God, please." He couldn't have been plainer, or needier, if he'd lain on his back and lifted his ass in the air.

He'd do that. He'd do that in a second, grab his thighs and spread his legs, giving Derek permission to ravage him and fuck him and....

The image alone, while Derek was plowing him from behind, made his balls ache.

"Grab yourself," Derek commanded, pulling back and giving a minithrust, teasing him. "It's gonna be quick."

Little patters of sweat from Derek's forehead hit Rico's bare shoulders, and their bodies schwacked together, sticky from the warm day, from the exertion, from the torture of being close, so close, of pounding each other until their bodies exploded into orgasm.

"I'll come on your closet," Rico threatened, barely able to form words.

"Better than being locked in one," Derek cracked, then threw himself forward hard.

"Augh! Amen!" Rico squeezed his own cock at the base, then stroked up while Derek thrust hard inside him, not teasing anymore, fucking, fucking mercilessly, hard and fast and huge.

Rico beat his hand faster, his balls bouncing off the bottom of his fist, his cheek bruising against the closet door, Derek's member stretching his ass so hard he could feel the throb in his thighs, in his spine, in his taint. "Oh God—*Derek!*"

Derek grasped hard, managed a grip on Rico's short hair, and Rico tipped his head back, exposing his throat, his chest, barely keeping his grip on the closet door.

And that dominance was all he needed. His vision washed white-blind and his muscles screamed in pleasure as his body convulsed, orgasm hitting him like a freight train, balls first. He clenched, squeezing Derek's cock with all his strength, and Derek cried out behind him, his next thrust deeper, harder than the others. He stayed there, buried inside Rico, shaking and spending deep in Rico's body, even as he leaned forward and rested his cheek on the back of Rico's shoulder.

His climax went on, the come sliding from Rico's stretched asshole, slipping down his thighs.

Rico moaned a little, his brain aroused by the feeling of Derek's semen, his body still recovering from the sex they'd had in the entryway, barely after they'd shut the door.

"Sore?" Derek asked, concerned.

"Turned on," Rico confessed, releasing his deflating cock and wiping his sticky hand on his stomach. His nipples tingled—hell, *everything* tingled. "I... God... ohhh...."

Because Derek apparently read his mind, dropping to a squat again and licking delicately at Rico's cheek, at his thigh, at his dilated entrance. Rico shook hard and begged some more. "A kiss," he pleaded. "Let me—"

Derek stood, whirled him around, and claimed his mouth again, letting him taste everything, all they had done, that he hadn't seen, his eyes filled with the closet door while his body had been ravaged by Derek's rough need.

By the time this kiss ended, he'd melted into Derek's arms, helpless against the sweetness and safety there.

Derek pulled away and nuzzled his temple. "Let me wash up," he said softly. "I'll make you dinner. We can do this again on the bed."

Rico licked the salt off Derek's neck, smiling to himself. Oh, the things he would do to Derek's body, sprawled beneath him, spread for pleasure. "I am *so* down with that," he murmured.

"Even if it means you get the shower second?" Derek asked fondly.

Rico tilted his head so he could see Derek's eyes. "Not together?"

"No." Derek bit his lip, looking abashed. "For one thing, my bathroom is pretty fuckin' small. For another, I... I *really* want to cook you dinner. That, uhm, wouldn't happen. You know. If...."

Rico laughed and kissed his cheek, then straightened and started picking up his clothes—and his overnight bag. "Show me the way. The naked tour it is!"

Derek laughed self-consciously, like a gawky teenager, and picked up his clothes. "Yeah. Well, get used to it. I never did get the hang of bathrobes."

Rico gasped, pretending to be shocked. "Blasphemy! It's like walking around in your underwear with a blanket on!"

Derek rolled his eyes. "It's like daring yourself not to get a boner when you've got easy access! I'd never get anything done!"

Rico chuckled as he followed Derek's perfect ass down the hall. "Buddy, the *last* thing you need is to be more sexed up."

DEREK GRILLED hamburgers and Rico made the salad—well, all the fixings were bagged; it was no big deal—and they sat on his little porch and ate dinner in the fading light.

Rico appreciated the misters as the concrete and brick held the heat in the backyard, even as the sky turned purple, and Derek filled his wineglass with just enough regularity to keep him mellow.

"I'd say you're trying to get me drunk to take advantage of me," Rico joked as they savored the last of the bottle. "But we both know *that* cow escaped."

Derek's chuckle sounded absolutely sinful. "We could catch her again and have even *more* fun letting her out of the barn," he said, eyes crinkling in the corners.

Rico nodded. "Wow. Sex and cows. I can't believe I'm turned on!"

"But you are, right? Turned on?" Derek looked at him slyly, and Rico could tell he didn't have any uncertainty whatsoever.

"Yeah, Derek. I'm pretty sure the barn door's gonna go flying open and that thing's escaping again—"

"Can it make more noise this time?" Derek asked avidly. "You did *not* make enough sex noises!"

Rico choked on his wine. "Holy God, Derek—what do you usually bang? Farm animals?"

It was Derek's turn to choke, and for a moment they were twelve years old, and they'd just cracked their first dirty joke.

When they'd recovered, Derek stood up and took Rico's wineglass. They'd cleared off the rest of the table already—this was the signal that the dishes needed to be done.

"Here," Rico said, making to rise. "Let me help you—"

"No," Derek replied, smiling a little. Those hidden moments of shyness in his own home were becoming more and more potent, twisting the wire of yearning tighter in Rico's stomach. "I mean, you know, eventually I'll be like, 'Jesus, clean up your own damned water glass,' right? But right now I sort of, you know. Want to make an impression."

Rico watched him take stuff into the kitchen and barely remembered to close his mouth.

Make an impression? *Make an impression?*

The wire of yearning that Rico had chalked up to lingering sexual tension snapped tight, and Rico swallowed.

He stood and walked into the house, then closed the glass door behind him, because it was still hot outside and the air-conditioning was running. Derek was bent over the sink, rinsing out the glasses. Rico waited until he'd put them into the dishwasher along with the other dishes and turned it on.

He was hosing out the sink when he realized Rico had walked in, and he looked up and smiled. "I was going to be out in—"

Rico took two steps into the kitchen, came up behind Derek, and put his hands on his hips. Oh Lord—his body heat alone was intoxicating.

"What's up?" Derek asked, but his voice had dropped in timbre, and he sounded sultry. Breathy.

Ready.

"You know how some shit just hits you?" Rico asked, running his lips down the side of Derek's neck.

Derek tilted his head to give him access. "Like, uhm, you're ready again?" Derek asked, his voice light.

"Like, I'm ready for everything," Rico whispered, licking his ear. "I... I am so gone on you, Derek," he said, pulling Derek into the cradle of his hips. "You... you don't ever have to impress me." He shuddered, wanting to engulf Derek, swallow him whole, wear his heat and his joy and his fierce, funny intelligence under his skin.

"No?" Derek asked, pushing back. Oh yeah. Rico wanted to top this time. Not fumbling or shy or shaking because he was afraid of hurting Derek. He wanted to *top*, to pleasure Derek until he was begging for Rico and Rico alone.

"I'm impressed," Rico told him. His hands shook on Derek's hips, and his body sang, begging for skin-on-skin like they hadn't just had screaming sex in the entryway not three hours earlier. "I'm...." His breath shuddered, and he shoved his hands under Derek's T-shirt. "I'm so fucking in love with you," he confessed, because if he didn't, his skin would shake off his body.

Derek turned and slid his wet hands through Rico's hair, holding him in place so he could lunge into a frantic, soul-rending kiss. Rico met the kiss with hunger—*God*, he was so hungry for this man. Dinner was not enough, dessert was not enough, *sex* was not enough. The thought of this man leaning over the sink in a simple, meaningful task *for Rico* was enough to make him need, like he needed oxygen, or water, or sunlight.

Derek tried to take over, but for once Rico didn't want his guidance or his aggressiveness—Rico just wanted *him*. He kept kissing, framing Derek's face with his hands to make him behave, make him *yearn* for Rico like Rico yearned for him. Kiss, parted lips, moist lip, rough tongue, again, again, again, Rico fed the fires of Derek's need until Derek was back against the sink, groaning deep from his stomach, hands shaking as much as Rico's.

"Bed," he begged. "Bed. This time we were gonna make it to—"

"Fuck bed," Rico rasped, and he sank to his knees, taking Derek's shorts and underwear with him.

Oh man. Something primal and real about actually *seeing* another man's cock, about grasping it, seeing his own brown hand wrapped around its pale length... God, it shook Rico in his vitals, made what they were doing intimate and real. Derek wasn't quite hard yet, and Rico stroked him loosely, enjoying the slip and slide of the foreskin around the bell.

"You're playing," Derek accused.

Rico pulled the little hood back and licked the head experimentally, and Derek closed his eyes and let a long hissing breath escape. "You're complaining?" Rico asked, letting his breath dust the damp, pink tenderness.

"Never seen one of those before?" Derek asked.

Rico prodded the space under Derek's foreskin with his tongue, then pulled the hood up experimentally, trying to see if he could keep his tongue trapped and wriggling. The maneuver didn't work, but it did make Derek let out a whimper of raw want.

"Nope." Rico played, pulling the hood between his lips and licking the extra skin like he wanted to do with Derek's nipples.

Derek didn't respond, and Rico looked up. He had one hand up under his shirt and was kneading his own chest, pinching restlessly.

"Ooh," Rico breathed. "I was just thinking about—"

"Please don't tease me," Derek said nakedly. "Oh hells, Rico—"

He kept his eyes open and locked his gaze with Derek's as he opened his mouth and engulfed the head, taking it in the back of his throat and holding the base to make up the extra. Derek leaned back against the sink and groaned, raising one hand to massage Rico's scalp.

Rico would have smiled if his mouth hadn't been stretched wide, and he swallowed to take it deeper.

"Nungh."

Rico pulled back and licked around the head and then thrust forward again, squeezing the base, letting his spit make Derek's cock sloppy. Derek was fully hard now, and the foreskin slid up and back as Rico stroked. The idea of it sliding over the widely flared thick bell and slipping down made Rico shudder. He pulled back with his fist and put his mouth over the cap, slithering his tongue around the head some more, feeling the silk of the skin, the looseness, the rigid strength of the shaft.

His thighs were starting to burn as he squatted, but except for that, he thought he could pull Derek's cock into his mouth and release it until the end of time.

Derek thought different.

He tightened his hold in Rico's hair and canted his shoulder back so he could rest his hand on the counter behind him. Rico gave a particularly hard suck, and Derek shook. Precome, tangy and sweet, hit Rico's tongue, and his throat convulsed.

"Harder," Derek whispered. "Grab my balls—"

Rico tightened his stroke and moved his other hand from Derek's thigh to his hanging testicles, fondling gently.

"*Harder!*" Derek begged.

Rico tightened his hand just a little, tugged ever so slightly, and Derek moaned from deep in his stomach. He cried out, and again, then held Rico's head still and thrust into his mouth until Rico gagged, letting his jaw drop a little. Semen filled his mouth, dribbled out, and Derek kept coming, thrusts shorter as Rico struggled to swallow, to hold him, to take it all.

The frenzy ended, and Derek's cock flopped limply out. Rico wrapped both arms around Derek's waist and buried his face against a sweaty thigh as Derek caught his breath. That hand in his hair relaxed, massaging gently, as the two of them remembered simple things, like breathing and standing and squatting on the kitchen floor.

"Rico?" Derek's voice sounded breathy and a little uncertain.

"Yeah?"

"Can we move to the bed *now*?"

Rico shuddered, his groin giving a vicious throb as his vision of sinking into Derek's flesh and giving him everything returned. "We got lube?"

Derek shuddered. "Yeah," he rasped.

"Gimme a hand up."

Derek's hand was damp in his, but he pulled Rico right up to him. Sweat made his face glossy, and his sandy hair clung to his forehead. His shirt was rucked up around his chest and his pants were still in a puddle around his feet. He looked delicious and used and dirty, and Rico wanted to roll around in him and soak up his smell.

Derek palmed the back of his head and pulled him into a kiss, a ruthless, messy, come-swapping kiss, and Rico groaned, needy and at Derek's mercy all over again.

That was okay. Mutual. The feeling was mutual. They would go to bed and roll like sweaty puppies and stay there until they smelled like each other.

Like family.

Weekends and Mondays

BED WAS just as lovely as Derek had promised.

They kissed naked for what felt like hours, until Rico's cock leaked steadily and even Derek was hard again.

Rico explored everywhere: Derek's mostly smooth chest; his tiny, tan nipples; the sensitive spot by the freckle under his ribs. He nibbled the crease under the cut of his stomach and ducked when Derek giggled like a tickled child.

Then he rolled Derek to his stomach and spread his thighs with both hands, diving into the crease of his ass like he'd dreamed of, licking, probing, fingering, until Derek was gasping into his pillow, mindless and begging, loose and ready.

Rico shuddered as he pulled to his knees, grabbing the lube from under the pillow. He dribbled it cold down the cleft of Derek's cheeks and then spread them, letting the slick mingle with the spit and softness and blowing gently on the tender pinkened opening.

Derek, sensitized, driven mad by teasing, screamed into the pillow. *"Please!"*

Rico positioned himself so quickly, Derek's scream was still vibrating the bed. He thrust slowly, because he wanted it to be good.

The sound—the hissing, sobbing, happy groan—that Derek let loose shivered through Rico's spine.

His body's focus narrowed to that One. Specific. Part. And that One. Specific. Part. Was sheathed tightly, stroked by Derek's clenching muscles, swelling in its prince's chamber, even as Rico started to rock back and forth.

Lost. He was lost inside Derek, lost in his body and his heat, in his joy. Derek gibbered and begged for *Rico.* Rico wanted to please him, would do anything, fucked him into the mattress, oh yes, oh God, *please* let him make Derek happy, let him be part of that joy, part of that pleasure, that glorious explosion of the two of them, bodies carnal, hearts thundering like the same horse.

Derek's cries grew sharper, and Rico adjusted his angle, suddenly right there.

"I'm gonna... oh Derek, I'm gonna—"

"*Come!*" Derek screamed, body rocking, clenching on Rico as he came.

Hips pistoning, ass clenching, cock *screaming*, locked in a sensual vise, Rico lost all control of his body, of his sex, pounding inside Derek blindly, his entire being exploding, sparkling with nerve-ending fireworks as his balls swelled and clenched and he came.

"Oooh...." Oh, his come sliding in the oven of Derek's body felt heavenly, and he spilled it in great spurts, until his well ran dry and only the twitches of the end of climax remained.

He collapsed on top of Derek, their bodies mashing together, slick with sweat.

"Don't move," Derek mumbled. "Stay right there."

"Yeah, good," Rico said back, content with the world as he'd never been. "Not moving."

"You know, I haven't come three times in a day since I was seventeen," Derek said conversationally, his voice muffled by his pillows and the mattress and Rico's body on top of him.

"You were a randy fucker," Rico teased, "because I always stopped at once."

Derek laughed, dirty, his body shaking. Rico slid out of him and to the side, closing his eyes as the overhead fan dusted their bodies with cool, cool air.

"Yeah, well, I just couldn't find anybody like you to bang me," Derek said, grinning.

It was Rico's turn to be shy. "I, uh... I mean, I never uhm—"

"Topped?" Derek moved way too quickly for the moment, pushing himself up in a panic, and Rico had to stop that industry at once.

"No, I topped," he corrected. "I just... not like *that*."

Derek's smile relaxed, and he was a dirty-minded teenager again. "Like what?" he asked, eyes lasciviously wide.

Rico responded with a slow, smug smile of his own. "I've never made anyone scream for it," he admitted. And suddenly he was matching Derek's cockiness, his playfulness, grin for grin. "I, uh, never fucked anyone until they couldn't talk before," he said, his chest swelling a little for pride. And just that sudden, his words became real. "I've never trusted anyone enough to be that… that powerful." Of course, there had only been Ezra, but they'd been so tender with each other.

Derek was stronger than that. Derek was made for loud, sweaty, playful sex, and tender touches afterward.

Rico gazed into those blue eyes and ran an easy hand down Derek's naked thigh. "You're just so damned happy," he said, giving a little pop to Derek's backside.

Derek smiled at him lazily. "Well, yanno, I just got *laid*. That makes a guy happy."

Rico shook his head, not wanting to wax lyrical about all of Derek's good points right now. He was too busy letting his heart swell with them. "As long as I can *keep* you happy," he said, a little serious.

Derek nodded, then rolled over and kissed his shoulder. "Here, I'm going to go wash up and get us some ice cream. Meet you back here in five minutes."

"Ice cream?" Rico asked, struggling to sit up. "In bed?"

Derek nodded like it was the most logical thing in the world. "Yes. Ice cream and boxer shorts. At least for me—man, my shit gets in the *way*."

Rico eyed his rather impressive "shit." "Yes," he said dryly. "I would imagine."

Derek's smile showed all his teeth. "Well, there's always a price to pay," he bragged.

Rico snorted. "Yeah, well, you appear to be rich in that area," he said. "I'm not feeling any pity."

Rico was pretty much as sexed out as he'd ever been in his life, but Derek's laughter, wicked and suggestive, made his stomach flutter and clench. "Good," he said smugly. "I'll be back in a sec."

He walked down the hall into the bathroom. Rico waited until his washing-up sounds stopped before venturing in there himself with his own boxer shorts. The tub and shower were pretty small—the entire house, actually, spoke to snug efficiency. Rico liked that idea. Derek himself was larger than life, but not on purpose. His joy and his enthusiasm made him that way, but he didn't buy the big ostentatious house or brag about his tailor or even try to cull an exclusive client list to be that way.

He just was.

Rico came out of the bathroom and Derek called, "Get back in bed! I'm bringing ice cream and cookies, and it's not nearly as decadent in the kitchen!"

"Roger that," Rico called back, smiling. He went into the bedroom, straightened the comforter, and plumped the pillows so they could sit on the bed and eat. He'd just finished when Derek came in, each hand holding a bowl with two Oreos balanced on the edge.

"You do know this is our second dessert," Rico said, taking his bowl from Derek and scooting to the far side of the bed so Derek could sit down.

"Yeah, but I always crave ice cream after good sex," Derek said seriously. "I mean"—he grinned, wicked and sensual—"I stocked up. So I've got rocky road, vanilla, and salted caramel too. Different flavor for each night."

Rico laughed, pushing himself back into the pillow, before taking a bite of vanilla and Oreo. "If we weren't having sex to earn this, it would make us fat," he said, but he didn't repent a single bite.

"Yup," Derek said. He turned his spoon in his mouth and sucked on it until it was shiny clean. Then he went for another bite. And when he was done with that and had licked the ice cream delicately from his palate, they began to talk.

Sometimes a late-night conversation in bed over ice cream could be a religious experience.

No, man! Transformers all the way. You didn't play with those? Adam used to make all these giant battle machines, right, and I would be the little human who ran interference for the superhero.

Dude, you didn't want to be the giant robot?

I hate guns. I couldn't have gone into the military like my cousin, not on your life.

And:

Yes, I woke up with no eyebrows. I swear to God, my sister used Nair as a face cream and left it on the washcloth. It wasn't until I went downstairs the next morning, my eyes all burning and shit, that my mom made the connection. And we both *looked like victims of a nuclear accident too. God, I started telling people I had the mange just so they'd leave me alone about the Nair!*

She sounds terrifying. Who did she marry again?

Hale was a friend of mine from school. He went to college to be an actuary, but he's working at my dad's store. Man deserves sainthood. I'd pay him *to keep her out of my hair.*

Hahahahahaha!

Shut up.

And:

Well, yeah, I believe in God. But watching the way my family treated Adam, and saying it's all justified and shit? It's like once I put that together, I couldn't go back to the church. I miss it. There's this sort of mystery there, you know?

Yeah. My parents drag me to their little church—which is very nice to me, by the way—on holidays. I don't like to admit it because I'm supposed to be grown, but it puts the magic in Christmas and Easter. I hear you.

Right? Like there's a grown-up there who still knows something more than I do.

Yeah! And if we fuck up, he's still going to tell us it's okay.

I really loved that. I've missed it.

Well, you know. You and me... we could go together.

Pause.

Yeah? We'll be together then?

God, Rico. I hope so. I want... I want so much for us. With all my heart.

Then I'll plan on it.

They kissed then, and set their bowls down, and although they didn't have a third dessert, they definitely earned it.

By the time Sunday night rolled around, Rico was well and truly in love. Not magical weekend love, just in plain "I love you forever— God, I'd have your babies if I could" sort of love. He was going to go to the office to work with Derek, and he wasn't tired of the man's company. He was looking forward to work. He was looking forward to seeing Derek all week. He was looking forward to sleepovers between weekends.

Rico was looking forward to forever.

But he'd settle for waking up next to Derek three mornings in a row, legs twined, bodies pressed together, their sex still filling the room even though Derek had changed and laundered at least three sets of sheets.

That morning he was letting Derek knot his tie, since the bathroom was too small for them both to look in the mirror, when a question occurred to him. "So, we don't just have to have sex for me to spend the night, do we?"

Derek stopped midknot and looked up at him, those wonderful wrinkles appearing in the corners of his eyes. "No. Not at all, why?"

"Well, I don't know. I was just... you know, not *tonight*, of course—"

"Why not?" Derek asked seriously.

"Well, for one thing, I owe Adam and Finn a walk with the dog. And for another, I don't want you to get tired of me."

Derek's mouth on his was hot and urgent and still minty fresh. "Not happening," he whispered, leaving Rico's knees weak. "And you can bring Clopper over here, you know."

Rico's eyes widened. "In your house? Are you kidding? He'll shed all over—"

"Well, yeah," Derek said, looking worried. "But, you know. You've got a dog; I want a dog. I wouldn't mind some shedding."

Rico thought about it—thought of Finn and Adam and how much they loved the dog. "Okay," he said slowly, thinking.

"Well, if you don't want to—" Oh no! He sounded hurt.

"No! That's not it at all!" Rico reassured him. Derek's tie hung around his neck, and Rico took his turn and started to fuss. "It's just... I mean, I love Clopper and all, but Finn and Adam... I mean, they *love* that dog. As much as I do, but... well, they're sort of needier. I can't explain it. It's like I had that dog for two years, and I was okay as a master for him and all, but really, the whole time I was holding him for my cousin."

Derek's face fell. "You mean I'm not inheriting a dog?"

"Well, you know. Maybe... I mean, not right away, and Clopper can still come over to play, but... you know. Maybe we can find a dog that was waiting for *me* the whole time. Like Clopper was waiting for my cousin."

And his face lit up from the inside. "So, like, *you and me* could get a dog."

Rico carefully knotted the raw silk tie, stroked the fiber a little, and then smiled into Derek's eyes, completely besotted. Ezra hadn't even liked staying over. He'd never talked about the future. Every moment had been stolen and precious.

Apparently the everyday nonstolen moments could be just as good as the precious ones.

"Yeah," he said. He held Derek's clean-shaven cheeks and kissed him because he could. "We could get a—"

Derek's phone rang, surprising them both.

Derek broke off from the kiss and pulled it off the charger and answered, sounding puzzled. "Hi. Yeah, hi, Adam. Yeah, he's with me—Oh, crap. He turned the phone off. You know that? Okay, so why—Seriously? Are you fucking *kidding* me? And you didn't think you should call us?" Derek blinked slowly. "Well, uhm, I can't say I blame you for that, and—" He blinked again. "Yeah, you're right. It was sweet of you to do that, but—" And now his eyes grew *really* wide. "You're absolutely right. You should definitely talk to Rico. Here he is." He handed Rico his cell phone.

"What is it?" Rico asked, more curious than alarmed.

"Your mom returned to their apartment yesterday morning. Apparently Finn's sister was there and words were exchanged, and... well, I think you need to go bail your mom out of jail."

Rico's mouth fell open. "I need to do what?" he asked, talking into the phone.

"Yeah. Well, we bailed Mari out yesterday," Adam said, sounding sullen. "Finn's parents paid the fine and said they were proud of her, and asked me if I wanted them to bail your mother out." Adam's chuckle was all evil. "I told them I wasn't really fuckin' family."

"You left my *mother* in *jail*?" Rico asked, not even angry, just stunned. "On what charge?"

"Assault," Adam said matter-of-factly. "It was a good thing Finn called the cops first, because they helped break it up. Your mom called Finn a faggot, and Mari apparently knows Spanish real good too. And not just the nice words, like Finn. Your mom left a couple of big scratches on Mari's face before we pulled her off."

Rico wasn't sure where the chuckle came from. It was horrible. *Inconceivable.* His mother had been arrested for assault, and nobody from her family had come to bail her out.

Well, they probably weren't sure it was the right thing to do.

"But...." Rico found his feet again, found that kernel of properly outraged good boy in himself. "But Adam, why didn't you tell *me*?"

Adam sounded absolutely smug. "Because. You turned off your phone so family didn't bother you, and it wasn't like this was a *real* emergency, right? I mean, if it was a *real* emergency, Grandma or your dad would have come bail her out. I left messages on their phones in case she didn't get to call."

"But, I mean—"

"Did you have a nice weekend?" Adam inquired, sounding like it was the most natural thing in the world.

Rico relaxed. "Best weekend of my life," he said, catching Derek's eyes so he'd know Rico meant it.

"Good. So I didn't want to fuck that up. Here, I'm waiting outside the courthouse—I can take you in to front bail if you want. You know where it is?"

"Yeah. Seventh and H. I'll be there in—" He grimaced at Derek.

"Twenty minutes," Derek supplied. "I'll take you there myself."

"Thanks," Rico said with a sigh. "This was *not*—"

Derek stopped him with a finger on his lips. "Don't stress it," he murmured. "Family. I get it."

And he did.

Rico shook his head. "So you'll be outside the courthouse?"

"Yeah," Adam said, his voice dry. "You can recognize me easy. I'll be the scary Mexican guy with the tats and the big fuckin' dog."

Well, all the better to eat Rico's mother, Rico supposed.

Especially since she'd been tenderized by a night in the hoosegow first.

Amends and Amens

RICO COULDN'T look at Adam objectively, so to Rico's eye he didn't look scary at all. But that didn't stop him from noticing the way people eyeballed the three of them—Adam, Rico, and Derek—as they stood in the concrete courtyard outside the relatively new jail on H Street.

"Don't sweat it," Adam said, watching the direction of Rico's gaze. "They probably think you're my lawyer. I've had three people ask me for cigarettes and two for beer, and I've only been here for five minutes."

"Oolf!"

Clopper had apparently missed Rico over the weekend, and thought an appropriate greeting would be to jump up and plant both paws on his chest while trying to headbutt him while flailing his tongue.

"Oh my God! Clop—Clopper, dammit—!"

Derek was regarding him with a smirk. "Not really your dog, huh?"

"He's a family animal," Adam said dryly. "Clopper, you asshole, get your balls down on the ground." He gave the short lead a solid yank and Clopper thunked heavily down on all four feet.

Rico made it up to him by rubbing his ears and scratching his ruff. "So now that I've fucked up my suit, should we go inside and spring the moms from the joint?" He looked up at Adam and tried to summon a little bit of recrimination, but he couldn't.

Adam didn't look tough—not to Rico. He looked wounded and irritated, but not tough. He'd been looking out for the family that loved him, and Rico couldn't make himself be mad at that.

Adam shrugged. "Don't need to. Mari's in there with *her* mom having some sort of girl-bonding bullshit with *your* mom so she doesn't have to press charges."

Rico's eyes were going to pop out of his head, he just knew it. "She's doing *what*?"

Adam shrugged, looking really uncomfortable. "Oh, I don't know, something about talking while they were in the cell like hamsters—Mari's word, I've never seen a jail cell and I'm not a hamster. But they were talking and… I don't know. I don't get it. It's like Finn's whole fuckin' family. They're just magic fuckin' happy people, and you don't want to get in their way."

Rico grunted and eyed Derek sideways. "Yeah. I know the type."

"What?" Derek asked, genuinely puzzled.

"I'm sure you do," Adam muttered. "Anyway, Mari texted me. They're on their way out. She said your mom's all weepy and she really wants to see you."

Rico's eyeballs really were going to explode. "I'm sure you got that wrong."

"Oh you wish. She's gonna come out here and get all sad on you, and you're gonna be great friends, and suddenly you'll be stuck doing family shit again."

Rico shook his head. "Oh *hell* no. Man, my last meal at Grandma Macias's was *your* last meal there. I went to New York to avoid another family Christmas."

"Charming. And ungrateful."

Rico's stomach sank. Adam's face twisted like he'd eaten a lemon, and Clopper started a low, angry rumble like the buzz of pissed-off bees.

He swallowed and turned to his father. "Well, *Papi*, it's not like you ever did anything at those gatherings to make them more pleasant."

Rico's father was tall and thin—he wore his suits like a clothes hanger and had an expression of disdain for their inability to fit him. Or something. Rico couldn't remember him with any other face besides the one with the deep lines at the mouth, alongside the nose, and the forehead. His *papi* had been finding things wrong with life since Rico was born.

"I didn't know it was my job to make your life easier," he said now, of course picking at the small thing Rico said. "I provide a good home, clothes, an education—unlike *this* one, you didn't need to join the service—"

"I'm fuckin' outta here," Adam snapped. "By the way, Mr. Gonzalves? My boyfriend's sister isn't pressing charges, so the next time you open your mouth about being ungrateful, you fuckin' remember that."

Adam turned away, jerking bitterly at Clopper's lead, and Rico looked at Derek unhappily. "Derek, could you go talk to Adam for a sec? *I'm* grateful, and I don't want him to forget that."

Derek nodded briefly, all business, but Rico couldn't do that to him. Not without a sign, something that said Rico's loyalties weren't the same as Ezra's. Rico knew where home was. He grabbed Derek's hand and pulled him forward for a brief kiss on the cheek, ignoring his father's hiss of disgust.

"Thanks," he said softly. "Let's see how this convo goes and we'll see if I even want you to meet him. He's embarrassing to me."

Derek looked at him reprovingly, but Rico shook his head.

"No, man. You don't even know." He nodded, and Derek walked toward Adam, casting a glance over his shoulder once, just to make sure.

"Was that the... *man* who made you decide to break your mother's heart?"

Rico turned toward his father and grimaced. In thirty years Rico might look like him, with a widow's peak and skin so tight the shape of his skull showed past his forehead. "I was gay before Derek," he said. "Derek just makes me really happy, but I guess that doesn't matter to you."

"Your mother is in *jail*—"

"Have you met them? Finn's family?"

"No." One syllable, chill and complete.

Rico glanced toward Derek and Adam talking desultorily and casting Rico's father dirty looks. "They're some of the nicest people," Rico said. "Mari—the girl *Mami* scratched until she bled? She fed me beignets and coffee the first day I met her. Just because, you know? Because I was Adam's family, and Adam made Finn happy, so they were going to treat me right. And she's in there now with her mother, trying to drop the charges after *your wife* called a boy she didn't know an ugly name. Do you know how much class that takes, *Papi*? They're trying to drop the charges, and it wasn't even their fault. *Adam* managed to keep his baggage from polluting their doorstep for four months. I've been here for two, and suddenly they are nose deep in our trash—"

His father slapped him across the face, *hard*, and glared at Rico with the first trace of emotion he'd seen. "That is your *mother* you are talking about!"

"Then she needs to act like it!" Rico shouted. "You never gave a *damn* about me, but *Mami* told me I was loved. If I was going to be loved, I've got to be loved for all of me, and not just the little clone businessman she thinks she's raised."

"*Sentiment!*" Eduardo Gonzalves spat. "You pretend to be grown—"

"I wasn't," Rico said, feeling this conviction deep inside—in the places Derek had touched, and had owned, over the past three days. "I wasn't grown up. I had to go to New York, get my heart broken, and come back *here*, and figure out how to fix it. *Now* I'm grown up, and as a grown-up? I say you and *Mami* have to either love who I am or leave me alone."

His father's lips had gone bloodless, and for a moment they stared at each other, his father's cheekbones and jawbones so prominent he looked like a skull. "I don't know who filled your head—"

Rico saw movement near the doors and looked up quickly as Mari and Mrs. Stewart emerged from the courthouse. Between the two women, Rico's mother walked tiredly, her strappy heels dangling from her fingers and her nylons shredding on the concrete. Her hair had long since fallen from its chignon, and she'd pulled it back into a serviceable ponytail. The rumpled jacket of her suit draped over one arm.

Her other arm was companionably linked with Finn's mother's. They were both wiping their eyes without self-consciousness.

She looked up and saw Rico and smiled apologetically. Then her eyes flickered to her husband's, and any spark shut down.

Mari looked up at them and waved happily, apparently as impervious to Rico's father as Finn was to a bad day. She said something to Rico's mom, who replied briefly. Mari's mom—the white-lady equivalent of Rico's mom, in a pale peach linen suit with a white shell underneath, stopped and hugged her tightly. To Rico's surprise, his mother returned the hug.

"Holy God," he breathed. "That family...."

Lydia Gonzalves-Macias broke away from them reluctantly, and Mari held up her phone and nodded. Lydia patted her purse and nodded back. Great. Apparently they'd exchanged numbers. Adam caught Rico's eyes in disbelief, and Rico shrugged back. Damn. Just...

Damn.

Lydia walked up to Rico and his father and, after a tentative look back at her new sisterhood, gave a tentative smile. "Hola, Ricardo."

Fucking surreal. "Hola, *Mami*. Uhm, new friends?"

Lydia's shoulders relaxed. "Sí." She smiled a little more naturally. "Mari and her mother—they're good people. I... they didn't need to come in and do that." She flushed and her gaze darted to her husband. "I didn't behave very well, Ricardo," she said after a moment. "You were right. I… I was upset, and I ran to my mami, and… and what we did, it wasn't nice." Her chin wobbled. "And it should have been between you and me—"

"Lydia!" his father said sharply, and she shook her head.

"You didn't raise him," she snapped. "*I* did. I kept him out of your way. Well, that's fine. It's what you wanted—a nice boy for the family pictures. But my sister—she's *never* going to see Adam again. And you know what? Rico's right. Adam didn't deserve that. He's been nothing but honorable this whole time—"

"Honorable—"

"I don't want to talk about what you think 'gay' is," she snapped, and Rico recoiled. He'd *never* heard her talk like that. Not to his father. "Those women were *nice* to me. I was hideous, and they were *kind*. And if they can be nice to me when my own family is ugly, then maybe Rico has the right of it. Maybe the people who are nice to you should be the people you care about. I don't *want* Rico to go away. I don't *want* to never see him again. Lucy is *horrible*—I've never wanted to be like her in anything. Why would I want to be like her in how she treats her son?"

"Lydia Gonzalves-Macias—"

"*I'm not your wayward child*!" she shouted. Her lower lip trembled, and her tears fell freely. "I'm a mother, and if it's a choice between loving my son and never seeing him again, this is my choice."

"Well, it's *not* mine," Eduardo snapped back. Then he spat at Rico's feet. "You're not my son, and we shall see if *she* remains my wife."

He turned around and stalked off, leaving Rico openmouthed, his hands shaking.

"*Mami*," he said, as shocked and saddened as a child.

His mother's hug surprised him. For a moment he held himself stiff from surprise, but the moment passed, and he fell into it, grateful, suddenly, *so* grateful that he hadn't lost this, the magic of those quiet meals in the kitchen. But this was better because there was no fear.

"Don't worry," she said softly. "He's my problem, not yours." She pulled back and wiped her eyes again. Rico had a kerchief in the pocket of his rumpled suit, and he pulled it out and offered it to her. For some reason this made her cry harder. "Such a gentleman," she sniffled. "Always such a gentleman. Your cousin's new family— they're really good people," she continued, surprising him. "You tell him I said I was glad. Tell him he deserves to be happy. He deserves to be loved." She sobbed a little into the kerchief. "Tell him I'm sorry I wasn't braver when he was little. It won't help him now, but I'm sorry."

"*Mami*," he said gently, hugging her again. He'd thought she'd break down, but she didn't.

"I've got to go," she said, nodding to where Rico's father paced angrily by the car. "And I've got to get angry to talk to him, so no more tears. But when you were little, I always picked him. No meals in the dining room, no pictures on the refrigerator, no weekends at the zoo. I sat in that jail cell with Mari, and she talked about how much she loved her little brother, and how her family always had such joy together, and how she couldn't let anybody say mean things. I realized that they picked *each other*. Her parents made the children happy, and the children made the parents happy. She would do *anything* to protect them. And I hadn't done anything—not one thing—to protect you or Adam."

Rico was crying. Oh goddammit—*crying*—on the lawn of the county jail. "I grew up fine," he said, voice tight.

"You grew up lonely," she corrected bitterly. "No wonder you love your cousin so much. But that's okay. He loves you back. You have family here. And your young man—"

"Do you want to meet him?" Rico asked, suddenly anxious that she would.

Lydia shook her head. "Later," she said softly, waving her hands around her face. "When we can pretend this never happened."

"The jail?" he asked, half-afraid. "Or the choosing me?"

"The jail," she reassured him. "Now give me one more hug, Rico. Tell your cousin he doesn't have to worry if I ever show up on his doorstep again. I don't understand about the gay thing, but I get the not being ugly now. Maybe I'll be better the next time I visit."

Rico thought of Derek's parents. In touch they were not—but kind? There was no doubt. "I'd like that," he said, hugging her. "I love you, *Mami*."

"I love you too," she said. And then she said the thing that leveled him. "And you are always my good boy."

She pulled away hurriedly and sprinted across the grass to where Rico's father stood in front of their car, glaring angrily at her. He started to yell as she approached, but his mother? Oh, she did him proud. She drew her shoulders back and, in an act of icy disdain worthy of her own mother, gestured to the door.

Flummoxed, Eduardo Gonzalves opened the door to the Lincoln, and Rico's mother swept regally in.

Oh, *Mami*.

By the time the car disappeared down the street, Derek was at his elbow. "Rico?" he asked softly.

Rico shook his head. "Uhm, she wanted Adam to know she was sorry," he said, glancing up at Adam. Adam was sandwiched between Mari and her mother, both of them talking to him earnestly, with lots of reassuring touches on the shoulder and the arms. Adam looked uncomfortable, like a dog being rubbed on by two sweet little kittens he didn't want to frighten. Well, good. Adam got to see that women could be nice creatures. It was a lesson Rico had once thought neither of them would learn.

"Baby," Derek said, sounding a little wrecked.

Rico looked back at him and realized he'd violated all of the personal space laws ever.

"What?" Rico asked, his voice thick in his throat.

"You're crying." He wiped under Rico's eyes with his thumbs, his nearness intimate and kind and God, such bedrock reassurance.

Rico nodded, feeling foolish. "She, uh, said she loved me," he said, his voice crackling all over the place. "And then she, uh, said I'm her good boy—" And that's when he lost it, Derek's arms around his shoulders while he cried honestly, like his mother had, because being a grown-up was hard, and sometimes love just fucking hurt, even if it was a good kind of pain.

THEY DIDN'T go to work immediately. Adam had apparently walked with Clopper, and in the middle of being half smothered by Finn's mom and sister, he looked at his watch and said loudly, "Oh hell— ladies, I need to go. I've got to drop Clopper off before I go to work!"

Rico met eyes with Derek, who nodded. They stepped apart, and Derek handed Rico his handkerchief before calling smoothly, "We'll take you home, Adam. We can drop you off at work too. We'll get some lunch while we're there."

Adam shot him a look of pure relief—that turned immediately hunted when Mari said, "Great! We'll see you all at River Burger. Finn's working, and I can't wait to tell him it all worked out!"

She and her mother took off across the lawn, waving as they trotted to their car.

Adam sighed and rubbed his eyes, then walked resignedly up to Rico and Derek. "Take your time," he muttered. "I've got, like, an hour and a half—I so totally could have made it."

Derek half laughed and clapped him on the shoulder. "Well, good. You need the practice if those are gonna be your in-laws."

Adam groaned and shook his head. "God. Women. I got... I mean, *no* idea, you know?"

"And yet," Rico said, laughing a little through the thickness in his head, "if he was straight, he'd be rolling around in them. They follow him *everywhere*."

Adam shuddered—a full-out body shudder. "You're mean," he muttered. "Just... just piss mean. Let your boyfriend take me home, okay?"

"Not without me," Rico returned, not because he was jealous but because their banter was doing a great job at bringing their world back to normal.

An hour later they pulled up to Candy Heaven and Adam hopped out. "You guys go on to River Burger. I've got to see what the schedule looks like anyway."

"But what about Finn?" Rico asked.

Adam grimaced. "Tell him I'll be by on my lunch break. Will I see you tonight?"

Rico glanced at Derek and nodded. "Yeah. I'll be home after work."

"That's funny," Adam muttered. "Neither of you *look* stupid, but whatever. I'm cooking. Be prepared for red meat and some sort of vegetable. Derek, you want some?"

Derek looked apologetic. "Sorry—actually, my sister's husband texted this morning. He wants to go bond, so I'm going to go play on Dad's company softball team tonight."

Adam grunted. "Lucky," he muttered.

"Well, I'll tell Dad you're open to a game," Derek laughed. "He sort of thinks you're a baseball god already."

Adam shrugged and ran inside, apparently having taken as much family goodwill as one guy could possibly stand.

"Was that a no?" Derek asked, a little puzzled.

"That was a 'he'd love to but he's afraid to ask or get his hopes up,'" Rico said dryly. "Did you not just *meet* my family?"

Derek grunted and put the car in drive, the better to find a parking spot closer to River Burger. "We should do something nice for him and Finn," he said thoughtfully. "Just… just because. Because he's got to get used to people being good to him."

Rico reached over and patted his knee. "I know I could get used to *you* being good to *me*," he said, and only part of it was innuendo.

Derek slanted him a smile. "Yeah?"

Rico nodded. "God, could I."

"Then we'll do something nice for him, and I'll do *lots* of nice stuff for you, how's that?"

"I can't thank you enough—you know that, right?"

Derek pulled the car up to a parking spot that God himself might have picked out, and slid right in. He hit the button for the top so they wouldn't be leaving the car wide open, and as they sat in the idling car, waiting for the vinyl to obscure the too-bright sun, he grabbed Rico's hand and kissed it, looking straight ahead. "You know what I didn't say this weekend?"

"Stop, that hurts?"

Derek startled and then flashed him a giant grin. "Well, that too. But I didn't say 'I love you.'"

Rico's breath caught in his chest.

"I love you, Rico. Your mom—she seems like a really classy lady. But she was right about one thing. You've always been a good boy. I… not *too* good," he qualified rapidly, and then he looked at him head-on. "I just really love you. Does that scare you?"

Rico leaned forward and kissed him, just to seal it. "No. But you know what?"

"What?" Derek asked, but he smirked like he knew what was coming.

"Now that we've had sex in a bed, we're not making out in the car. Let's go get lunch!"

They enjoyed lunch. Mari and her mom told a simple version of what they'd talked about, the thing that had turned Rico's mom around and given the heart of sweetness to what could have been a truly awful moment.

Turned out, they'd just explained things.

"It's like nobody talks about it," Mari said, waving her hands in frustration. "I mean, everyone who's allied with the LGBTQ community expects people to either be awful *or* expects them to be on our side. Nobody ever accounts for the learning curve. She needed someone to explain how both Rico and Adam could be gay—that it's DNA. She needed someone to explain that just because they were gay didn't mean they didn't have the same morals as everyone else." Mari shuddered. "I actually had to *say* that just because I grew up in the house with my brothers, that didn't mean I was going to have sex with them. Ugh. Now I have to live with that in my brain. You people owe me."

Rico laughed kindly. "Well, I for one appreciate it. She… she was really ready to understand, I think, when she came out. Let's hear it for jailhouse education."

"Let's hear it for family worth fighting for," Mari said back, and then she hugged Finn, who had just rounded the corner with a tray full of sandwiches.

Finn made a show of "get off me!" but once he'd unloaded his tray, he kissed his sister on the cheek. "Yeah, yeah—now I've got to think of something nice to do back. Thanks a lot."

Mari and her mother laughed, but Rico thought his mom had been right. Finn's family really *was* that tight, and yeah. There was a lot you could learn from just being around them.

Fortunately for Rico, Finn and Adam weren't going anywhere. Also fortunately, Derek's family was pretty supportive too. Rico had already learned the hard way that a love could stand or fall when it leaned on the wrong load-bearing walls.

IT WAS a good thing Rico had arrived at that conclusion, because Derek's meeting with his brother-in-law had unforeseen consequences of the familial variety.

A few weeks after Rico's mom got out of jail (and he wasn't ever going to get tired of thinking of it like that), Rico had a family dinner to attend, and once again, he was dependent on Finn for a good impression.

"A tie?" Finn asked, scandalized. "To a meeting with his friend and his sister?"

"We're going out to dinner!" Rico objected. "It's supposed to be a really nice—"

"Does it *require* a tie?" Finn asked straight up, hands on hips. That kid had *really* long arms, and the effect was more frightening than comic. If Finn ever started using his Finn-power for evil, he could probably beat the crap out of people without a lot of effort.

"His parents are going to be there!" Rico told him.

Finn waved his hand as if that meant nothing. "You've already met them. They're like sitcom parents—real parents are not possibly that adorable."

Rico stared at him openmouthed. "You mean like *your entire family*? You know, your freaky womenfolk who sweet-talked my *mami* out of jail?" His mother had called him twice since that week: once to tell him she'd made it home safely, and once to tell him she'd moved out and was in her own apartment now. He'd tried to awkwardly offer his sympathies, but her response had been pure Lydia Gonzalves-Macias.

"It is not for you to worry about, Ricardo. Your father chose his side, I chose mine, and that is all."

But his father had obviously not chosen *Rico*, and Rico was a little relieved. Cowardly? Maybe. But he didn't feel the loss of his father in his life like he would have felt the loss of his mother. Perhaps that was what his father got for not being there when Rico *wasn't* out, but Rico wasn't going to try to change that now.

No, *now* Rico had to worry about a semiformal family dinner, and his new best gayfriend didn't think he was going to pass muster.

"I have no idea what you're talking about," Finn said blankly. "My family is what?"

Rico shook his head. "Nothing. They're awesome. For one thing, they'd never drag Adam anyplace he'd have to wear a tie."

Finn laughed evilly. "That's what you think. I'm gonna marry that man someday, and I expect him to wear a suit."

Rico stared at him. "Uhm. Okay. Awesome. Adam's wearing a suit to his wedding, and I'm wearing *my underwear* to meet my in-laws!"

"Cool your jets and keep your boxers on," Finn muttered, rifling through the drawers under the television. The kid knew his clothes better than Rico at this point. "You know what I don't understand?"

"That your family is like fairy-elf angels sent straight from heaven to make all gay people happy?" Rico *still* couldn't believe Finn thought that was normal.

Finn shot him an annoyed look over his shoulder as he pulled out Rico's casual shirts in a clump. "Are you high? I mean, I didn't think Derek did drugs, but—"

"*No!*" Rico snapped. "Get to the point?"

"Oh. Yeah. Well, what I don't understand is how Adam, who hates 90 percent of all people on general principle and is awkward in most social situations, knows what to wear during all those social situations, even if he can't afford to buy clothes."

Rico narrowed his eyes. "He. Is. An. *Artist!*"

"Yeah, I know! And you're a professional! Shouldn't you know wardrobe rules?"

"It didn't come with the gay," Rico said sullenly. "Do we have anything yet? I'm supposed to be there in forty-five minutes."

"Yeah, but it's in Old Sac, so you got time. You're going home with Derek, right?"

"Yeah, I told you that."

"But I'm making sure, because I want to pick Adam up, and I don't want to feel like we're deserting you."

"Didn't Adam take the bus for *months*—"

Finn's glance raked him from top to toe. "You're not a bus-taking guy, Rico. And you're picking a fight with me why?"

He held a khaki green shirt made of a nice silky blend, with button-down pockets, and a pair of khaki shorts. "See? It's July, but this says semiformal, 'I want to impress my in-laws, but I'm not stupid enough to show up in a tie and slacks when it's 106 today.'"

Rico squinted, puzzled. "I didn't even know I had that shirt."

"You're hopeless. I mean, all your *suits* are top rate, but your, you know, living for you clothes? Dude. I hope Derek takes you shopping or something. You're driving *me* bugshit."

Rico's pocket buzzed, which was awesome because that meant it was a text, and he didn't have to answer that. The truth was, he was coming to treasure these sparring matches with Finn. He was bright, funny, and endlessly entertaining—and extremely protective of Adam. Rico had never actually had a *friend* who was gay, and it was apparent Finn knew all about being someone's gay friend, because he was awesome at it. Rico really hoped Finn didn't get tired of him—not so early in his relationship, anyway. Rico might need help for a little while longer.

"It's Derek," he said. "He wants to meet up at Candy Heaven. I guess he wanted to introduce everyone to Adam."

"Oh God," Finn muttered. "Get your ass in gear, Rico! This is an emergency!"

Rico nodded, taking the clothes Finn tossed at him and getting dressed in record speed. "Okay, I need to get my hair and my breath—"

"Yeah, wait—I'll be right there with gel. I bought some new product for Adam, but I want you to try it out."

"Adam wears product?" Rico asked dubiously. Because that ranked right up there with *Adam wears nylons and a corset?*

"Well, not yet! Now go!"

Rico paused to fasten his cargo shorts and then asked, a little hesitantly, "I, uhm, don't really drive you bugshit, right? 'Cause you're sort of my best platonic friend outside of work *ever*."

Finn gaped at him, big blue eyes wide as an angel's. He closed his mouth after a moment and grinned. "That's awesome," he said, nodding. "'Cause, you know, friends from school don't always stick, but you're sort of stuck with family for life. So that works for us. Now hurry—Adam's going to seriously plotz in his shorts if suddenly Derek's whole family shows up and we're not there."

They were too late.

By the time Finn and Rico found parking and hopped out of the car, Adam was pinned behind the counter, surrounded by Derek's well-meaning parents, a pretty woman who looked a lot like Derek, and a massive six-five plus man-mountain with black hair and a sweet smile.

"Who is *that*?" Finn asked, a little bit of awe in his voice.

"Hale and Renee," Rico replied, awed too. "Hale is Derek's friend from college."

"Jesus, he's all muscle!"

Rico would have made a crack about Finn only having eyes for Adam, but it was the truth. This guy studied to be an *actuary*? No wonder he felt more comfortable in a hardware store. That body would have been wasted behind a desk.

Derek's little marshmallow-cheeked mother was busy talking to Adam, and Rico had a whole other thing to worry about.

"So, Adam! My husband and I really loved seeing you play softball last month. Did you not play professionally because you were gay?"

They actually watched Adam's eyes grow larger and his mouth fall open. "Uh, no, uh, school, uh, Army, oh...."

"Mom," Derek said good-naturedly, coming up behind Rico and touching his shoulder in passing. "What did I say about waiting until I got here?"

"But Derek, we already *sort* of know each other! Besides, Adam's happy to meet us, aren't you, Adam?"

"I know *I'm* thrilled," Darrin said, walking from the back offices and meeting Adam's eyes. Everybody turned to look at Darrin, who was wearing another androgynous peasant blouse over his blue jeans today and whose shoulder-length shag was pulled up in a clip at his nape. Adam practically slumped against the back wall. "To what do we owe the, uhm, pleasure?"

Derek looked at him sheepishly. "Sorry, Darrin. I told my family to meet me *out in front* of the store—I didn't think they'd swarm all over Adam."

Darrin arched a sculpted eyebrow. "Well, as fun as it is to swarm over Adam, we should probably try to avoid making him piddle like a schnauzer in the corner. Adam, how about you show Derek's parents where their favorite candy is, and I'll help everybody else."

"'Kay, boss," Adam said weakly. He moved from behind the counter and caught Rico's eye, mouthing, "You so fuckin' owe me."

Rico nodded, covering his mouth so Adam couldn't see him smile, and then turned to where Renee was complimenting Darrin on his earrings and asking for the artisan who designed them. Okay, good. One in-law down, the other to go.

"He's lucky," Hale told him, swallowing Rico's hand in his massive paw and shaking delicately, like he was picking up a porcelain doll. "Kevin and Dillon wanted to come too, but Derek told them to back off, he didn't want to scare you. He didn't even mention making your cousin piss himself."

"He was just overwhelmed," Finn snapped.

Rico put a hand on his shoulder. "Maybe go run interference?" he said quietly. "You know, translate nice parents to Adam? He doesn't speak that language."

Finn shook his head. "Everybody wants to know Adam better. Nobody wants to know that he likes to be left alone." But he trotted down toward the fudge cooler and started asking Sylvie and Edgar what they were planning to eat that night and whether they were going out for ice cream.

"Nice to meet you," Hale said, grinning. God, he even had a leviathan grin! "Derek has told us a *lot* about you."

"Well, I'd say the same, but apparently he forgot to mention you were as big as a bus."

Hale's laugh was as big as the man. Renee left off her chatter with Darrin to look at him in puzzlement. "But why *wouldn't* he tell Rico how big you are?" she asked. "Isn't that, like, the first thing people notice? Because that's what *I* noticed—honey, you're like Andre the Giant, but cuter. You know, like in *Princess Bride*?"

Rico blinked hard, but his eyes were still drying out because he couldn't seem to stop staring. "Derek has *definitely* told me about *you*," he said, smiling widely so she wouldn't suspect exactly what he'd been saying.

"He thinks I'm an airhead," she said flatly, eyeing her brother with dislike.

"Oh, honey, you know he just gets impatient when you don't get his jokes." Hale draped his arm over his wife's thin shoulders, dwarfing her tiny body, before winking at Rico.

"But they're not *funny*!" she protested.

He squeezed her shoulder. "It's a sibling thing," Hale reassured her. "I know I've got a brother at home that I cannot *stand*, but my parents tell me that it's entirely hormonal."

Rico infused all of the sincerity he could muster into his smile. "Well, I'm sure that's Derek's problem, because you are definitely charming."

She narrowed her eyes. "As opposed to what?"

Hale patted her arm. "The opposite of charming, sweetheart. Let's go see what your parents are getting!"

Rico watched them go with mixed feelings of relief and distress. "Wasn't the whole point to get people *away* from Adam?"

"And possibly out of my store," Darrin said behind them, sounding only a little annoyed. "Not that I mind customers *or* sales, but I'm expecting my newest employee to wander in, and these things are always tricky when they haven't met you yet."

Rico gaped at him. "Please tell me it's some sort of exchange program?" he begged, because otherwise that sounded… well, a little weird.

"And please tell *me* why you two aren't moved in together and setting off car alarms with your loud annoying monkey sex every night!" Darrin demanded.

Rico took two flailing steps back. "You know, that's a little personal—"

"You don't like it? Then resolve your love life and get out of my Pixy Stix powder. It's *irritating* how long you two are taking. I would *like* to focus on the poor feral little kitten who's going to walk through my door, but now I've got two metrosexuals who apparently can't find commitment with two hands and a backhoe!"

"I *beg* your pardon?" Rico asked, still freaking out.

Darrin shook his head and then looked over at the door on Front Street. "Bzzz," he said, waving his hand. "Go bother your cousin some more. I've got at least four more years to straighten *him* out!"

"But I was going to offer him more work!" Derek said, sounding genuinely upset.

Darrin smiled and waved at a tiny waif in the gauzy dress who was standing at the door and then made a hurried gesture to a stocky girl wearing a Candy Heaven work apron with brutally short hair and horn-rimmed glasses. "Yes, Joni dear, that's *her*." Then he turned to Derek. "*You* will do no such thing. He can be yours when he gets out of school, but right now he's mine. Do you have *any* idea how much damage I have to clean up in that one before I set him loose on the world? *Do you?*"

Derek stopped short and looked at Rico, who looked soberly back.

"I've got some idea, yes," Derek said, pinching the bridge of his nose.

"Then could you possibly butt out of his life and let him stay here where he feels safe for a while? He'll work for you through school too. He's a good boy, that one. Works hard. He'll be fine."

"But—" Derek began, probably about to tell Adam's boss that Adam could make a lot more money working for him full time, and possibly he'd get through school faster too.

"He's right," Rico said, grabbing his arm and going to bail Adam out of the family that wouldn't leave him alone. Over his shoulder he said, "Thank you, Darrin. You're right. We'll stop worrying you and get out of your way."

"*What?*" Derek asked, outraged. "Rico—!"

"My mom said she was sorry," Rico said softly. "Adam's never will. Look at him." They both looked as Adam found his footing and started offering truffle samples to everyone and taking orders and filling them quickly and efficiently. "It's simple work—and we both know he can do a lot more. But he's capable. He's dealing with people, and I never thought he could do this in a million years. He needs this. It's his happy place. Let him stay here until it chafes, okay?"

Derek paused and squeezed his hand. "Yeah, okay. You're right, you know that? But I thought you didn't believe in—"

"I'll believe in anything that makes him happy," Rico said and then took a deep breath and prepared to launch himself back into Derek's family. "Just like you."

Derek kissed his cheek right there in the store. "That's sweet," he said. "And nice outfit! Did Finn pick that out for you?"

"You'd better believe it," Rico said grimly. "Now be nice to your sister or this whole exercise was a waste of time."

Well, a good steak was *never* a waste of time, and since Derek took them to a steakhouse in Old Sac, at the end of the day, Rico figured it was worth his time. They ate, drank good wine, and Rico and Derek pressed their knees together under the table when Renee went off on a ramble about margarine, butter, and vegan margarine substitute that lasted ten minutes and was punctuated with Hale's besotted prompts of "That's real smart, sweetheart. What else do you know about soluble fats?"

Derek's parents asked him the "Does he talk in his sleep?" question again, and this time, Rico was able to answer with a solid negatory. "No, actually. I haven't heard him once."

"*See!*" Derek crowed in triumph. "I *told* you it was Dillon!"

"So Dillon was asleep when he told me to piss off the other day?" Renee asked, sounding confused.

"No, darlin'," Hale said, the epitome of patience. "He was getting a sandwich and you were trying to make lemonade under his arms. You were actually being annoying."

Renee opened and closed her mouth a few times and looked at her husband in shock, and then she closed her eyes, took a deep breath, and sighed. "Yeah, I probably was. It's really easy to forget I'm a grown-up when we're all at my parents' house, you know?"

Rico suddenly felt a bit of kinship for her that he never expected, and they started a conversation about when adulthood *really* began that actually involved the entire table through dessert.

A good meal—a pleasant family meal—and as Derek and Rico were walking back to the parking structure near Candy Heaven, Rico grabbed Derek's hand and kissed it.

"What?" Derek asked.

"Just... you know. Your sister *is* an airhead, but you know what?"

"What?"

"She's part of your family, and I love her too."

"Aw," Derek said, holding his face to the breeze off the river. The sweltering air was finally cooling down at nearly ten o'clock at night. "That kind of talk *will* get you laid."

"Promise?" Rico asked breathily. Because even though they'd been having sex for nearly a month, it wasn't getting *any* less exciting. The thought of it still squeezed his breath, and the touch of Derek's skin against his own still sent an uncomfortable wash of heat through him.

It was beginning to dawn on him that this relationship had lasted almost as long as his and Ezra's, and that this one didn't have any reason to go away.

Here, under the stars and with the smell of water drifting over them, that promise was becoming more and more necessary to breathe.

Summer's End

AT THE beginning of August, Rico and Derek took Adam and Finn to a Giants game. This took subterfuge and planning, and Rico was surprised they managed to pull it off.

He couldn't say exactly where the idea took root—sure, he'd semipromised to take Adam earlier in the year, but suddenly, after that day in the candy store, the idea seemed to sprout full grown.

Rico wanted to give Adam something amazing.

He tried to explain it about two weeks after the dinner with Derek's parents. They were sitting in the living room, watching professional wrestling—which was an extremely odd choice, but Derek had left the remote on the coffee table and was now lying on Rico, head on his chest. They were both too comfortable to move, so guys in rainbow leotards mauled each other mercilessly. Rico gave up staring at them and trying with half his brain to figure out if they were fighting or just really well choreographed.

"So," Rico said after thirty seconds of trying to decide if the guy in the purple cape had a really big jock strap or a really big erection, "he's starting school, and he's going to be working two jobs, and you know? He keeps asking when I want him to move out, and the thing is, I don't. And I don't think he gets that. I don't *want* him to move. He's happy there with Finn. I'd rather give *them* the apartment and—"

"Move in with me?" Derek said, turning to look at him earnestly.

The question wasn't unexpected. Rico was spending, at most, three days a week over at the apartment, and that was to help take care of the animals when Finn and Adam were busy.

But it was also to walk to work with Adam and talk to Finn and have an excuse to pet his dog. It was just that now that Rico knew how family worked, he was happy. He was comfortable. He was sort of reluctant to go start one on his own—he didn't want to screw this up.

His uncertainty must have shown on his face.

Derek raised a hand to his cheek and stroked gently. "What are you afraid of?"

"This is as good as my life's ever gotten," Rico said honestly. "I mean… in a million years, I didn't think I could be this happy."

Derek widened his eyes and blinked. "So you don't want to move in with me because…."

Rico cleared his throat and shifted, feeling superstitious and silly. "Uhm… you know. What if I mess with what we're doing and it breaks?"

Derek pushed himself up awkwardly and reached for the remote to turn off the television. "You're afraid that moving in will break us," he said slowly, like the concept was foreign to him.

"Uh, yeah." Rico tried a quick smile. "I mean, I'm *happy*. I know this happens to you a little more often, and I just want to make sure it's all stable and shit before I go jinxing it by trying to do too much."

It occurred to him that he sounded about twelve years old, and he didn't know how to fix that, and he didn't know how to *not* be afraid either.

Derek stood up and stretched and then offered his hand to Rico. "C'mon," he said, smiling sleepily.

"Where we going?"

"Well, first we're going to my laptop to buy four tickets and to reserve two hotel rooms in the city."

Rico smiled. "Yeah?" Oh good. They were going to forget completely about Rico being superstitious and dragging his feet and not wanting to rock the—

"And then we're going into my bedroom, where first we're going to watch porn for, like an *hour*, and then we're going to have *real sex*, and you're going to see the difference."

Rico flushed. "I, uhm… I mean, I've seen porn before, Derek. I know the difference between what's on screen and what you and I do in real life."

Derek arched an eyebrow. "Are you sure?"

Rico flushed harder. "Yeah. I mean, I was celibate for seven years. Real life is better."

"But not as pretty," Derek said soberly. "And you usually have to clean stuff up afterwards."

Rico couldn't meet his eyes. "Your point is…?"

"That I'm not positive this is going to work out—but I sure do hope it will. I get being a little bit nervous, but don't let that… that *fear* keep this from becoming something amazing. 'Cause no matter how good something looks in fantasy, real life is better."

Rico looked away. "We already are," he said softly.

Derek sighed and shook his head. "Yeah. Okay. I get it. Let's go prove to *Adam* that happiness exists."

Derek turned to the kitchen table, where his laptop was set up. They'd both needed to wrap up some work that evening, and they'd eaten takeout companionably as they'd finished.

Derek apparently had the page bookmarked.

"You were making plans?" Rico asked, looking over his shoulder.

Derek's grunt was a little wounded. "I thought you and I were going to go sometime this summer. I didn't think we'd be taking Adam and Finn."

"We don't have to—"

"No, no—it's a good idea," Derek said on a sigh. "It's just... I don't know. I get the whole family thing, okay? I have one of my own, and they love you. Hell, they love *Adam* at this point."

"Adam's won two softball games for them so far." That meeting at Candy Heaven had resulted in Adam's draft onto the family business softball team. Finn got time off to go to his games and cheer him on. "And I liked them too—"

"Then why are you so worried about leaving your own couch?"

Rico shrugged, feeling miserable. "I don't know. I mean, except for with you, it's the only place in the world I feel safe."

Derek blinked slowly. "Nice save," he said after a moment.

Rico smiled hopefully and nuzzled his ear. "Nice enough to get me some non-porn-flavored action?"

Derek squinted at the screen. "I am not sure if that's good or not."

Rico *hmm*ed in his ear again, letting his tongue flicker out and tease the whorls. Derek shivered as he selected seats and prepared to buy the tickets.

"Think of it like movie popcorn without the butter," Rico purred. "Same great flavor, none of the slimy, fatty aftertaste."

Derek actually turned and looked at him. "I may need porn now just to get it up after that."

Rico winced. "Uhm, okay. Well, if you come to bed and undress voluntarily, I may, perhaps, find a way to fix that."

Derek shook his head. "You may have to coax me out of my clothes," he said seriously. "And I can't even look at the lube."

Rico giggled. "You afraid I'm going to butter your buns and pop your corn?"

"Out!" Derek commanded, a smile twitching at his lips. "Out, I say! Go make thee naked, heathen, and try to find some way to assuage my wounded sensibilities!" He waved Rico imperiously toward the bedroom while he pulled out his credit card to pay for the tickets and the reservations.

Rico paused. "Hey, wait. Do you want my card? I can totally spring—"

Derek continued to gesture without breaking character. "Did I say go?" he thundered. "I think I said something about naked and stroking your cock in one hand while violating yourself with the other—"

"I could always use the new sex toy in the drawer," Rico suggested hopefully.

Derek pretended to consider this, but given that Rico had found the thing, fresh and sealed in the box, in the lube drawer after one of his rare nights in his own apartment, he was pretty sure Derek was *dying* to see him use that thing.

"It may soothe my annoyance," he said sagely. "Yes, indeed. I think I should find you in miduse of that instrument when I come in." He looked away from the computer and allowed his full wicked grin to take over his features. "Please?" he added with a little nibble of his lower lip.

Rico bowed completely at the waist. "Anything to please you, my liege," he said throatily, so very grateful. Derek had been hurt, but he'd dropped the subject. And Rico had a little more time to revel in this relationship like Clopper reveled in a field full of daisies, before reality called him home.

Derek harrumphed royally as his fingers flew over the keyboard, and Rico turned and trotted down the hallway to get ready.

The naked was no problem.

Outside was another scorching summer day, but Derek had turned on the misters and the fans the moment they arrived, giving the AC a much-needed boost. In the back bedroom, with a fan on the ceiling and one on the floor, the air was cool enough to tantalize, cool enough to titillate, so stripping the bedding and lying naked in the center of the big bed was an erotic pleasure and not a discomfort.

But it wasn't until he *was* lying naked on his side in the middle of the bed, the long, heavily veined purple sex toy and lube on a towel in front of him, that he realized he had more than the joy of being naked going on here.

He was alone, as vulnerable as any human being could be in front of another, on Derek's bed.

"Have you started?" Derek called. Rico could hear him moving around, probably turning off the lights and the television and such.

"Right now," he answered breathily.

He had to close his eyes at first, forgetting that it was Derek's bed, forgetting that the lights were on and he was sprawled in the middle of white sheets. He had to concentrate only on the cool air moving over his heated skin, on the way his nipples puckered as he drifted his fingertips over them.

That felt nice. He pinched his nipple a little more forcefully, and a full-body shudder racked him. He rolled over to his back and let his thighs fall open, shivering again when a burst of air from the fan hit his crease, his taint, his balls. His cock, already semierect, swelled thickly against his thigh.

He didn't palm it. Not yet. The moment stretched out, all about teasing himself, about being lost in sex when Derek finally walked in— about trusting that Derek wouldn't hurt him or laugh or leave him hanging.

The thought of Derek walking in, seeing him sprawled out with the toy shoved in his ass, made his cock harder. His breathing quickened, and he fumbled for the toy and the lube. His cock he left, throbbing, *aching* for attention, because he hoped it would be the first thing Derek touched.

Derek's going to touch me.

Ah! One of those whole-body shivers again. He propped his feet up, spreading himself as much as possible to the air, and dumped lube on his fingers.

Cold.

Cold, right at the tender heat of his orifice, smoothing, penetrating, stretching. He was panting now, and every now and then a faint, breathy moan issued from his throat.

He bore down on his own fingers, wanting more, practically gibbering to himself for *somebody* to *for God's sake* touch his cock and fuck his ass.

He fumbled for the toy then, and it was slippery, *tantalizingly* slippery, sliding through his fingers, pushing against his opening before skimming off, and he groaned in frustration.

"Need help?" Derek asked.

Rico's eyes flew open, and it was just like he'd imagined: Derek leaning against his closed door, shirt unbuttoned and unbelted pants hanging to his knees. His erection bulged against his boxers, peeking out from under the elastic on the top, shining with precome.

With a burst of determination, Rico shoved the toy *hard*, and the head popped in. "Nungh...."

He shuddered again and his whole body started to vibrate like a piano string tapped frantically at perfect pitch.

"So," Derek said, semiamused but mostly aroused, "you're just going to make me watch?"

Rico shoved the seven-inch length of the toy in to the base, feeling every veined ridge as it slid in. "You do what you have to," he taunted. "But I haven't touched my cock yet, so—"

"Don't," Derek commanded. His clothes hit the ground before Rico had time to withdraw the toy. "Let go." He crawled across the bed, and Rico's hand left the base of the dildo before his mind had time to catch up.

"*No!*" he whined. It just hung there, the head inside of him, the rest of it on the bed, and every whoosh of the fan teased him, from the crack of his ass to the head of his dripping cock.

"Trust me," Derek purred, seizing the base and pushing in just a little at a time.

"*Nnn*...." Rico flailed for a moment as his body—which had been given to pleasure—was now taken over by Derek.

Derek licked the dripping head of his cock with a flat tongue. "Trust me," he commanded again, and Rico had no choice. Of *course* he trusted Derek. He knotted his fingers in that careless sand-colored hair and held on.

"Trust. You." His throat felt raw and tortured. When Derek engulfed his cooling cockhead with a hot mouth, he arched up hard, trusting that Derek knew what he was doing.

Oh *God*, did Derek know what he was doing. He sucked viciously, squeezing Rico's shaft with his mouth and thrusting the toy in slow, tantalizing strokes.

Rico's noises had gone from faint moans to full-out repeated cries.

Derek shoved the dildo in to the hilt while he bottomed Rico's cock in the back of his throat, and Rico arched his shoulders off the bed and screamed—

But he didn't come.

His body shook with the effort, and he spurted enough precome to make Derek swallow, but he held on to himself.

"You waiting for something?" Derek asked, teasing Rico's frenulum with his tongue.

Rico tugged at his head. "You," he said gruffly.

Derek's mouth tasted like precome and sweat, and Rico knotted his fingers in his hair and pulled him close, welcoming the warmth of his lean body over Rico's chilled skin.

Their bodies ground together, and Rico's ass clenched tightly around the silicone invader. Every beat of his heart drove the ridges more tightly against his muscle ring, and he smoothed Derek's hair back from his face with shaking hands.

"Me?" Derek asked, smiling impishly. "That's what you're waiting for?"

Rico didn't feign the desperation. "Please?"

Derek's grin turned sultry, and he grabbed the lubricant from next to Rico and squeezed it on his fingers, then reached behind his back. Rico watched avidly as Derek grimaced at the invasion, and then… then….

His face relaxed in total welcome of his fingers.

Derek shuddered hard and wrapped his slippery fingers around Rico's cock, squeezing, slicking. And before Rico could whine, could beg some more, Derek positioned Rico at his entrance and slid down, slow, so slow, taking Rico's cock and riding him, making his own needy sex noises as he sat.

He hit bottom, shuddering, his thighs clenching Rico's hips, and Rico reached up and stroked his stomach. Derek clasped one of his hands and leaned forward, starting to rock, while Rico moved his hand to fist Derek's dripping cock.

For a moment they were complete and completely equal. Derek rocked forward and backward, his body tight and hot and around Rico, and Rico kept up his own pump on Derek's shaft, rubbing his thumb across the slickness of the head.

Ah… God… yes. Now that he and Derek were one, *now* he could relax, could let go, could let the orgasm ride through his asshole, his taint, that sweet grip on his cock. *Now* he could arch up and lose himself in Derek's body, could let the pressure in his own body peak and crest and wash through him, tumbling him weightlessly into the surf of come.

Above him Derek tilted his head back and cried out, shuddering, ejaculating messily over Rico's stomach and across his mouth and cheekbone. As Rico sank down against the mattress, he licked his lips, tasting the clotted salt-tang of it. Derek slumped forward and Rico popped out, both of them running with Rico's semen, neither of them caring.

It took a few minutes for them to catch up with their breathing, to come back to themselves.

"After," Rico panted.

"Afterwards?" Derek asked muzzily. "Afterglow? Afterlife?"

"After the game," Rico said, smiling a little. He kissed Derek's temple tenderly. "After we take my cousin and his boyfriend to the city and show them a good time. That's what, three weeks? So then. After I get used to leaving my dog with Adam. After we get back. Ask me again."

"Ask you what again?" Derek asked, but he didn't sound muzzy or out of it anymore. He sounded careful.

Rico regarded him soberly. "Ask me when we're moving in together. I'm pretty sure you'll get a better answer."

Derek smiled slowly. "So, after?"

Rico nodded, closing his eyes in the aftermath of sex in spite of his best intentions of staying awake for this conversation. "Yeah," he said. "After. 'Cause you know I love you, right?"

"Yeah," Derek whispered, kissing his jaw, by his ear. "And I love you too."

"Good. Then we should move in together soon. 'Cause that's how you trust someone when you're in love."

He heard Derek's sleepy chuckle and figured that "after" would be good enough for them both.

AT FIRST Finn was going to try to get Mari to watch the animals, and she was all for it. But at the last minute, her kid got sick, and Derek called on Miguel.

Miguel had lost his business financing at the last moment, and Derek had already filled his position with another intern. At present Derek had him on the payroll as a freelance manager, but he'd actually gone back to work for Darrin at Candy Heaven to make ends meet and to raise money for another attempt.

Derek and Rico were picking Adam up at work for another softball game when Derek saw Miguel and brought it up.

"Babysit your dog?" Miguel said, looking like Derek had just chopped off his finger and Miguel was waiting for the pain.

Derek winced, and Rico smacked him on the arm. He'd never seen Derek make a social misstep before, but when Finn had called them that morning to say they might not be able to leave the next day because Joshie was having a bad reaction to the chicken-pox vaccine and Mari couldn't leave him, Derek had looked stricken. Rico figured it had something to do with that promise—made three weeks ago on this day—that he'd give Derek a solid answer on the moving-in thing. If anything, he spent more time at Derek's house than ever—if it wasn't for the time he took to walk the dog and help Finn and Adam with transportation, he'd say he *was* living at Derek's house. But there was something about that promise—having all of your possessions in a place, and your name on the bills, and the address on your driver's license—that made "living together" much more a thing.

"It's more like Adam's dog," Rico said, glaring at Derek.

Derek had the grace to look ashamed. "Sorry. You know, forget it. We can just do this some other weekend or—"

Miguel had been restocking the fudge in the refrigerator case, and suddenly he shook himself like a dog shedding water. "You know what? That's fine. I mean, it's a stupid crush, and it's not like he's been anything but decent to me." He looked over his shoulder to where Adam was busy running stock from the loft down the stairs like he was running ammo to the front lines of a bitter and brutal war. Intent on saving the world through sugar supply, Adam almost didn't look up, and when he did, he paused to wave.

"How's it hanging, guys? Too bad about Joshie—man, that game would have been nice." He set down the two boxes in his arms and called, "Katia, if you could fill this stock for me? That'd be great, and you can go eat afterwards."

The waifish girl with blue hair who had showed up the last time Rico had been there looked at Adam with adoring eyes and nodded, trotting to the boxes with enthusiasm.

Miguel watched the by-play with a pained expression and turned back to Rico and Derek. "See? Finn was in here yesterday getting *so* enthused about the trip to the city, and Adam was like, 'No, man—don't get too excited, we don't have our plans made yet.' It was…

yeah. I'd like to do something nice for the guy. Katia doesn't talk to anybody but Adam and Darrin, you know? Not even Joni, who's totally in love with her." Miguel shrugged resignedly. "It'd be spiteful not to help him out."

Rico shook his head. "You're like... like a TV person, do you know that? That's really nice of you."

Miguel shrugged again. "Do I need a key or something?"

"Yeah. Can you stop by tomorrow morning? I'll text you the address."

As Rico pulled out his phone and started tapping, Adam came down the stairs again, balancing two boxes on his hip.

"Hey, Adam! Miguel says he can watch Clopper while we're gone—the game's still on!"

Adam stumbled down the last step. Darrin—who just happened to be walking by—steadied him. "Oh thank God," Darrin said, taking one of the boxes and walking toward the sour barrels. "He goes to the baseball game, you guys can *finally* get your shit together, and I can start figuring out who this blue-eyed kid with the Star of David is who keeps fucking up my dreams."

Rico froze right after hitting Send. "You've been dreaming about Ezra?" he asked, his entire body still. Next to him, Derek quit breathing.

Darrin's eyes widened and he shook his head frantically. "No. I absolutely have *not* been dreaming about someone who may or may not put you two yuppies on hold. Nope. Not Ezra, not big blue eyes... just, you two, move the hell in already, you're messing up my vibe!"

With that Darrin flounced off, leaving the four of them in his wake, three of them staring at Rico.

Surprisingly, Adam spoke up first. "Well, even if he does show up, it's not like you'd go back to him anyway. What-the-fuck ever." He turned on his heel and resumed stocking.

"Who's Ezra?" Miguel asked, puzzled.

Rico shifted uncomfortably. "Uhm, you know. Exes."

Miguel's eyes widened and he stared at Derek like Derek might not have heard.

"Yes," Derek said shortly. "I know about Ezra. And how lovely that Darrin is apparently dreaming about him. Isn't that nice? I think that's nice, don't you think that's nice?"

"No!" Rico said, appalled. "I think it's creepy as hell. *I* don't dream about him. I'd really prefer it if nobody here gave him a second thought!"

Derek regarded him through narrowed eyes. "Yeah?"

"Swear!" Rico held his hand up like he was testifying. "Not a single dream—not since...." He looked at Miguel and smiled gamely. "Uh, come over tomorrow morning, okay?"

Miguel nodded, holding his hands up and backing away. "Deal."

Rico let out a sigh of relief, grabbed Derek's biceps through his T-shirt, and hauled him out of the store through the side entrance, which was not assaulted by the full fury of the sun in early evening.

"Adam, we'll be outside—hurry it up a little!" he called through the open door, although he and Derek had plenty of time to get to the game. He just didn't want this conversation to last any longer than absolutely necessary.

"No," he snapped as soon as they were clear of the doorway—and any listening ears.

"I'm not a child—"

"I said no! I'm not having any thoughts about Ezra. I *promise* you, Derek, that's not what the wait was about."

Derek swallowed and nodded. "Okay," he said, looking away. "I mean, I sort of rushed you. I just didn't want—"

Rico grabbed his hand and leaned in, talking closely because kissing him senseless was not an option—not here. "Look, you didn't rush me. You didn't pressure me. You and me? We happened with full consent and the blessing of the stars, okay? Ezra was almost five months ago—and even if he was yesterday, he wasn't what I've got going inside for you. And you have exes too—"

"Not in a while," Derek said quietly.

Rico nodded, because he'd known that too. "Yeah. You were waiting for me. I mean, you don't want to say it, because it doesn't sound all... educated and businessman, but I get it." He did too. Underneath Derek's business plan and his perfect capability of being Captain of the Universe was a little boy who watched his parents raise children and grow old together. Derek wanted that. He *believed* in it. And whether he said it or not, he thought Rico might just be that chance.

"I want to be that guy for you," Rico said quietly. "I want to be the guy you grow old with, okay? I said afterward, and I meant it. It was a promise. I haven't broken one of those yet—not to you."

Derek sighed and nodded and then gave one of those brilliant smiles like the moment of sulkiness had never been. "Yeah, okay. I get it. I'll borrow my dad's truck if you want—just let me know when."

Rico hoped Derek's overcasualness was fooling Derek, because it sure wasn't fooling Rico. "This weekend we go to the Giants game?"

"Yeah."

"Next weekend I move my shit to your house. I don't have much. We can do it in the cars—it'll take two trips."

Derek smiled a little. "You have more stuff than that."

"No. Adam has most of it. The rest is in storage. So you want me, you got me. I'm a freeloader. None of the shit in storage is worth moving."

"You'll want to keep some—"

Rico grimaced. "You *so* do not get how my life started the day I met you."

Derek's smile relaxed a notch, turned soft and a little wounded. "Neither do you—for me."

Rico nodded. "I'm starting to get it," he said. "I promise I am. Just have a little faith, right? I'll tell Adam in San Francisco."

Derek grinned then, and it wasn't forced, and it wasn't tinged with melancholy either. "I'll make sure me and Finn are getting food and beer!"

"Yeah, but not garlic fries—that kid's digestive system is a *trip*."

Winners and Losers

THERE WAS something lovely about a Giants game. San Francisco could be downright chilly, even in the summer, and Derek and Rico wore their matching River Cats sweatshirts for fun. It was a bright, windy day, and the sky over the Bay was the color of heartbreak and August. Even the scads of tourists couldn't dim their mood as they made their way down the Embarcadero to find dinner. Finn and Rico had chattered the whole trip down, and Adam and Derek responded laconically during the pauses, so even the traffic at the Bay Bridge didn't seem like a bother.

Derek took them to a really nice seafood place with a fire pit inside, that served an awesome seafood Alfredo. While they were there, Adam kept looking self-consciously at the other patrons. It took Rico most of the meal to realize he was fingering the frayed cuffs of his hooded blue sweatshirt, and he almost smacked his forehead with his palm.

After their late lunch/early dinner, Rico got Finn to help him haul Adam into a tourist shop, where he and Derek bought them matching orange zippered hoodies with *Giants* scrawled across the front.

"Oh God," Adam said as Finn zipped him up outside the store. "You can see these things from space!"

"Yeah, I know," Rico said quietly. "So when it starts to fall apart, I'll see it and I can get you another one."

Adam shrugged, and Rico tried not to think about the tattered state of the jacket in the bag. Finn had made a passing remark about how it had been Adam's winter jacket until he'd pulled Rico's old peacoat from the closet, and Rico had died a little inside.

Finn grabbed Adam's hand and hauled him to the back end of the pier so they could look out over the ocean, and Derek hung back next to Rico.

"What are you thinking?" he asked quietly.

"I'm thinking that I'm really glad you and I will live blocks away from the two of them—at least until he's out of school."

"Yeah?" Derek was staring at him avidly, and Rico helped the wind clear his hair from his eyes.

"Yeah. I like that you and me and Finn and Darrin can take care of him. I know it's stupid—I mean, he can obviously take care of himself—"

"But you two need family," Derek said softly. "I hear you. I've always heard you. He's in, Rico. Don't worry."

Rico smiled. "With you? Never. You're the one guy I'd trust to get that about me and Adam. I'm not worried at all."

Derek kissed him softly under the bright August sun, and they went to go find Finn and Adam, because it was time to catch a cab to the stadium before there were none to be found.

The Giants played horribly in the first two innings, but by the third they had four runs to Chicago's three, so there was hope. Derek and Finn went for beer and food in the fifth inning, leaving Adam and Rico sitting in the stands. Rico watched for a second as Adam raised his face to the breeze coming off the Bay. His eyes were closed and his mouth relaxed, and for that moment, Rico could see the gentle little kid he would always think of as his cousin—the boy who would follow Rico anywhere, Rico's dependable bastion against loneliness.

Funny how Adam had actually led the way here, shown Rico how to live his life with no apologies and with a healthy amount of happiness when it was offered on a silver platter. It wasn't his years in the military that made Adam brave.

"Good game?" Rico asked, because you don't talk about things like "You're my hero" when you're family.

"Let's see if they can keep it up," Adam said, opening his eyes. "Are they really getting garlic fries?"

Rico flashed a smile. "For your sake, I hope not."

Adam nodded. "I had *plans* for that kid," he muttered darkly.

Rico laughed. Gassy Finn or not, they would probably still have "plans." Finn's sparkly excitement would have rubbed off on the most dour, cynical, withered, bitchy old misanthropist who ever lived. In Adam's case, he had this sweet half smile whenever he looked at Finn or responded to his enthusiastic babble, or Finn touched Adam's hand.

Or looked at Adam. Or moved. Or breathed in and out without stopping.

"You and Finn probably make good plans," Rico said. "He makes you really happy."

Adam kept his eyes on the game, but the smile that split his face wasn't going anywhere. "Yup."

"You guys really helped me find my feet when I got here," Rico said, feeling awkward. "I appreciate it."

Adam actually darted his gaze off the field and to Rico's face. "Course," he said, surprised. "You're my family."

Rico nodded and smiled. "So, uhm, I'd still be family if I moved into Derek's, right?"

Bless him, Adam didn't even look surprised. "Course." He shrugged. "'Bout time I started paying rent on the apartment anyway. Me and Finn've been feeling bad about that."

Rico shrugged. Rent on that apartment was pretty low, and it had been worth it to have Adam and Finn there, making him feel like a part of a group. Making him feel normal. "You were saving for school, right?"

Adam kept his eyes on the field, and his smile turned shy. Apparently just hoping about the future did that to him. "Yeah. Twelve units this semester. Worth the wait so I could build up the money. 'Preciate the free rent."

"My pleasure," Rico said. On the field, Chicago's pitcher threw high and outside, but the batter swung anyway. Pop fly to right field, catch, and out. "Uhm, just 'cause I'm living with Derek, that… I mean, we can still have dinner once a week, and I'll still want to visit my dog, and we still haven't gone dancing, and you and Finn can still ask me for rides and—" Oh God. He'd made such a fuss about being worried about Adam, but it was *Rico's* voice that wobbled, and *Rico* who sounded like a kid leaving home for the first time.

But it didn't even knock Adam out of the game. "Course," he said. The batter was walking into the box, which was probably why Adam felt like he could shoot a look at Rico and meet his eyes. "You'll have a key. You're not leaving me. I mean"—he shrugged—"it's a few blocks, right?"

Adam turned his attention back to the field, and the twist to his lips wasn't quite as happy or quite as free as it had been. "There's family and family, Rico. You and me, we're the good kind. Didn't go away when I was deployed, isn't going away when you'll live less than a mile away."

Rico wasn't as stoic as Adam—he'd never had to hide under the bed. His eyes burned, and suddenly no amount of pride or manly posturing was enough to keep him from throwing his arm around Adam's shoulders and kissing him unapologetically on the temple. "I love you, cousin," he said, his voice rough. "You and me will *always* be family."

Adam leaned into Rico's arm for a second and accepted the kiss on the temple. In that second, Rico felt like they were boys again, being tucked into the guest bedroom for their nap. That had been the safest part of their day, and the one time he knew he and Adam would have peace.

"Love you back," Adam rasped, and at that moment San Francisco hit one over the wall and out into the Bay. Bells, whistles, a steamboat horn—and the crowd going wild, of course. Adam leapt to his feet and cheered, with Rico not far behind, and Finn and Derek walked up with dogs and beer and ice cream in lieu of garlic fries.

San Francisco won eight to six. Best game Rico had ever seen.

SEX WITH Derek that night was sweet and hot—and a little awkward, because it was the hotel room and not Derek's familiar bed, but maybe that was just Rico.

But in the end, Derek's cock, breathtaking and huge, thrusting inside Rico's ass and Derek's lithe, fit body pounding Rico into the mattress, made Rico forget all about the strange bed and the bright lights while he lost himself in orgasm and the clench of Derek's fingers at his hips.

Derek cried out and shuddered, spending himself inside Rico with force and enthusiasm, and then he collapsed, sweaty and breathless, on Rico's back. His harsh breaths puffed against Rico's ear and interrupted the sound of Rico's heart thundering in his ears.

"Good?" Derek asked when he could talk.

"Do you even need to ask?" Rico retorted. Ah! Derek's come was hot and slippery, sliding down his thighs, and his own cock twitched in response. So good.

Derek nuzzled his nape, blowing to clear the hair out of his way. "Getting long. Ready to get it cut yet?"

Rico turned his head and looked at Derek through his lashes. "Can I say no? I like having hair again."

"You can say whatever you want," Derek said, smiling. He rested his cheek on Rico's. "As long as you tell me it's 'after.'"

"Afterglow? After sex? After midnight?" Rico teased.

Derek groaned and rolled off him onto the bed, sprawling on his back with his arms over his head.

Rico couldn't repress the little grunt of loss at the absence of his cock from the depths of Rico's body. "I'll want that back in a few minutes," he said seriously.

"You'll get nothing and like it if I don't get a better answer," Derek growled. Well, he'd been pretty patient so far, right?

Rico rolled so he could rest his chin on Derek's chest. "Yes, Derek, it's after. I talked to Adam, he's fine. *I* was the one who needed reassurance."

"Did you get it?" Derek searched his face.

"We're going to have them for dinner a lot," Rico said thoughtfully. "And we may be spending some time playing video games on their couch." It felt silly telling Derek that he'd be forsaking his nice house in the thirty block for the small apartment on F Street, but Derek didn't even bat an eyelash.

"I'd love to play video games. I'm sort of hurt you haven't asked me before."

He wasn't, but it was kind of him to say so. Rico smiled slowly. "You're so good at everything," he said, without agenda or envy. "I just didn't want you to win all the games."

To his surprise, Derek blushed and rolled to his side, hiding his face in the bright white comforter on the bed.

"What?" Rico asked, laughing.

Derek laughed and shook his head.

"No, seriously—what?"

"M-mmflll…," he confessed, facedown in the covers.

"Stop talking to the bed!" Rico demanded, still laughing, a little alarmed at how red Derek's face *had* turned when he came up for air. "What?"

"I'm *awful*!" Derek actually choked on his own laughter. "I'm the worst video game player *ever*. I lost *money* in college. I get *annihilated*!"

Rico started to chuckle. "No, really?"

Derek shook his head, still laughing. "God, *Clopper* could beat me!"

"Well, awesome! We'll make it a thing!" For a moment Rico couldn't stop laughing, and Derek couldn't either. Then, as quickly as the laughter sprang up, it died into a sober moment, when Rico met Derek's eyes and Derek seemed to probe directly into his soul.

"You're moving in. It's a thing. We're a couple."

"For as long as you can stand me," Rico said, and he leaned in to take Derek's mouth and push him against the bed. This man—not Ezra, not any guy he'd crushed on during his long period of loneliness—was all he needed.

IT WAS like saying his name—even in Rico's mind—was all the magic the universe needed.

The trip back was full of details: where Rico would leave his car, since Derek's garage only held one car and Rico had covered parking behind the apartment. Where Clopper would go and how visiting rights would work, and would the big doofus even care one way or the other as long as one of the four of them was actually in the room. How Jake the cat got to stay at the apartment too, because Derek's one flaw as a human being was a slight cat allergy. He said he could buy the medication to fix that, but Rico said that if he did, it would be for a cat he helped pick out, and Jake sort of loved Adam and Finn most anyway. This was a slight fabrication. As far as Rico could tell, if the cat was allowed to sleep for at least twenty-two hours a day, he was all good, but Finn seemed especially happy to keep the big comatose drool monkey, so that worked out.

The planning made the trip go fast, as did the gentle kidding about how now Finn and Adam could have loud hyena sex again as well as free use of the couch if they needed. Rico took some ribbing about being sure he wasn't going from one couch to another, but he didn't laugh at that.

"No," he said simply. "I've finally found a home."

The noise in the car quieted, but since it was right at the exit into the city, the silence didn't last long.

As they pulled up to the apartment, Finn said, "Hey, Adam, who's that guy? In the slacks and the polo shirt? He has to be sweltering—God, it's 110 today."

Rico glanced up at the front porch and then hurt his neck doing a double take as Derek swung the car around. "Oh holy fuck," he breathed, sure it was the last time he *could* breathe. "That's Ezra."

Spell of the Third

THERE WAS a thump as Derek drove the car up on the curb and dropped it back onto the street.

"I bit my tongue!" Finn wailed, and Adam checked for blood as Derek straightened the car.

"Ezra your ex?" Derek asked, sounding a little panicked.

Rico turned toward him, planning to laugh off the fear in his voice, but then he caught sight of Derek's face.

He was terrified.

"I should go see what he wants," Rico said, squeezing his knee. "And then I'll get my suitcases. We can bring them back to the—"

"Don't worry about it," Derek said. The car was idling in park, and Derek was looking stoically ahead. "However this goes, call me later, okay?"

"However this—"

"Rico, I'm sorry to interrupt," Adam said quietly, "but he's going to need some Advil and some ice. He's bleeding."

Derek and Rico looked at each other in horror and then looked back at Finn, who stuck his tongue out apologetically. Yes. Bleeding.

"Holy fuck that looks painful," Rico said. "I'm getting, I'm getting!" He hurried out of the car and pulled the seat down so Finn and Adam could duck under the convertible top and flee for the house. "You," he said to Derek, "turn off the car and go inside with them—I swear, this won't take a minute!"

Derek's face held no recrimination, just a bone-deep sadness. "You... I mean, I should have waited," he said, almost to himself. "You weren't ready. I should have made you call him again."

Oh Jesus. "Derek—c'mon, man, give me the benefit of the doubt!"

Derek's eyes were bleak. "I do, Rico. But he's your first love—and he came back for you. No contest, right?"

And with that he put the car in gear and started to pull away from the curb. "I'll bring Adam and Finn's bags to work tomorrow." And then he drove away, giving Rico no choice but to close the door and turn to the forlorn figure sweating his way down the sidewalk.

"God*dammit!*" he snarled, turning to Ezra with murder in his eyes. "Do you have *any* idea what you just did?"

Ezra recoiled, his lower lip trembling, and Rico felt like shit. Hell. He hadn't done anything wrong except love his father and be afraid.

And tell Rico to go away.

"I'm sorry?" he said, sounding improbably young.

Rico scrubbed his face with his hands. "How did you find me?"

Ezra shrugged. Yes, his eyes were still shocking blue, and his long face was still vulnerable and pretty. But the place he'd held in Rico's heart wasn't open for him anymore, and his looks didn't catch Rico's breath or make him want to run to the moon and back—or come out to his parents.

He'd done that already. He'd done that for himself, and then he'd held on to Derek and Adam and stayed out.

Rico would run to hell and back for Derek; he hardly wanted to walk up the stairs to talk to Ezra.

"This was the last address on your résumé," Ezra said, eyes pleading for understanding. "You talked about having your cousin house-sit—I took a chance." Ezra pointed to the stoop, where Miguel was walking Clopper down the stairs. "That guy said you'd be home soon."

Adam was talking to Miguel and shooing Finn up the stairs and petting an excited Clopper all at once, and Rico nodded to him and waved him on. Rico could do this, and it wasn't going to hurt anywhere near like he'd once predicted.

"Yeah," he said, trying not to be cruel. "Me and my boyfriend took Adam and Finn out to a game in San Francisco."

Ezra grimaced. "Uh... so, your boyfriend. You're out?"

Rico nodded. "To everyone," he said softly. "My dad and grandma disowned me, but fuck 'em. My mom stood tough in the end."

Ezra couldn't seem to stop studying his feet in their shiny wingtips. "I, uh... well, after you left, I... I mean, I tried to toe the line for a little while. But I couldn't." He shot Rico a naked look. "I missed you so bad. You were the only reason I could work there. I had no idea how horrible it had been... how close I was to dying every day. And then you left, and I...." He swallowed and held out his hands. His knuckles were healing from what looked to be injuries that would come from hitting something. "I lost it one day," he said, shrugging like it was no big deal. "I just started banging on my cubicle until I'd destroyed it, and I was bleeding and crying, and nobody knew what to do. And my dad sent me to the doctor, and the doctor sent me to the shrink, and the shrink talked to my dad for fifteen minutes and then came to me and told me I could come out and make another future or the next time I wouldn't be able to stop. And when the dust cleared, I realized…." He shook his head. "I hoped…."

Rico closed his eyes and swallowed. "I'm so sorry," he said softly. He'd had no idea how fragile Ezra had been. None. "I… I should have known." How could he? "If I'd been a better person, I would have known," he said, fractured for a moment. Destroyed.

"How could you?" Ezra said, raising his hand to cup Rico's cheek. "I didn't know. It wasn't… I mean, I would have done it earlier without you. I just… I kept thinking, 'I need something to make me feel alive.' And then you did."

"And then I left." Fuck.

Ezra shook his head and waved his hand like he was swatting flies. "No—this is *not* about guilt!" he said, sounding angry. "I told you to go—you didn't think you had a choice. I don't want to guilt you into this. I… I spent the last four months getting *better*, dammit, and I don't want this to be a consideration."

Rico closed his eyes, saw the vulnerability in Derek's face as he'd pulled away. "Good," he said quietly. "Because the guy who just drove away—he… I can't hurt him. I'd die before I hurt him. Not even for…." He swallowed. In March it would have been a very different story.

Ezra nodded. "Not even for me. I get it," he said softly. "He's a good guy?"

"Oh God—you got no idea," Rico said, his throat raw. "He's… I mean, maybe someday I'll tell you all the good things this guy is. But I can't. He just drove away thinking I'd choose you, and I can't let him do that, you understand?"

Ezra, God love him, wiped his eyes with his palms and nodded. His chin crumpled, but he nodded. "Yeah. I… uh, you got some recommendations for a hotel or something?" he asked after a minute. He gestured to the stoop, where three big suitcases stood. "My apartment, most of my clothes, I left all of it behind. I think my dad's burning it or something. I… I sort of got nowhere to go."

Rico half laughed. "I'll tell you what," he said, taking a tentative step forward. He didn't want what he was about to do to be misconstrued. "I, uh... I'm about to move out of my apartment. I'm leaving behind a really comfortable couch, a couple of drawers, and my big fucking dog to guard my cousin and his boyfriend. You can have my spot, okay?"

Ezra gaped. "No, seriously—"

Rico shook his head. "No, seriously. And you know what? My cousin works in a candy store—it's not great pay, but I'm pretty sure they have a spot for you."

"A candy store?" Ezra wrinkled his nose.

Rico had to laugh. "Yeah. I'll let him explain it." He called to Miguel, who had Clopper out on the lawn, probably so he could take a dump. "Miguel, look. I'm going to walk Clopper over to Derek's. I'll probably be gone until tomorrow, and then tell Adam I'm coming back to get my stuff, okay?"

"Yeah, no problem," Miguel said, drinking in Ezra's misery with concern. "Uhm, this is—"

"This is Ezra Kellerman," Rico said, standing back and letting the two of them shake hands. "He's a real good guy, and I need you to tell Adam he's sleeping on the couch until he's got himself a place to stay. I'll pay the rent, no worries."

"Rico, you don't have to—"

Rico cut him off by hugging him sure and tight and kissing him platonically on the cheek. "You and me aren't ever going to be a thing again," he said softly. "But I still care what happens to you. This is a good place. Adam and Finn'll take care of you. But I've got to go get Derek. He thinks I'm walking out of his life. I can't let him think that, you know?" Rico knew what it felt like.

Ezra nodded and held on extra tight for a minute.

And then let go.

Rico smiled at Miguel for a minute. "Make sure Adam knows me and Ezra are cool, or he's going to think this is bullshit," he cautioned. Then he took Clopper's lead and started walking.

He'd measured once in Derek's car. Derek lived about a mile away. He could be there in twenty-five minutes if he didn't want to kill himself and Clopper in the heat.

Derek found him in the front yard, hosing himself and Clopper off and trying not to pass out.

"Oh my God, don't you have a car?"

"I'm leaving it at the apartment, remember?" Rico panted, bending over and letting the hose play on the back of his neck and then turning his head to gulp some more water. He'd actually stopped and run him and Clopper through someone's sprinklers on the way, but the refreshment hadn't lasted long. Fucking *Jesus*, Sacramento could suck in the summer.

"I thought you were leaving the dog at the apartment too," Derek said, and Rico grunted. He'd gotten a good look at Derek's face, and for all his bullshit, his eyes were red-rimmed and his cheekbones stood out on high alert—a man who was pale and sad and crying.

"I thought it was shared custody." They *had* worked out the details on the way home, right? "What can I say, Derek, the dog needed to crap and I needed to tell you not to be an asshole, because I wasn't leaving you." He'd actually planned that better a thousand times in his head on the way over, but he still had spots dancing in front of his eyes and apparently the pretty words had been cooked out of him, like fat.

"You just left your ex-boyfriend on the lawn?" Derek asked in horror.

Rico scowled at him and then decided he might not get sick if he stood up, as long as he kept the hose going. "Well, I gave him my spot on the couch," Rico said, not sure how this would go over. "And I told Adam to get him a job. But…." He'd spent some time on the walk over getting indignant, and now that came back to him as well.

"You *left* me, you asshole. Jesus, the next time some ghost from the past shows up on our doorstep, would you do me a favor and stick around long enough to fight for me?"

"I was *trying* to be a good guy!"

"You *are* a good guy! Stop trying so hard—you do too much!" Rico's voice pitched plaintively on that last note, and a reluctant smile played with the corners of Derek's mouth.

"Here, baby," he said softly. "Let's go through the garage to the backyard, and you can take off your clothes and get inside to the air-conditioning."

"That would be much appreciated," Rico said, trying for dignity. "That right there would make you a good guy." He wasn't sure if it was the brush with heat stroke or the brush with the ex-boyfriend or the *watching Derek drive away thinking it was the end*, but he felt dangerously near tears himself.

Derek's firm hand on the small of his back helped take the shakiness away, and so did a big glass of ice water and a cool shower.

Twenty minutes later Clopper flopped on the cool tiles of the kitchen floor, eschewing the bed Derek had bought him for his visits. Rico sprawled on the couch next to Derek, wearing a towel and nothing else. He sipped his third glass of water and prodded Derek's shin with his toe.

"You going to tell me why you left me on the lawn talking to my ex-ex-ex-boyfriend?" he asked softly.

Derek's expression should have been sheepish, but it was, in fact, that bare, vulnerable look that Rico had caught only glimpses of before. "You know," he said, failing at a casual smile, "it's… it's like when I caught my old boyfriend cheating and knew it was my fault. I… I knew you were on the rebound, but…. God, I just wanted you so bad. Just that first meeting. Went home and dreamed about you. Called you out of the blue. Wanted to hear your voice. And I told myself it was okay that I got you on the rebound, because you weren't bouncing back across the country to see him again. You were making this your home, right? But there he was… I mean, what right did I have to get in the way? You'd put off moving in, and it was like… I don't know. A sign."

Rico grunted. "Yeah—it was a sign that you haven't been listening to me." His prodding on Derek's shin became a slow caress. "You and me, Derek? We're the best thing I ever could have imagined. Ezra and I were… like you said. I wasn't home. *He* wasn't home. You are."

"Yeah?"

Rico continued his caress. "Swear. You're… you're the best home I could imagine. I saw him there on the lawn, and I was shocked. And worried about *him*, if you must know the truth, because…." Rico thought about those scars on his knuckles and wanted to cry. "He's fragile. I mean, I knew he was a little, but he's… he's fragile. And I'll give him a place on Adam's couch, and I'll let Adam get him a job—hell, I'll even ask you to give him a job—and we might even have to let him beat you at video games. But he can't have that place in my heart anymore, Derek. You live there. You've set up this *beautiful* house"—he gestured to Derek's living room, now graced with one of Adam's brightest paintings and so warm and so full of beauty and comfort that it made Rico's throat close—"and you've sort of set up the same place inside of me. I can't leave this place—not to comfort Ezra. Not to make you feel like 'the good guy.' It's my home now. We made it my home with every plan we made." Suddenly his stomach clenched, the memory of the rather void apartment in New York, of the apartment on F Street that he'd never made his, of the dormitories he'd lived in without even a poster, of his room in his parents' house with the plain white comforter and not a picture on the wall, all assailing him at the same time.

Any of them could have been his home, if only Derek had lived there too.

But Derek lived *here*, and Rico couldn't leave.

"Please don't make me leave," Rico said, the wobbliness coming back. "Being with you is the only home I've ever had."

Derek leaned forward on the couch so he could look Rico in the eyes. "How you feeling?" he asked quietly. "Going to throw up or pass out?"

Rico shook his head. "Naw. But I might cry."

Derek nodded and very carefully took his glass of ice water away, then set it on the glass-topped coffee table without a coaster. "That's okay," he said, giving Rico a shaky smile. "Me too."

He felt so good in Rico's arms. Warm, solid, beautiful.

"I'm not going anywhere," Rico said against his shoulder.

"I believe that with all I got," Derek said back.

There were a few tears then, but then the tears turned to kisses, and the kisses turned to making love on the couch, Rico on his knees with Derek's cock erupting into his mouth, the taste of his come suffusing Rico with heat and bitterness and joy.

He rested his head against Derek's thigh when it was done, palming his own cock while Derek caught his breath and played with Rico's hair.

"So," Derek breathed, still coming down, "is this 'after'?"

"Sure," Rico said, content and aching all at once. "But I'm still hard."

Derek laughed and leaned over, pulling Rico up gently by the hair and taking his come-slicked mouth with a full-tongue kiss. He pulled back and smiled. "We'll have to take care of that hard-on," he promised. "There's no 'after' without the 'happy' first, right?"

Rico grinned and stood, his erection bobbing, teasing Derek's lips. "Then come on and make me happy," he said playfully.

Derek stuck his tongue out and teasingly licked a drop of precome off, watching as Rico closed his eyes and bit his lip.

"I will *always* work to make you happy," he promised, and then he opened his mouth and pulled Rico in, and words were the last thing on either of their minds.

Stray Thoughts and Stray People

DARRIN WAS rarely caught unaware, but when Adam and Miguel walked into Candy Heaven with the pretty young man he'd been dreaming about for the past week, you could have knocked him over with a feather.

"Really?" he asked Adam sharply. "Really? You're responsible for this one too?"

"Hey, don't look at me!" Adam defended. "Rico brought this one. Finn and I were finally going to get sex on the couch, but Rico said he's ours, so I brought him here."

Darrin looked the slick young man over, wrinkling his nose. "You smell like Manhattan," he said with distaste. "We need to fix that."

"I like Manhattan," the young man said uncertainly.

No. "No, you don't. You've been *told* you like Manhattan, but you really like Sacramento much better." He looked at Adam. "Is this some sort of punishment? Your damned cousin haunted me for *four* months. You and Finn at least had the good sense to fall in love over the course of one. This one's a project—what did I ever do to you?"

Adam blinked those big liquid brown eyes at him. "You hired me and sicced Finn on me like a love-struck schnauzer. You're getting what you deserve. Now do you have a job for him?"

"And be nice," Miguel said, his own sloe eyes wide and shiny like one of those hideous paintings of big-eyed children. "He needs some extra care."

Darrin opened his mouth, closed it again, and then looked at Miguel's protective hand hovering at the small of the newcomer's back.

"Of course," he said simply. Oh, this was convenient. Perhaps not easy, but, well, convenient. He put on his best smile and extended his hand. "Welcome to Candy Heaven," he said sweetly. "I'm Darrin and I'll be dispensing candy for all your emotional needs. What can I do for you today?"

The young man swallowed and smiled uncertainly. "I'm, uh, Ezra Kellerman, and I was told you could give me a job."

Of course Darrin could. But that wasn't all the young man needed—and that was the challenge, wasn't it? "Go get him an apron," he said to Adam. "And you get to train him."

Adam shrugged. "Yeah, boss. Whatever."

Ezra watched Adam disappear into the office like he was a last, best hope. Aw, poor puppy. Darrin succumbed to the urge to ruffle his carefully coifed hair.

"Hey!" The explosion of big hands and elbows was the closest thing Darrin had seen to spirit coming from the young man. "Watch the do!"

Darrin laughed, enjoying the sound, low and evil, from the pit of his stomach. "Ezra?" he said, smiling prettily.

"Yeah?" Ezra patted his hair carefully back into place.

"It's going to be a *very* sweet day."

AMY LANE is a mother of two college students, two grade-schoolers, and two small dogs. She is also a compulsive knitter who writes because she can't silence the voices in her head. She adores fur-babies, knitting socks, and hawt menz, and she dislikes moths, cat boxes, and knuckle-headed macspazzmatrons. She is rarely found cooking, cleaning, or doing domestic chores, but she has been known to knit up an emergency hat/blanket/pair of socks for any occasion whatsoever, or sometimes for no reason at all. Her award-winning writing has three flavors: twisty-purple alternative universe, angsty-orange contemporary, and sunshine-yellow happy. By necessity, she has learned to type like the wind. She's been married for twenty-plus years to her beloved Mate and still believes in Twu Wuv, with a capital Twu and a capital Wuv, and she doesn't see any reason at all for that to change.

Website: www.greenshill.com
Blog: www.writerslane.blogspot.com
E-mail: amylane@greenshill.com
Facebook: www.facebook.com/amy.lane.167
Twitter: @amymaclane

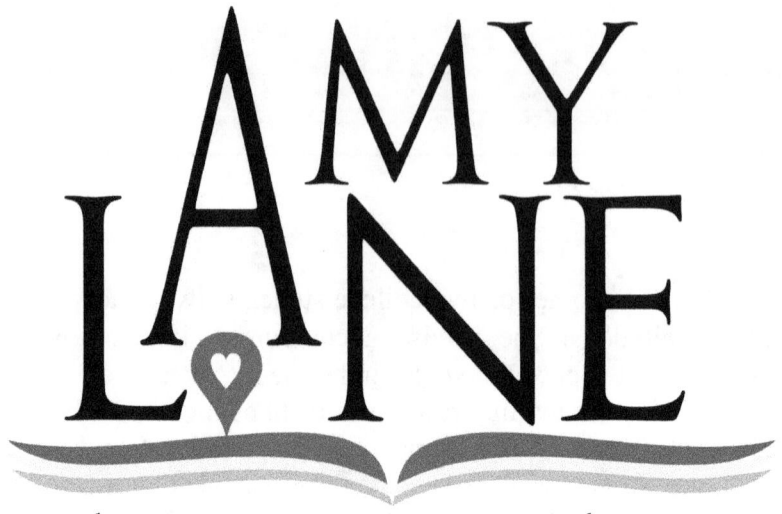

Choose your Lane to love!

Yellow

Amy Lane Lite

Contemporary Romance

Available at
http://www.dreamspinnerpress.com

Terrell Washington's childhood was a trifecta of suck: being black, gay, and poor in America has no upside. Terrell climbed his way out of the hood only to hit a glass ceiling and stop, frozen, a chain restaurant bartender with a journalism degree. His one bright spot is Colby Meyers, a coworker who has no fear, no inhibitions, and sees no boundaries. Terrell and Colby spend their summers at the river and their breaks on the back dock of Papiano's. As terrified as Terrell is of coming out, he's helpless to stay away from Colby's magnetic smile and contagious laughter.

But Colby is out of college now, and he has grand plans for the future—plans Terrell is sure will leave his scrawny black ass in the Sacramento dust until a breathless moment stolen from the chaos of the restaurant tells Terrell he might be wrong. When the moment is shattered by a mystery and an act of violence, Terrell and Colby are left with two puzzles: who killed their scumbag manager, and how to fit their own lives—the black and the white of them—into a single shining tomorrow.

http://www.dreamspinnerpress.com

Meet Patrick Cleary: party boy, loser, and spaz. Patrick's been trying desperately to transform himself, and the results have been so spectacular, they've almost killed him. Meet Wes "Whiskey" Keenan: he's a field biologist wondering if it's time to settle down. When the worst day of Patrick's life ends with Whiskey saving it, Patrick and Whiskey find themselves sharing company and an impossibly small berth on the world's tackiest houseboat.

Patrick needs to get his life together—and Whiskey wants to help—but Patrick is not entirely convinced it's doable. He's pretty sure he's a freak of nature. But Whiskey, who works with real freaks of nature, thinks all Patrick needs is a little help to see the absolute beauty inside his spastic self, and Whiskey is all about volunteering. Between anomalous frogs, a homicidal ex-boyfriend, and Patrick's own hangups, Whiskey's going to need all of his patience and Patrick's going to need to find the best of himself before these two men ever see clear water.

http://www.dreamspinnerpress.com

GAMBLING MEN:
THE NOVEL
Amy Lane

Quent Jackson has followed Jason Spade's every move in business and in poker since their first day as college freshmen. Eight years later, when Jace finally decides Quent is the one man he can't live without, he sees no reason for that to change.

But as much as Jace believes that poker is life, no one gave Quent the same playbook. After their first passionate night, the real game of love and trust begins, and Jace has been playing alone too long to make teaching the rules easy. Jace only speaks two languages: one of them is sex, and the other one is poker. Between the two, he needs to find a way to convince himself to take a chance on love—and Quent to take a chance on him. It's a lucky thing they're good at reading the odds, because they're playing for keeps, and this is one high-stakes relationship that's definitely worth the gamble.

http://www.dreamspinnerpress.com

Carson O'Shaughnessy has one task: track down his boss's flighty nephew, Stassy, and return the kid to Chicago. Then Carson can go back to waiting tables and being productively bitter about his life. He didn't count on finding a dead body in Stassy's bed, and he certainly didn't count on the guy in the flip-flops and cutoffs at the local café helping him get to the bottom of the crime.

But Dale Arden is no ordinary surfing burnout—he's actually a pretty sharp guy with a seductive voice and a bossy streak wider than the Florida panhandle. When he decides to boss Carson right into his bed, Carson realizes Stassy's not the only one who's been lost. Carson likes to think he's got his life all figured out, that sex with guys is your basic broom-closet transaction; he may just have to revise his priorities, because nobody plans on taking a left at St. Truth-be-Well and finding love at the Bates Parrot Hotel.

http://www.dreamspinnerpress.com

Will Lafferty and Kenny Scalia are both having sort of a day. Will gets fired for letting fifth graders read Harry Potter, and Kenny finds his boyfriend and his sex toys in bed with a complete stranger. When Will knocks over Kenny's trash can—and strews Kenny's personal business all over the street—it feels like the perfect craptastic climax to the sewage of suckage that has rained down on them both.

But ever-friendly, ever-kind Will asks snarky Kenny out for a beer—God knows they both need one—and two amazing things occur: Kenny discovers talking to Will might be the best form of intercourse ever, and Will discovers he's gay.

Their unlikely friendship seems like the perfect platonic match until Will reveals how very much more he's been feeling for Kenny almost since the beginning. But Kenny's worried. Will's newfound sexuality is bright and glittery and shiny, but what happens when that wears off? Is Will's infatuation with Kenny strong enough to stay real?

http://www.dreamspinnerpress.com

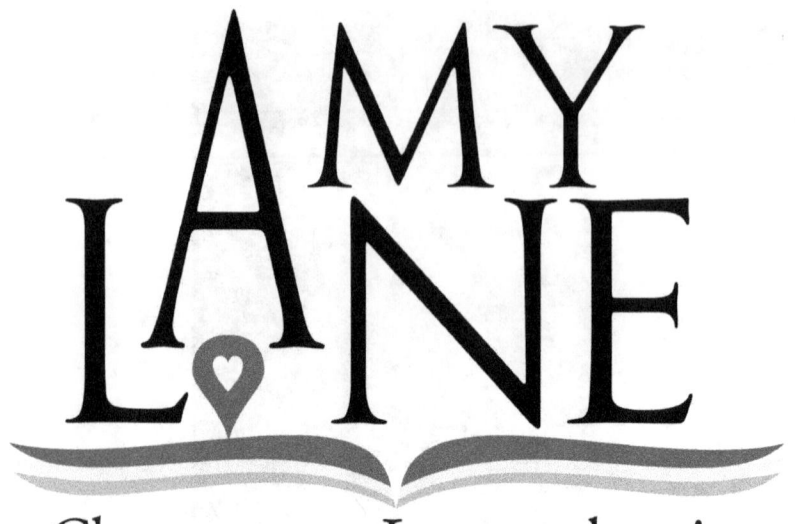

Choose your Lane to love!

Orange

Amy's

Dark Contemporary Romance

Available at
http://www.dreamspinnerpress.com

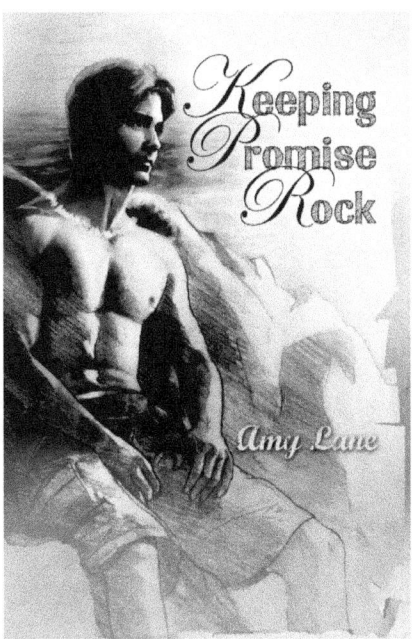

http://www.dreamspinnerpress.com

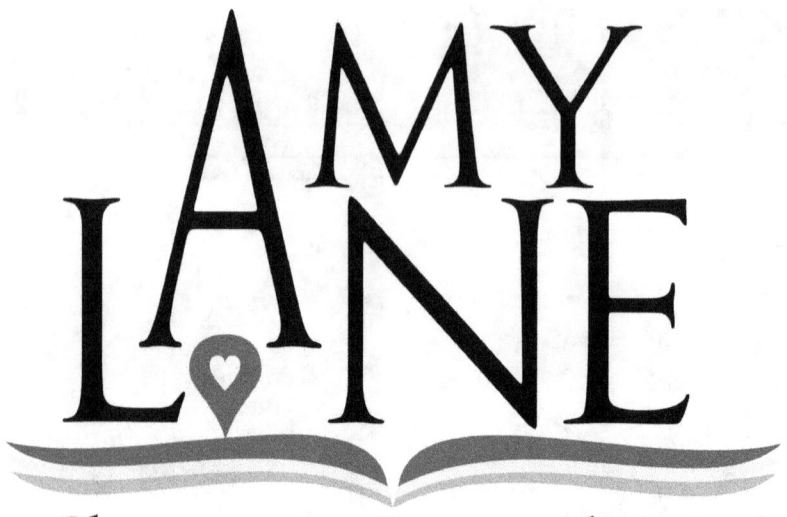

Choose your Lane to love!

Purple

Amy's Alternative Universe Romance

Available at
http://www.dreamspinnerpress.com

http://www.dreamspinnerpress.com

FOR **MORE** OF THE **BEST GAY** ROMANCE

DREAMSPINNER
PRESS
dreamspinnerpress.com